Elr
Stormbr

The Michael Moorcock Collection

The Michael Moorcock Collection is the definitive library of acclaimed author Michael Moorcock's SF & fantasy, including the entirety of his Eternal Champion work. It is prepared and edited by John Davey, the author's long-time bibliographer and editor, and will be published, over the course of two years, in the following print omnibus editions by Gollancz, and as individual eBooks by the SF Gateway (see http://www.sfgateway.com/authors/m/moorcock-michael/ for a complete list of available eBooks).

A Cornelius Calendar
    comprising –
    *The Adventures of Una Persson
        and Catherine Cornelius in
        the Twentieth Century*
    The Entropy Tango
    The Great Rock 'n' Roll Swindle
    The Alchemist's Question
    *Firing the Cathedral/Modem
        Times 2.0*

Von Bek
    comprising –
    *The War Hound and the World's
        Pain*
    The City in the Autumn Stars

The Eternal Champion
    comprising –
    The Eternal Champion
    Phoenix in Obsidian
    The Dragon in the Sword

The Dancers at the
End of Time
    comprising –
    An Alien Heat
    The Hollow Lands
    The End of all Songs

Kane of Old Mars
    comprising –
    Warriors of Mars
    Blades of Mars
    Barbarians of Mars

Moorcock's Multiverse
    comprising –
    The Sundered Worlds
    The Winds of Limbo
    The Shores of Death

The Nomad of Time
    comprising –
    The Warlord of the Air
    The Land Leviathan
    The Steel Tsar

Travelling to Utopia
    comprising –
    The Wrecks of Time
    The Ice Schooner
    The Black Corridor

The War Amongst the Angels
    comprising –
    Blood: A Southern Fantasy
    Fabulous Harbours
    The War Amongst the Angels

Tales From the End of Time
    comprising –
    Legends from the End of Time
    Constant Fire
    Elric at the End of Time

Behold the Man

Gloriana; or, The Unfulfill'd Queen

SHORT FICTION
My Experiences in the Third World
War and Other Stories: The Best
Short Fiction of Michael Moorcock
Volume 1

The Brothel in Rosenstrasse and
Other Stories: The Best Short Fiction
of Michael Moorcock Volume 2

Breakfast in the Ruins and Other
Stories: The Best Short Fiction of
Michael Moorcock Volume 3

Elric: Stormbringer!

MICHAEL MOORCOCK

Edited by John Davey

This edition published in Great Britain in 2014 by
Gollancz
An imprint of the Orion Publishing Group
Orion House, 5 Upper St Martin's Lane,
London WC2H 9EA

An Hachette UK Company

3 5 7 9 10 8 6 4 2

A CIP catalogue record for this book is
available from the British Library

ISBN 978 0 575 11438 8

Typeset by Jouve (UK), Milton Keynes

Printed and bound by CPI Group (UK) Ltd, Croydon, CR0 4YY

The Orion Publishing Group's policy is to use papers
that are natural, renewable and recyclable products and
made from wood grown in sustainable forests. The logging
and manufacturing processes are expected to conform to
the environmental regulations of the country of origin.

www.multiverse.org
www.sfgateway.com
www.gollancz.co.uk
www.orionbooks.co.uk

Introduction to
The Michael Moorcock Collection
John Clute

H E IS NOW over 70, enough time for most careers to start and
end in, enough time to fit in an occasional half-decade or so
of silence to mark off the big years. Silence happens. I don't think
I know an author who doesn't fear silence like the plague; most of
us, if we live long enough, can remember a bad blank year or so,
or more. Not Michael Moorcock. Except for some worrying
surgery on his toes in recent years, he seems not to have taken
time off to breathe the air of peace and panic. There has been no
time to spare. The nearly 60 years of his active career seems to
have been too short to fit everything in: the teenage comics; the
editing jobs; the pulp fiction; the reinvented heroic fantasies;
the Eternal Champion; the deep Jerry Cornelius riffs; NEW WORLDS;
the 1970s/1980s flow of stories and novels, dozens upon dozens
of them in every category of modern fantastika; the tales of the
dying Earth and the possessing of Jesus; the exercises in postmodernism that turned the world inside out before most of us had
begun to guess we were living on the wrong side of things; the
invention (more or less) of steampunk; the alternate histories; the
Mitteleuropean tales of sexual terror; the deep-city London riffs:
the turns and changes and returns and reconfigurations to which
he has subjected his oeuvre over the years (he expects this new
Collected Edition will fix these transformations in place for good);
the late tales where he has been remodelling the intersecting
worlds he created in the 1960s in terms of twenty-first-century
physics: for starters. If you can't take the heat, I guess, stay out of
the multiverse.

His life has been full and complicated, a life he has exposed and hidden (like many other prolific authors) throughout his work. In *Mother London* (1988), though, a nonfantastic novel published at what is now something like the midpoint of his career, it may be possible to find the key to all the other selves who made the 100 books. There are three protagonists in the tale, which is set from about 1940 to about 1988 in the suburbs and inner runnels of the vast metropolis of Charles Dickens and Robert Louis Stevenson. The oldest of these protagonists is Joseph Kiss, a flamboyant self-advertising fin-de-siècle figure of substantial girth and a fantasticating relationship to the world: he is Michael Moorcock, seen with genial bite as a kind of G.K. Chesterton without the wearying punch-line paradoxes. The youngest of the three is David Mummery, a haunted introspective half-insane denizen of a secret London of trials and runes and codes and magic: he too is Michael Moorcock, seen through a glass, darkly. And there is Mary Gasalee, a kind of holy-innocent and survivor, blessed with a luminous clarity of insight, so that in all her apparent ignorance of the onrushing secular world she is more deeply wise than other folk: she is also Michael Moorcock, Moorcock when young as viewed from the wry middle years of 1988. When we read the book, we are reading a book of instructions for the assembly of a London writer. The Moorcock we put together from this choice of portraits is amused and bemused at the vision of himself; he is a phenomenon of flamboyance and introspection, a poseur and a solitary, a dreamer and a doer, a multitude and a singleton. But only the three Moorcocks in this book, working together, could have written all the other books.

It all began – as it does for David Mummery in *Mother London* – in South London, in a subtopian stretch of villas called Mitcham, in 1939. In early childhood, he experienced the Blitz, and never forgot the extraordinariness of being a participant – however minute – in the great drama; all around him, as though the world were being dismantled nightly, darkness and blackout would descend, bombs fall, buildings and streets disappear; and in the morning, as though a new universe had taken over from the old one and the world had become portals, the sun would rise on glinting rubble, abandoned tricycles, men and women going about their daily tasks as though nothing had happened, strange shards of ruin poking into altered air. From a very early age, Michael Moorcock's security reposed in a sense that everything might change, in the blinking of an eye, and be *rejourneyed* the next day (or the next book). Though as a writer he has certainly elucidated the fears and alarums of life in Aftermath Britain, it does seem that his very early years were marked by the epiphanies of war, rather than the inflictions of despair and beclouding amnesia most adults necessarily experienced. After the war ended, his parents separated, and the young Moorcock began to attend a pretty wide variety of schools, several of which he seems to have been expelled from, and as soon as he could legally do so he began to work full time, up north in London's heart, which he only left when he moved to Texas (with intervals in Paris) in the early 1990s, from where (to jump briefly up the decades) he continues to cast a Martian eye: as with most exiles, Moorcock's intensest anatomies of his homeland date from after his cunning departure.

But back again to the beginning (just as though we were rimming a multiverse). Starting in the 1950s there was the comics and pulp work for Fleetway Publications; there was the first book (*Caribbean Crisis*, 1962) as by Desmond Reid, co-written with his early friend the artist James Cawthorn (1929–2008); there was marriage, with the writer Hilary Bailey (they divorced in 1978), three children, a heated existence in the Ladbroke Grove/Notting Hill Gate region of London he was later to populate with Jerry Cornelius and his vast family; there was the editing of NEW WORLDS, which began in 1964 and became the heartbeat of the British New Wave two years later as writers like Brian W. Aldiss and J.G. Ballard, reaching their early prime, made it into a tympanum, as young American writers like Thomas M. Disch, John T. Sladek, Norman Spinrad and Pamela Zoline found a home in London for material they could not publish in America, and new British writers like M. John Harrison and Charles Platt began their careers in its pages; but before that there was Elric. With *The Stealer of Souls* (1963) and

Stormbringer (1965), the multiverse began to flicker into view, and the Eternal Champion (whom Elric parodied and embodied) began properly to ransack the worlds in his fight against a greater Chaos than the great dance could sustain. There was also the first SF novel, *The Sundered Worlds* (1965), but in the 1960s SF was a difficult nut to demolish for Moorcock: he would bide his time.

We come to the heart of the matter. Jerry Cornelius, who first appears in *The Final Programme* (1968) – which assembles and co-ordinates material first published a few years earlier in NEW WORLDS – is a deliberate solarisation of the albino Elric, who was himself a mocking solarisation of Robert E. Howard's Conan, or rather of the mighty-thew-headed Conan created for profit by Howard epigones: Moorcock rarely mocks the true quill. Cornelius, who reaches his first and most telling apotheosis in the four novels comprising *The Cornelius Quartet*, remains his most distinctive and perhaps most original single creation: a wide boy, an agent, a *flaneur*, a bad musician, a shopper, a shapechanger, a trans, a spy in the house of London: a toxic palimpsest on whom and through whom the *zeitgeist* inscribes surreal conjugations of 'message'. Jerry Cornelius gives head to Elric.

The life continued apace. By 1970, with NEW WORLDS on its last legs, multiverse fantasies and experimental novels poured forth; Moorcock and Hilary Bailey began to live separately, though he moved, in fact, only around the corner, where he set up house with Jill Riches, who would become his second wife; there was a second home in Yorkshire, but London remained his central base. *The Condition of Muzak* (1977), which is the fourth Cornelius novel, and *Gloriana; or, The Unfulfill'd Queen* (1978), which transfigures the first Elizabeth into a kinked Astraea, marked perhaps the high point of his career as a writer of fiction whose font lay in genre or its mutations – marked perhaps the furthest bournes he could transgress while remaining within the perimeters of fantasy (though *within* those bournes vast stretches of territory remained and would, continually, be explored). During these years he sometimes wore a leather jacket constructed out of numerous patches of varicoloured material, and it sometimes seemed perfectly fitting that he bore the semblance, as his jacket flickered and fuzzed from across a room or road, of an illustrated man, a map, a thing of shreds and patches, a student fleshed from dreams. Like the stories he told, he seemed to be more than one thing. To use a term frequently applied (by me at least) to twenty-first-century fiction, he seemed equipoisal: which is to say that, through all his genre-hopping and genre-mixing and genre-transcending and genre-loyal returnings to old pitches, *he was never still*, because 'equipoise' is all about *making stories move*. As with his stories, he cannot be pinned down, because he is not in one place. In person and in his work, it has always been sink or swim: like a shark, or a dancer, or an equilibrist...

The marriage with Jill Riches came to an end. He married Linda Steele in 1983; they remain married. The Colonel Pyat books, *Byzantium Endures* (1981), *The Laughter of Carthage* (1984), *Jerusalem Commands* (1992) and *The Vengeance of Rome* (2006), dominated these years, along with *Mother London*. As these books, which are non-fantastic, are not included in the current *Michael Moorcock Collection*, it might be worth noting here that, in their insistence on the irreducible difficulty of gaining anything like true sight, they represent Moorcock's mature modernist take on what one might call the rag-and-bone shop of the world itself; and that the huge ornate postmodern edifice of his multiverse *loosens* us from that world, gives us room to breathe, to juggle our strategies for living – allows us ultimately to escape from prison (to use a phrase from a writer he does not respect, J.R.R. Tolkien, for whom the twentieth century was a prison train bound for hell). What Moorcock may best be remembered for in the end is the (perhaps unique) interplay between modernism and postmodernism in his work. (But a plethora of discordant understandings makes these terms hard to use; so enough of them.) In the end, one might just say that Moorcock's work as a whole represents an extraordinarily multifarious execution of the fantasist's main task: which is to *get us out of here*.

Recent decades saw a continuation of the multifarious, but with a more intensely applied methodology. The late volumes of the long Elric saga, and the Second Ether sequence of meta-fantasies – *Blood: A Southern Fantasy* (1995), *Fabulous Harbours* (1995) and *The War Amongst the Angels: An Autobiographical Story* (1996) – brood on the real world and the multiverse through the lens of Chaos Theory: the closer you get to the world, the less you describe it. *The Metatemporal Detective* (2007) – a narrative in the Steampunk mode Moorcock had previewed as long ago as *The Warlord of the Air* (1971) and *The Land Leviathan* (1974) – continues the process, sometimes dizzyingly: as though the reader inhabited the eye of a camera increasing its focus on a closely observed reality while its bogey simultaneously wheels it backwards from the desired rapport: an old Kurasawa trick here amplified into a tool of conspectus, fantasy eyed and (once again) rejourneyed, this time through the lens of SF.

We reach the second decade of the twenty-first century, time still to make things new, but also time to sort. There are dozens of titles in *The Michael Moorcock Collection* that have not been listed in this short space, much less trawled for tidbits. The various avatars of the Eternal Champion – Elric, Kane of Old Mars, Hawkmoon, Count Brass, Corum, Von Bek – differ vastly from one another. Hawkmoon is a bit of a berk; Corum is a steely solitary at the End of Time: the joys and doleurs of the interplays amongst them can only be experienced through immersion. And the Dancers at the End of Time books, and the Nomad of the Time Stream books, and the Karl Glogauer books, and all the others. They are here now, a 100 books that make up one book. They have been fixed for reading. It is time to enter the multiverse and see the world.

September 2012

Introduction to
The Michael Moorcock Collection

Michael Moorcock

B Y 1964, AFTER I had been editing NEW WORLDS for some months and had published several science fiction and fantasy novels, including *Stormbringer*, I realised that my run as a writer was over. About the only new ideas I'd come up with were miniature computers, the multiverse and black holes, all very crudely realised, in *The Sundered Worlds*. No doubt I would have to return to journalism, writing features and editing. 'My career,' I told my friend J.G. Ballard, 'is finished.' He sympathised and told me he only had a few SF stories left in him, then he, too, wasn't sure what he'd do.

In January 1965, living in Colville Terrace, Notting Hill, then an infamous slum, best known for its race riots, I sat down at the typewriter in our kitchen-cum-bathroom and began a locally based book, designed to be accompanied by music and graphics. *The Final Programme* featured a character based on a young man I'd seen around the area and whom I named after a local greengrocer, Jerry Cornelius, 'Messiah to the Age of Science'. Jerry was as much a technique as a character. Not the 'spy' some critics described him as but an urban adventurer as interested in his psychic environment as the contemporary physical world. My influences were English and French absurdists, American noir novels. My inspiration was William Burroughs with whom I'd recently begun a correspondence. I also borrowed a few SF ideas, though I was adamant that I was not writing in any established genre. I felt I had at last found my own authentic voice.

I had already written a short novel, *The Golden Barge*, set in a nowhere, no-time world very much influenced by Peake and the surrealists, which I had not attempted to publish. An earlier auto-biographical novel, *The Hungry Dreamers*, set in Soho, was eaten by rats in a Ladbroke Grove basement. I remained unsatisfied with my style and my technique. *The Final Programme* took nine days to complete (by 20 January, 1965) with my baby daughters sometimes cradled with their bottles while I typed on. This, I should say, is my memory of events; my then wife scoffed at this story when I recounted it. Whatever the truth, the fact is I only believed I might be a serious writer after I had finished that novel, with all its flaws. But Jerry Cornelius, probably my most successful sustained attempt at unconventional fiction, was born then and ever since has remained a useful means of telling complex stories. Associated with the 60s and 70s, he has been equally at home in all the following decades. Through novels and novellas I developed a means of carrying several narratives and viewpoints on what appeared to be a very light (but tight) structure which dispensed with some of the earlier methods of fiction. In the sense that it took for granted the understanding that the novel is among other things an internal dialogue and I did not feel the need to repeat by now commonly understood modernist conventions, this fiction was post-modern.

Not all my fiction looked for new forms for the new century. Like many 'revolutionaries' I looked back as well as forward. As George Meredith looked to the eighteenth century for inspiration for his experiments with narrative, I looked to Meredith, popular Edwardian realists like Pett Ridge and Zangwill and the writers of the *fin de siècle* for methods and inspiration. An almost obsessive interest in the Fabians, several of whom believed in the possibility of benign imperialism, ultimately led to my Bastable books which examined our enduring British notion that an empire could be essentially a force for good. The first was *The Warlord of the Air*.

I also wrote my *Dancers at the End of Time* stories and novels under the influence of Edwardian humourists and absurdists like Jerome or Firbank. Together with more conventional generic books like *The Ice Schooner* or *The Black Corridor*, most of that work was done in the 1960s and 70s when I wrote the Eternal Champion supernatural adventure novels which helped support my own and others' experiments via NEW WORLDS, allowing me also to keep a family while writing books in which action and fantastic invention were paramount. Though I did them quickly, I didn't write them cynically. I have always believed, somewhat puritanically, in giving the audience good value for money. I enjoyed writing them, tried to avoid repetition, and through each new one was able to develop a few more ideas. They also continued to teach me how to express myself through image and metaphor. My Everyman became the Eternal Champion, his dreams and ambitions represented by the multiverse. He could be an ordinary person struggling with familiar problems in a contemporary setting or he could be a swordsman fighting monsters on a far-away world.

Long before I wrote *Gloriana* (in four parts reflecting the seasons) I had learned to think in images and symbols through reading John Bunyan's *Pilgrim's Progress*, Milton and others, understanding early on that the visual could be the most important part of a book and was often in itself a story as, for instance, a famous personality could also, through everything associated with their name, function as narrative. I wanted to find ways of carrying as many stories as possible in one. From the cinema I also learned how to use images as connecting themes. Images, colours, music, and even popular magazine headlines can all add coherence to an apparently random story, underpinning it and giving the reader a sense of internal logic and a satisfactory resolution, dispensing with certain familiar literary conventions.

When the story required it, I also began writing neo-realist fiction exploring the interface of character and environment, especially the city, especially London. In some books I condensed, manipulated and randomised time to achieve what I wanted, but in others the sense of 'real time' as we all generally perceive it was more suitable and could best be achieved by traditional nineteenth-century means. For the Pyat books I first looked back to the great German classic, Grimmelshausen's *Simplicissimus* and other early picaresques. I then examined the roots of a certain kind of moral fiction from Defoe through Thackeray and Meredith then to modern times where the picaresque (or rogue tale) can take the form of a road movie, for instance. While it's probably fair to say that Pyat and *Byzantium Endures* precipitated the end of my second marriage (echoed to a degree in *The Brothel in Rosenstrasse*), the late 70s and the 80s were exhilarating times for me, with *Mother London* being perhaps my own favourite novel of that period. I wanted to write something celebratory.

By the 90s I was again attempting to unite several kinds of fiction in one novel with my Second Ether trilogy. With Mandelbrot, Chaos Theory and String Theory I felt, as I said at the time, as if I were being offered a chart of my own brain. That chart made it easier for me to develop the notion of the multiverse as representing both the internal and the external, as a metaphor and as a means of structuring and rationalising an outrageously inventive and quasi-realistic narrative. The worlds of the multiverse move up and down scales or 'planes' explained in terms of mass, allowing entire universes to exist in the 'same' space. The result of developing this idea was the *War Amongst the Angels* sequence which added absurdist elements also functioning as a kind of mythology and folklore for a world beginning to understand itself in terms of new metaphysics and theoretical physics. As the cosmos becomes denser and almost infinite before our eyes, with black holes and dark matter affecting our own reality, we can explore them and observe them as our ancestors explored our planet and observed the heavens.

At the end of the 90s I'd returned to realism, sometimes with a dash of fantasy, with *King of the City* and the stories collected in *London Bone*. I also wrote a new Elric / Eternal Champion sequence, beginning with *Daughter of Dreams*, which brought the fantasy worlds of Hawkmoon, Bastable and Co. in line with my realistic and autobiographical stories, another attempt to unify all my fiction; and also offer a way in which disparate genres could be reunited, through notions developed from the multiverse and the Eternal Champion, as one giant novel. At the time I was finishing the Pyat sequence which attempted to look at the roots of the Nazi Holocaust in our European, Middle Eastern and American cultures and to ground my strange survival guilt while at the same time examining my own cultural roots in the light of an enduring anti-Semitism.

By the 2000s I was exploring various conventional ways of story-telling in the last parts of *The Metatemporal Detective* and through other homages, comics, parodies and games. I also looked back at my earliest influences. I had reached retirement age and felt like a rest. I wrote a 'prequel' to the Elric series as a graphic novel with Walter Simonson, *The Making of a Sorcerer*, and did a little online editing with FANTASTIC METROPOLIS.

By 2010 I had written a novel featuring Doctor Who, *The Coming of the Terraphiles*, with a nod to P.G. Wodehouse (a boyhood favourite), continued to write short stories and novellas and to work on the beginning of a new sequence combining pure fantasy and straight autobiography called *The Whispering Swarm* while still writing more Cornelius stories trying to unite all the various genres and sub-genres into which contemporary fiction has fallen.

Throughout my career critics have announced that I'm 'abandoning' fantasy and concentrating on literary fiction. The truth is, however, that all my life, since I became a professional writer and editor at the age of 16, I've written in whatever mode suits a story best and where necessary created a new form if an old one didn't work for me. Certain ideas are best carried on a Jerry Cornelius story, others work better as realism and others as fantasy or science fiction. Some work best as a combination. I'm sure I'll write whatever I like and will continue to experiment with all the ways there are of telling stories and carrying as many themes as possible. Whether I write about a widow coping with loneliness in her cottage or a massive, universe-size sentient spaceship searching for her children, I'll no doubt die trying to tell them all. I hope you'll find at least some of them to your taste.

One thing a reader can be sure of about these new editions is that they would not have been possible without the tremendous and indispensable help of my old friend and bibliographer John Davey. John has ensured that these Gollancz editions are definitive. I am indebted to John for many things, including his work at

Moorcock's Miscellany, my website, but his work on this edition has been outstanding. As well as being an accomplished novelist in his own right John is an astonishingly good editor who has worked with Gollancz and myself to point out every error and flaw in all previous editions, some of them not corrected since their first publication, and has enabled me to correct or revise them. I couldn't have completed this project without him. Together, I think, Gollancz, John Davey and myself have produced what will be the best editions possible and I am very grateful to him, to Malcolm Edwards, Darren Nash and Marcus Gipps for all the considerable hard work they have done to make this edition what it is.

Michael Moorcock

Contents

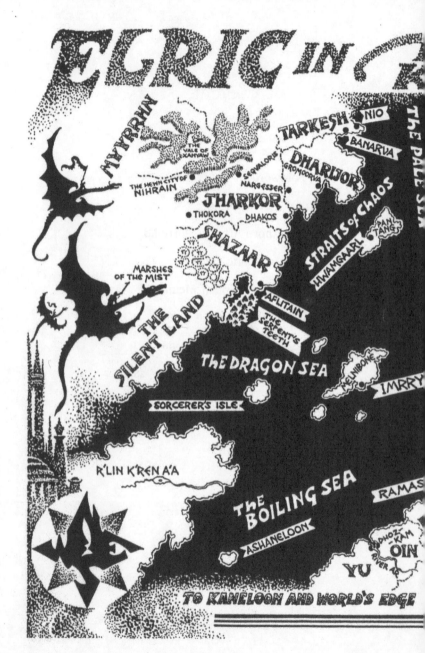

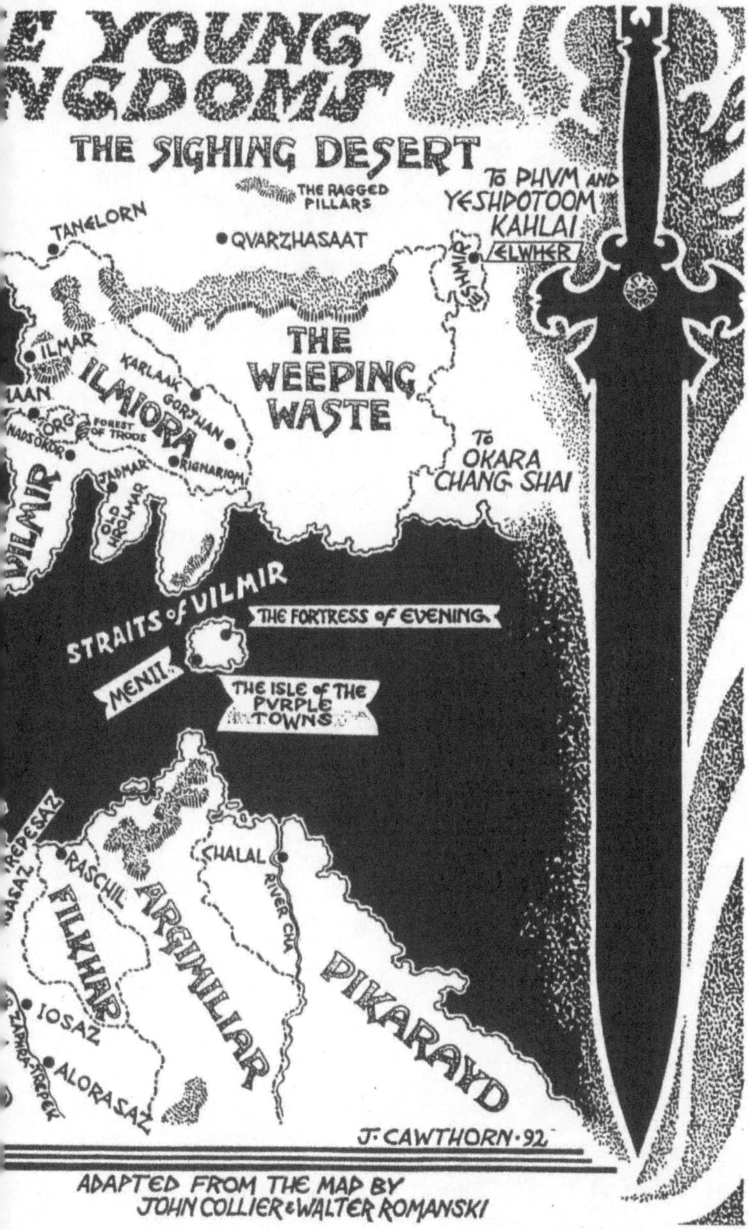

ADAPTED FROM THE MAP BY
JOHN COLLIER & WALTER ROMANSKI

Foreword
by Tad Williams

M ICHAEL MOORCOCK IS my religion.
I'll explain that, I promise. It may take me a few minutes...
First off, if you're standing in a store reading this and you don't
know Moorcock's work, just buy the book. There. You've done
yourself a favor.

If you're one of my readers (I feel presumptuous even mentioning it) and you haven't read any Moorcock, you must. He is one of
the field's few living legends, and has had a gigantic influence on
me (and on most other writers of speculative fiction my age).

If you're new to his work and want to know more about Moorcock's background, go get the first volume of this series and read
Alan Moore's introduction. In fact, get the whole series. That's
not what this introduction's about.

And no, I haven't forgotten that I said I'd explain the religion
thing.

See, I sat down to write this introduction and realized that the
other writers who had talked about Moorcock in the previous volumes had said pretty much all the general stuff about the man
and his work that needed to be said. He's an artist who knocked
people's socks off when he was a wunderkind, but he has continued to get better and better every damn year of his life. The
scope of his work is probably unmatched in the field – science
fiction, fantasy, black humor, surrealism, you name it – and he's
had a life full of adventures as well. As editor of NEW WORLDS he
helped spawn the modern age of science fiction. He's been
onstage with Hawkwind. God knows, he probably undertakes
secret missions in his spare time to defeat smirking archvillains

and save the Earth from destruction. Mike Moorcock just RULES. That's all there is to it. Discovering his work changed my life as a reader and a writer.

But everyone else has said pretty much the same thing in *their* introductions. So what's left for me?, I wondered.

Well, besides all those other things, Michael Moorcock is the prophet of my own personal religion. Yes, now I'm explaining.

First off, you have to understand that I'm one of those folks who grew up in the sixties and seventies, the years in which Moorcock was fizzing up into grand prominence in the fields of SF and Fantasy. I read everything you would imagine – Tolkien, Bradbury, Leiber, Howard, Lovecraft, and too many others to relate – but Michael Moorcock's books were the first things in the genre that seemed to be truly of my era, even though his fantasy heroes like Elric and Corum lived in timeless fantasy worlds. Something about the melancholy and absurdity of Moorcock's worlds, even during his greenest and most melodramatic beginnings as a writer, struck a note of familiarity that thrilled me. And in his other work, I soon began to discover, the implicit became explicit: the Jerry Cornelius books and *The Dancers at the End of Time* were surreal but nevertheless revealing and accurate mirrors of our shared era, an age when everything fell apart, but also when even the ruins themselves seemed to contain the excitement of new possibility.

Years later, long after I'd become a writer myself (and begun to realize to my chagrin that many of my best and most creative ideas were actually fuzzy memories of things I'd read in a well-thumbed Moorcock paperback twenty years earlier) I moved to England. My wife was, for a while, Mr M.'s British publisher, and because of that I had the great good fortune to meet him in person and even get to know him. The first social get-together was especially exciting, of course, even when we had a mild argument about Tolkien. (Mike, although admiring *The Lord of the Rings*, seemed to be irritated about the little-England-ness of Tolkien's Shire and what Mike felt was the romanticization of the peasant-landowner relationship. Or something like that.) But of course mainly I was just thrilled to be talking to him.

During the time I lived in the UK we spent a few evenings with Mike and his wife Linda. It was always great, but after a while it wasn't like going backstage to meet the Beatles anymore. It was almost... normal.

Then one night Mike called us and invited us over for dinner. He and Linda were moving to the United States in a couple of weeks, he reminded us, and he thought we should get together before they left. Of course we said yes.

Comes the appointed night. I was having a crappy day for some reason – small irritations, perhaps a squabble with my publishers, maybe I was just being a jerk for no reason (God knows, it happens). In any case, I was not in a good mood. Deborah came home a little late from work and I was worried about being late. (I don't like being late.) We got a cab and headed across London to the Moorcocks'.

I can still remember that night far better than I remember most of the other important moments of my life. It was raining, not enough to be interesting but too much to ignore, and cross-town traffic was jerky and slow. The taxi windows were striped with orange sodium glow from the streetlights and I was feeling really tense and grumpy. Deb had sensibly stopped talking to me and was looking out the window. I was probably reviewing some silent list of my grievances against Fate at that moment, when suddenly the sky opened, the trumpets blared, the angels sang!

Well, no. The windshield wipers kept thumping and the sodium light kept strobing in slow motion over the windows (which was frankly a bit migrainous and probably why Deb wasn't talking). But at the moment, the angels should have sung. Because I was having a Revelation.

(I'm not the spiritual type, by the way. This is the only Revelation I've ever had.)

'Look at yourself,' a voice told me. I think it was my own voice, and I think it was just in my head, but it seemed really *loud*. 'You're in a cab going across London with your beautiful publisher wife. You write books for a living. You get up when you want to and dress the way you want to, and take naps at any hour of the day and call it "plotting". But even more importantly, you idiot man, you are on your way to MICHAEL MOORCOCK'S HOUSE! He called you up – he knows your first name! He invited you to come over just like you were ANOTHER HUMAN BEING and not a slobbering fanboy. He even seems to LIKE you.'

'HELLO!' the inner voice thundered. 'Michael Moorcock called you up and invited you over to dinner. Nobody paid him or put a gun to his head or ANYTHING. He just called you up and said, "Come over."

'So why are you being such a @$%#head?'

And instantly, as if the sky truly had opened up and the top of the cab had popped off and the heavenly sunshine of wisdom had poured down on me, I ceased my @$%#headedness forever. (Or at least for the rest of the evening.)

'Hosanna,' I cried, or something like that. 'My own fifteen-year-old self would shake his head in awe and tell me that I am the luckiest human being in the world – and he would be right. I must never forget that.'

And I never have. And that's why, above all the other reasons (and those reasons are plentiful, among them his writerly skill, his wit, imagination, fiery compassion and gloriously cracked poetic soul), above even the immense influence he's had on my writing... that's why Michael Moorcock is my religion.

He changed my life forever. Twice.

Hosanna!

Tad Williams
November 2008

Stormbringer

And Elric, who had within him
a greater destiny than he knew, now dwelt
in Karlaak with Zarozinia, his wife,
and his sleep was troubled, his dream
dark, one brooding night in the
Month of Anemone...

For J.G. Ballard, whose enthusiasm for Elric gave me encouragement to begin this particular book, my first attempt at a full-length novel, and for Jim Cawthorn, whose illustrations based on my ideas in turn gave me inspiration for certain scenes in this book, and for Dave Britton, who kept the magazines in which the serial first appeared and who kindly loaned them to me so that I could restore this novel to its original shape and length.

Prologue

THERE CAME A time when there was great movement upon the Earth and above it, when the destiny of Men and Gods was hammered out upon the forge of Fate, when monstrous wars were brewed and mighty deeds were designed. And there rose up in this time, which was called the Age of the Young Kingdoms, heroes. Greatest of these heroes was a doom-driven adventurer who bore a crooning runeblade that he loathed.

His name was Elric of Melniboné, king of ruins, lord of a scattered race that had once ruled the ancient world. Elric, sorcerer and swordsman, slayer of kin, despoiler of his homeland, white-faced albino, last of his line.

Elric, who had come to Karlaak by the Weeping Waste and had married a wife in whom he found some peace, some surcease from the torment in him.

And Elric, who had within him a greater destiny than he knew, now dwelt in Karlaak with Zarozinia, his wife, and his sleep was troubled, his dream dark, one brooding night in the Month of Anemone...

Book One

Dead God's Homecoming

In which, at long last, Elric's fate begins to be revealed to him as the forces of Law and Chaos gather strength for the final battle which will decide the future of Elric's world...

Chapter One

ABOVE THE ROLLING Earth great clouds tumbled down and bolts of lightning charged groundwards to slash the midnight black, split trees in twain and sear through roofs that cracked and broke.

The dark mass of forest trembled with the shock and out of it crept six hunched, unhuman figures who paused to stare beyond the low hills towards the outline of a city. It was a city of squat walls and slender spires, of graceful towers and domes; and it had a name which the leader of the creatures knew. Karlaak by the Weeping Waste it was called.

Not of natural origin, the storm was ominous. It groaned around the city of Karlaak as the creatures skulked past the open gates and made their way through shadows towards the elegant palace where Elric slept. The leader raised an axe of black iron in its clawed hand. The group came to a stealthy halt and regarded the sprawling palace which lay on a hill surrounded by languorously scented gardens. The earth shook as lightning lashed it and thunder prowled across the turbulent sky.

'Chaos has aided us in this matter,' the leader grunted. 'See – already the guards fall in magic slumber and our entrance is thus made simple. The Lords of Chaos are good to their servants.'

He spoke the truth. Some supernatural force had been at work and the warriors guarding Elric's palace had dropped to the ground, their snores echoing the thunder. The servants of Chaos crept past the prone guards, into the main courtyard and from there into the darkened palace. Unerringly they climbed twisting staircases, moved softly along gloomy corridors, to arrive at length outside the room where Elric and his wife lay in uneasy sleep.

As the leader laid a hand upon the door, a voice cried out from within the room: '*What's this? What things of hell disrupt my rest?*'

'He sees us!' sharply whispered one of the creatures.

'No,' the leader said, 'he sleeps – but such a sorcerer as this Elric is not so easily lulled into a stupor. We had best make speed and do our work, for if he wakes it will be the harder!'

He twisted the handle and eased the door open, his axe half raised. Beyond the bed, heaped with tumbled furs and silks, lightning gashed the night again, showing the white face of the albino close to that of his dark-haired wife.

Even as they entered, he rose stiffly in the bed and his crimson eyes opened, staring out at them. For a moment the eyes were glazed and then the albino forced himself awake, shouting: 'Begone, you creatures of my dreams!'

The leader cursed and leapt forward, but he had been instructed not to slay this man. He raised the axe threateningly.

'Silence – your guards cannot aid you!'

Elric jumped from the bed and grasped the thing's wrist, his face close to the fanged muzzle. Because of his albinism he was physically weak and required magic to give him strength. But so quickly did he move that he had wrested the axe from the creature's hand and smashed the shaft between its eyes. Snarling, it fell back, but its comrades jumped forward. There were five of them, huge muscles moving beneath their furred skins.

Elric clove the skull of the first as others grappled with him. His body was spattered with the thing's blood and brains and he gasped in disgust at the foetid stuff. He managed to wrench his arm away and bring the axe up and down into the collarbone of another. But then he felt his legs gripped and he fell, confused but still battling. Then there came a great blow on his head and pain blazed through him. He made an effort to rise, failed and fell back insensible.

Thunder and lightning still disturbed the night when, with throbbing head, he awoke and got slowly to his feet using a bedpost as support. He stared dazedly around him.

Zarozinia was gone. The only other figure in the room was the stiff corpse of the beast he had killed. His black-haired girl-wife had been abducted.

Shaking, he went to the door and flung it open, calling for his guards, but none answered him.

His runesword Stormbringer hung in the city's armoury and would take time to get. His throat tight with pain and anger, he ran down the corridors and stairways, dazed with anxiety, trying to grasp the implications of his wife's disappearance.

Above the palace, thunder still crashed, eddying about in the noisy night. The palace seemed deserted and he had the sudden feeling that he was completely alone, that he had been abandoned. But as he ran out into the main courtyard and saw the insensible guards he realised at once that their slumber could not be natural. Realisation was coming even as he ran through the gardens, through the gates and down to the city, but there was no sign of his wife's abductors.

Where had they gone?

He raised his eyes to the shouting sky, his white face stark and twisted with frustrated anger. There was no sense to it. Why had they taken her? He had enemies, he knew, but none who could summon such supernatural help. Who, apart from himself, could work this mighty sorcery that made the skies themselves shake and a city sleep?

To the house of Lord Voashoon, Chief Senator of Karlaak and father of Zarozinia, Elric ran panting like a wolf. He banged with his fists upon the door, yelling at the astonished servants within.

'Open! It is Elric. Hurry!'

The doors gaped back and he was through them. Lord Voashoon came stumbling down the stairs into the chamber, his face heavy with sleep.

'What is it, Elric?'

'Summon your warriors. Zarozinia has been abducted. Those who took her were demons and may be far from here by now – but we must search in case they escaped by land.'

Lord Voashoon's face became instantly alert and he shouted terse orders to his servants between listening to Elric's explanation of what had happened.

'And I must have entrance into the armoury,' Elric concluded. 'I must have Stormbringer!'

'But you renounced the blade for fear of its evil power over you!' Lord Voashoon reminded him quietly.

Elric replied impatiently. 'Aye – but I renounced the blade for Zarozinia's sake, too. I must have Stormbringer if I am to bring her back. The logic is simple. Quickly, give me the key.'

In silence Lord Voashoon fetched the key and led Elric to the armoury where the weapons and armour of his ancestors were held, unused for centuries. Through the dusty place strode Elric to a dark alcove that seemed to contain something which lived.

He heard a soft moaning from the great black battle-blade as he reached out a slim-fingered white hand to take it. It was heavy, yet perfectly balanced, a two-handed broadsword of prodigious size, with its wide crosspiece and its blade smooth and broad, stretching for over five feet from the hilt. Near the hilt, mystic runes were engraved and even Elric did not know what they fully signified.

'Again I must make use of you, Stormbringer,' he said as he buckled the sheath about his waist, 'and I must conclude that we are too closely linked now for less than death to separate us.'

With that he was striding from the armoury and back to the courtyard where mounted guards were already sitting nervous steeds, awaiting his instructions.

Standing before them, he drew Stormbringer so that the sword's strange, black radiance flickered around him, his white face, as pallid as bleached bone, staring out of it at the horsemen.

'You go to chase demons this night. Search the countryside, scour forest and plain for those who have done this thing to our princess! Though it's likely that her abductors used supernatural means to make their escape, we cannot be sure. So search – and search well!'

All through the raging night they searched but could find no trace of either the creatures or Elric's wife. And when dawn came, a smear of blood in the morning sky, his men returned to Karlaak where Elric awaited them, now filled with the nigromantic vitality which his sword supplied.

'Lord Elric – shall we retrace our trail and see if daylight yields a clue?' cried one.

'He does not hear you,' another murmured as Elric gave no sign.

But then Elric turned his pain-racked head and he said bleakly, 'Search no more. I have had time to meditate and must seek my wife with the aid of sorcery. Disperse. You can do nothing further.'

Then he left them and went back towards his palace, knowing that there was still one way of learning where Zarozinia had been taken. It was a method which he ill-liked, yet it would have to be employed.

Curtly, upon returning, Elric ordered everyone from his chamber, barred the door and stared down at the dead thing. Its congealed blood was still on him, but the axe with which he had slain it had been taken away by its comrades.

Elric prepared the body, stretching out its limbs on the floor. He drew the shutters of the windows so that no light filtered into the room, and lit a brazier in one corner. It swayed on its chains as the oil-soaked rushes flared. He went to a small chest by the window and took out a pouch. From this he removed a bunch of dried herbs and with a hasty gesture flung them on the brazier so that it gave off a sickly odour and the room began to fill with smoke. Then he stood over the corpse, his body rigid, and began to sing an incantation in the old language of his forefathers, the Sorcerer Emperors of Melniboné. The song seemed scarcely akin to human speech, rising and falling from a deep groan to a high-pitched shriek.

The brazier speared flaring red light over Elric's face and grotesque shadows skipped about the room. On the floor the dead corpse began to stir, its ruined head moving from side to side. Elric drew his runesword and placed it before him, his two hands on the hilt. 'Arise, soulless one!' he commanded.

Slowly, with jerky movements, the creature raised itself stiffly upright and pointed a clawed finger at Elric, its glazed eyes staring as if beyond him.

'All this,' it whispered, 'was preordained. Think not that you can escape your fate, Elric of Melniboné. You have tampered with my corpse and I am a creature of Chaos. My masters will avenge me.'

'How?'

'Your destiny is already laid down. You will know soon enough.'

'Tell me, dead one, why did you come to abduct my wife? Who sent you hither? Where has my wife been taken?'

'Three questions, Lord Elric. Requiring three answers. You know that the dead who have been raised by sorcery can answer nothing directly.'

'Aye – that I know. So answer as you can.'

'Then listen well for I may recite only once my rede and then must return to the nether regions where my being may peacefully rot to nothing. Listen:

> *'Beyond the ocean brews a battle;*
> *Beyond the battle blood shall fall.*
> *If Elric's kinsman ventures with him*
> *(Bearing a twin of that he bears)*
> *To a place where, man-forsaken,*
> *Dwells the one who should not live,*
> *Then a bargain shall be entered.*
> *Elric's wife shall be restored.'*

With this the thing fell to the floor and did not stir thereafter.

Elric went to the window and opened the shutters. Used as he was to enigmatic verse-omens, this one was difficult to unravel. As daylight entered the room, the rushes sputtered and the smoke faded. *Beyond the ocean...* There were many oceans.

He resheathed his runesword and climbed onto the disordered bed to lie down and contemplate the rede. At last, after long minutes of this contemplation, he remembered something he had heard from a traveller who had come to Karlaak, from Tarkesh, a nation of the Western Continent, beyond the Pale Sea.

The traveller had told him how there was trouble brewing between the land of Dharijor and the other nations of the West. Dharijor had contravened treaties she had signed with her neighbouring kingdoms and had signed a new one with the Theocrat of

Pan Tang. Pan Tang was an unholy island dominated by its dark aristocracy of warrior-wizards. It was from here that Elric's old enemy, Theleb K'aarna, had come. Its capital of Hwamgaarl was called the City of Screaming Statues and until recently its residents had had little contact with the folk of the outside world. Jagreen Lern was the new Theocrat and an ambitious man. His alliance with Dharijor could only mean that he sought more power over the nations of the Young Kingdoms. The traveller had said that strife was sure to break out at any moment since there was ample evidence that Dharijor and Pan Tang had entered a war alliance.

Now, as his memory improved, Elric related this information with the news he had had recently that Queen Yishana of Jharkor, a neighbouring kingdom to Dharijor, had recruited the aid of Dyvim Slorm and his Imrryrian mercenaries. And Dyvim Slorm was Elric's only kinsman. This meant that Jharkor must be preparing for battle against Dharijor. The two facts were too closely linked with the prophecy to be ignored.

Even as he thought upon it, he was gathering his clothes together and preparing for a journey. There was nothing for it but to go to Jharkor and speedily, for there he was sure to meet his kinsman. And there, also, there would soon be a battle if all the evidence were true.

Yet the prospect of the journey, which would take many days, caused a cold ache to grow in his heart as he thought of the weeks to come in which he would not know how his wife fared.

'No time for that,' he told himself as he laced up his black quilted jacket. 'Action is all that's required of me now – and speedy action.'

He held the sheathed runeblade before him, staring beyond it into space. 'I swear by Arioch that those who have done this, whether they be man or immortal, shall suffer from their deed. Hear me, Arioch! That is my oath!'

But his words found no answer and he sensed that Arioch, his patron demon, had either not heard him or else heard his oath and was unmoved.

Then he was striding from the death-heavy chamber, yelling for his horse.

Chapter Two

WHERE THE SIGHING Desert gave way to the borders of Ilmiora, between the coasts of the Eastern Continent and the lands of Tarkesh, Dharijor, Jharkor and Shazaar, there lay the Pale Sea.

It was a cold sea, a morose and chilling sea, but ships preferred to cross from Ilmiora to Dharijor by means of it, rather than chance the weirder dangers of the Straits of Chaos which were lashed by eternal storms and inhabited by malevolent sea-creatures.

On the deck of an Ilmioran schooner, Elric of Melniboné stood wrapped in his cloak, shivering and staring gloomily at the cloud-covered sky.

The captain, a stocky man with blue, humorous eyes, came struggling along the deck towards him. He had a cup of hot wine in his hands. He steadied himself by clinging to a piece of rigging and gave the cup to Elric.

'Thanks,' said the albino gratefully. He sipped the wine. 'How soon before we make the port of Banarva, captain?'

The captain pulled the collar of his leather jerkin about his unshaven face. 'We're sailing slow, but we should sight the Tarkesh peninsula well before sunset.' Banarva was in Tarkesh, one of its chief trading posts. The captain leaned on the rail. 'I wonder how long these waters will be free for ships now that war's broken out between the kingdoms of the West. Both Dharijor and Pan Tang have been notorious in the past for their piratical activities. They'll soon extend them under the guise of war, I'll warrant.'

Elric nodded vaguely, his mind on other things than the prospect of piracy.

Disembarking in the chilly evening at the port of Banarva, Elric soon saw ample evidence that war darkened the lands of the

Young Kingdoms. There were rumours rife, talk of nothing but battles gained and warriors lost. From the confused gossip, he could get no clear impression of how the war went, save that the decisive battle was yet to be fought.

Loquacious Banarvans told him that all over the Western Continent men were marching. From Myyrrhn, he heard, the winged men were flying. From Jharkor, the White Leopards, Queen Yishana's personal guard, ran towards Dharijor, while Dyvim Slorm and his mercenaries pressed northwards to meet them.

Dharijor was the strongest nation of the West and Pan Tang was a formidable ally, more for her people's occult knowledge than for her numbers. Next in power to Dharijor came Jharkor, who, with her allies Tarkesh, Myyrrhn and Shazaar, was still not as strong as those who threatened the security of the Young Kingdoms.

For some years Dharijor had sought an opportunity for conquest and the hasty alliance against her had been made in an effort to stop her before she had fully prepared for conquest. Whether this effort would succeed, Elric did not know, and those who spoke to him were equally uncertain.

The streets of Banarva were packed with soldiers and supply trains of horses and oxen. The harbour was filled with warships and it was difficult to find lodgings since most inns and many private houses had been requisitioned by the army. And it was the same all over the Western Continent. Everywhere, men strapped metal about them, bestrode heavy chargers, sharpened their arms, and rode beneath bright silken banners to slay and to despoil.

Here, without doubt, Elric reflected, he would find the battle of the prophecy. He tried to forget his tormented longing for news of Zarozinia and turned his moody eyes towards the west. Stormbringer hung like an anchor at his side and he fingered it constantly, hating it even as it fed him his vitality.

He spent the night in Banarva and by morning had hired a good horse and was riding through the sparse grassland towards Jharkor.

Across a war-torn world rode Elric, his crimson eyes burning with a fierce anger at the sights of wanton destruction he witnessed. Although he had himself lived by his sword for many years and had committed acts of murder, robbery and urbicide, he disliked the senselessness of wars such as this, of men who killed one another for only the vaguest of reasons. It was not that he pitied the slain or hated the slayers; he was too remote from ordinary men to care greatly about what they did. Yet, in his own tortured way, he was an idealist who, because he lacked peace and security himself, resented the sights of strife which the war brought to him. His ancestors, he knew, had also been remote, yet they had delighted in the conflicts of the men of the Young Kingdoms, observing them from a distance and judging themselves above such activities; above the morass of sentiment and emotion in which these new men struggled. For ten thousand years the Sorcerer Emperors of Melniboné had ruled this world, a race without conscience or moral creed, unneedful of reasons for their acts of conquest, seeking no excuses for their natural malicious tendencies. But Elric, the last in the direct line of emperors, was not like them. He was capable of cruelty and malevolent sorcery, had little pity, yet could love and hate more violently than ever his ancestors. And these strong passions, perhaps, had been the cause of his breaking with his homeland and travelling the world to compare himself against these new men since he could find none in Melniboné who shared his feelings. And it was because of these twin forces of love and hate that he had returned to have vengeance on his cousin Yyrkoon who had put Cymoril, Elric's betrothed, into a magic slumber and usurped the kingship of Melniboné, the Dragon Isle, the last territory of the fallen Bright Empire. With the aid of a fleet of reavers, Elric had razed Imrryr in his vengeance-taking, destroyed the Dreaming City and scattered for ever the race who had founded it so that the last survivors were now mercenaries roaming the world to sell their arms to whoever bid highest. Love and hate; they had led him to kill Yyrkoon who deserved death and, inadvertently, Cymoril, who did not. Love and hate. They welled in him now as bitter smoke stung his throat and he passed a straggling group of townspeople who were fleeing, without knowledge of their direction, from the latest depredation of the roving Dharijorian troops who had struck far into this part of Tarkesh and had met little hindrance from the armies of King Hilran of Tarkesh whose main force was concentrated further north, readying itself for the major battle.

Now Elric rode close to the Western Marches, near the Jharkorian border. Here lived sturdy foresters and harvesters in better times. But now the forests were blackened and burned and the crops of the fields were ruined.

His journey, which was speedy for he wasted no time, took him through one of the stark forests where remnants of trees cast cold silhouettes against the grey, seething sky. He raised the hood of his cloak over his head so that the heavy black fabric completely hid his face, and rode on as rain rushed suddenly down and beat through the skeleton trees, sweeping across the distant plains beyond so that all the world seemed grey and black with the hiss of the rain a constant and depressing sound.

Then, as he passed a ruined hovel which was half cottage and half hole in the earth, a cawing voice called out:

'*Lord Elric!*'

Astonished that he should be recognised, he turned his bleak face in the direction of the voice, pushing his hood back as he did so. A ragged figure appeared in the hole's opening. It beckoned him closer. Puzzled, he walked his horse towards the figure and saw that it was an old man, or perhaps a woman, he couldn't tell.

'You know my name. How?'

'Thou art a legend throughout the Young Kingdoms. Who could not recognise that white face and heavy blade thou art carrying?'

'True, perhaps, but I have a notion there is more to this than chance recognition. Who are you and how do you know the High Speech of Melniboné?' Elric deliberately used the coarse common speech.

'Thou shouldst know that all who practise dark sorcery use the High Tongue of those who are past masters in its arts. Wouldst thou guest with me a while?'

Elric looked at the hovel and shook his head. He was fastidious at the best of times. The wretch smiled and made a mock bow, resorting to the common speech and saying: 'So the mighty lord disdains to grace my poor home. But does he not perhaps wonder why the fire which raged through this forest a while ago did not, in fact, harm me?'

'Aye,' said Elric thoughtfully, 'that is an interesting riddle.'

The hag took a step towards him. 'Soldiers came not a month gone – from Pan Tang they were. Devil Riders with their hunting tigers running with them. They despoiled the harvest and burned even the forests that those who fled them might not eat game or berries here. I lived in this forest all my life, doing a little simple magic and prophecy for my needs. But when I saw the walls of flame soon to engulf me, I cried the name of a demon I knew – a thing from Chaos which, latterly, I had dared not summon. It came.

'"Save me," I cried, "And what would ye do in return?" said the demon. "Anything," I quoth. "Then bear this message for my masters," it said. "When the kinslayer known as Elric of Melniboné shall pass this way, tell him that there is one kinsman he shall not slay and he will be found in Sequaloris. If Elric loves his wife, he will play his rôle. If he plays it well, his wife shall be returned." So I fixed the message in my mind and now give it thee as I swore.'

'Thanks,' said Elric, 'and what did you give in the first place for the power to summon such a demon?'

'Why, my soul, of course. But it was an old one and not of much worth. Hell could be no worse than this existence.'

'Then why did you not let yourself burn, your soul unbartered?'

'I wish to live,' said the wretch, smiling again. 'Oh, life is good. My own life, perhaps, is squalid, yet the life around me, that is what I love. But let me not keep you, my lord, for you have weightier matters on your mind.' Once more the wretch gave a mock bow as Elric rode off, puzzled, but encouraged. His wife still lived and was safe. But what bargain must he strike before he could get her back?

Savagely he goaded his horse into a gallop, heading for Sequaloris in Jharkor. Behind him, faintly through the beating rain, he heard a cackling at once mocking and miserable.

Now his direction was not so vague, and he rode at great speed, but cautiously, avoiding the roving bands of invaders, until at length the arid plains gave way to the lusher wheatlands of the Sequa province of Jharkor. Another day's ride and Elric entered the small walled city of Sequaloris which had so far not suffered attack. Here, he discovered preparations for war and learned news that was of greater interest to him.

The Imrryrian mercenaries, led by Dyvim Slorm, Elric's cousin and son of Dyvim Tvar, Elric's old friend, were due to arrive next day in Sequaloris.

There had been a certain enmity between Elric and the Imrryrians since the albino had been the direct cause of their need to leave the ruins of the Dreaming City and live as mercenaries. But those times were past, long since, and on two previous occasions he and the Imrryrians had fought on the same side. He was their leader by right and the ties of tradition were strong in the elder race. Elric prayed to Arioch that Dyvim Slorm would have some clue to his wife's whereabouts.

At noon of the next day the mercenary army rode swaggering into the city. Elric met them close to the city gate. The Imrryrian warriors were obviously weary from the long ride and were loaded with booty since, before Yishana sent for them, they had been raiding in Shazaar close to the Marshes of the Mist. They were different from any other race, these Imrryrians, with their tapering faces, slanting eyes and high cheekbones. They were pale and slim with long, soft hair drifting to their shoulders. The finery they wore was not stolen, but definitely Melnibonéan in design; shimmering cloths of gold, blue and green, metals of delicate workmanship and intricately patterned. They carried lances with long, sweeping heads and there were slender swords at their sides. They sat arrogantly in their saddles, convinced of their superiority over other mortals, and were, as Elric, not quite human in their unearthly beauty.

He rode up to meet Dyvim Slorm, his own sombre clothes contrasting with theirs. He wore a tall-collared jacket of quilted leather, black and buckled in by a broad, plain belt at which hung a poignard and Stormbringer. His milk-white hair was held from his eyes by a fillet of black bronze and his breeks and boots were also black. All this black set off sharply his white skin and crimson, glowing eyes.

Dyvim Slorm bowed in his saddle, showing only slight surprise.

'Cousin Elric. So the omen was true.'

'What omen, Dyvim Slorm?'

'A raven's – your name bird if I remember.'

It had been customary for Melnibonéans to identify newborn children with birds of their choice; thus Elric's was a raven, a wise, if unpopular, bird.

'What did it tell you, cousin?' Elric asked eagerly.

'It gave a puzzling message. While we had barely gone from the Marshes of the Mist, it came and perched on my shoulder and spoke in human tongue. It told me to come to Sequaloris and there I would meet my king. From Sequaloris we were to journey together to join Yishana's army and the battle, whether won or lost, would resolve the direction of our linked destinies thereafter. Do you make sense of that, cousin?'

'Some,' Elric frowned. 'But come – I have a place reserved for you at the inn. I will tell you all I know over wine – if we can find decent wine in this forsaken hamlet. I need help, cousin; as much help as I can obtain, for Zarozinia has been abducted by supernatural agents and I have a feeling that this and the wars are but two elements in a greater play.'

'Then quickly, to the inn. My curiosity is further piqued. This matter increases in interest for me. First ravens and omens, now abductions and strife! What else, I wonder, are we to meet!'

With the Imrryrians straggling after them through the cobbled streets, scarcely a hundred warriors but hardened by their outlawed life, Elric and Dyvim Slorm made their way to the inn and there, in haste, Elric outlined all he had learned.

Before replying, his cousin sipped his wine and carefully placed the cup upon the board, pursing his lips. 'I have a feeling in my bones that we are puppets in some struggle between the gods. For all our blood and flesh and will, we can see none of the bigger conflict save for a few scarcely related details.'

'That may be so,' said Elric impatiently, 'but I'm greatly angered at being involved and require my wife's release. I have no notion why we, together, must make the bargain for her return, neither can I guess what it is we have that those who captured her want. But, if the omens are sent by the same agents, then we had best do as we are told, for the meantime, until we can see matters more clearly. Then, perhaps, we can act upon our *own* volition.'

'That's wise,' Dyvim Slorm nodded, 'and I'm with you in it.' He smiled slightly and added: 'Whether I like it or not, I fancy.'

Elric said: 'Where lies the main army of Dharijor and Pan Tang? I heard it was gathering.'

'It has gathered – and marches closer. The impending battle will decide who rules the Western lands. I'm committed to Yishana's side, not only because she has employed us to aid her, but because I felt that if the warped lords of Pan Tang dominate these nations, then tyranny will come upon them and they will threaten the security of the whole world. It is a sad thing when a Melnibonéan has to consider such problems.' He smiled ironically. 'Aside from that, I like them not, these sorcerous upstarts – they seek to emulate the Bright Empire.'

'Aye,' Elric said. 'They are an island culture, as ours was. They are sorcerers and warriors as our ancestors were. But their sorcery is less healthy than ever ours was. Our ancestors committed frightful deeds, yet it was *natural* to them. These newcomers, more human than we, have perverted their humanity whereas we never possessed it in the same degree. There will never be another Bright Empire, nor can their power last more than ten thousand years. This is a fresh age, Dyvim Slorm, in more than one way. The time of subtle sorcery is on the wane. Men are finding new means of harnessing natural power.'

'Our knowledge is ancient,' Dyvim Slorm agreed, 'yet, so old is it that it has little relation to present events, I think. Our logic and learning are suited to the past...'

'I think you are right,' said Elric, whose mingled emotions

were suited neither to past, present nor future. 'Aye, it is fitting that we should be wanderers, for we have no place in this world.'

They drank in silence, moodily, their minds on matters of philosophy. Yet, for all this, Elric's thoughts were forever turning to Zarozinia and the fear of what might have befallen her. The very innocence of this girl, her vulnerability and her youth had been, to some degree at least, his salvation. His protective love for her had helped to keep him from brooding too deeply on his own doom-filled life and her company had eased his melancholy. The strange rede of the dead creature lingered in his memory. Undoubtedly the rede had referred to a battle, and the raven which Dyvim Slorm had seen had spoken of one also. The battle was sure to be the forthcoming one between Yishana's forces and those of Sarosto of Dharijor and Jagreen Lern of Pan Tang. If he was to find Zarozinia then he must go with Dyvim Slorm and there take part in the conflict. Though he might perish, he reasoned that he had best do as the omens ordered – otherwise he could lose even the slight chance of ever seeing Zarozinia again. He turned to his cousin.

'I'll make my way with you tomorrow, and use my blade in the battle. Whatever else, I have the feeling that Yishana will need every warrior against the Theocrat and his allies.'

Dyvim Slorm agreed. 'Not only *our* doom but the doom of nations will be at stake in this...'

Chapter Three

TEN TERRIBLE MEN drove their yellow chariots down a black mountain which vomited blue and scarlet fire and shook in a spasm of destruction.

In such a manner, all over the globe, the forces of nature were disrupted and rebellious. Though few realised it, the Earth was changing. The Ten knew why, and they knew of Elric and how their knowledge linked with him.

The night was pale purple and the sun hung a bloody globe over the mountains, for it was late summer. In the valleys, cottages were burning as smoking lava smacked against the straw roofs.

Sepiriz, in the leading chariot, saw the villagers running, a confused rabble – like ants whose hills had been scattered. He turned to the blue-armoured man behind him and he smiled almost gaily.

'See them run,' he said. 'See them run, brother. Oh, the joy of it – such forces there are at work!'

''Tis good to have woken at this time,' his brother agreed, shouting over the rumbling noise of the volcano.

Then the smile left Sepiriz and his eyes narrowed. He lashed at his twin horses with a bull-hide whip, so that blood laced the flanks of the great black steeds as they galloped even faster down the steep mountain.

In the village, one man saw the Ten in the distance. He shrieked, voicing his fear in a warning:

'The fire has driven them out of the mountain. Hide – escape! The men from the volcano have awakened – they are coming. The Ten have awakened according to the prophecy – it is the end of the world!' Then the mountain gushed a fresh spewing of hot rock and flaming lava and the man was struck down, screamed as he burned, and died. He died needlessly, for the Ten had no interest in him or his fellows.

Sepiriz and his brothers rode straight through the village, their chariot wheels rattling on the coarse street, the hoofs of their horses pounding.

Behind them, the mountain bellowed.

'To Nihrain!' cried Sepiriz. 'Speedily, brethren, for there is much work to do. A blade must be brought from limbo and a pair of men must be found to carry it to Xanyaw!'

Joy filled him as he saw the earth shuddering about him and heard the gushing of fire and rock behind him. His black body glistened, reflecting the flames of the burning houses. The horses leaned in their harness, dragging the bucking chariot at wild speed, their hoofs blurred movement over the ground so that it often seemed they flew.

Perhaps they did, for the steeds of Nihrain were known to be different from ordinary beasts.

Now they flung themselves along a gorge, now up a mountain path, making their speedy way towards the Chasm of Nihrain, the ancient home of the Ten who had not returned there for two thousand years.

Again, Sepiriz laughed. He and his brothers bore a terrible responsibility, for though they had no loyalty to men or gods, they were Fate's spokesmen and thus bore an awful knowledge within their immortal skulls.

For centuries they had slept in their mountain chamber, dwelling close to the dormant heart of the volcano since extremes of heat and cold bothered them little. Now the spewing rock had awakened them and they knew that their time had come – the time for which they had been waiting for millennia.

This was why Sepiriz sang in joy. At last he and his brothers were to be allowed to perform their ultimate function. And this involved two Melnibonéans, the two surviving members of the royal line of the Bright Empire.

Sepiriz knew they lived – they had to be alive, for without them Fate's scheme was impossible. But there were those upon the Earth, Sepiriz knew, who were capable of cheating Fate, so powerful were they. Their minions lay everywhere, particularly among the new race of men, but ghouls and demons were also their tools.

This made his chosen task the harder.

But now – to Nihrain! To the hewn city and there to draw the threads of destiny into a finer net. There was still a little time, but it was running short; and Time the Unknown was master of all...

The pavilions of Queen Yishana and her allies were grouped thickly about a series of small, wooded hills. The trees afforded cover from a distance and no campfires burned to give away their position. Also the sounds of the great army were as muted as possible. Outriders went to and fro, reporting the enemy's positions and keeping wary eyes open for spies.

But Elric and his Imrryrians were unchallenged as they rode in, for the albino and his men were easily recognisable and it was well-known that the feared Melnibonéan mercenaries had elected to aid Yishana.

Elric said to Dyvim Slorm: 'I had best pay my respects to Queen Yishana, on account of our old bond, but I do not want her to know of my wife's disappearance – otherwise she may try to hinder me. We shall just say that I have come to aid her, out of friendship.'

Dyvim Slorm nodded, and Elric left his cousin to tend to making camp, while he went at once to Yishana's tent where the tall queen awaited him impatiently.

The look in her eyes was shielded as he entered. She had a heavy, sensuous face that was beginning to show signs of ageing. Her long hair was black and shone around her head. Her breasts were large and her hips broader than Elric remembered. She was sitting in a padded chair and the table before her was scattered with battle-maps and writing materials, parchment, ink and quills.

'Good morning, wolf,' said she with a half-smile that was at once sardonic and provocative. 'My scouts reported that you were riding with your countrymen. This is pleasant. Have you forsaken your new wife to return to subtler pleasures?'

'No,' he said.

He stripped off his heavy riding cloak and flung it on a bench. 'Good morning, Yishana. You do not change. I've half a suspicion that Theleb K'aarna gave you a draught of the waters of Eternal Life before I killed him.'

'Perhaps he did. How goes your marriage?'

'Well,' he said as she moved closer and he felt the warmth of her body.

'And now I'm disappointed,' she smiled ironically and shrugged. They had been lovers on different occasions, in spite of the fact that Elric had been partially responsible for her brother's death during the raid on Imrryr. Dharmit of Jharkor's death had put her on the throne and, being an ambitious woman, she had not taken the news with too much sadness. Elric had no wish to resume the relationship, however.

He turned immediately to the matter of the forthcoming battle.

'I see you're preparing for more than a skirmish,' he said. 'What forces have you and what are your chances of winning?'

'There are my own White Leopards,' she told him, 'five hundred picked warriors who run as swiftly as horses, are as strong as mountain cats and as ferocious as blood-mad sharks – they are trained to kill and killing is all they know. Then there are my other troops – infantry and cavalry, some eighty lords in command. The best cavalry are from Shazaar, wild riders but clever fighters and well-disciplined. Tarkesh has sent fewer men since I understand King Hilran needed to defend his southern borders against a heavy attack. However, there are almost a thousand and fifty foot soldiers and some two hundred mounted men from Tarkesh. In all we can put perhaps six thousand trained warriors on the field. Serfs, slaves and the like are also fighting, but they will of course serve only to meet the initial onslaught and will die in the early part of the battle.'

Elric nodded. These were standard military tactics. 'And what of the enemy?'

'We have more numbers – but they have Devil Riders and hunting tigers. There are also some beasts they keep in cages – but we cannot guess what they are since the cages are covered.'

'I heard that the men of Myyrrhn are flying hither. The import must be great for them to leave their eyries.'

'If we lose this battle,' she said gravely, 'Chaos could easily engulf the Earth and rule over it. Every oracle from here to Shazaar says the same thing, that Jagreen Lern is but the tool of less natural masters, that he is aided by the Lords of Chaos. We are not only fighting for our lands, Elric, we are fighting for the human race!'

'Then let us hope we win,' he said.

Elric stood among the captains as they surveyed the mobilising army. Tall Dyvim Slorm was by his side, his golden shirt loose on his slim body and his manner confident, arrogant. Also here were hardened soldiers of many smaller campaigns; short, dark-faced men from Tarkesh with thick armour and black, oiled hair and beards. The half-naked winged men from Myyrrhn had arrived, with their brooding eyes, hawklike faces, their great wings folded on their backs, quiet, dignified, seldom speaking. The Shazaarian commanders were there also, in jackets of grey, brown and black, in rust-coloured bronze armour. With them stood the captain of Yishana's White Leopards, a long-legged, thick-bodied man with blond hair tied in a knot at the back of his bull-necked head, silver armour bearing the emblazon of a leopard, albino like Elric, rampant and snarling.

The time of the battle was drawing close...

Now, in the grey dawn, the two armies advanced upon each other, coming from opposite ends of a wide valley, flanked by low, wooded, hills.

The army of Pan Tang and Dharijor moved, a tide of dark metal, up the shallow valley to meet them. Elric, still unarmoured, watched as they approached, his horse stamping the turf. Dyvim Slorm, beside him, pointed and said: 'Look – there are the plotters – Sarosto on the left and Jagreen Lern on the right!'

The leaders headed their army, banners of dark silk rustling above their helms. King Sarosto and his thin ally, aquiline Jagreen Lern in glowing scarlet armour that seemed to be red-hot and may have been. On his helm was the Merman Crest of Pan Tang, for he claimed kinship with the sea-people. Sarosto's armour was dull, murky yellow, emblazoned with the Star of Dharijor upon which was the Cleft Sword which history said was borne by Sarosto's ancestor Atarn the City-Builder.

Behind them, instantly observable, came the Devil Riders of Pan Tang on their six-legged reptilian mounts, bred by sorcery it was said. Swarthy and with introspective expressions on their sharp faces, they carried long, curved sabres, naked at their belts. Prowling among them came over a hundred hunting tigers, trained like dogs, with tusklike teeth and claws that could rend a man to the bone with a single sweep. Beyond the rolling army as it moved towards them, Elric could just see the tops of the mysterious cage-wagons. What weird beasts did *they* contain? he wondered.

Then Yishana shouted a command.

The archers' arrows spread a rattling black cloud above them as Elric led the first wave of infantry down the hill to meet the van of the enemy army. That he should be forced to risk his life embittered him, but if he was ever to discover Zarozinia's whereabouts he had to play out his ordered part and pray that he lived.

The main force of cavalry followed the infantry, flanking it with orders to encircle the enemy if possible. Brightly clad Imrryrians and bronze-armoured Shazaarians were to one side. Blue-armoured Tarkeshites with brilliant plumes of red, purple and white, long lances levelled, and gold-armoured Jharkorians, longswords already unscabbarded, galloped on the other side. In the centre of Elric's advance phalanx loped Yishana's White Leopards and the queen herself rode beneath her banner, behind the first phalanx, leading a battalion of knights.

Down they rushed towards the enemy whose own arrows rose upwards and then swept down to clash against helmets or thud into flesh.

Now the sound of war-shouts smashed through the still dawn as they streaked down the slopes and clashed.

Elric found himself confronting lean Jagreen Lern, and the snarling Theocrat met Stormbringer's swing with a flame-red buckler which successfully protected him – proving the shield to be treated against sorcerous weapons.

Jagreen Lern's features wrinkled into a malicious smile as he recognised Elric. 'I was told you'd be here, Whiteface. I know you Elric and I know your doom!'

'Too many men appear to know my destiny better than I,' said the albino. 'But perhaps if I slay you, Theocrat, I may force the secret from you before you die?'

'Oh, no! That is not my masters' plan at all.'

'Well, mayhap 'tis mine!'

He struck again at Jagreen Lern, but again the blade was turned, screaming its anger. He felt it move in his hand, felt it throb with chagrin, for normally the hell-forged blade could slice through metal however finely tempered.

In Jagreen Lern's gauntleted right hand was a huge war-axe which he now swung at the unprotected head of Elric's horse. This was odd since he was in a position to strike at Elric himself. The albino jerked his steed's head to one side, avoided the blow and drove again point first at Jagreen Lern's midriff. The rune-blade shrieked as it failed to pierce the armour. The war-axe swung again and Elric brought up his sword as protection but, in astonishment, was driven back in his saddle by the force of the blow, barely able to control his horse, one foot slipping from the stirrup.

Jagreen Lern struck again and successfully split the skull of Elric's horse which crumpled to its knees, blood and brains gushing, great eyes rolling as it died.

Flung from the beast, Elric rose painfully and readied himself for Jagreen Lern's next blow. But to his surprise, the sorcerer-king turned away and moved into the thick of the battle.

'Sadly your life is not mine to take, Whiteface! That is the prerogative of other powers. If you live and we are the victors – I will seek you out, perhaps.'

Unable, in his dazed condition, to make sense of this, Elric

looked desperately around for another horse and saw a Dharijorian mount, its head and foreparts well protected by dented black
armour, running loose and away from the fight.

Swiftly, he leapt for its harness and caught a dangling rein,
steadied the beast, got a foot into a stirrup and swung himself up
in the saddle which was uncomfortable for an unarmoured man.
Standing in the stirrups, Elric rode it back into the battle.

He hewed his way through the enemy knights, slaying now a
Devil Rider, now a hunting tiger that lashed at him with bared
fangs, now a gorgeously armoured Dharijorian commander, now
two foot soldiers who struck at him with halberds. His horse
reared like a monster and, desperately, he forced it closer to the
standard of Yishana until he could see one of the heralds.

Yishana's army was fighting bravely, but its discipline was lost.
It must regroup if it was to be most effective.

'Recall the cavalry!' Elric yelled. 'Recall the cavalry!'

The young herald looked up. He was badly pressed by two
Devil Riders. His attention diverted, he was skewered on a Devil
Rider's blade and shrieked as the two men butchered him.

Cursing, Elric rode closer and struck one of the attackers in the
side of the head. The man toppled and fell into the churned mud
of the field. The other Rider turned, only to meet howling Stormbringer's point, and he died yelling, as the runeblade drank his
soul.

The herald, still mounted, was dead in the saddle, his body a
mass of cuts. Elric leaned forward, tearing the bloody horn from
around the corpse's neck. Placing it to his lips, he sounded the
Cavalry Recall and caught a glimpse of horsemen turning. Now
he saw the standard itself begin to fall and realised that the stand-
ard-bearer was slain. He rose in the saddle and grasped the pole
which bore the bright flag of Jharkor and, with this in one hand,
the horn at his lips, attempted to rally his forces.

Slowly, the remnants of the battered army gathered around
him. Then Elric, taking control of the battle, did the only thing he
could – took the sole course of action which might save the day.

He sounded a long, wailing note on the horn. In response to

this he heard the beating of heavy wings as the men of Myyrrhn rose into the air.

Observing this, the enemy released the traps of the mysterious cages.

Elric groaned with despair.

A weird hooting preceded the sight of giant owls, thought extinct even in Myyrrhn the land of their origin, circling skyward.

The enemy had prepared against a threat from the air and, by some means, had produced the age-old enemies of the men of Myyrrhn.

Only slightly daunted by this unexpected sight, the men of Myyrrhn, armed with long spears, attacked the great birds. The embattled warriors on the ground were showered with blood and feathers. Corpses of men and birds began to flop downwards, crushing infantry and cavalry beneath them.

Through this confusion, Elric and the White Leopards of Yishana cut their way into the enemy to join up with Dyvim Slorm and his Imrryrians, the remnants of the Tarkeshite cavalry, and about a hundred Shazaarians, who had survived. Looking upwards, Elric saw that most of the great owls were destroyed, but only a handful of the men of Myyrrhn had survived the fight in the air. These, having done what they could against the owls, were themselves circling about preparing to leave the battle. Obviously they realised the hopelessness of it all.

Elric called to Dyvim Slorm as their forces joined: 'The battle's lost – Sarosto and Jagreen Lern rule here now!'

Dyvim Slorm hefted his longsword in his hand and gave Elric a look of assent. 'If we're to live to keep our destiny, we'd best make speed away from here!' he cried.

There was little more they could do.

'Zarozinia's life is more important to me than anything else!' Elric yelled. 'Let's look to our own predicament!'

But the weight of the enemy forces was like a vice, crushing Elric and his men. Blood covered Elric's face from a blow he had received on the forehead. It clogged his eyes so that he had to keep raising his left hand to his face to get rid of the stuff.

His right arm ached as he lifted Stormbringer again and again, hacking and stabbing about him, desperate now, for although the dreadful blade had a life, almost an intelligence, of its own, even it could not supply the vitality which Elric needed to remain entirely fresh. In a way he was glad, for he hated the runesword, though he had to depend on the force which flowed from it to him.

Stormbringer more than slew Elric's attackers – it drank their souls, and some of that life-force was passed on to the Melnibonéan monarch...

Now the ranks of the enemy fell back and seemed to open. Through this self-made breach, animals came running. Animals with gleaming eyes and red, fang-filled jaws. Animals with claws.

The hunting tigers of Pan Tang.

Horses screamed as the tigers leapt and rent them, tearing down mount and man and slashing at the throats of their victims. The tigers raised bloody snouts and stared around for a new prey. Terrified, many of Elric's small force fell back shouting. Most of the Tarkeshite knights broke and fled the field, precipitating the flight of the Jharkorians whose maddened horses bore them away and were soon followed by the few remaining Shazaarians still mounted. Soon only Elric, his Imrryrians and about forty White Leopards stood against the might of Dharijor and Pan Tang.

Elric raised his horn and sounded the Retreat, wheeled his black steed about and raced up the valley, Imrryrians behind him. But the White Leopards fought on to the last. Yishana had said that they knew nothing but how to kill. Evidently they also knew how to die.

Elric and Dyvim Slorm led the Imrryrians up the valley, half-thankful that the White Leopards covered their retreat. The Melnibonéan had seen nothing of Yishana since he had clashed with Jagreen Lern. He wondered what had become of her.

As they turned a bend in the valley, Elric understood the full battle plan of Jagreen Lern and his ally – for a strong, fresh force of foot soldiers and cavalry had assembled at the other end of the valley, for the purpose of cutting off any retreat made by his army.

Scarcely thinking, Elric urged his horse up the slopes of the

hills, his men following, ducking beneath the low branches of the birch trees as the Dharijorians rushed towards them, spreading out to cut off their escape.

Elric turned his horse about and saw that the White Leopards were still fighting around the standard of Jharkor and he headed back in that direction, keeping to the hills. Over the crest of the hills he rode, Dyvim Slorm and a handful of Imrryrians with him, and then they were galloping for open countryside while the knights of Dharijor and Pan Tang gave chase. They had obviously recognised Elric and wished either to kill or to capture him.

Ahead Elric could see that the Tarkeshites, Shazaarians and Jharkorians who had earlier fled had taken the same route out as he had. But they no longer rode together, were scattering away.

Elric and Dyvim Slorm fled westwards across unknown country while the other Imrryrians, to take attention off their leaders, rode to the north-east towards Tarkesh and perhaps a few days of safety.

The battle was won. The minions of evil were the victors and an age of terror had settled on the lands of the Young Kingdoms in the West.

Some days later, Elric, Dyvim Slorm, two Imrryrians, a Tarke-shite commander called Yedn-pad-Juizev, badly wounded in the side, and a Shazaarian foot soldier, Orozn, who had taken a horse away from the battle, were temporarily safe from pursuit and were trudging their horses wearily towards a range of slim-peaked mountains which loomed black against the red evening sky.

They had not spoken for some hours. Yedn-pad-Juizev was obviously dying and they could do nothing for him. He knew this also and expected nothing, merely rode with them for company. He was very tall for a Tarkeshite, his scarlet plume still bobbing on his dented blue-metal helmet, his breastplate scarred and smeared with his own blood and others'. His beard was black and shiny with oil, his nose a jutting crag on the rock of his soldier's face, his eyes half-glazed. He was bearing the pain well. Though they were impatient to reach the comparative safety of the mountain range, the others matched their pace to his, half in respect and half in fascination that a man could cling to life for so long.

Night came and a great yellow moon hung in the sky over the mountains. The sky was completely clear of cloud and stars shone brightly. The warriors wished that the night had been dark, storm-covered, for they could have then sought more security in the shadows. As it was the night was lighted and they could only hope that they reached the mountains soon – before the hunting tigers of Pan Tang discovered their tracks and they died under the rending claws of those dreadful beasts.

Elric was in a grim and thoughtful mood. For a while the Dharijorian and Pan Tang conquerors would be busy consolidating their new-won empire. Perhaps there would be quarrels between them when this was done, perhaps not. But soon, anyway, they would be very powerful and threatening the security of other nations on the Southern and Eastern Continents.

But all this, however much it overshadowed the fate of the whole world, meant little to Elric for he still could not clearly see his way to Zarozinia. He remembered the dead creature's prophecy, part of which had now come about. But still it meant little. He felt as if he were being driven constantly westwards, as if he must go further and further into the sparsely settled lands beyond Jharkor. Was it here his destiny lay? Was it here that Zarozinia's captors were? *Beyond the ocean brews a battle; Beyond the battle blood shall fall...*

Well, had the blood fallen, or was it yet to fall? What was the 'twin' that Elric's kinsman, Dyvim Slorm, bore? Who was the one who should not live?

Perhaps the secret lay in the mountains ahead of them?

Beneath the moon they rode, and at last came to a gorge. Half-way along it they located a cave and lay down inside to rest.

In the morning, Elric was awakened by a sound outside the cave. Instantly he drew Stormbringer and crept to the mouth of the cave. What he saw caused him to sheathe the blade and call in a soft voice to the battered man who was riding up the gorge towards the cave. 'Here, herald! We are friends!'

The man was one of Yishana's heralds. His surcoat was in ribbons, his armour crumpled on his body. He was swordless and without a helmet, a young man with his face made gaunt by weariness and despair. He looked up and relief came when he recognised Elric.

'My lord Elric – they said you were slain on the field.'

'I'm glad they did, since that makes pursuit less likely. Come inside.'

The others were awake now – all but one. Yedn-pad-Juizev had died, sleeping, in the night. Orozn yawned and jerked a thumb at the corpse. 'If we do not find food soon, I'll be tempted to eat our dead friend.'

The man looked at Elric for response to this jest, but seeing the albino's expression he was abashed and retreated to the depths of the cave grumbling and kicking at loose stones.

Elric leaned against the wall of the cave near the opening. 'What news have you?' he asked.

'Dark news, my lord. From Shazaar to Tarkesh black misery prevails and iron and fire beat across nations like an unholy storm. We are fully conquered. Only small bands of men carry on a hopeless struggle against the enemy. Some of our folk are already talking of turning bandit and preying on each other, so desperate have times become.'

Elric nodded. 'Such is what happens when foreign allies are beaten on friendly soil. What of Queen Yishana?'

'She fared ill, my lord. Clad in metal, she battled against a score of men before expiring – her body torn asunder by the force of their attack. Sarosto took her head for a keepsake and added it to other trophies including the hands of Karnarl, his half-brother who opposed him over the Pan Tang alliance, the eyes of Penik of Nargesser, who raised an army against him in that province. Theocrat Jagreen Lern ordered that all other prisoners be tortured to death and hanged in chains through the lands as warning against insurrection. They are an unholy pair, my lord!'

Elric's mouth grew tight when he heard this. Already it was becoming clear to him that his only route was westwards, for the conquerors would soon search him out if he went back. He turned to Dyvim Slorm. The Imrryrian's shirt was in rags and his left arm covered in dried blood.

'Our destiny appears to lie in the west,' he said quietly.

'Then let us make speed,' said his cousin, 'for I am impatient to get it over and at least learn whether we live or perish in this enterprise. We gained nothing by our encounter with the enemy, but wasted time.'

'I gained something,' Elric said, remembering his fight with Jagreen Lern. 'I gained the knowledge that Jagreen Lern *is* connected in some way with the kidnapping of my wife – and if he had aught to do with it, I'll claim my vengeance no matter what.'

'Now,' said Dyvim Slorm. 'Let us make haste to the west.'

Chapter Four

THEY DROVE DEEPER into the mountains that day, avoiding the few hunting parties sent out by the conquerors, but the two Imrryrians, recognising that their leaders were on a special journey, left to go in another direction. The herald was gone southward to spread his gloomy news so that only Elric, Dyvim Slorm and Orozn were left. They did not welcome Orozn's company, but bore with it for the meanwhile.

Then, after a day, Orozn disappeared and Elric and Dyvim Slorm ranged deeper into the black crags, riding through towering, oppressive canyons or along narrow paths.

Snow lay on the mountains, bright white against sharp black, filling gorges, making paths slippery and dangerous. Then one evening they came to a place where the mountains opened out into a wide valley and they rode with difficulty down the foothills of the mountains, their tracks making great black scars in the snow and their horses steaming, their breath billowing white in the cold air.

They observed a rider coming across the valley floor towards them. One rider they did not fear, so they waited for him to approach. To their surprise it was Orozn, clad in fresh garments of wolfskin and deer hide. He greeted them in a friendly manner.

'I have come seeking you both. You must have taken a more difficult route than mine.'

'From where have you come?' Elric asked; his face was drawn, his cheekbones emphasised by the sunken skin. He looked more like a wolf than ever with his red eyes gleaming. Zarozinia's fate weighed heavily on his mind.

'There is a settlement nearby. Come, I will take you to it.'

They followed Orozn for some way and it was getting near nightfall, the setting sun staining the mountains scarlet, when they reached the opposite side of the valley, dotted with a few birch trees and, further up, a cluster of firs.

Orozn led them into this grove.

They came screaming out of the dark, a dozen swarthy men, possessed by hatred – and something else. Weapons were raised in mailed hands. By their armour, these men were from Pan Tang. Orozn must have been captured and persuaded to lead Elric and his cousin into ambush.

Elric turned his horse, rearing.

'Orozn! You betrayed us!'

But Orozn was riding. He looked back once, his pale face tortured with guilt. Then his eyes darted away from Elric and Dyvim Slorm and he frowned, rode down the moss-wet hill back into the howling darkness of the night.

Elric lifted Stormbringer from his belt, gripped the hilt, blocked a blow from a brass-studded mace, slid his sword down the handle and sheared off his attacker's fingers. He and Dyvim Slorm were soon surrounded, yet he fought on, Stormbringer shrilling a wild, lawless song of death.

But Elric and Dyvim Slorm were still weak from the rigours of their past adventures. Not even Stormbringer's evil strength was sufficient fully to revitalise Elric's deficient veins and he was filled with fear – not of the attackers, but of the fact that he was doomed to die or be captured. And he had the feeling that these warriors had no knowledge of their master's part in the matter of the prophecy, did not realise that, perhaps, he was not meant to die at that moment.

In fact, he decided, as he battled, a great mistake was about to be perpetrated...

'Arioch!' he cried in his fear to the demon-god of Melniboné. 'Arioch! Aid me! Blood and souls for thine aid!'

But that intractable entity sent no aid.

Dyvim Slorm's long blade caught a man just below his gorget and pierced him through the throat. The other Pan Tang horsemen threw themselves at him but were driven back by his sweeping sword. Dyvim Slorm shouted: 'Why do we worship such a god when whim decides him so often?'

'Perhaps he thinks our time has come!' Elric yelled back as his runeblade drank another foe's life-force.

Tiring fast, they fought on until a new sound broke above the clash of arms – the sound of chariots and low, moaning cries.

Then they were sweeping into the mêlée, black men with handsome features and thin, proud mouths, their magnificent bodies half-naked as their cloaks of white fox fur streamed behind them and their javelins were flung with terrible accuracy at the bewildered men of Pan Tang.

Elric sheathed his sword and remained ready to fight or flee. 'This is the one – the white-faced one!' cried a black charioteer as he saw Elric. The chariots rolled to a halt, tall horses stamping and snorting. Elric rode up to the leader.

'I am grateful,' he said, half falling from his saddle in weariness. He turned the droop of his shoulders into a bow. 'You appear to know me – you are the third I've met while on this quest who recognises me without my being able to return the compliment.'

The leader tugged the fox cape about his naked chest and smiled with his thin lips. 'I'm named Sepiriz and you will know me soon enough. As for you, we have known of you for thousands of years. Elric are you not – last king of Melniboné?'

'That is true.'

'And you,' Sepiriz addressed Dyvim Slorm, 'are Elric's cousin. Together you represent the last of the pure line of Melniboné.'

'Aye,' Dyvim Slorm agreed, curiosity in his eyes.

'Then we have been waiting for you to pass this way. There was a prophecy...'

'*You* are the captors of Zarozinia?' Elric reached for his sword.

Sepiriz shook his head. 'No, but we can tell you where she is. Calm yourself. Though I realise the agony of mind you must be suffering, I will be better able to explain all I know back in our own domain.'

'First tell us who you are,' Elric demanded.

Sepiriz smiled slightly. 'You know us, I think – or at least you know of us. There was a certain friendship between your ancestors and our folk in the early years of the Bright Empire.' He paused a moment before continuing: 'Have you ever heard legends, in Imrryr perhaps, of the Ten from the mountain? The Ten who sleep in the mountain of fire?'

'Many times.' Elric drew in his breath. 'Now I recognise you by description. But it is said that you sleep for centuries in the mountain of fire. Why are you roaming abroad in this manner?'

'We were driven by an eruption from our volcano home which had been dormant for two thousand years. Such movements of nature have been taking place all over the Earth of late. Our time, we knew, had come to awaken again. We are servants of Fate – and our mission is strongly bound up with your destiny. We bear a message for you from Zarozinia's captor – and another from a different source. Would you return now, with us, to the Chasm of Nihrain and learn all we can tell you?'

Elric pondered for a moment, then he lifted his white face and said: 'I am in haste to claim vengeance, Sepiriz. But if what you can tell me will lead me closer to claiming it, I'll come.'

'Then come!' The black giant jerked the reins of his horse and turned the chariot about.

It was a journey of a day and a night to the Chasm of Nihrain, a huge gaping fissure high in the mountains, a place avoided by all; it had supernatural significance for those who dwelt near the mountains.

The lordly Nihrain conversed little on the journey and at last they were above the chasm, driving their chariots down the steep path which wound into its dark depths.

About half a mile down no light penetrated, but they saw ahead of them flickering torches that illuminated part of the carved outline of an unearthly mural or betrayed a gaping opening in the solid rock. Then, as they guided their horses down further, they saw, in detail, the awe-inspiring city of Nihrain which outsiders had not glimpsed for many centuries. The last of the Nihrain now lived here; ten immortal men of a race older even than that of Melniboné which had a history of twenty thousand years.

Huge columns rose above them, hewn ages before from the living rock, giant statues and wide balconies, many-tiered. Windows a hundred feet high and sweeping steps cut into the face of the chasm. The Ten drove their yellow chariots through a mighty gate and into the caverns of Nihrain, carved to their entire extent with strange symbols and stranger murals. Here slaves, wakened from a sleep of centuries to tend their masters, ran forward. Even these did not fully bear resemblance to the men that Elric knew.

Sepiriz gave the reins to a slave as Elric and Dyvim Slorm dismounted, staring about them in awe.

He said: 'Now – to my own chambers and there I'll inform you of what you wish to know – and what you must do.'

Led by Sepiriz, the kinsmen stalked impatiently through galleries and into a large chamber full of dark sculpture. A number of fires burned behind this hall, in big grates. Sepiriz folded his great body in a chair and bade them sit in two similar chairs, carved from solid blocks of ebony. When they were all seated before one of the fires, Sepiriz took a long breath, staring around the hall, perhaps remembering its earlier history.

Somewhat angered by this show of casualness, Elric said impatiently: 'Forgive me, Sepiriz – but you promised to pass on your message to us.'

'Yes,' Sepiriz said, 'but so much do I have to tell you that I must pause one moment to collect my thoughts.' He settled himself in the chair before continuing.

'We know where your wife is,' he said at last, 'and know also that she is safe. She will not be harmed since she is to be bargained for something which you possess.'

'Then tell me the *whole* story,' Elric demanded bleakly.

'We were friendly with your ancestors, Elric. And we were friendly with those they superseded, the ones who forged that blade you bear.'

Elric was interested in spite of his anxiety. For years he had attempted to rid himself of the runesword, but had never succeeded. All his efforts had failed and he still needed to carry it, although drugs now gave him most of his strength.

'Would you be rid of your sword, Elric?' Sepiriz said.

'Aye – it's well known.'

'Then listen to this tale.

'We know for whom and for what the blade – and its twin – were forged. They were made for a special purpose and for special men. Only Melnibonéans may carry them, and of those only the blood of the royal line.'

'There is no hint of any special purpose for the swords in Melnibonéan history or legend,' Elric said leaning forward.

'Some secrets are best kept fully guarded,' Sepiriz said calmly. 'Those blades were forged to destroy a group of very powerful beings. Among them are the Dead Gods.'

'The Dead Gods – but, by their very name, *you* must know that they perished long ages ago.'

'They "perished" as you say. In human terms they are dead. But they *chose* to die, chose to rid themselves of material shape and hurled their lifestuff into the blackness of eternity, for in those days they were full of fear.'

Elric had no real conception of what Sepiriz described but he accepted what the Nihrainian said and listened on.

'One of them has returned,' Sepiriz said.

'Why?'

'To get, at any cost, two things which endanger him and his fellow gods – wherever they may be they can still be harmed by these things.'

'They are...?'

'They have the earthly appearance of two swords, runecarved and sorcerous – Mournblade and Stormbringer.'

'This!' Elric touched his blade. 'Why should the gods fear this? And the other went to limbo with my cousin Yyrkoon whom I killed many years ago. It is lost.'

'That is not true. We recovered it – that was part of Fate's purpose for us. We have it here in Nihrain. The blades were forged for your ancestors who drove the Dead Gods away by means of them.

They were made by other unhuman smiths who were also enemies of the Dead Gods. These smiths were compelled to combat evil *with* evil, although they, themselves, were not pledged to Chaos, but to Law. They forged the swords for several reasons – ridding the world of the Dead Gods was but one!'

'The other reasons?'

'Those you shall learn in times to come – for our relationship will not be ended until the whole destiny has been worked out. We are obliged not to reveal the other reasons until the proper time. You have a dangerous destiny, Elric, and I do not envy it.'

'But what is the message you have?' Elric said impatiently.

'Due to the disturbance created by Jagreen Lern, one of the Dead Gods has been enabled to return to Earth, as I told you. He has gathered acolytes about him. They kidnapped your wife.'

Elric felt a mood of deep despair creep over him. Must he defy such power as this?

'Why...?' he whispered.

'Darnizhaan is aware that Zarozinia is important to you. He wishes to barter her for the two swords. We, in this matter, are merely messengers. We must give up the sword we keep, at the request of you or Dyvim Slorm, for they rightfully belong to any of the royal line. Darnizhaan's terms are simple. He will dispatch Zarozinia to limbo unless you give him the blades which threaten his existence. Her death, it would not be death as we know it, would be unpleasant and eternal.'

'And if I agreed to do that, what would happen?'

'All the Dead Gods would return. Only the power of the swords keeps them from doing so now!'

'And what would happen if the Dead Gods came back?'

'Even without the Dead Gods, Chaos threatens to conquer the planet, but with them it would be utterly invincible, its effect immediate. Evil would sweep the world. Chaos would plunge this Earth into a stinking inferno of terror and destruction. You have already had a taste of what is happening, and Darnizhaan has only been back for a short time.'

'You mean the defeat of Yishana's armies and the conquest by Sarosto and Jagreen Lern?'

'Exactly. Jagreen Lern has a pact with Chaos – all the Lords of Chaos, not merely the Dead Gods – for Chaos fears Fate's plan for Earth's future and would attempt to tamper with it by gaining domination of our planet. The Lords of Chaos are strong enough without the help of the Dead Gods. Darnizhaan must be destroyed.'

'I have an impossible choice, Sepiriz. If I give up Stormbringer I can probably survive on herbs and the like. But if I do give it up for Zarozinia, then Chaos will be unleashed to its full extent and I will have a monstrous crime upon my conscience.'

'The choice is yours alone to make.'

Elric deliberated but could think of no way of solving the problem.

'Bring the other blade,' he said at last.

Sepiriz rejoined them a while later, with a scabbarded sword that seemed little different from Stormbringer.

'So, Elric – is the prophecy explained?' he asked, still keeping hold of Mournblade.

'Aye – here is the twin of that I bear. But the last part – where are we to go?'

'I will tell you in a moment. Though the Dead Gods, and the powers of Chaos, are aware that we possess the sister blade, they do not know whom we really serve. Fate, as I told you, is our master, and Fate has wrought a fabric for this Earth which would be hard to alter. But it *could* be altered and we are entrusted to see that Fate is not cheated. You are about to undergo a test. How you fare in it, what your decision is, will decide what we must tell you upon your return to Nihrain.'

'You wish me to return here?'

'Yes.'

'Give me Mournblade,' Elric said quickly.

Sepiriz handed him the sword and Elric stood there with one twin blade in each hand, as if weighing something between them.

Both blades seemed to moan in recognition and the powers swam through his body so that he seemed to be built of steel-hard fire.

'I remember now that I hold them both that their powers are greater than I realise. There is one quality they possess when paired, a quality we may be able to use against this Dead God.' He frowned. 'But more of that in a moment.' He stared sharply at Sepiriz. 'Now tell me, where is Darnizhaan?'

'The Vale of Xanyaw in Myyrrhn!'

Elric handed Mournblade to Dyvim Slorm who accepted it gingerly.

'What will your choice be?' Sepiriz asked.

'Who knows?' Elric said with bitter gaiety. 'Perhaps there is a way to beat this Dead God...

'But I tell you this, Sepiriz – given the opportunity I shall make that god rue his homecoming, for he has done the one thing that can move me to real anger. And the anger of Elric of Melniboné and his sword Stormbringer can destroy the world!'

Sepiriz rose from his chair, his eyebrows lifting.

'And gods, Elric, can it destroy gods?'

Chapter Five

ELRIC RODE LIKE a giant scarecrow, gaunt and rigid on the massive back of the Nihrainian steed. His grim face was set fast in a mask that hid emotion and his crimson eyes burned like coals in their sunken sockets. The wind whipped his hair this way and that, but he sat straight, staring ahead, one long-fingered hand gripping Stormbringer's hilt.

Occasionally Dyvim Slorm, who bore Mournblade both proudly and warily, heard the blade moan to its sister and felt it shudder at his side. Only later did he begin to ask himself what the blade might make him, what it would give him and demand of him. After that, he kept his hand away from it as much as possible.

Close to the borders of Myyrrhn, a pack of Dharijorian hirelings – native Jharkorians in the livery of the conquerors – came upon them. Unsavoury louts they were, who should have known better than to ride across Elric's path. They steered their horses towards the pair, grinning. The black plumes of their helmets nodded, armour straps creaked and metal clanked. The leader, a squint-eyed bully with an axe at his belt, pulled his mount short in front of Elric.

At a direction from its master, the albino's horse came to a stop. His expression unchanged, Elric drew Stormbringer in an economic, catlike gesture. Dyvim Slorm copied him, eyeing the silently laughing men. He was surprised at how easily the blade sprang from its scabbard.

Then, with no challenges, Elric began to fight.

He fought like an automaton, quickly, efficiently, expressionlessly, cleaving the leader's shoulder plate in a stroke that cut through the man from shoulder to stomach in one raking movement which peeled back armour and flesh, rupturing the body so that a great scarlet gash appeared in the black metal and the leader wept as he slowly died, sprawling for a moment over his horse before slumping from the mount, one leg high, caught in a stirrup strap.

Stormbringer let out a great metallic purr of pleasure and Elric directed arm and blade about him, emotionlessly slaying the horsemen as if they were unarmed and chained, so little chance did they have.

Dyvim Slorm, unused to the semi-sentient Mournblade, tried to wield her like an ordinary sword but she moved in his hand, making cleverer strokes than he. A peculiar sense of power, at once sensual and cool, poured into him and he heard his voice yelling exultantly, realised what his ancestors must have been like in war.

The fight was quickly done with and leaving the soul-drained corpses on the ground behind them, they were soon in the land of Myyrrhn. Both blades had now been commonly blooded.

Elric was now better able to think and act coherently, but he could spare nothing for Dyvim Slorm while intratemporally asking nothing of his cousin who rode at his side, frustrated in that he was not called upon for his help.

Elric let his mind drift about in time, encompassing past, present and future and forming it into a whole – a pattern. He was suspicious of pattern, disliking shape, for he did not trust it. To him, life was chaotic, chance-dominated, unpredictable. It was a trick, an illusion of the mind, to be able to see a pattern to it.

He knew a few things, judged nothing.

He knew he bore a sword which physically and psychologically he needed to bear. It was an unalterable admission of a weakness in him, a lack of confidence in either himself or the philosophy of cause and effect. He believed himself a realist.

He knew that he loved, obscurely at times, his wife Zarozinia and would die if it meant she would not be harmed.

He knew that, if he were to survive and keep the freedom he had won and fought to hold, he must journey to the Dead God's lair and do what he saw fit to do when he had managed to assess the situation. He knew that for all his admission of Chaos he would be better able to do what he wished in a world ordered by some degree of Law.

The wind had been warm but now, nearing dusk, it grew colder. A low, cloudy sky with the heavy banks of grey picked out against the lighter shades of grey like islands in a cold sea. And there was a smell of smoke in Elric's nostrils, the frantic chirruping of birds in his ears and the sound of a whistling boy heard over the droning wind.

Dyvim Slorm turned his horse in the direction of the whistling, rode into scrub, leaned down in the saddle and hauled himself up with a wriggling youngster gripped by the slack of his shirt.

'Where are you from, lad?' Dyvim Slorm asked.

'From a village a mile or two away, sir,' the boy replied, out of breath and scared.

He looked with wide eyes at Elric, fascinated by the tall albino's stern and pitiless mien.

He turned his head sharply to stare up at Dyvim Slorm. 'Is that not Elric Friendslayer?' he said.

Dyvim Storm released the boy and said, 'Where lies the Vale of Xanyaw?'

'North-west of here – it is no place for mortals. Is that not Elric Friendslayer, sir, tell me?'

Dyvim Slorm glanced miserably at his cousin and did not reply to the boy. Together they urged their horses north-west and Elric's pace was even more urgent.

Through the bleak night they rode, buffeted by a vicious wind.

And as they came closer to the Vale of Xanyaw, the whole sky, the earth, the air became filled with heavy, throbbing music. Melodious, sensual, great chords of sound, on and on it rose and fell, and following it came the white-faced ones.

Each had a black cowl and a sword which split at the end into three curved barbs. Each grinned a fixed grin. The music followed them as they came running like mad things at the two men who reined in their horses, restraining the urge to turn and flee. Elric had seen horrors in his life, had seen much that would make others insane, but for some reason these shocked him more deeply than any. They were men, ordinary men by the look of them – but men possessed by an unholy spirit.

Prepared to defend themselves, Elric and Dyvim Slorm drew their blades and waited for the encounter, but none came. The music and the men rushed past them and away beyond them in the direction from which they had come.

Overhead, suddenly, they heard the beat of wings, a shriek from out of the sky and a ghastly wail. Fleeing, two women rushed by and Elric was disturbed to see that the women were from the winged race of Myyrrhn, but were wingless. These, unlike a woman Elric remembered, had had their wings deliberately hacked off. They paid no attention to the two riders, but disappeared, running into the night, their eyes blank and their faces insane.

'What is happening, Elric?' cried Dyvim Slorm, resheathing his runeblade, his other hand striving to control the prancing horse.

'I know not. What *does* happen in a place where the Dead Gods' rule has come back?'

All was rushing noise and confusion; the night was full of movement and terror.

'Come!' Elric slapped his sword against his mount's rump and sent the beast into a jerking gallop, forcing himself and the steed forward into the terrible night.

Then mighty laughter greeted them as they rode between hills into the Vale of Xanyaw. The valley was pitch-black and alive with menace, the very hills seeming sentient. They slowed their pace as they lost their sense of direction, and Elric had to call to his unseen cousin, to make sure he was still close. The echoing laughter sounded again, roaring from out of the dark, so that the earth shook. It was as if the whole planet laughed in ironic mirth at their efforts to control their fears and push on through the valley.

Elric wondered if he had been betrayed and this was a trap set by the Dead Gods. What proof had he that Zarozinia was here? Why had he trusted Sepiriz? Something slithered against his leg as it passed him and he put his hand on the hilt of his sword, ready to draw it.

But then, shooting upwards into the dark sky, there arose, seemingly from the very earth, a huge figure which barred their way. Hands on hips, wreathed in golden light, a face of an ape, somehow blended with another shape to give it dignity and wild grandeur, its body alive and dancing with colour and light, its lips grinning with delight and knowledge – Darnizhaan, the Dead God!

'Elric!'

'Darnizhaan!' cried Elric fiercely, craning his head to stare up at the Dead God's face. He felt no fear now. 'I have come for my wife!'

Around the Dead God's heels appeared acolytes with wide lips and pale, triangular faces, conical caps on their heads and madness in their eyes. They giggled and shrilled and shivered in the light of Darnizhaan's grotesque and beautiful body. They gibbered at the two riders and mocked them, but they did not move away from the Dead God's heels.

Elric sneered. 'Degenerate and pitiful minions,' he said.

'Not so pitiful as you, Elric of Melniboné,' laughed the Dead God. 'Have you come to bargain, or to give your wife's soul into my custody, so that she may spend eternity dying?'

Elric did not let his hate show on his face.

'I would destroy you; it is instinctive for me to do so. But –'

The Dead God smiled, almost with pity. '*You* must be destroyed, Elric. You are an anachronism. Your time is gone.'

'Speak for yourself, Darnizhaan!'

'I *could* destroy you.'

'But you will not.' Though passionately hating the being, Elric also felt a disturbing sense of comradeship for the Dead God.

Both of them represented an age that was gone; neither was really part of the new Earth.

'Then I will destroy her,' the Dead God said. 'That I could do with impunity.'

'Zarozinia! Where is she?'

Once again Darnizhaan's mighty laughter shook the Vale of Xanyaw. 'Oh, what have the old folk come to? There was a time when no man of Melniboné, particularly of the royal line, would admit to caring for another mortal soul, especially if they belonged to the beast-race, the new race of the age you call that of the Young Kingdoms. What? Are you mating with animals, King of Melniboné? Where is your blood, your cruel and brilliant blood? Where the glorious malice? Where the evil, Elric?'

Peculiar emotions stirred in Elric as he remembered his ancestors, the Sorcerer Emperors of the Dragon Isle. He realised that the Dead God was deliberately awakening these emotions and, with an effort, he refused to let them dominate him.

'That is past,' he shouted, 'a new time has come upon the Earth. Our time will soon be gone – and yours is *over*!'

'No, Elric. Mark my words, whatever happens. The dawn is over and will soon be swept away like dead leaves before the wind of morning. The Earth's history has not even begun. You, your ancestors, these men of the new races even, you are nothing but a *prelude to history*. You will all be forgotten if the real history of the world begins. But we can avert that – we can survive, conquer the Earth and hold it against the Lords of Law, against Fate herself, against the Cosmic Balance – we *can* continue to live, but you *must* give me the swords!'

'I fail to understand you,' Elric said, his lips thin and his teeth tight in his skull. 'I am here to bargain or do battle for my wife.'

'You do not understand,' the Dead God guffawed, 'because we are all of us, gods and men, but shadows playing puppet parts before the true play begins. You would best not fight me – rather side with me, for I know the truth. We share a common destiny. We do not, any of us, exist. The old folk are doomed, you, myself and my brothers, unless you give me the swords. We must not fight one another. Share our frightful knowledge – the knowledge that turned us insane. There is nothing, Elric – no past, present, or future. *We do not exist, any of us!'*

Elric shook his head quickly. 'I do not understand you, still. I would not understand you if I could. I desire only the return of my wife – not baffling conundrums!'

Darnizhaan laughed again. 'No! You shall not have the woman unless we are given control of the swords. You do not realise their properties. They were not only designed to destroy us or exile us – their destiny is to destroy the world as we know it. If you retain them, Elric, you will be responsible for wiping out your own memory for those who come after you.'

'I'd welcome that,' Elric said.

Dyvim Slorm remained silent, not altogether in sympathy with Elric. The Dead God's argument seemed to contain truth.

Darnizhaan shook his body so that the golden light danced and its area widened momentarily. 'Keep the swords and all of us will be as if we had *never* existed,' he said impatiently.

'So be it,' Elric's tone was stubborn, 'do you think I wish the memory to live on – the memory of evil, ruin and destruction? The memory of a man with deficient blood in his veins – a man called Friendslayer, Womanslayer and many other such names?'

Darnizhaan spoke urgently, almost in terror. 'Elric, you have been duped! Somewhere you have been given a conscience. You must join with us. Only if the Lords of Chaos can establish their reign will we survive. If they fail, we shall be obliterated!'

'Good!'

'Limbo, Elric. *Limbo*! Do you understand what that means?'

'I do not care. Where is my wife?'

Elric blocked the truth from his mind, blocked out the terror in the meaning of the Dead God's words. He could not afford to listen or fully to comprehend. He must save Zarozinia.

'I have brought the swords,' said he, 'and wish my wife to be returned to me.'

'Very well,' the Dead God smiled hugely in his relief. 'At least if we keep the blades, in their true shape, beyond the Earth, we may be able to retain control of the world. In your hands they could destroy not only us but you, your world, all that you represent. Beasts would rule the Earth for millions of years before the age of intelligence began again. And it would be a duller age than this. We do not wish it to occur. But if you had *kept* the swords, it would have come about almost inevitably!'

'Oh, be silent!' Elric cried. 'For a god, you talk too much. Take the swords – and give me back my wife!'

At the Dead God's command, some of the acolytes scampered away. Elric saw their gleaming bodies disappear into the darkness. He waited nervously until they returned, carrying the struggling body of Zarozinia. They set her on the ground and Elric saw that her face bore the blank look of shock.

'Zarozinia!'

The girl's eyes roamed about before they saw Elric. She began to move towards him, but the acolytes held her back, giggling.

Darnizhaan stretched forward two gigantic, glowing hands.

'The swords first.'

Elric and Dyvim Slorm put them into his hands. The Dead God straightened up, clutching his prizes and roaring his mirth. Zarozinia was now released and she ran forward to grasp her husband's hand, weeping and trembling. Elric leaned down and stroked her hair, too disturbed to say anything.

Then he turned to Dyvim Slorm, shouting: 'Let us see if our plan will work, cousin!'

Elric stared up at Stormbringer writhing in Darnizhaan's grasp. 'Stormbringer! *Kerana soliem, o'glara...*'

Dyvim Slorm also called to Mournblade in the High Tongue of Melniboné, the mystic, sorcerous tongue which had been used for rune-casting and demon-raising all through Melniboné's twenty thousand years of history.

Together, they commanded the blades, as if they were actually wielding them in their hands, so that merely by shouting orders, Elric and Dyvim Slorm began their work. This was the remembered quality of both blades when paired in a common fight. The blades twisted in Darnizhaan's glowing hands. He started backwards, his shape faltering, sometimes manlike, sometimes beastlike, sometimes totally alien. But he was evidently horrified, this god.

Now the swords wrenched themselves from the clutching hands and turned on him. He fought against them, fending them off as they wove about in the air, whining malevolently, triumphantly, attacking him with vicious power. At Elric's command, Stormbringer slashed at the supernatural being and Dyvim Slorm's Mournblade followed its example. Because the runeblades were also supernatural, Darnizhaan was harmed dreadfully whenever they struck his form.

'Elric!' he raved, 'Elric – you do not know what you are doing! Stop them! Stop them! You should have listened more carefully to what I told you. Stop them!'

But Elric in his hate and malice urged on the blades, made them plunge into the Dead God's being time after time so that his shape sometimes faltered, faded, the colours of its bright beauty dulling. The acolytes fled upwards into the vale, convinced that their lord was doomed. Their lord, also, was so convinced. He made one lunge towards the mounted men and then the fabric of his being began to shred before the blades' attack; wisps of his body-stuff seemed to break away and drift into the air to be swallowed by the black night.

Viciously and ferociously, Elric goaded the blades while Dyvim Slorm's voice blended with his in a cruel joy to see the bright being destroyed.

'Fools!' he screamed, 'in destroying me, you destroy yourselves!'

But Elric did not listen and at last there was nothing left of the Dead God and the swords crept back to lie contentedly in their masters' hands.

Quickly, with a sudden shudder, Elric scabbarded Stormbringer.

He dismounted and helped his girl-wife onto the back of his great stallion and then swung up into the saddle again. It was very quiet in the Vale of Xanyaw.

Chapter Six

THREE PEOPLE, BENT in their saddles with weariness, reached the Chasm of Nihrain days later. They rode down the twisting paths into the black depths of the mountain city and were there welcomed by Sepiriz whose face was grave, though his words were encouraging.

'So you were successful, Elric,' he said with a small smile.

Elric paused while he dismounted and aided Zarozinia down. He turned to Sepiriz. 'I am not altogether satisfied with this adventure,' he said grimly, 'though I did what I had to in order to save my wife. I would speak with you privately, Sepiriz.'

The black Nihrainian nodded gravely. 'When we have eaten,' he said, 'we will talk alone.'

They walked wearily through the galleries, noting that there was considerably more activity in the city now, but there was no sign of Sepiriz's nine brothers. He explained their absence as he led Elric and his companions towards his own chamber. 'As servants of Fate they have been called to another plane where they can observe something of the several different possible futures of the Earth and thus keep me informed of what I must do here.'

They entered the chamber and found food ready and, when they had satisfied their hunger, Dyvim Slorm and Zarozinia left the other two.

The fire from the great hearth blazed. Elric and Sepiriz sat together, unspeaking, hunched in their chairs.

At last, without preamble, Elric told Sepiriz the story of what had happened, what he remembered of the Dead God's words, how they had disturbed him – even struck him as being true.

When he had finished, Sepiriz nodded. 'It is so,' he said. 'Darnizhaan spoke the truth. Or, at least, he spoke most of the truth, as he understood it.'

'You mean we will all soon cease to exist? That it will be as if we had never breathed, or thought, or fought?'

'That is likely.'

'But why? It seems unjust.'

'Who told you that the world was just?'

Elric smiled, his own suspicions confirmed. 'Aye, as I expected, there is no justice.'

'But there *is*,' Sepiriz said, 'justice of a kind – justice which must be carved from the chaos of existence. Man was not born to a world of justice. But he can *create* such a world!'

'I'd agree to that,' Elric said, 'but what are all our strivings for if we are doomed to die and the results of our actions with us?'

'That is not absolutely the case. Something will continue. Those who come after us will inherit something from us.'

'What is that?'

'An Earth free of the major forces of Chaos.'

'You mean a world free of sorcery, I presume...?'

'Not entirely free of sorcery, but Chaos and sorcery will not dominate the world of the future as it does this world.'

'Then that *is* worth striving for, Sepiriz,' Elric said almost with relief. 'But what part do the runeblades play in the scheme of things?'

'They have two functions. One, to rid this world of the great dominating sources of evil –'

'But they *are* evil, themselves!'

'Just so. It takes a strong evil to battle a strong evil. The days that will come will be when the forces of good can overcome those of evil. They are not yet strong enough. That, as I told you, is what we must strive for.'

'And what is the other purpose of the blades?'

'That is their final purpose – your destiny. I can tell you now. I *must* tell you now, or let you live out your destiny unknowing.'

'Then tell me,' Elric said impatiently.

'Their ultimate purpose is to destroy this world!'

Elric stood up. 'Ah, no, Sepiriz. That I cannot believe. Shall I have such a crime on my conscience?'

'It is not a crime, it is in the nature of things. The era of the Bright Empire, even that of the Young Kingdoms, is drawing to a close. Chaos formed this Earth and, for aeons, Chaos ruled. Men were created to put an end to that rule.'

'But my ancestors worshipped the powers of Chaos. My patron demon, Arioch, is a Duke of Hell, one of the prime Lords of Chaos!'

'Just so. You, and your ancestors, were not true men at all, but an intermediary type created for a purpose. You understand Chaos as no true men ever could understand it. You can control the forces of Chaos as no true men ever could. And, as a manifestation of the Champion Eternal, you can weaken the forces of Chaos – for you know the qualities of Chaos. Weaken them is what you *have* done. Though worshipping the Lords of Chance, your race was the first to bring some kind of order to the Earth. The people of the Young Kingdoms have inherited this from you – and have consolidated it. But, as yet, Chaos is still that much stronger. The runeblades, Stormbringer and Mournblade, this more orderly age, the wisdom your race and mine have gained, all will go towards creating the basis for the true beginnings of mankind's history. That history will not begin for many thousands of years, the type may take on a lowlier form, become more beast-like before it re-evolves, but when it does, it will re-evolve into a world bereft of the stronger forces of Chaos. It will have a fighting chance. We are all doomed, but *they* need not be.'

'So that is what Darnizhaan meant when he said we were just puppets, acting out our parts before the true play began...' Elric sighed deeply, the weight of his mighty responsibility was heavy on his soul. He did not welcome it; but he accepted it.

Sepiriz said gently: 'It is your purpose, Elric of Melniboné. Hitherto, your life has appeared comparatively meaningless. All through it you have been searching for some purpose for living, is that not true?'

'Aye,' Elric agreed with a slight smile, 'I've been restless for many a year since my birth; restless the more between the time when Zarozinia was abducted and now.'

'It is fitting that you should have been,' Sepiriz said, 'for there *is* a purpose for you – Fate's purpose. It is this destiny that you have sensed all your mortal days. You, the last of the royal line of Melniboné, must complete your destiny in the times which are to follow closely upon these. The world is darkening – nature revolts and rebels against the abuses to which the Lords of Chaos put it. Oceans seethe and forests sway, hot lava spills from a thousand mountains, winds shriek their angry torment and the skies are full of awful movement. Upon the face of the Earth, warriors are embattled in a struggle which will decide the fate of the world, linked as the struggle is, with greater conflicts among gods. Women and little children die on a million funeral pyres upon this continent alone. And soon the conflict will spread to the next continent and the next. Soon all the men of the Earth will have chosen sides and Chaos might easily win. It would win but for one thing: you and your sword Stormbringer.'

'Stormbringer. It has brought enough storms for me. Perhaps this time it can calm one. And what if Law should win?'

'And if Law should win – then that, too, will mean the decline and death of this world – we shall all be forgotten. But if Chaos should win – then doom will cloud the very air, agony will sound in the wind and foul misery will dominate a plunging, unsettled world of sorcery and evil hatred. But you, Elric, with your sword and our aid, could stop this. It must be done.'

'Then let it be done,' Elric said quietly, 'and if it must be done – then let it be done well.'

Sepiriz said: 'Armies will soon be marshalled to drive against Pan Tang's might. These must be our first defence. Thereafter, we shall call upon you to fulfil the rest of your destiny.'

'I'll play my part, willingly,' Elric replied, 'for, whatever else, I have a mind to pay the Theocrat back for his insults and the inconvenience he has caused me. Though perhaps he didn't instigate Zarozinia's abduction, he aided those who did, and he shall die slowly for that.'

'Go then, speedily, for each moment wasted allows the Theocrat to consolidate further his new-won empire.'

'Farewell,' said Elric, now more than ever anxious to leave Nihrain and return to familiar lands. 'I know we'll meet again, Sepiriz, but I pray it be in calmer times than these.'

Now the three of them rode eastwards, towards the coast of Tarkesh where they hoped to find a secret ship to take them across the Pale Sea to Ilmiora and thence to Karlaak by the Weeping Waste. They rode their magical Nihrain horses, careless of danger, through a war-wasted world, strife-ruined and miserable under the heel of the Theocrat.

Elric and Zarozinia exchanged many glances, but they did not speak much, for they were both moved by a knowledge of something which they could not speak of, which they dared not admit. She knew they would not have much time together even when they returned to Karlaak, she saw that he grieved and she grieved also, unable to understand the change that had come upon her husband, only aware that the black sword at his side would never, now, hang in the armoury again. She felt she had failed him, though this was not the case.

As they topped a hill and saw smoke drifting, black and thick across the plains of Toraunz, once beautiful, now ruined, Dyvim Slorm shouted from behind Elric and his bride: 'One thing, cousin – whatever happens, we must have vengeance on the Theocrat and his ally.'

Elric pursed his lips.

'Aye,' he said, and glanced again at Zarozinia whose eyes were downcast.

Now the Western lands from Tarkesh to Myyrrhn were sundered by the servitors of Chaos. Was this truly to be the final conflict that would decide whether Law or Chaos would dominate the future? The forces of Law were weak and scattered. Could this possibly be the final paroxysm on Earth of the great Lords of Evil? Now, between armies, one part of the world's fate was being decided. The lands groaned in the torment of bloody conflict.

What other forces must Elric fight before he accomplished his final destiny and destroyed the world he knew? What else before the Horn of Fate was blown – to herald in the night?

Sepiriz, no doubt, would tell him when the time came.

But meanwhile more material scores had to be settled. The lands to the east must be made ready for war. The sea-lords of the Purple Towns must be approached for aid, the kings of the South marshalled for attack on the Western Continent. It would take time to do all this.

Part of Elric's mind welcomed the time it would take.

Part of him was reluctant to continue his heavy destiny, for it would mean the end of the Age of the Young Kingdoms, the death of the memory of the Age of the Bright Empire which his ancestors had dominated for ten thousand years.

The sea was at last in sight, rolling its troubled way towards the horizon to meet a seething sky. He heard the cry of gulls and smelled the tang of the salt air in his nostrils.

With a wild shout he clapped his steed's flanks and raced down towards the sea...

Book Two

Black Sword's Brothers

In which a million blades decide an issue between
Elric and the Lords of Chaos...

Chapter One

ONE DAY THERE came a gathering of kings, captains, and warlords to the peaceful city of Karlaak in Ilmiora by the Weeping Waste.

They did not come in great pomp or with grandiose gestures. They came grim-faced and hurriedly to answer the summons of Elric, who dwelt again in Karlaak with his lately-rescued wife Zarozinia. And they gathered in a great chamber which had once been used by the old rulers of Karlaak for the planning of wars. To this same purpose Elric now put it.

Illuminated by flaring torches, a great coloured map of the world was spread behind the dais on which Elric stood. It showed the three major continents of the East, West and South. That of the West, comprising Jharkor, Dharijor, Shazaar, Tarkesh, Myyr-rhn and the Isle of Pan Tang, was shaded black, for all these lands were now the conquered Empire of the Pan Tang-Dharijor alliance which threatened the security of the assembled nobles.

Some of the men who stood armoured before Elric were exiles from the conquered lands – but there were few. Few also were Elric's Imrryrian kinsmen who had fought at the Battle of Sequa and had been defeated with the massed army that had sought to resist the combined might of the evil alliance. At the head of the eldritch Imrryrians stood Dyvim Slorm, Elric's cousin. At his belt, encased in a sturdy scabbard, was the runesword Mournblade, twin to the one Elric wore.

Here also was Montan, Lord of Lormyr, standing with fellow rulers from the Southlands – Jerned of Filkhar, Hozel of Argimiliar, and Kolthak of Pikarayd, adorned in painted iron, velvet, silk and wool.

The sea-lords from the Isle of the Purple Towns were less gaudily clad with helms and breastplates of plain bronze, jerkins, breeks and boots of unstained leather and great broadswords at their hips. Their faces were all but hidden by their long shaggy hair and thick, curling beards.

All these, kings and sea-lords alike, were inclined to stare at Elric suspiciously, since years before he had led their royal predecessors on the raid of Imrryr – though it had left many thrones clear for those who now sat on them.

In another group stood the nobles of that part of the Eastern Continent lying to the east of the Sighing Desert and the Weeping Waste. Beyond these two barren stretches of land were the kingdoms of Eshmir, Chang Shai and Okara, but there was no contact between Elric's part of the world and theirs – save for the small, red-headed man beside him – his friend Moonglum of Elwher, an Eastern adventurer.

The Regent of Vilmir, uncle of the ten-month-old king, headed this last group made up of senators from the city-states comprising Ilmiora; the red-clothed archer Rackhir representing the city of Tanelorn; and various merchant princes from towns coming under the indirect rule of Vilmir as protectorates.

A mighty gathering, representing the massed power of the world.

But would even this be sufficient, Elric wondered, to wipe out the growing menace from the Westlands?

His white albino's face was stern, his red eyes troubled as he addressed the men he had caused to come here.

'As you know, my lords, the threat of Pan Tang and Dharijor is not likely to remain confined to the Western Continent for much longer. Though barely two months have passed since their victory was achieved, they are already marshalling a great fleet aimed at crushing the power of those kings dependent, largely, on their ships for livelihood and defence.'

He glanced at the sea-lords of the Purple Towns and the kings of the Southern Continent.

'We of the East, it seems, are not regarded as so much of a danger to their immediate plans and, if we did not unite now, they would have a greater chance of success by conquering first the

Southern sea power and then the scattered cities of the East. We must form an alliance which can match their strength.'

'How do you know this is their plan, Elric?'

The voice was that of Hozel of Argimiliar, a proud-faced man inclined it was said to fits of insanity, the inbred offspring of a dozen incestuous unions.

'Spies, refugees – and supernatural sources. They have all reported it.'

'Even without these reports, we could be sure that this is, indeed, their plan,' growled Kargan Sharpeyes, spokesman for the sea-lords. He looked directly at Hozel with something akin to contempt. 'And Jagreen Lern of Pan Tang might also seek allies amongst the Southerners. There are some who would rather capitulate to a foreign conqueror than lose their soft lives and easily earned treasure.'

Hozel smiled coldly at Kargan. 'There are some, too, whose animal suspicions might cause them to make no move against the Theocrat until it was too late.'

Elric said hastily, aware of age-old bitternesses between the hardy sea-lords and their softer neighbours: 'But worst of all they would be best aided by internal feuds in our ranks, brothers. Hozel – take it for granted that I speak truly and that my information is exact.'

Montan, Lord of Lormyr, his face, beard and hair all shaded grey, said haughtily: 'You of the North and East are weak. We of the South are strong. Why should we lend you our ships to defend your coasts? I do not agree with your logic, Elric. It will not be the first time it has led good men astray – to their deaths!'

'I thought we had agreed to bury old disputes!' Elric said, close to anger, for the guilt of what he had done was still in him.

'Aye,' nodded Kargan. 'A man who can't forget the past is a man who cannot plan for the future. I say Elric's logic is good!'

'You traders were always too reckless with your ships and too gullible when you heard a smooth tongue. That's why you now envy our riches.' Young Jerned of Filkhar smiled in his thin beard, his eyes on the floor.

Kargan fumed. 'Too honest, perhaps, is the word you should have used, Southerner! Belatedly our forefathers learned how the fat Southlands were cheating them. Their forefathers raided your coasts, remember? Maybe we should have continued their practice! Instead, we settled, traded – and your bellies swelled from the profits of our sweat! Gods! I'd not trust the word of a Southern –'

Elric leaned forward to interrupt, but was interrupted himself by Hozel who said impatiently: 'The fact is this. The Theocrat is more likely to concentrate his first attacks on the East. For these reasons: The Eastlands are weak. The Eastlands are poorly defended. The Eastlands are closer to his shores and therefore more accessible. Why should he risk his recently united strength on the stronger Southlands, or risk a more hazardous sea-crossing?'

'Because,' Elric said levelly, 'his ships will be magic-aided and distance will not count. Because the South is richer and will supply him with metals, food –'

'Ships and men!' spat Kargan.

'So! You think we already plan treachery!' Hozel glanced first at Elric and then at Kargan. 'Then why summon us here in the first place?'

'I did not say that,' Elric said hastily. 'Kargan spoke his own thoughts, not mine. Calm yourselves – we *must* be united – or perish before superior armies and supernatural might!'

'Oh, no!' Hozel turned to the other Southern monarchs. 'What say you, my peers? Shall we lend them our ships and warriors to protect their shores as well as ours?'

'Not when they are so ungratefully spurned,' Jerned murmured. 'Let Jagreen Lern expend his energies upon them. When he looks towards the South he will be weakened, and we shall be ready for him!'

'You are fools!' Elric cried urgently. 'Stand with us or we'll all perish! The Lords of Chaos are behind the Theocrat. If he succeeds in his ambitions it will mean more than conquest by a human schemer – it will mean that we shall all be subjected to the horror of total anarchy, on the Earth and above it. The human race is threatened!'

Hozel stared hard at Elric and smiled. 'Then let the human race protect itself and not fight under an unhuman leader. 'Tis well-known that the men of Melniboné are not true men at all.'

'Be that as it may.' Elric lowered his head and lifted a thin, white hand to point at Hozel. The king shivered and held his ground with obvious effort. 'But I know more than that, Hozel of Argimiliar. I know that the men of the Young Kingdoms are only the gods' first mouldings – shadow-things who precede the race of real men, even as we preceded you. And I know more! I know that if we do not vanquish both Jagreen Lern and his supernatural allies, then men will be swept from the boiling face of a maddened planet, their destiny unfulfilled!'

Hozel swallowed and spoke, his voice trembling.

'I've seen your muttering kind in the market places, Elric. Men who prophesy all kinds of dooms that never take place – mad-eyed men such as you. But we do not let them live in Argimiliar. We fry them slowly, finger by finger, inch by inch until they admit their omens are fallacious! Perhaps we'll have that opportunity, yet!'

He swung about and half-ran from the hall. For a moment the other Southern monarchs stood staring irresolutely after him.

Elric said urgently: 'Heed him not, my lords. I swear on my life that my words are true!'

Jerned said softly, half to himself: 'That could mean little. There are rumours you're immortal.'

Moonglum came close to his friend and whispered: 'They are unconvinced, Elric. 'Tis plain they're not our men.'

Elric nodded. To the Southern nobles he said: 'Know this: Though you foolishly reject my offer of an alliance, the day will come when you will regret your decision. I have been insulted in my own palace, my friends have been insulted and I curse you for the upstart fools you are. But when the time comes for you to learn the error of this decision I swear that we shall aid you, if it is in our power. Now go!'

Disconcerted, the Southerners straggled from the hall in silence.

Elric turned to Kargan Sharpeyes. 'What have you decided, sea-lord?'

'We stand with you,' Kargan said simply. 'My brother Smiorgan Baldhead always spoke well of you and I remember his words rather than the rumours which followed his death under your leadership. Moreover,' he smiled broadly, 'it is in our nature to believe that whatever a Southern weakling decides must therefore be wrong. You have the Purple Towns as allies – and our ships, though fewer than the combined fleets of the South, are smooth-sailing fighting ships and well-equipped for war.'

'I must warn you that we stand little chance without Southern aid,' Elric said gravely.

'I'm doubtful if they'd have been more than an encumbrance with their guile and squabblings,' Kargan replied. 'Besides – have you no sorcery to help us in this?'

'I plan to seek some tomorrow,' Elric told him. 'Moonglum and myself will be leaving my cousin Dyvim Slorm in charge here while we go to Sorcerers' Isle, beyond Melniboné. There, among the hermit practitioners of the White Arts, I might find means of contacting the Lords of Law. I, as you know, am half-sworn to Chaos, though I fight it, and am finding increasingly that my own demon-god is somewhat loath to aid me these days. At present, the White Lords are weak, beaten back, just as we are on Earth, by the increasing power of the Dark Ones. It is hard to contact them. The hermits can likely help me.'

Kargan nodded. ''Twould be a relief to us of the Purple Towns to know that we were not too strongly leagued with dark spirits, I must admit.'

Elric frowned. 'I agree, of course. But our position is so weak that we must accept *any* help – be it black or white. I presume that there is dispute among the Masters of Chaos as to how far they should go – that is why some of my own help still comes from Chaos. This blade that hangs at my side, and the twin which Dyvim Slorm bears, are both evil. Yet they were forged by creatures of Chaos to bring an end, on Earth at least, to the Masters' rule here. Just as my blood-loyalties are divided, so are the swords' loyalties. We have no supernatural allies we can wholly rely upon.'

'I feel for you,' Kargan said gruffly, and it was obvious that he did. No man could envy Elric's position or Elric's destiny.

Orgon, Kargan's cousin-in-law, said bluntly: 'We'll to bed now. Has your kinsman your full confidence?'

Elric glanced at Dyvim Slorm and smiled. 'My full confidence – he knows as much as I about this business. He shall speak for me since he knows my basic plans.'

'Very well. We'll confer with him tomorrow and, if we do not see you before we leave, do well for us on Sorcerers' Isle.'

The sea-lords left.

Now, for the first time, the Regent of Vilmir spoke. His voice was clear and cool. 'We, too, have confidence in you and your kinsman, Elric. Already we know you both for clever warriors and cunning planners. Vilmir has good cause to know it from your exploits in Bakshaan and elsewhere throughout our territories. We, I feel, have the good sense to bury old scores.' He turned to the merchant princes for confirmation and they nodded their agreement.

'Good,' Elric said. He addressed the gaunt-faced archer, Rackhir, his friend, whose legend almost equalled his own.

'You come as a spokesman of Tanelorn, Rackhir. This will not be the first time we have fought the Lords of Chaos.'

'True,' Rackhir nodded. 'Most recently we averted a threat with certain aid from the Grey Lords – but Chaos had caused the gateways to the Grey Lords to be closed to mortals. We can offer you only our warriors' loyalty.'

'We shall be grateful for that.' Elric paced the dais. There was no need to ask the senators of Karlaak and the other cities of Ilmiora, for they had agreed to support him, come what may, long before the other rulers were called.

The same was true of the bleak-faced band who made up the refugees from the West, headed by Viri-Sek, the winged youth from Myyrrhn, last of his line since all the other members of the ruling family had been slain by Jagreen Lern's minions.

Just beyond the walls of Karlaak was a sea of tents and pavilions over which the banners of many nations waved sluggishly in
the hot, moist wind. At this moment, Elric knew, the proud lords
of the South were uprooting their standards and packing their
tents, not looking at the war-battered warriors of Shazaar, Jharkor and Tarkesh who stared at them in puzzlement. Sight of those
dull-eyed veterans should have decided the Southern nobles to
ally themselves with the East, but evidently it had not.

Elric sighed and turned his back on the others to contemplate
the great map of the world with its shaded dark areas.

'Now only a quarter is black,' he said softly to Moonglum. 'But
the dark tide spreads farther and faster and soon we may all be
engulfed.'

'We'll dam the flow – or try to – when it comes,' Moonglum
said with attempted jauntiness. 'But meanwhile your wife would
spend some time with you before we leave. Let's both to bed and
trust our dreams are light!'

Chapter Two

Two nights later they stood on the quayside in the city of Jadmar while a cold wind sliced its way inland.

'There she is,' Elric said, pointing down at the small boat rocking and bumping in the water below.

'A small craft,' Moonglum said dubiously. 'She scarcely looks seaworthy.'

'She'll stay afloat longer than a larger vessel in a heavy storm.' Elric clambered down the iron steps. 'Also,' he added, as Moonglum put a cautious foot on the rung above him, 'she'll be less noticeable and won't draw the attention of any enemy vessels which might be scouting in these waters.'

He jumped and the boat rocked crazily. He leaned over, grasped a rung and steadied the boat so that Moonglum could climb aboard.

The cocky little Eastlander pushed a hand through his shock of red hair and stared up at the troubled sky.

'Bad weather for this time of year,' he noted. 'It's hard to understand. All the way from Karlaak we've had every sort of weather, freak snowstorms, thunderstorms, hail and winds as hot as a furnace blast. Those rumours were disturbing, too – a rain of blood in Bakshaan, balls of fiery metal falling in the west of Vilmir, unprecedented earthquakes in Jadmar a few hours before we arrived. It seems nature has gone insane.'

'Not far from the truth,' Elric said grimly, untying the mooring line. 'Lift the sail will you, and tack into the wind?'

'What do you mean?' Moonglum began to loosen the sail. It billowed into his face and his voice was muffled. 'Jagreen Lern's hordes haven't reached this part of the world yet.'

'They haven't needed to. I told you the forces of nature were being disrupted by Chaos. We have only experienced the backwash of what is going on in the West. If you think these weather conditions are peculiar, you would be horrified by the effect which Chaos has on those parts of the world where its rule is almost total!'

'I wonder if you haven't taken on too much in this fight.' Moonglum adjusted the sail and it filled to send the little boat scudding between the two long harbour walls towards the open sea.

As they passed the beacons, guttering in the cold wind, Elric gripped the tiller tighter, taking a south-westerly course past the Vilmirian peninsula. Overhead the stars were sometimes obscured by the tattered shreds of clouds streaming before the cold, unnatural blast of the wind. Spray splashed in his face, stinging it in a thousand places, but he ignored it. He had not answered Moonglum, for he also had doubts about his ability to save the world from Chaos.

Moonglum had learned to judge his friend's moods. For some years before they had travelled the world together and had learned to respect one another. Lately, since Elric had near-permanent residence in his wife's city of Karlaak, Moonglum had continued to travel and had been in command of a small mercenary army patrolling the Southern Marches of Pikarayd, driving back the barbarians inhabiting the hinterland of that country. He had immediately relinquished this command when Elric's news reached him and now, as the tiny ship bore them towards a hazy and peril-fraught destiny, savoured the familiar mixture of excitement and perturbation which he had felt a dozen times before when their escapades had led them into conflict with the unknown supernatural forces so closely linked with Elric's destiny. He had come to accept as a fact that his destiny was bound to Elric's and felt, in the deepest places of his being, that when the time came they would both die together in some mighty adventure.

Is this death imminent? he wondered, as he concentrated on the sail and shivered in the blasting wind. Not yet, perhaps, but he felt, fatalistically, that it was not far away, for the time was looming when the only deeds of men would be dark, desperate and great and even these might not serve to form a bastion against the inrush of the creatures of Chaos.

Elric, himself, contemplated nothing, kept his mind clear and relaxed as much as he could. His quest for the aid of the White Lords was one which could well prove fruitless, but he chose not to dwell on this until he knew for certain whether their help could be invoked or not.

Dawn came swimming over the horizon, showing a heaving waste of grey water with no land in sight. The wind had dropped and the air was warmer. Banks of purple clouds bearing veins of saffron and scarlet poured into the sky, like the smoke of some monstrous pyre. Soon they were sweating beneath a moody sun and the wind had dropped so that the sail hardly moved and yet, at the same time, the sea began to heave as if lashed by a storm.

The sea was moving like a living entity thrashing in nightmare-filled sleep. Moonglum glanced at Elric from where he lay sprawled in the prow of the boat. Elric returned the gaze, shaking his head and releasing his half-conscious grip of the tiller. It was useless to attempt steering the boat in conditions like these. The boat was being swept about by the wild waves, yet no water seemed to enter it, no spray wet them. Everything had become unreal, dreamlike and for a while Elric felt that even if he had wished to speak, he would not have been able to.

Then, in the distance at first, they heard a low droning which grew to a whining shriek and suddenly the boat was sent half-flying over the rolling waves and driven down into a trench. Above them, the blue and silver water seemed for a moment to be a wall of metal – and then it came crashing down towards them.

His mood broken, Elric clung to the tiller, yelling: 'Hang on to the boat, Moonglum! Hang on, or you're lost!'

Tepid water groaned down and they were flattened beneath it as if swatted by a gigantic palm. The boat dropped deeper and deeper until it seemed they would be crushed on the bottom by the surging blow. Then, they were flung upwards again, and down, and as he glimpsed the boiling surface, Elric saw three mountains pushing themselves upwards, gouting flame and lava. The boat wallowed, half-full of water, and they set to frantically baling it out as the boat was swirled back and forth, being driven nearer and nearer to the new-formed volcanoes.

Elric dropped his baling pan and flung his weight against the tiller, forcing the boat away from the mountains of fire. It responded sluggishly, but began to drift in the opposite direction.

Elric saw Moonglum, pale-faced, attempting to shake out the sodden sail. The heat from the volcanoes was hardly bearable. He glanced upwards to try and get some kind of bearing, but the sun seemed to have swollen and broken so that he saw a million fragments of flame.

'This is the work of Chaos, Moonglum!' he shouted. 'And only a taste, I fancy, of what it can become!'

'They must know we are here and seek to destroy us!' Moonglum swept sweat from his eyes with the back of his hand.

'Perhaps, but I think not.' Now he looked up again and the sun seemed almost normal. He took a bearing and began to steer the boat away from the mountains of fire, but they were many miles off their original course.

He had planned to sail to the south of Melniboné, Isle of the Dragon, and avoid the Dragon Sea lying to the north, for it was well-known that the last great sea-monsters still roamed this stretch. But now it was obvious that they were, in fact, north of Melniboné and being driven further north all the time – towards Pan Tang!

There was a no chance of heading for Melniboné itself – he wondered if the Isle of the Dragon had even survived the monstrous upheavals. He would have to make straight for Sorcerers' Isle if he could.

The ocean was calmer now, but the water had almost reached boiling point so that every drop that fell on his skin seemed to scald him. Bubbles formed on the surface and it was as if they sailed in a gigantic witch's cauldron. Dead fish and half-reptilian forms drifted about, as thick as seaweed, threatening to clog the boat's passage. But the wind, though strong, had begun to blow in one direction and Moonglum grinned in relief as it filled the sail.

Slowly, through the death-thick waters, they managed to steer a south-westerly course towards Sorcerers' Isle as clouds of steam formed on the ocean and obscured their view.

Hours later, they had left the heated waters behind and were sailing beneath clear skies on a calm sea. They allowed themselves to doze. In less than a day they would reach Sorcerers' Isle, but now they were overcome by the reaction to their experience and wondered, dazedly, how they had lived through the awful storm.

Elric jerked his eyes open with a shock. He was certain he had not slept long, yet the sky was dark and a cold drizzle was falling. As the drops touched his head and face, they oozed down it like viscous jelly. Some of it entered his mouth and he hastily spat out the bitter-tasting stuff.

'Moonglum,' he called through the gloom, 'what's the hour, do you know?'

The Eastlander's sleep-heavy voice answered dazedly. 'I know not. I'd swear it is not night already.'

Elric gave the tiller a tentative push. The boat did not respond. He looked over the side.

It seemed they were sailing through the sky itself. A dully luminous gas seemed to swirl about the hull, but he could see no water. He shuddered. Had they left the plane of Earth? Were they sailing through some frightful, supernatural sea? He cursed himself for sleeping, feeling helpless; more helpless than when he had fought the storm. The heavy, gelatinous rain beat down strongly and he pulled the hood of his cloak over his white hair. From his belt pouch he took flint and tinder and the tiny light was just sufficient to show him Moonglum's half-mad eyes. The little Eastlander's face was taut with fear. Elric had never seen such fear on his friend's face, and knew that with a little less self-control, his own face would assume a similar expression.

'Our time has ended,' Moonglum trembled. 'I fear that we're dead, at last, Elric.'

'Don't prattle such emptiness, Moonglum. I have heard of no

afterlife such as this.' But secretly, Elric wondered if Moonglum's words were true. The ship seemed to be moving rapidly through the gaseous sea, being driven or drawn to some unknown destination. Yet Elric could swear that the Lords of Chaos had no knowledge of his boat.

Faster and faster the little craft moved and then, with relief, they heard the familiar splash of water about its keel and it was surging through the salt-sea again. For a short while longer the viscous rain continued to fall and then even that was gone.

Moonglum sighed as the blackness slowly gave way to light and they saw again a normal ocean about them.

'What was it, then?' he ventured, finally.

'Another manifestation of ruptured nature,' Elric attempted to keep his voice calm. 'Some warp in the barrier between the realm of men and the realm of Chaos, perhaps? Don't question our luck in surviving it. We are again off course, and,' he pointed to the horizon, 'a natural storm seems to be brewing yonder.'

'A natural storm I can accept, no matter how dangerous,' Moonglum murmured, and made swift preparations, furling the sail as the wind increased and the sea churned.

In a way, Elric welcomed the storm when it finally struck them. At least it obeyed natural laws and could be fought by natural means. The rain refreshed their faces, the wind swept through their hair and they battled the storm with fierce enjoyment, the plucky boat riding the waves.

But, in spite of this, they were being driven further and further north-east, towards the conquered coasts of Shazaar, in the opposite direction to their goal.

The healthy storm raged on until all thoughts of destiny and supernatural danger were driven from their minds and their muscles ached and they gasped with the shock of cold waves on their drenched bodies.

The boat reeled and rocked, their hands were sore from the tightness of their grip on wood and rope, but it was as if Fate had singled them out to live, or perhaps for a death that would be less clean, for they continued to ride the heaving waters.

Then, with a shock, Elric saw rocks rearing and Moonglum shouted in recognition: *'The Serpent's Teeth!'*

The Serpent's Teeth lay close to Shazaar and were one of the most feared hazards of the shore-hugging traders of the West. Elric and Moonglum had seen them before, from a distance, but now the storm was driving them nearer and nearer, and though they struggled to keep the boat away, they seemed bound to be smashed to their deaths on the jagged rocks.

A wave surged under the boat, lifted them and bore them down. Elric clung to the side of the boat and thought he heard Moonglum's wild shout above the noise of the storm before they were flung towards the Serpent's Teeth.

'Farewell!'

And then there was a terrifying sound of smashing timbers, the feel of sharp rock lacerating his rolling body, and he was beneath the waves, fighting his way to the surface to gasp in air before another wave tossed him and grazed his arm against the rocks.

Desperately, encumbered by the life-giving runesword at his belt, he attempted to swim for the looming cliffs of Shazaar, conscious that even if he lived, he had returned to enemy soil and his chances of reaching the White Lords were now almost non-existent.

Chapter Three

ELRIC LAY EXHAUSTED on the cold shingle, listening to the musical sound that the tide made as it drew back over the stones. Another sound joined that of the surf, and he recognised it as the crunch of boots. Someone was coming towards him. In Shazaar it was most likely to be an enemy. He rolled over and began scrambling to his feet, drawing the last reserves from his worn-out body. His right hand had half-drawn Stormbringer from its scabbard before he realised that it was Moonglum, bent with weariness, standing grinning before him.

'Thank the gods, you live!' Moonglum lowered himself to the shingle and leaned back with his arms supporting his weight, regarding the now calm sea and the towering Serpent's Teeth in the distance.

'Aye, we live,' Elric squatted down, moodily, 'but for how long in this ruined land, I cannot guess. Somewhere, perhaps, we can find a ship – but it will mean seeking a town or city and we're a marked pair, easily recognised by our physical appearance.'

Moonglum shook his head and laughed lightly. 'You're still the gloomy one, friend. Be thankful for your life, say I.'

'Small mercies are all but useless in this conflict,' Elric said. 'Rest, now, Moonglum, while I watch, then you can take my place. There was no time to lose when we began this adventure, and now we've lost days.'

Moonglum gave no argument, but allowed himself immediately to sleep and when he awoke, much refreshed though aching still, Elric slept until the moon was high and shining brightly in the clear sky.

They trudged through the night, the sparse grass of the coast region giving way to wet, blackened ground. It was as if a holocaust had raged over the countryside, followed by a rainstorm which had left behind it a marsh of ashes. Remembering the grassy plains of this part of Shazaar, Elric was horrified, unable to tell whether men or the creatures of Chaos had caused such wanton ruin.

Noon was approaching, with a hint of weird disturbances in the bright-clouded sky, when they saw a long line of people coming towards them. They flattened themselves behind a small rise and peered cautiously over it as the party drew nearer. These were no enemy soldiers, but gaunt women and starving children, men who staggered in rags, and a few battered riders, obviously the remnants of some defeated band of partisans who had held out against Jagreen Lern.

'I think we'll find friends, of sorts, here,' Elric muttered thankfully, 'and perhaps some information which will help us.'

They arose and walked towards the wretched herd. The riders quickly grouped around the civilians and drew their weapons, but before any challenges could be given, someone cried from the enclosed ranks:

'Elric of Melniboné! Elric – have you returned with news of rescue?'

Elric didn't recognise the voice, but he knew his face was a legend, with its dead white skin and glowing crimson eyes.

'I'm seeking rescue myself, friend,' he said with poorly assumed cheerfulness. 'We were shipwrecked on your coasts while on a journey which we hoped would help us lift the yoke of Jagreen Lern from off the Westlands, but unless we find another ship, our chances are poor.'

'Which way did you sail, Elric?' said the unseen spokesman.

'We sailed to Sorcerers' Isle in the south-west, there to invoke the aid, if we could, of the White Lords,' Moonglum replied.

'Then you were going in the wrong direction!'

Elric straightened his back and tried to peer into the throng. 'Who are you to tell us that?'

There was a disturbance in the crowd and a bent, middle-aged man with long, curling moustachios adorning his fair-skinned

face broke from the ranks and stood leaning on a staff. The riders
drew back their horses so that Elric could see him properly.

'I am named Ohada the Seer, once famous in Aflitain as an
oracle. But Aflitain was razed in the sack of Shazaar and I was
lucky enough to escape with these few people who are all from
Aflitain, one of the last cities to fall before Pan Tang's sorcerous
might. I have a message of great import for you, Elric. It is for
your ears only and I received it from one you know – one who
may help you and, indirectly, us.'

'You have piqued my curiosity and raised my hopes,' Elric
beckoned with his hand. 'Come, seer, tell me your news and let's
all trust it is as good as you hint.'

Moonglum took a step back as the seer approached. Both he
and the Aflitainians watched with curiosity as Ohada whispered
to Elric. Elric himself had to strain to catch the words. 'I bear a
message from a strange man called Sepiriz. He says that what you
have failed to do, he has done, but there is something which you
must do that he cannot. He says to go to the carved city and there
he will enlighten you further.'

'Sepiriz! How did he contact you?'

'I am clairvoyant. He came to me in a dream.'

'Your words could be treacherous, designed to lead me into
Jagreen Lern's hands.'

'Sepiriz added one thing to me – he told me that we should
meet on this very spot. Could Jagreen Lern know that?'

'Unlikely – but, by the same reckoning, could *anyone* know
that?' He nodded. 'Thanks, seer.' Then he shouted to the riders.
'We need a pair of horses – your best!'

'Our horses are valuable to us,' grumbled a knight in torn
armour, 'they are all we have.'

'My companion and I need to move swiftly if we are to save the
world from Chaos. Come, risk a pair of horses against the chance
of vengeance on your conquerors.'

'Aye, very well.' The knight dismounted and so did the man
beside him. They led their steeds up to Elric and Moonglum.

'Use them with care, Elric.'

Elric took the reins and swung himself into the saddle, the huge runesword slapping at his side. 'I will,' said he. 'What are your plans now?'

'We'll fight on, as best we can.'

'Would it not be wiser to hide in the mountains or the Marshes of the Mist?'

'If you had witnessed the depravity and terror of Jagreen Lern's rule, you would not make such an enquiry,' the knight said bleakly. 'Though we cannot hope to win against a warlock whose servants can command the very earth to heave like the ocean, pull down floods of salt water from the sky, and send green clouds scudding down to destroy helpless children in nameless ways, we shall take what vengeance we can. This part of the continent is calm beside what is going on elsewhere. Dreadful geological changes are taking place. You would not recognise a hill or forest ten miles north. And those that you passed one day might well have changed or disappeared the next.'

'We have witnessed something of the like on our sea journey,' Elric nodded. 'I wish you a long life of revenge, friend. I myself have scores to settle with Jagreen Lern and his accomplice.'

'His accomplice? You mean King Sarosto of Dharijor?' A thin smile crossed the knight's haggard face. 'You'll take no vengeance on Sarosto. He was assassinated soon after our forces were vanquished at the battle of Sequa. Though nothing was proved, it is common knowledge that he was killed at the orders of the Theocrat who now rules unchallenged.' The knight shrugged. 'And who can stand for long against Jagreen Lern, let alone his captains?'

'Who are these captains?'

'Why, he has summoned all the Dukes of Hell to him. Whether they will accept his mastery much longer, I do not know. It is our belief that Jagreen Lern will be the next to die – and hell unchecked will rule in his place!'

'I hope not,' Elric said softly, 'for I won't be cheated of my vengeance.'

The knight sighed. 'With the Dukes of Hell as his allies, Jagreen Lern will soon rule the world.'

'Let us hope I can find a means of disposing of that dark aristocracy, and keeping my vow to slay Jagreen Lern,' Elric said and, with a wave of thanks to the seer and the two knights, turned his horse towards the mountains of Jharkor, Moonglum in his wake.

They got little rest on their perilous ride to the mountain home of Sepiriz, for, as the knight had told them, the ground itself seemed alive and anarchy ruled everywhere. Afterwards, Elric remembered little, save a feeling of utter horror and the noise of unholy screechings in his ear, dark colours, gold, reds, blues, black, and the flaring orange that was everywhere the sign of Chaos on Earth.

In the mountain regions close to Nihrain, they found that the rule of Chaos was not so complete as in other parts. This proved that Sepiriz and his nine black brothers were exerting at least some control against the forces threatening to engulf them.

Through steep gorges of towering black rock, along treacherous mountain paths, down slopes that rattled with loose stones and seemed likely to start an avalanche, they pressed deeper and deeper into the heart of the ancient mountains. These were the oldest mountains in the world, and they held one of the Earth's most ancient secrets – the domain of the immortal Nihrain who had ruled for centuries even before the coming of the Melnibonéans. At last, they came to the Hewn City of Nihrain, its towering palaces, temples and fortresses carved into the living black granite, hidden in the depths of the chasm that might have been bottomless. Virtually cut off from all but the faintest filterings of sunlight, it had brooded here since earliest times.

Down the narrow paths they guided their reluctant steeds until they had reached a huge gateway, its pillars carved with the figures of titans and half-men looming above them, so that Moonglum gasped and immediately fell silent, overawed by the genius which could accomplish the twin feats of gigantic engineering and powerful art.

In the caverns, also carved to represent scenes from the legends of the Nihrain, Sepiriz awaited them, a welcoming smile on his thin-lipped ebony face.

'Greetings, Sepiriz,' Elric dismounted and allowed slaves to lead his horse away. Moonglum did likewise, a trifle warily.

'I was informed correctly,' Sepiriz clasped Elric's shoulders in his hands. 'I am glad for I learned you were bound to Sorcerers' Isle to seek the White Lords' help.'

'True. Is their help, then, unobtainable?'

'Not yet. We ourselves are trying to contact them, with the aid of the hermit magicians of the island, but so far Chaos has blocked our attempts. But there is work for you and your sword closer to home. Come to my chamber and refresh yourselves. We have some wine which will revitalise you and when you have drunk your fill I'll tell you what task Fate has decided for you now.'

Sitting in his chair, sipping his wine and glancing around Sepiriz's dark chamber, lighted only by the fires which burned in its several grates, Elric searched his mind for some clue to the unidentifiable impressions which seemed to drift just below the surface of his conscious brain. There was something mysterious about the chamber, a mystery that was not solely created by its vastness and the shadows that filled it. Without knowing why, Elric thought that though it was bounded by miles of solid rock in all directions, it had no proper dimensions that could be measured by the means normally employed; it was as if it extended into planes that did not conform to the Earth's space and time – planes that were, in fact, timeless and spaceless. He felt that he might attempt to cross the chamber from one wall to the other – but could walk for ever without ever reaching the far wall. He made an attempt to dismiss these thoughts and put down his cup, breathing in deeply. There was no doubt that the wine relaxed and invigorated him. He pointed to the wine jar on the stone table and said to Sepiriz: 'A man might easily become addicted to such a brew!'

'I'm addicted already,' Moonglum grinned, pouring himself another cup.

Sepiriz shook his head. 'It has a strange quality, our Nihrain wine. It tastes pleasant and refreshes the weary, yet once his strength is regained, the man who drinks it then is nauseated. That is why we still have some of it left. But our stocks are low – the vines from which it was made have long since passed from the Earth.'

'A magic potion,' Moonglum said, replacing his cup on the table.

'If you like so to designate it. Elric and I are of an earlier age when what you call magic was part of normal life and Chaos ruled entirely, if more quietly than now. You men of the Young Kingdoms are perhaps right to be suspicious of sorcery, for we hope to ready the world for Law soon and then, perhaps, you'll find similar brews by more painstaking methods, methods you can understand better.'

'I doubt it,' Moonglum laughed.

Elric sighed. 'If we are not luckier than we have been, we'll see Chaos unleashed on the globe and Law forever vanquished,' he said gloomily.

'And no luck for us if Law is triumphant, eh?' Sepiriz poured himself a cup of the wine.

Moonglum looked sharply at Elric, understanding that much more of his friend's unenviable predicament.

'You said there was work for me and my sword, Sepiriz.' Elric said. 'What's its nature?'

'You have already learned that Jagreen Lern has summoned some of the Dukes of Hell to captain his men and keep his conquered lands under control?'

'Yes.'

'You understand the import of this? Jagreen Lern has succeeded in making a sizeable breach in the Law-constructed barrier which once kept the creatures of Chaos from wholly ruling the planet. He is forever widening this breach as his power increases. This explains how he could summon such a mighty assembly of hell's nobility where, in the past, it was hard to bring one to our plane. Arioch is among them...'

'Arioch!' Arioch had always been Elric's patron demon, the principal god worshipped by his ancestors. That matters had reached such a stage conveyed to him, deeper than anything else, that he was now a total outcast, unprotected either by Law or Chaos.

'Your only close supernatural ally is your sword,' Sepiriz said grimly. 'And, perhaps, its brothers.'

'What brothers? There is only the sister sword Mournblade, which Dyvim Slorm has!'

'Do you remember that I told you how the twin swords were actually only an earthly manifestation of their supernatural selves?' Sepiriz said calmly.

'I do.'

'Well, I can tell you now that Stormbringer's "real" being is related to other supernatural forces on another plane. I know how to summon them, but these entities are also creatures of Chaos and therefore, as far as you're concerned, somewhat hard to control. They could well get out of hand – perhaps even turn against you. Stormbringer, as you have discovered in the past, is bound to you by ties even stronger than those which bind it to its brothers who are lesser beings altogether, but its brothers outnumber it, and Stormbringer might not be able to protect you against them.'

'Why have I never known this?'

'You *have* known it, in a way. Do you remember times when you have called to the Dark Ones for help and help has come?'

'Yes. You mean that this help has been supplied by Stormbringer's brethren?'

'Much of the time, yes. Already they are used to coming to your help. They are not what you and I would call intelligent, though sentient, and are therefore not so strongly bound to Chaos as its reasoning servants. They can be controlled, to a degree, by anyone who has power such as you have over one of their brothers. If you need their help, you will need to remember a rune which I shall tell you later.'

'And what is my task?'

'To destroy the Dukes of Hell.'

'Destroy the – Sepiriz, that's *impossible*. They are Lords of Chaos, one of the most powerful groups in the whole Realm of Chance. Sepiriz, I could not do it!'

'True. But you control one of the mightiest weapons. Of course, no mortal can destroy the dukes entirely – all he can hope to do is banish them to their own plane by wrecking the substance which they use for bodies on Earth. That is your task. Already there are hints that the Dukes of Hell – namely Arioch, and Balan, and Maluk – have taken some of Jagreen Lern's power from him. The fool still thinks he can rule over such supernatural might as they represent. It suits them, perhaps, to let him think so, but it is certain that with these friends Jagreen Lern can defeat the Southlands with a minimum of expenditure in arms, ships or men. Without them, he could do it – but it would take more time and effort and therefore give us a slight advantage to prepare against him while he subdues the Southlands.'

Elric did not bother to ask Sepiriz how he knew of the Southerners' decision to fight Jagreen Lern alone. Sepiriz obviously had many powers as was proved by his ability to contact Elric through the seer. 'I have sworn to help the Southlands in spite of their refusal to side with us against the Theocrat,' he said calmly.

'And you'll keep your oath – by destroying the dukes if you can.'

'Destroying Arioch, and Balan, and Maluk...' Elric whispered the names, fearful that even here he might invoke them.

'Arioch has always been an unhelpful demon,' Moonglum pointed out. 'Many's the time in the past he has refused to aid you, Elric.'

'Because,' Sepiriz said, 'he already had some knowledge that you and he were to fight in the future.'

Though the wine had refreshed his body, Elric's mind was close to snapping. The strain on his soul was almost at breaking point. To fight the demon-god of his ancestors... The old blood was still strong in him, the old loyalties still present.

Sepiriz rose and gripped Elric's shoulder, staring with black eyes into the dazed and smouldering crimson ones.

'You have pledged yourself to this mission, remember?'

'Aye, pledged – but Sepiriz – the Dukes of Hell – Arioch – I – oh, I wish that I were dead now...'

'You have much to do before you'll be allowed to die, Elric,' Sepiriz said quietly. 'You must realise how important you and your great sword are to Fate's cause. Remember your pledge!'

Elric drew himself upright, nodded vaguely. 'Even had I been given this knowledge before I made that pledge, I would still have made it. But...'

'What?'

'Do not place too much faith on my ability to fulfil this part, Sepiriz.'

The black Nihrain said nothing. Moonglum's normally animated face was grave and miserable as he looked at Elric standing in the mighty hall, the firelight writhing around him, his arms folded on his chest, the huge broadsword hanging straight at his side, and a look of stunned shock on his white face. Sepiriz walked away into the darkness and returned later with a white tablet on which old runes were engraved. He handed it to the albino.

'Memorise the spell,' Sepiriz said softly, 'and then destroy the tablet. But remember, only use it in extreme adversity for, as I warned you, Stormbringer's brethren may refuse to aid you.'

Elric made an effort and controlled his emotions. Long after Moonglum had gone to rest, he studied the rune under the guidance of the Nihrainian, learning not only how to vocalise it, but also the twists of logic which he would have to understand, and the state of mind into which he must put himself if it were to be effective.

When both he and Sepiriz were satisfied, Elric allowed a slave to take him to his sleeping chamber, but slumber came hard to him and he spent the night in restless torment until the slave came to wake him the next morning and found him fully dressed and ready to ride for Pan Tang where the Dukes of Hell were assembled.

Chapter Four

THROUGH THE STRICKEN lands of the West rode Elric and Moonglum, astride sturdy Nihrain steeds that seemed to need no rest and contained no fear. The Nihrain horses were a special gift, for they had certain additional powers to their unnatural strength and endurance. Sepiriz had told them how, in fact, the steeds did not have full existence on the earthly plane and that their hoofs did not touch the ground in the strict sense, but touched the stuff of their other plane. This gave them the ability to appear to gallop on air – or water.

Scenes of terror were everywhere to be found. At one time they saw a frightful sight; a wild and hellish mob destroying a village built around a castle. The castle itself was in flames and on the horizon a mountain gouted smoke and fire – yet another volcano in lands previously free of them. Though the looters had human shape, they were degenerate creatures, spilling blood and drinking it with equal abandon. And directing them without joining their orgy, Elric and Moonglum saw what seemed to be a corpse astride the living skeleton of a horse, bedecked in bright trappings, a flaming sword in its hand and a golden helm on its head.

They skirted the scene and rode fast away from it, through mists that looked and smelled like blood, over steaming rivers dammed with death, past rustling forests that seemed to follow them, beneath skies often filled with ghastly, winged shapes bearing even ghastlier burdens.

At other times, they met groups of warriors, many of them in the armour and trappings of the conquered nations, but depraved and obviously sold to Chaos. These they fought or avoided, depending on circumstance and, when at last they reached the cliffs of Jharkor and saw the sea which would take them to the Isle of Pan Tang, they knew they had ridden through a land to which hell had come.

Along the cliffs they galloped, high above the churning, grey sea, the lowering sky dark and cold; down to the beaches to pause for a second time on the water's edge.

'Come!' Elric cried, urging his horse forward. 'To Pan Tang!'

Scarcely stopping, they rode their magical steeds over the water towards the evil-heavy island of Pan Tang, where Jagreen Lern and his terrible allies prepared to sail with their giant fleet and smash the sea power of the South before conquering the Southlands themselves.

'Elric!' Moonglum called above the whining wind. 'Should we not proceed with more caution?'

'Caution? What need of that when the Dukes of Hell must surely know their turncoat servant comes to fight them!'

Moonglum pursed his long lips, disturbed, for Elric was in a wild, maddened mood. He got little comfort, also, from the knowledge that Sepiriz had charmed his shortsword and his sabre both, with one of the few white spells he had at his command.

Now the bleak cliffs of Pan Tang rose into sight, spray-lashed and ominous, the sea moaning about them as if in some special torture which Chaos could inflict on nature itself.

And also around the island a peculiar darkness hovered, shifting and changing.

They entered the darkness as the Nihrain steeds pounded up the steep, rocky beach of Pan Tang, a place that had always been ruled by its black priesthood, a grim theocracy that had sought to emulate the legendary Sorcerer Emperors of the Bright Empire of Melniboné. But Elric, last of those emperors, and landless now, with few subjects, knew that the dark arts had been natural and lawful to his ancestors, whereas these human beings had perverted themselves to worship an unholy hierarchy they barely understood.

Sepiriz had given them their route and they galloped across the turbulent land towards the capital – Hwamgaarl, City of Screaming Statues.

Pan Tang was an island of green, obsidian rock that gave off bizarre reflections; rock that seemed alive.

Soon they could see the looming walls of Hwamgaarl in the distance. As they drew nearer, an army of black-cowled swordsmen, chanting a particularly horrible litany, seemed to rise from the ground ahead and block their way.

Elric had no time to spare for these, recognisable as a detachment of Jagreen Lern's warrior-priests.

'Up, steed!' he cried, and the Nihrain horse leapt skywards, passing over the disconcerted priests with a fantastic bound. Moonglum did likewise, his laughter mocking the swordsmen as he and his friend thundered on towards Hwamgaarl. Their way was clear for some distance, since Jagreen Lern had evidently expected the detachment to hold the pair for a long time. But, when the City of Screaming Statues was barely a mile away, the ground began to grumble and gaping cracks split its surface. This did not overly disturb them, for the Nihrain horses had no use for earthly terrain in any case.

The sky above heaved and shook itself, the darkness became flushed with streaks of luminous ebony, and from the fissures in the ground, monstrous shapes sprang up!

Vulture-headed lions, fifteen feet high, prowled in hungry anticipation towards them, their feathered manes rustling as they approached.

To Moonglum's frightened astonishment, Elric laughed and the Eastlander knew his friend had gone mad. But Elric was familiar with this ghoulish pack, since his ancestors had formed it for their own purposes a dozen centuries before. Evidently, Jagreen Lern had discovered the pack lurking on the borders between

Chaos and Earth and had utilised it without being aware of how it had been created.

Old words formed on Elric's pale lips, and he spoke affectionately to the towering bird-beasts. They ceased their progress towards him, and glanced uncertainly around them, their loyalties evidently divided. Feathered tails lashed, claws worked in and out of pads, scraping great gashes in the obsidian rock. And, taking advantage of this, Elric and Moonglum walked their horses through them, and emerged just as a droning but angry voice rapped from the heavens, ordering, in the High Tongue of Melniboné: *'Destroy them!'*

One lion-vulture bounded uncertainly towards the pair. Another followed it, and another, till the whole pack raced to catch them.

'Faster!' Elric whispered to the Nihrain horse, but the steed could hardly keep the distance separating them. There was nothing for it but to turn. Deep in the recesses of his memory, he recalled a certain spell he had learned as a child. All the old spells of Melniboné had been passed on to him by his father, with the warning that, in these times, many of them were virtually useless. But there had been one – the spell for calling the vulture-headed lions, and another spell... Now he remembered it! The spell for sending them back to the domain of Chaos. Would it work?

He adjusted his mind, sought the words he needed as the beasts plunged on towards him.

> *'Creatures! Matik of Melniboné made thee*
> *From stuff of unformed madness!*
> *If thou wouldst live as thou art now,*
> *Get hence, or Matik's brew again shall be!'*

The creatures paused and, desperately, Elric repeated the spell, afraid that he had made a small mistake, either within his mind, or in the words.

Moonglum, who had drawn his horse up beside Elric, did not dare speak his fears, for he knew the albino sorcerer must not be hindered whilst spell-making. He watched in trepidation as the leading beast gave voice to a cawing roar.

But Elric heard the sound with relief, for it meant the beasts had understood his threat and were still bound to obey the spell. Slowly, half-reluctantly, they crawled down into the fissures, and vanished.

Sweating, Elric said triumphantly: 'Luck is with us so far! Jagreen Lern either underestimated my powers, or else this is all he could summon with his own! More proof, perhaps, that Chaos uses him, and not the other way about!'

'Tempt not such luck by speaking of it,' Moonglum warned. 'From what you'd told me, these are puny things compared with what we must soon face.'

Elric shot an angry look at his friend. He did not like to think of his coming task.

Now they neared the huge walls of Hwamgaarl. At intervals along these walls, which slanted outwards at an angle to encumber potential besiegers, they saw the screaming statues – once men and women whom Jagreen Lern and his forefathers had turned to rock but allowed them to retain their life and ability to speak. They spoke little, but screamed much, their ghastly shouts rolling over the disgusting city like the tormented voices of the damned – and damned they were. These sobbing waves of sound were horrifying, even to Elric's ears, familiar with such sounds. Then another noise blended with this as the mighty portcullis of Hwamgaarl's main gate squealed upwards and from it poured a host of well-armed men.

'Evidently, Jagreen Lern's powers of sorcery have been exhausted for the meantime and the Dukes of Hell disdain to join him in a fight against a pair of mere mortals!' Elric said, reaching for the hilt of the black runesword.

Moonglum was beyond speech. Wordlessly, he drew both his own charmed blades, knowing he must fight and vanquish his own fears before he could encounter the men who ran at him.

With a wild howl that drowned out the screams from the statues, Stormbringer climbed from the scabbard and stood in Elric's hand, waiting in anticipation for the new souls it might drink, for the lifestuff which it could pass on to Elric and fill him with dark and stolen vitality.

Elric half-cringed at the feel of his blade in his damp hand. But he shouted to the advancing soldiers: 'See, jackals! See the sword! Forged by Chaos to vanquish Chaos! Come, let it drink your souls and spill your blood! We are ready for you!'

He did not wait but, with Moonglum behind him, spurred the Nihrain horse into their ranks, hewing about him with something of the old delight.

Now, so symbiotically linked with the hellblade was he that a hungry joy of killing swept through him, the joy of soul-stealing which drew a surging, unholy vitality into his deficient veins.

Though there were over a hundred warriors blocking his path, he smashed a bloody trail through them and Moonglum, seized by something akin to his friend's mood, was equally successful in dispatching all who came against him. Familiar with horror as they were, the soldiers soon became loath to approach the screaming runesword as it shone with a peculiarly brilliant light – a black light that pierced the blackness itself.

Laughing in his half-insane triumph, Elric felt the callous joy that his ancestors must have felt long ago, when they conquered the world and made it kneel to the Bright Empire. Chaos was, indeed, fighting Chaos – but Chaos of an older, cleaner sort, come to destroy the perverted upstarts who thought themselves as mighty as the wild Dragon Lords of Melniboné! Through the red ruin they had made of the enemy's ranks the pair plunged until the gateway gaped like a monster's maw before them. Without pausing, Elric rode laughing through it and people scuttled to hiding as he entered, in bizarre triumph, the City of Screaming Statues.

'Where now?' gasped Moonglum, all fear driven from him.

'To the Theocrat's Temple-Palace, of course. There Arioch and his fellow dukes no doubt await us!'

Through the echoing streets of the city they rode, proud and terrible, as if with an army at their backs. Dark buildings towered above them, but not a face dared peep from a window. Pan Tang had planned to rule the world – and it might yet – but, for the moment, its denizens were fully demoralised by the sight of two men taking their huge city by storm.

As they reached the wide plaza, Elric and Moonglum pulled their horses to a halt and observed the huge bronze shrine swinging on its chains in the centre. Beyond it rose Jagreen Lern's palace, all columns and towers, ominously quiet. Even the statues had ceased to scream, and the horses' hoofs made no sound as Elric and Moonglum approached the shrine. The blood-reddened runesword was still in Elric's two hands and he raised it upwards and to one side as he reached the brazen shrine. Then he took a mighty sweep at the chains supporting it. The supernatural blade bit into the metal and severed the links. The crash as the shrine dropped and smashed, scattering the bones of Jagreen Lern's ancestors, was magnified a thousand times by the silence. The noise echoed throughout Hwamgaarl and every inhabitant left alive knew what it signified.

'Thus I challenge thee, Jagreen Lern!' Elric shouted, aware that these words would also be heard by everyone. 'I have come to pay the debt I promised! Come, puppet!' He paused, even his triumph not sufficient fully to quench his hesitation at what he must do now. 'Come! Bring hell's dukes with you –'

Moonglum swallowed, his eyes rolling as he studied Elric's twisted face, but the albino continued:

'Bring Arioch. Bring Balan. Bring Maluk! Bring the proud princes of Chaos with you, for I have come to send them back to their own realm for ever!'

The silence again enfolded his high challenge, and he heard its echoes die away in the far places of the city.

Then, from somewhere inside the palace, he heard a movement. His heart pounded against his rib cage, threatening to break through the bones and hang throbbing on his chest as proof of his mortality. He heard a sound like the clopping of monstrous hoofs and, ahead of this noise, the measured steps that must be those of a man.

His eyes fixed themselves on the great, golden doors of the palace, half-hidden in the shadows that the columns threw. The doors silently began to open. Then a high-shouldered figure, dwarfed by the size of the doors, stepped forth and stood there, regarding Elric with a horrible anger smouldering in its face.

On his body, scarlet armour glowed as if red-hot. On his left arm was a shield of the same stuff and in his hand a steel sword. He had a narrow, aquiline head with a closely trimmed black beard and moustache. On his elaborate helm was the Merman Crest of Pan Tang. Jagreen Lern said, in a voice that trembled with rage: 'So, Elric, you have kept part of your word, after all. How I wish I'd been able to kill you at Sequa when I had the chance, but then I had a bargain with Darnizhaan...'

'Step forward, Theocrat,' Elric said with sudden calm. 'I'll give you the chance again and meet you fairly in single combat.'

Jagreen Lern sneered. 'Fairly? With that blade in your hands? Once I met it and did not perish, but now it burns with the souls of my best warrior-priests. I know its power. I would not be so foolish as to stand against it. No – let those you have challenged meet you.'

He stepped to one side. The doors gaped wider and, if Elric expected to see giant figures to emerge, he was disappointed. The dukes had assumed human proportions and the forms of men. But there was a power about them that filled the air as they moved to stand, disdainful of Jagreen Lern, upon the topmost step of the palace.

Elric looked upon their beautiful, smiling faces and shuddered again, for there was a kind of love on their faces, love mingled with pride and confidence, so that, for a moment, he was filled with the wish to jump from his horse and fling himself at their feet to plead forgiveness for what he had become. All the longing and the loneliness within him seemed to well up and he knew that these lovely beings would claim him, protect him, care for him...

'Well, Elric,' said Arioch, the leader, softly. 'Would you repent and return to us?'

The voice was silvery in its beauty, and Elric half-made to dismount, but then he clapped his hands to his ears, the runesword hanging by its wrist-throng, and cried: *'No! No! I must do what I must! Your time, like mine, is over!'*

'Do not speak thus, Elric,' Balan said persuasively, 'our rule has hardly begun. Soon the Earth and all its creatures will be part of the Realm of Chaos and a wild and splendid era will begin!' His words passed Elric's hands and whispered in his skull. 'Chaos has never been so powerful on Earth – not even in earliest days. We shall make you great. We shall make you a Lord of Chaos, equal to ourselves! We give you immortality, Elric. If you behave so foolishly, you will bring yourself only death, and none shall remember you.'

'I know that! I would not wish to be remembered in a world ruled by Law!'

Maluk laughed softly. 'That will never come to pass. We block every move that Law makes to try to bring help to Earth.'

'And this is why you must be destroyed!' Elric cried.

'We are immortal – we can never be slain!' Arioch said, and there was a tinge of impatience in his voice.

'Then I shall send you back to Chaos in such a way that you shall never have power on the Earth again!'

Elric swung his runeblade into his hand and it trembled there, moaning quietly, as if unsure of itself, just as he was.

'See!' Balan walked partway down the steps. 'See – even your trusted sword knows that we speak truth!'

'You speak a sort of truth,' Moonglum said in a quavering tone, astonished at his own bravery. 'But I remember something of a greater truth – a law that should bind both Chaos and Law – the Law of the Balance. That balance is held over the Earth and it has been ordained that Chaos and Law must keep it straight. Sometimes the Balance tips one way, sometimes another – and thus are the ages of the Earth created. But an unequal balance of this magnitude is *wrong*. In your struggling, you of Chaos may have forgotten this!'

'We have forgotten it for good reason, mortal. The Balance has tipped to such an extent in our favour that it is no longer adjustable. We triumph!'

Elric used this pause to collect himself. Sensing his renewed strength, Stormbringer responded with a confident purr.

The dukes also sensed it and glanced at one another.

Arioch's beautiful face seemed to flare with anger and his pseudo-body glided down the steps towards Elric, his fellow dukes following.

Elric's steed backed away a few paces.

A blot of living fire appeared in Arioch's hand and it shot towards the albino. He felt cold pain in his chest and he staggered in the saddle.

'Your body is unimportant, Elric. But think of a similar blow to your soul!' The façade of patience was dropping from Arioch.

Elric flung back his head and laughed. Arioch had betrayed himself. If he had remained calm, he would have had a greater advantage, but now he showed himself perturbed, whatever he had said to the contrary.

'Arioch, you aided me in the past, aided me to live. You will regret that!'

'There's still time to undo my folly, upstart man!' Another bolt came streaking towards him, but he passed Stormbringer before it and, in relief, saw that it deflected the unholy weapon.

But against such might they were surely doomed, unless they could invoke some supernatural aid. But Elric dared not risk summoning his runesword's brothers. Not yet. He must think of some other means. As he retreated before the searing bolts, Moonglum behind him whispering almost impotent charms, he thought of the vulture-lions he had sent back to Chaos. Perhaps he could recall them – for a different purpose.

The spell was fresh in his mind, requiring a slightly changed mental state and scarcely changed wording. Calmly, mechanically deflecting the bolts of the dukes, whose features had changed hideously to retain their previous beauty but take on an increasingly malevolent look, he uttered the spell.

> *'Creatures! Matik of Melniboné made thee,*
> *From stuff of unformed madness!*
> *If thou wouldst live, then aid me now.*
> *Come hither, or Matik's brew again shall be!'*

From out of the rolling darks of the plaza, the beaked beasts prowled. Elric yelled at the dukes. 'Mortal weapons cannot harm you! But these are beasts of your own plane! Sample their ferocity!' In the bizarre tongue of Melniboné, he ordered the vulture-lions upon the dukes.

Apprehensively, Arioch and his fellows backed towards the steps again, calling their own commands to the giant animals, but the things advanced, gathering speed.

Elric saw Arioch shout, rave, and then his body seemed to split asunder and rise in a new, less recognisable shape as the beasts attacked. All was suddenly ragged colour, shrill sound and dis- ordered matter. Behind the embattled demons, Elric saw Jagreen Lern running back into his palace. Hoping that the creatures he had summoned would hold the dukes, Elric rode his horse around the boiling mass and galloped up the steps.

Through the doors the two men rode, catching a glimpse of the terrified Theocrat running before them.

'Your allies were not so strong as you believed, Jagreen Lern!' Elric yelled as he bore down upon his enemy. 'Why, you foolish latecomer, did you think your knowledge matched that of a Melnibonéan!'

Jagreen Lern began to climb a winding staircase, labouring up the steps, too afraid to look back. Elric laughed again and pulled his horse to a stop, watching the running man.

'Dukes! Dukes!' sobbed Jagreen Lern as he climbed. 'Do not desert me now!'

Moonglum whispered. 'Surely those creatures will not defeat the aristocracy of hell?'

Elric shook his head. 'I do not expect them to, but if I finish Jagreen Lern, at least it could put an end to his conquests and demon-summoning.' He spurred the Nihrain steed up the steps after the Theocrat who heard him coming and flung himself into a room. Elric heard a bar fall and bolts squeal.

When he reached the door, it fell in at a blow of his sword and he was in a small chamber. Jagreen Lern had disappeared.

Dismounting, Elric went to a small door in the farthest corner

of the room and again demolished it. A narrow stair led upwards, obviously into a tower. Now he could take his vengeance, he thought, as he reached yet another door at the top of the stair and drew back his sword to smite it. The blow fell, but the door held.

'Curse the thing, it is protected by charms!'

He was just about to aim another blow, when he heard Moonglum's urgent calling from below.

'Elric! Elric – they've defeated the creatures. They are returning to the palace!'

He would have to leave Jagreen Lern for the meantime. He sprang down the steps, into the chamber and out onto the stair. In the hall he saw the flowing shapes of the unholy trinity. Halfway up the stair, Moonglum was quaking.

'Stormbringer,' said Elric, 'it is time to summon your brothers.'

The sword moved in his hand, as if in assent. He began to chant the difficult rune that Sepiriz had taught him. Stormbringer moaned a counterpoint to the dirge as the battle-worn dukes assumed different shapes and began to rise menacingly towards Elric.

Then, in the air all about him, he saw shapes appear, shadowy shapes half on his own plane, half on the plane of Chaos. He saw them stir and suddenly it seemed as if the air was filled with a million swords, each a twin to Stormbringer!

Acting on instinct, Elric released his grip on his blade and flung it towards the rest. It hung in the air before them and they seemed to acknowledge it. 'Lead them, Stormbringer! Lead them against the dukes – or your master perishes and you'll not drink another human soul again!'

The sea of swords rustled and a dreadful moaning emanated from them. The dukes flung themselves upwards towards the albino and he recoiled before the evil hatred that poured from the twisting shapes.

Glancing down, he saw Moonglum slumped in his saddle and did not know if he had perished or fainted.

Then the swords rushed upon the reaching dukes and Elric's head swam with the sight of a million blades plunging into the stuff of their beings.

The ululating noise of the battle filled his ears, the dreadful sight of the toiling conflict clouded his vision. Without Stormbringer's vitality, he felt weak and limp. He felt his knees shake and crumple and he could do nothing to aid the Black Sword's brothers as they clashed with the Dukes of Hell.

He collapsed, aware that if he witnessed further horror he would become totally insane. Thankfully, he felt his mind go blank and then, at last, he was unconscious, unable to know which would win.

Chapter Five

H IS BODY ITCHED. His arms and back ached. His wrists pounded with agony. Elric opened his eyes.

Immediately opposite him, spreadeagled in chains against the wall he saw Moonglum. Dull flame flickered in the centre of the place and he felt pain on his naked knee, looked down and saw Jagreen Lern.

The Theocrat spat at him.

'So,' Elric said thickly, 'I failed. You triumph after all.'

Jagreen Lern did not look triumphant. Rage still burned in his eyes.

'Oh, how shall I punish you?' he whispered.

'Punish me? Then –?' Elric's heartbeat increased.

'Your final spell succeeded,' the Theocrat said flatly, turning away to contemplate the brazier. 'Both your allies and mine vanished and all my attempts to contact the dukes have proved fruitless. You achieved your threat – or your minions did – you sent them back to Chaos for ever!'

'My sword – what of that?'

The Theocrat smiled bitterly. 'That's my only pleasure. Your sword vanished with the others. You are weak and helpless now, Elric. You are mine to maim and torture until the end of my life.'

Elric was dumbfounded. Part of him rejoiced that the dukes

had been beaten. Part of him lamented the loss of his sword. As Jagreen Lern had emphasised, without the blade, he was less than half a man, for his albinism weakened him. Already, his eyesight was dimmer and he felt no response in his limbs.

Jagreen Lern looked up at him.

'Enjoy the comparatively painless days left you, Elric. I leave you to anticipate what I have in store for you. I must away and instruct my men in the final preparations for the war-fleet soon to sail against the South. I won't waste time with crude torture now, for all the while I shall be scheming the most exquisite tortures conceivable. You shall take long years to die, I swear.'

He left the cell and, as the door slammed, Elric heard Jagreen Lern instructing the guard.

'Keep the brazier at full blast. Let them sweat like damned souls. Feed them enough to keep them alive, once every three days. They will soon be crying for water. Give them only sufficient to sustain their lives. They deserve far worse than this and they'll get their deserts when my mind has had time to work on the problem.'

A day later, the real agony began. Their bodies gave out the last of their sweat. Their tongues were swollen in their heads and all the time as they groaned in their torment they were aware that this terrible torture would be nothing to what they might expect. Elric's weakened body would not respond to his desperate struggling and at length his mind dulled, the agony became constant and familiar, and time was non-existent.

Finally, through a pain-thick daze, he recognised a voice. It was the hate-filled voice of Jagreen Lern.

Others were in the chamber. He felt their hands seize him and his body was suddenly light as he was borne, moaning, from the cell.

Though he heard disjointed phrases, he could make no sense of Jagreen Lern's words. He was taken to a dark place that rolled about, hurting his scorched chest.

Later, he heard Moonglum's voice and strained to hear the words.

'Elric! What's happening? We're aboard a ship at sea, I'd swear!'

But Elric mumbled without interest. His deficient body was weakening faster than would a normal man's. He thought of Zarozinia, whom he would never see again. He knew he would not live to know whether Law or Chaos finally won, or even if the Southlands would stand against the Theocrat.

And these problems were fading in his mind again.

Then the food started to come and the water and it revived him somewhat. At one stage, he opened his eyes and stared upwards into the thinly smiling face of Jagreen Lern.

'Thank the gods,' said the Theocrat. 'I feared we'd lost you. You're a delicate case to be sure, my friend. You must stay alive longer than this. To begin my entertainment, I have arranged for you to sail on my own flagship. We are now crossing the Dragon Sea, our fleet well-protected by charms against the monsters roaming these parts.' He frowned. 'Thanks to you, we haven't the same call for the charms which would have borne us safely through the Chaos-torn waters. The seas are almost normal for the moment. But that will soon be changed.'

Elric's old spirit returned for a moment and he glared at his enemy, too weak to voice the loathing he felt.

Jagreen Lern laughed softly and stirred Elric's gaunt white head with the toe of his boot. 'I think I can brew a drug which will give you a little more vitality.'

The food, when it came, was foul-tasting, and had to be forced between Elric's mumbling lips, but after a while he was able to sit up and observe the huddled body of Moonglum. Evidently, the little man had totally succumbed to his torture. To his surprise, Elric discovered he was unfettered and he crawled the agonising distance between himself and the Eastlander, shaking Moonglum's shoulder. He groaned, but did not otherwise respond.

A shaft of light suddenly struck through the darkness of the hold and Elric blinked, looking up to see that the hatch cover had been prised aside and Jagreen Lern's bearded face stared down at him.

'Good, good. I see the brew had its effect. Come, Elric, smell the invigorating sea and feel the warm sun on your body. We are not many miles from the coasts of Argimiliar and our scout ships report quite a sizeable fleet sailing hence.'

Elric cursed. 'By Arioch, I hope they send you all to the bottom!'

Jagreen Lern pursed his lips, mockingly. 'By whom? Arioch? Do you not remember what ensued in my own palace? Arioch cannot be invoked. Not by you – not by me. Your stinking spells saw to that.'

He turned to an unseen lieutenant. 'Bind him and bring him on deck. You know what to do with him.'

Two warriors dropped into the hold and grasped the still-weak Elric, tying his arms and legs and manhandling him onto the deck. He gasped as the sun's glare struck his eyes.

'Prop him up so he may see all,' Jagreen Lern ordered.

The warriors obeyed, and Elric was lifted to a standing position, seeing Jagreen Lern's huge, black flagship with its silken deck canopies flapping in a steady westerly breeze, its three banks of straining oarsmen and its tall ebony mast, bearing a sail of dark red.

Beyond the ship's rails, Elric saw a massive fleet surging in the flagship's wake. As well as the vessels of Pan Tang and Dharijor, there were many from Jharkor, Shazaar and Tarkesh, but on every scarlet sail the Merman blazon of Pan Tang was painted.

Despair filled Elric, for he knew that the Southlands, however strong, could not match a fleet like this.

'We have been at sea for only three days,' said Jagreen Lern, 'but thanks to a witch-wind, we're almost at our destination. A scout ship has recently reported that the Lormyrian navy, hearing rumours of our superior sea power, is sailing to join with us. A wise move of King Montan – for the moment, at any rate. I'll make use of him for the time being and, when his usefulness is over, I'll kill him for a treacherous turncoat.'

'Why do you tell me all this?' Elric whispered, his teeth gritted against the pain that came with any slight movement of his face or body.

'Because I want you to witness for yourself the defeat of the

South. The merchant princes sail against us – and we shall easily crush them. I want you to know that what you sought to avert will come to pass. After we have subdued the South and sucked her of her treasures, we'll vanquish the Isle of the Purple Towns and press forward to sack Vilmir and Ilmiora. That will be an easy matter, don't you agree? We have allies other than those you defeated.'

When Elric did not reply, Jagreen Lern gestured impatiently to his men.

'Tie him to the mast so that he may get a good view of the battle. I'll put a protective charm around his body, for I do not want him to be killed by a stray arrow and cheat me of my full vengeance.'

Elric was borne up and roped to the mast, but he was scarcely aware of it, for his head lolled on his right shoulder, only semi-conscious.

The massive fleet plunged onwards, certain of victory.

By mid-afternoon, Elric was aroused from his stupor by the shout of the helmsman.

'Sail to the south-east! Lormyrian fleet approaches!'

With impotent anger, Elric saw the fifty two-masted ships, their bright sails contrasting with the sombre scarlet of Jagreen Lern's vessels, come into line with the others.

Lormyr, though a smaller power than Argimiliar, had a larger navy. Elric judged that King Montan's treachery had cost the South more than a quarter of its strength.

Now he knew there was absolutely no hope for the South and that Jagreen Lern's certainty of victory was well-founded.

Night fell and the huge fleet lay at anchor. A guard came to feed Elric a mushy porridge containing another dose of the drug. As he revived, his anger increased, and Jagreen Lern paused by the mast on two occasions, taunting him savagely.

'Soon after dawn we shall meet the Southern fleet,' Jagreen Lern smiled, 'and by noon what is left of it will float as bloody driftwood behind us as we press on to establish our reign over those nations who so foolishly relied on their sea power as defence.'

Elric remembered how he had warned the kings of the Southlands that this was likely to happen if they stood alone against the Theocrat. But he wished that he had been wrong. With the defeat of the South, the conquest of the East seemed bound to follow and, when Jagreen Lern ruled the world, Chaos would dominate and the Earth revert to the stuff from which it had been formed millions of years before.

All through that moonless night, he brooded. He pulled his thoughts together, summoning all his strength for a plan that was, as yet, only a shadow in the back of his mind.

Chapter Six

T HE RATTLE OF anchors woke him.

Blinking in the light of the watery sun, he saw the Southern fleet on the horizon, riding gracefully in hollow pomp towards the ships of Jagreen Lern. Either, he thought, the Southern kings were very brave, or else they did not understand the strength of their enemies.

Beneath him, on Jagreen Lern's foredeck, a great catapult rested, and slaves had already filled its cup with a large ball of flaming pitch. Normally, Elric knew, such catapults were an encumbrance, since when they reached that size they were difficult to rewind and gave lighter war-engines the advantage. Yet obviously Jagreen Lern's engineers were not fools. Elric noted extra mechanisms on the big catapult and realised they were equipped to rewind rapidly.

The wind had dropped and five hundred pairs of muscles strove to row Jagreen Lern's galley along. On the deck, in disciplined order, his warriors took their posts beside the great boarding platforms that would drop down on the opponent's ships and grapple them at the same time as they formed a bridge between the vessels.

Elric was forced to admit that Jagreen Lern had used foresight. He had not relied wholly on supernatural aid. His ships were the best equipped he had ever seen. The Southern fleet, he decided, was doomed. To fight Jagreen Lern was insanity.

But the Theocrat had made one mistake. He had, in his gnawing desire for vengeance, ensured that Elric's vitality was restored for a few hours and this vitality extended to his mind as well as his body.

Stormbringer had vanished. With the sword he was, among men, all but invincible. Without it, he was helpless. These were

115

facts. Therefore he must somehow regain the blade. But how? It had returned to the plane of Chaos with its brothers, presumably drawn back there by the overwhelming power of the rest.

He must contact it.

He dare not summon the entire horde of blades with the spell, that would be tempting providence too far.

He heard the sudden *thwack* and roar as the giant catapult discharged its first shot. The flame-shrouded pitch went arching over the ocean and landed short, boiling the sea around it as it guttered and sank. Swiftly the war-engine was rewound, and Elric marvelled at the speed as another ball of flaring pitch was forked into its cup. Jagreen Lern looked up at him and laughed.

'My pleasure will be short. There are not enough of them to put up a long fight. Watch them perish, Elric!'

Elric said nothing, pretended to be dazed and frightened.

The next fireball struck one of the leading ships directly and Elric saw tiny figures scampering about, striving desperately to quench the spreading pitch, but within a minute the whole ship was ablaze, a gouting mass of flame as the figures now jumped overboard, unable to save their vessel.

The air around him sounded to the rushing heat of the fireballs and, within range now, the Southerners retaliated with their lighter machines until it seemed the sky was filled with a thousand comets and the heat almost equalled that which Elric had experienced in the torture chamber. Black smoke began to drift as the brass beaks of the ships' rams ground through timbers, impaling ships like skewered fish. The hoarse yells of fighting men began to be heard, and the clash of iron as the first few opposing warriors met.

But now he only vaguely heard the sounds, for he was thinking deeply.

Then, when at last his mind was ready, he called in a desperate and agonised voice that human ears could not hear above the noise of war: 'Stormbringer!'

His straining mind echoed the shout and he seemed to look beyond the turbulent battle, beyond the ocean, beyond the very

Earth to a place of shadows and terror. Something moved there. Many things moved there.

'*Stormbringer!*'

He heard a curse from beneath him and saw Jagreen Lern pointing up at him. 'Gag the white-faced sorcerer,' Jagreen Lern's eyes met Elric's and the Theocrat sucked in his lips, deliberating a bare moment before adding: 'And if that doesn't put an end to his babbling – best slay him!'

The lieutenant began to climb the mast towards Elric.

'Stormbringer! Your master perishes!'

He struggled in the biting ropes, but could hardly move.

'*Stormbringer!*'

All his life he had hated the sword he relied on so much; which he was relying on more and more, but now he called for it as a lover calls for his betrothed.

The warrior grasped his foot and shook it. 'Silence! You heard my master!'

With insane eyes, Elric looked down at the warrior who shuddered and drew his sword, hanging to the mast with one hand and readying himself to make a stab at Elric's vitals.

'*Stormbringer!*' Elric sobbed the name. He *must* live. Without him, Chaos would surely rule the world.

The man lunged at Elric's body – yet the blade did not reach the albino. Then Elric remembered, with sudden humour, that Jagreen Lern had placed a protective spell about him! The Theocrat's own magic had saved his enemy!

'*Stormbringer!*'

Now the warrior gasped and the sword dropped from his fingers. He seemed to grapple with something invisible at his throat and Elric saw the man's fingers sliced off and blood spurt from the stumps. Then, slowly, a shape materialised and, with bounding relief, the albino saw that it was a sword – his own runesword impaling the warrior and sucking out his soul!

The warrior dropped, but Stormbringer hung in the air and then turned to slash the ropes restraining Elric's hands and then nestled firmly, with horrid affection, in its master's right fist.

At once the stolen lifestuff of the warrior began to pour through Elric's being and the pain of his body vanished. Quickly he grasped a piece of the sail's rigging and cut away the rest of his bonds until he was swinging by one hand on the rope.

'Now, Jagreen Lern, we'll see who takes vengeance, finally,' he grimaced as he swung towards the deck and dropped lightly upon it, the unholy vitality from the sword surging through him to fill him with a godlike ecstasy. He had never known it so strong before.

But then he noted that the boarding platforms had been lowered and only a skeleton crew remained on the flagship. Jagreen Lern must have led his main strength onto the ship which was now held fast by grapples.

Close by was a great barrel of pitch, used to form the fireballs. Close to that was a flaring torch used to ignite them. Elric seized the brand and flung it into the pitch.

'Though Jagreen Lern may win this battle, his flagship shall go to the bottom with the Southern fleet,' he said grimly, and dashed for the hold where he had been imprisoned, aware that Moonglum lay helpless there.

He wrenched up the hatch cover and stared down at the pitiful figure of his friend. Evidently, he had been left to starve to death. A rat chittered away as the light shone down.

Elric jumped into the hold and saw, with horror, that part of Moonglum's right arm had been gnawed already. He heaved the body onto his shoulder, aware that the heart still beat, though faintly, and clambered back up to the deck. How to ensure his friend's safety and still take vengeance on Jagreen Lern was a problem. But Elric moved towards the boarding platform which he guessed the Theocrat to have crossed. As he did so, three warriors leapt towards him. One of them cried: 'The albino! The reaver escapes!'

Elric struck him down with a blow that required only a slight movement of his wrist. The Black Sword did the rest. The others retreated, remembering how Elric had entered Hwamgaarl.

New energy flowed through him. For every corpse he created,

his strength increased – a stolen strength, but necessary if he was to survive and win the day for Law.

He ran, untroubled by his burden, over the boarding platform and onto the deck of the Southern ship. Up ahead he saw the standard of Argimiliar and a little group of men around it, headed by King Hozel himself, his face gaunt as he stared at the knowledge of his own death. A deserved death thought Elric grimly, but nonetheless when Hozel died it would mean another victory for Chaos.

Then he heard a shout of a different quality, thought for a moment that he had been observed, but one of Hozel's men was pointing to the north and mouthing something.

Elric looked in that direction and saw the brave sails of the Purple Towns. They were fighting ships, better equipped for battle than those of the merchant princes. Their brightly painted sails caught the light. The only rich decoration the austere sea-lords allowed themselves was upon their sails. Elric's ally Kargan must command them.

But they had arrived belatedly. Even if they had sailed with the other Southern vessels it would have been unlikely that they could have turned the day against Pan Tang.

At that moment, staring around him, Jagreen Lern saw Elric and bellowed at his men who moved forward warily and reluctantly, approaching the albino in a wide semicircle.

Elric cursed the brave sea-lords who had added a further factor to his indecision.

Menacingly he swung the moaning runeblade about him as he advanced to meet the half-terrified Pan Tang warriors. They dropped back, some of them groaning as the blade touched them. The way was now clear to Jagreen Lern.

But the ships of the Purple Towns were drawing closer, almost within catapult range.

Elric looked directly into Jagreen Lern's frightened face and snarled: 'I doubt if my blade has the strength to pierce your burning armour with one blow, and one blow is all I have time for. I leave you now, Theocrat, but remember that even if you conquer all the world including the unmapped lands of the East, I'll have my sword drink your black soul at length.'

With that he dropped Moonglum's unconscious body overboard and dived after it into the choppy sea.

The blade gave him superhuman strength and he swam towards the leading ship of the sea-lords, which he recognised as Kargan's, dragging Moonglum's body after him.

Now, behind him, Jagreen Lern and his men saw their own flagship blazing. Elric had done his work well.

That, too, would serve to divert attention from Kargan's fleet.

Trusting to the sea-lords' famed seamanship, he swam directly in the path of the leading galleon, shouting Kargan's name.

The ship veered slightly and he saw bearded faces at the rail, saw ropes flicker towards him and grasped one, letting them haul him upwards with his burden.

As the seamen pulled them both over the rail, Elric saw Kargan staring at him with shocked eyes. The sea-lord was dressed in the tough brown leather armour of his folk. He had an iron cap on his massive head and his black beard bristled. 'Elric! We thought you dead – lost on your voyage south!'

Elric spat salt water from his mouth and said urgently: 'Turn your fleet, Kargan! Turn it back the way it has come, there is no hope of saving the Southlanders – they are doomed. We must preserve our forces for a later struggle.'

Hesitating momentarily, Kargan gave the order which was swiftly relayed to the rest of his sixty-strong fleet.

As the ships turned away, Elric noted that hardly a Southern ship remained afloat. For more than a mile the water burned and the sputtering of the flaming, sinking ships was blended with the screams of the maimed and drowning.

'With the Southern sea power crushed so decisively,' Kargan said, watching the physician who was tending to Moonglum, 'the lands will not last long before Pan Tang's marching hordes. Like us, the South relied too much on its ships. It has taught me that we must strengthen our land defences if we are to have any chance at all.'

'From now on we'll use your island as our main headquarters,' Elric said. 'We'll fortify the whole place and from there keep in close touch with what is happening in the South. How is my friend, physician?'

The physician looked up. 'These are no battle-made wounds. He's been hurt sorely, but he'll live. He should recover to perfect fitness given a month or so of rest.'

'He'll have it,' Elric promised. He gripped the runesword at his belt and wondered what other tasks lay in store for them before the last great battle between Law and Chaos was joined.

Chaos would soon rule more than half the world, in spite of the powerful blow he had dealt it in forever sentencing the Dukes of Hell to their own plane; the more power that Jagreen Lern gathered, the more the threat from Chaos would increase.

He sighed and looked northwards.

Two days later they returned to the Isle of the Purple Towns, the fleet remaining in the largest harbour of Utkel since it was thought wise to have it at hand and not disperse it.

All that following night, Elric talked with the sea-lords, ordered messengers to Vilmir and Ilmiora and, towards morning, there came a polite knock on the door of the room.

Kargan got up to open it and stared in astonishment at the tall, black-faced man who stood there.

'Sepiriz!' Elric cried. 'How did you come here?'

'On horseback,' smiled the giant, 'and you know the power of the Nihrain steeds. I had come to warn you. We have, at last, managed to contact the White Lords but they can do little as yet. Somehow a path to their plane must be made through the barricades which Chaos has constructed against them. Jagreen Lern's ships have vomited their contents on the Southern shores and his warriors swarm inland. There is nothing we can do now to stop his conquests there. Once consolidated, his earthly power increased, he will be able to summon more and more allies from Chaos.'

'Then where does my next task lie?' Elric asked softly.

'I am not sure yet. But that is not what I came for. Your blade's sojourn with its brothers has strengthened it. You notice how swiftly it pours power into your body now?'

'True. Yet I seem ever more reliant upon that power.' He spoke flatly. 'The power is stronger, but I am weaker, it seems.'

Sepiriz said gravely: 'That power is evilly gained and evil in itself. The blade's strength will continue to increase but as Chaos-begotten power fills your being, you will have to fight yet more strongly to control the force within you. That also will take strength. So, you see, you must use part of the strength to fight the strength itself.'

Elric sighed and grasped Sepiriz's arm.

'Thanks for the warning, friend, but when I beat the Dukes of Hell, to whom I formerly pledged allegiance, I did not expect to escape with a mere scratch or a flesh wound. Know this, Sepiriz,' he turned to the watching sea-lords, 'and know this all of you.'

He drew the groaning runeblade from its scabbard and held it aloft so that it shone and flared in its awful power.

'This blade was forged by Chaos to conquer Chaos and that is my destiny, too. Though the world crumbles and turns to boiling gas, I shall live now. I swear by the Cosmic Balance that Law shall triumph and the New Age come to this Earth.'

Taken aback by this grim vow, the sea-lords glanced at one another and Sepiriz smiled.

'Let us hope so, Elric,' he said. 'Let us hope so.'

Book Three

Sad Giant's Shield

Thirteen times thirteen, the steps to the sad giant's lair;
And the Chaos Shield lies there.
Seven times seven are the elder trees
Twelve times twelve warriors he sees
But the Chaos Shield lies there.
And the hero fair will the sad giant dare
And a red sword wield for the sad giant's shield
On a mournful victory day.

— The Chronicle of the Black Sword

Chapter One

A CROSS THE WHOLE world the shadow of anarchy had fallen. Neither god, nor man, nor that which ruled both could clearly read the future and see the fate of Earth as the forces of Chaos increased their strength both personally and through their human minions.

From Westland mountain, over the agitated ocean to Southland plain, Chaos now held its monstrous sway. Tormented, miserable, unable to hope any longer for liberation from the corroding, warping influence of Chaos, the remnants of races fled over the two continents already fallen to the human minions of Disorder, led by their warped Theocrat Jagreen Lern of Pan Tang, aquiline, high-shouldered and greedy for power, in his glowing scarlet armour, controlling human vultures and supernatural creatures alike as he widened his black boundaries.

Upon the face of the Earth all was disruption and roaring anguish, save for the thinly populated, already threatened Eastern Continent and the Isle of the Purple Towns, which now readied itself to withstand Jagreen Lern's initial onslaught. The onrushing tide of Chaos must soon sweep the world unless some great force could be summoned to halt it.

Bleakly, bitterly, the few who still resisted Jagreen Lern, under the command of Elric of Melniboné, talked of strategy and tactics in the full knowledge that more than these were needed to beat back Jagreen Lern's unholy horde.

Desperately, Elric attempted to utilise the ancient sorcery of his emperor forefathers to contact the White Lords of Law; but he was unused to seeking such aid and, as well, the forces of Chaos were now so strong that those of Law could no longer gain easy access to the Earth as they had contrived to do in earlier times.

As they prepared for the coming fight, Elric and his allies went about the preparation with heavy souls and a sense of the futility of such action. And in the back of Elric's mind was the constant knowledge that even if he won against Chaos, the very act of winning would destroy the world he knew and leave it ripe for the forces of Law to rule – and there would be no place in such a world for the wild albino sorcerer.

Beyond the earthly plane, in their bordering realms, the Lords of the Higher Worlds watched the struggle, and even they did not realise Elric's entire destiny.

Chaos triumphed. Chaos blocked the efforts of Law on each occasion they tried to pass through the domain of Chaos, now the only road to Earth. And the Lords of Law shared Elric's frustration.

And, if Chaos and Law were observing the Earth and her struggle, who watched these? For Chaos and Law were but the twin weights in a balance and the hand that held the Balance, though it rarely deigned to interfere in their struggle, still less in the affairs of men, had reached the rare state of a decision to alter the status quo. Which weight would drop? Which rise? Could men decide? Could the lords decide? Or could only the Cosmic Hand remould the pattern of the Earth, reforming her stuff, changing her spiritual constituents and placing her on a different path, a fresh course of destiny?

Perhaps all would play some part before the outcome was decided.

The great zodiac influencing the universe and its Ages had completed its twelve cycles and the cycles would soon begin again. The wheel would spin and, when it stopped its spinning, which symbol would dominate, how changed would it be?

Great movements on the Earth and beyond it; great destinies being shaped, great deeds being planned and, marvellously, could it just be possible that in spite of the Lords of the Higher Worlds, in spite of the Cosmic Hand, in spite of the myriad supernatural denizens that swarmed the multiverse, that Man might decide the issue?

Even one man?

One man, one sword, one destiny?

*

Elric of Melniboné sat hunched in his saddle, watching the warriors bustle to and fro around him in the city square of Bakshaan. Here, years before, he had conducted a siege against the city's leading merchant, tricked others and left rich, but such scores that they held against him were now forgotten, pushed from their minds by the threat of war and the knowledge that if Elric's command could not save them, nothing could. The walls of the city were being widened and heightened, warriors being trained in the use of unfamiliar war-engines. From being a lazy merchant city, Bakshaan had become a functional place, ready for battle when it came.

For a month, Elric had been riding the length and breadth of the Eastern kingdoms of Ilmiora and Vilmir, overseeing preparations, building the strength of the two nations into an efficient war machine.

Now he studied parchments handed him by his lieutenants and, recalling all the old tactical skill of his ancestors, gave them his decisions.

The sun was setting and heavy black clouds hung against a sharp, metallic blue sky, stretching over the horizon. Elric loosened his cloak strings and allowed the folds of the garment to enclose him, for a chill had come.

Then, as he silently regarded the sky to the west, he frowned as he noticed something like a flashing golden star appear, moving swiftly towards him.

Ever wary for signs of the coming of Chaos, he turned in his saddle shouting:

'Every man to his position! 'Ware the golden globe!'

The thing approached rapidly until soon it was hanging over the city, all men looking up at it in astonishment, their hands on their weapons. As black night fell, the clouds admitting no moonlight, the globe began to fall towards the spires of Bakshaan, a strange luminescence pulsing from it. Elric tugged Stormbringer from its scabbard and black fire flickered along the blade as it gave out a low moaning sound. The globe touched the cobbles of the city square – broke into a million fragments that glowed for a moment before vanishing.

Elric laughed in relief, resheathing Stormbringer as he saw who now stood in the place of the golden globe.

'Sepiriz, my friend. You choose strange means of transport to carry you from the Chasm of Nihrain.'

The tall, black-faced seer smiled, his white pointed teeth gleaming. 'I have so few carriages of that type that I must only use them when pressed. I come with news for you – much news.'

'I hope it is good, for we have enough bad to last us for ever.'

'It is mixed. Where can we converse in private?'

'My headquarters are in yonder mansion,' Elric pointed at a richly decorated house on the far side of the square.

Inside, Elric poured yellow wine for his guest. Kelos the merchant, whose house this was, had not accepted the requisitioning altogether willingly and, partly because of this, Elric maliciously made free with all Kelos's best.

Sepiriz took the goblet and sipped the strong wine.

'Have you succeeded in contacting the White Lords again, Sepiriz?' Elric asked.

'We have.'

'Thank the gods. Are they willing to give their aid to us?'

'They have always been so willing – but they have not yet made a sufficient breach in the defences that Chaos has set up around this planet. However, the fact that I have at last managed to contact them is a better sign than we've had these past months.'

'So – the news *is* good,' Elric said cheerfully.

'Not altogether. Jagreen Lern's fleet has set sail again – and they head towards the Eastern Continent, with thousands of ships – and supernatural allies, too.'

'It was only what I expected, Sepiriz. My work's done here, anyway. I'll ride for the Isle of the Purple Towns at once, for I must lead the fleet against Jagreen Lern.'

'Your chances of winning will be all but non-existent, Elric,' Sepiriz warned him gravely. 'Have you heard of the Ships of Hell?'

'I've heard of them – do they not sail the depths of the sea, taking on board dead mariners as crews?'

'They do – they're things of Chaos and far larger than even the largest mortal warship. You'd never withstand them, even if you did not have the Theocrat's fleet to fight as well.'

'I'm aware the fight will be hard, Sepiriz – but what else can we do? I have a weapon against Chaos in my blade here – or so you tell me.'

'Not enough, that bodkin – you still have no *protection* against the Dark Lords. That is what I have to tell you of – a personal armament for yourself to help you in your struggle, though you'll have to win it from its present possessor.'

'Who owns it?'

'A giant who broods in eternal misery in a great castle on the edge of the world, beyond the Sighing Desert. Mordaga is his name and he was once a god, but is now made mortal for sins he committed against his fellow gods long ages ago.'

'Mortal? Yet he has lived so long?'

'Aye. Mordaga is mortal – though his life-span's considerably greater than an ordinary man's. He is obsessed with the knowledge that he must one day die. That is what saddens him.'

'And the weapon?'

'Not a weapon exactly – a shield. A shield with a purpose – one that Mordaga had made for himself when he raised a rebellion in the domain of the gods and sought to make himself greatest of them, and even wrest the Eternal Balance from He who holds it. For this he was banished to Earth and informed that he would one day die – slain by a mortal's blade. The shield, as you might guess, is proof against the workings of Chaos.'

'How so?'

'The chaotic forces, if powerful enough, can disrupt any defence made of lawful matter; no construction based on the principles of order can withstand for long the ravages of sheer chaos, as we know.' Sepiriz leaned forward a little. 'Stormbringer has shown you that the only weapon effective against Chaos is something of Chaos-manufacture. The same can be said for the Chaos Shield. This itself is chaotic in nature and therefore there is nothing organised in it on which the random forces can act and destroy. It meets Chaos with Chaos, and so the hostile powers are subverted.'

'If I had only had such a shield of late – things might have gone better for us all!'

'I could not tell you of it. I am merely the servant of Fate and cannot act unless it is sanctioned by that which I serve. Perhaps, as I have guessed, it is willing to see Chaos sweep the world before it is defeated – if indeed it *is* defeated – so that it can completely change the nature of our planet before the new cycle begins. Change it will – but whether it will be ruled in the future primarily by Law or Chaos, that is in your hands, Elric!'

'How would I recognise this shield?'

'By the eight-arrowed Sign of Chaos which radiates from its boss. It is a heavy, round shield, made as a buckler for a giant. But, with the vitality you receive from your runesword, you will have the strength to carry it, have no fear. But first you must have the courage to win it from its current holder. Mordaga is aware of the prophecy, told him by his fellow gods before they cast him forth.'

'Are you, too, aware of it?'

'I am. In our language it forms a simple rhyme:

> 'Mordaga's pride; Mordaga's doom,
> Mordaga's fate shall be
> To die as men when slain by men,
> Four men of destiny.'

'Four men? Who are the other three?'

'Those you will know of when the time comes for you to seek the Chaos Shield. Which will you do? Go to the Purple Towns – or will you go to find the shield?'

'I wish that I had the time to embark on a quest of that kind, but I have not. I must go to rally my men, shield or no.'

'You will be defeated.'

'We shall see, Sepiriz.'

'Very well, Elric. Since so little of your destiny is in your own hands, we should allow you to take just one decision at times,' Sepiriz said sympathetically.

'Fate is kind,' Elric commented ironically. He rose from his seat. 'I'll begin the journey straightway, for there's no time to lose.'

Chapter Two

WITH HIS MILK-WHITE hair streaming behind him and his red eyes blazing with purpose, Elric lashed his stallion through the cold darkness of the night, through a disturbed land which awaited Jagreen Lern's attack in trepidation, for it could mean not only their deaths, but the drawing of their souls into the servitude of Chaos.

Already the standards of a dozen Western and Southern monarchs fluttered with Jagreen Lern's as the kings of the conquered lands chose his command rather than death – and placed their peoples under his dominance so that they became marching, blank-faced creatures with enslaved souls, their wives and children dead, tormented or feeding the blood-washed altars of Pan Tang where the priests send up invocations to the Chaos Lords, and, ever-willing to further their power on Earth, the lords answered with support.

And not only the entities themselves, but the stuff of their own weird cosmos was entering the Earth, so that where their power was the land heaved like the sea, or the sea flowed like lava, mountains changed shape and trees sprouted ghastly blossoms never seen on Earth before – all nature was unstable and it could not be long until Earth was wholly one with the Realm of Chaos.

Wherever Jagreen Lern conquered, the warping influence of Chaos was manifest. The very spirits of nature were tortured into becoming what they should not be – air, fire, water and earth, all became unstable, for Jagreen Lern and his allies were tampering not only with the lives and souls of men, but the very constituents of the planet itself. And there was none of sufficient power to punish them for these crimes. None.

★

With this knowledge within him, Elric's progress was swift and wild, as he strove to reach the Isle of the Purple Towns before his pitifully inadequate fleet sailed to do battle with Chaos.

Two days later he arrived in the port of Uhaio, at the tip of the smallest of the three Vilmirian peninsulas, and took ship at once to the Isle of the Purple Towns, where he disembarked and rode into the interior towards the ancient fortress *Ma-ha-kil-agra*, which had withstood every siege ever made against it, and was regarded as the most impregnable construction in the whole of the lands still free from Chaos. Its name was in an older language than any known to those who lived in the current Age of the Young Kingdoms. Only Elric knew what the name signified. The fortress had been there long before the present races came to dominance, even before Elric's ancestors had begun their conquerings. *Ma-ha-kil-agra* – the Fortress of Evening, where long ago, a lonely race had come to die.

As he arrived in the courtyard, Moonglum, the Eastlander, came rushing from the entrance of a tower.

'Elric! We have been awaiting your arrival, for time grows scarce before we must embark against the enemy. We have sent out ship-borne spies to estimate the size and power of Jagreen Lern's fleet. Only four returned and all were uselessly insane. The fifth has just come back, but –'

'But what?'

'See for yourself. He has been – altered, Elric.'

'Altered! Altered! Let me see him. Take me to him.' Elric nodded curtly to the other captains who had come out to greet him. He passed them and followed behind Moonglum through the stone corridors of the fortress, lit badly by sputtering rushes.

Leading Elric to an antechamber, Moonglum stopped outside, running his fingers through his thick, red hair. 'He is therein. Would you care to interview him alone? I'd rather not set eyes on him again!'

'Very well,' Elric opened the door, wondering how this spy would be changed. Sitting at the plain wooden table was the

remains of a man. It looked up. As Moonglum had warned him –
it had been altered.

Elric felt pity for the man, but he was not nauseated or horrified
like Moonglum, for in his sorcery-working he had seen far worse
creatures. It was as if the whole of one side of the spy's body had
become at one stage viscous, had flowed, and then coiled in a random shape. Side of head, shoulder, arm, torso, leg, all were
replaced by streamers of flesh like rat's tails, lumps of matter like
swollen boils, weirdly mottled. The spy spread his good hand and
some of the streamers seemed to jerk and wave in unison.

Elric spoke quietly. 'What magic wrought this drastic change?'

A kind of chuckle came from the lopsided face.

'I entered the Realm of Chaos, lord. And Chaos did this, it
changed me as you see. The boundaries are being extended. I did
not know it. I was inside before I realised what had happened. *The
area of Chaos is being widened!*' He leaned forward, his shaking voice
almost screaming. 'With it sail the massed fleets of Jagreen Lern –
great waves of warships, squadrons of invasion craft, thousands of
transports, ships mounting great war-engines, fire-ships – ships of
all kinds, bearing a multitude of standards – the kings of the South
left alive have sworn loyalty to Jagreen Lern and he has used all
their resources and his own to marshal this sea-horde! As he sails,
he extends the area of Chaos, so whereas his sailing is slower than
normal, when he reaches us here – Chaos will be with him. I saw
such ships that could be of no earthly contriving – the size of
castles – each one seeming to be a dazzling combination of all
colours!'

'So he *has* managed to bring more supernatural allies to his
standard,' Elric mused. 'Those are the Ships of Hell, Sepiriz
mentioned...'

'Aye – and even if we beat the natural craft,' the messenger
said, hysterically, 'we could not beat both the ships of Chaos and
the stuff of Chaos which boils around them and did to me what
you observe! It boils, it warps, it changes constantly. That is all I
know, save that Jagreen Lern and his human allies are unharmed

by it as I was harmed. When this change began to take place in my body, I fled to the Dragon Isle of Melniboné, which seems to have withstood the process and is the only safe land in all the waters of the world. My body – healed – swiftly, and I chanced another sailing to bring me here.'

'You were courageous,' Elric said hollowly. 'You will be well rewarded, I promise.'

'I want only one reward, my lord.'

'What is that?'

'Death. I can no longer live with the horror of my body mirroring the horror in my brains!'

'I will see to it,' Elric promised. He remained brooding for a few seconds before nodding farewell to the spy and leaving the room.

Moonglum met him outside.

'It looks black for us, Elric,' he said softly.

Elric sighed. 'Aye – perhaps I should have gone to seek the Chaos Shield *first*.'

'What's that?'

Elric explained all Sepiriz had told him.

'We could do with such a defence,' Moonglum agreed. 'But there it is – the priority is tomorrow's sailing. Your captains await you in the conference chamber.'

'I will see them in a short while,' Elric promised. 'First I wish to go to my own room to collect my thoughts. Tell them I'll join them when that's done.'

When he reached his room, Elric locked the door behind him, still thinking of the spy's information. He knew that without supernatural aid no ordinary fleet, no matter how large or how courageously manned, could possibly withstand Jagreen Lern. And the fact was that he had only a comparatively small fleet, no supernatural entities for allies, no means of combatting the disrupting chaotic forces. If only he had the Chaos Shield beside him now... But it was useless to regret a decision of the kind he'd made. If he sought the shield now, he couldn't fight the battle in any case.

For weeks he had consulted the grimoires that, in the form of scrolls, tablets, books and sheets of precious metals engraved with ancient symbols, littered his room. The elementals had helped him in the past, but so disrupted were they by Chaos that they were weak for the most part.

He unstrapped his hellsword and flung it on the bed of tumbled silks and furs. Wryly he thought back to earlier times when he had given in to despair and how those incidents which had engendered the mood seemed merely gay escapades in comparison to the task which now weighed on his mind. Though weary, he chose not to draw Stormbringer's stolen energy into himself, for the feeling that was so close to ecstasy was leavened by the guilt – the guilt which had possessed him since a child when he had first realised that the expression on his remote father's face had not been one of love, but of disappointment that he should have spawned a deficient weakling – a pale albino, good for nothing without the aid of drugs or sorcery.

Elric sighed and went to the window to stare out over the low hills and beyond them to the sea. He spoke aloud, perhaps subconsciously, hoping that the release of the words would relieve some of the tension within him.

'I do not care for this responsibility,' he said. 'When I fought the Dead God he spoke of both gods and men as shadow-things, playing puppet parts before the true history of Earth began and men found their fate in their own hands. Then Sepiriz tells me I must turn against Chaos and help destroy the whole nature of the world I know or history might never begin again, and Fate's great purpose would be thwarted. Therefore I am the one who must be split and tempered to fulfil my destiny – I must know no peace of mind, must fight men and gods and the stuff of Chaos without surcease, must bring about the death of this age so that, in some far dawn-age, men who know little of sorcery or the Lords of the Higher Worlds may move about a world where the major forces of Chaos can no longer enter, where justice may actually exist as a reality, and not as a mere concept in the minds of all philosophers.'

He rubbed his red eyes with his fingers.

'So fate makes Elric a martyr that Law might rule the world. It gives him a sword of ugly evil that destroys friends and enemies alike and sucks their soul-stuff out to feed him the strength he needs. It binds me to evil and to Chaos, in order that I may *destroy* evil and Chaos – but it does not make me some senseless dolt easily convinced and a willing sacrifice. No, it makes me Elric of Melniboné and floods me with a mighty misery...'

'My lord speaks aloud to himself – and his thoughts are gloomy. Speak them to me, instead, so that I might help you bear them, Elric.'

Recognising the soft voice, but astonished nonetheless, Elric turned quickly towards the source and saw his wife Zarozinia standing there, her arms outstretched and a look of deep sympathy on her young face.

He took a step towards her before stopping and saying angrily: 'When did you come here? Why? I told you to remain in your father's palace at Karlaak until this business is done, if ever!'

'If ever...' she repeated, dropping her arms to her sides with a little shrug. Though scarcely more than a girl, with her full red lips and long black hair, she bore herself as a princess must and seemed more than her age.

'Ask not *that* question,' he said cynically. 'It is not one we ask ourselves here. But answer mine. How did you come here and why?' He knew what her reply would be, but he spoke only to emphasise his anger which in turn was a result of his horror that she should have come so close to danger – danger which he had already rescued her from once.

'I came with my cousin Opluk's two thousand,' she said, lifting her head defiantly, 'when he joined the defenders of Uhaio. I came to be near my husband at a time when he may need my comforting. The gods know I've had little opportunity to discover if he does!'

Elric paced the room in agitation. 'As I love you, Zarozinia, believe that I would be in Karlaak now with you had I any excuse at all. But I have not – you know my rôle, my destiny, my doom.

137

You bring sorrow with your presence, not help. If this business has a satisfactory end, then we'll meet again in joy – not in misery as we now must!'

He crossed to her and took her in his arms. 'Oh, Zarozinia, we should never have met, never have married. We can only hurt one another at this time. Our happiness was so brief...'

'If you would be hurt by me, then hurt you shall be,' she said softly, 'but if you would be comforted, then I am here to comfort my lord.'

He relented with a sigh. 'These are loving words, my dear – but they are not spoken in loving times. I have put love aside for the nonce. Try to do likewise and thus we'll both dispense with added complication.'

Without anger, she drew slowly away from him and with a slight smile that had something of irony in it, pointed to the bed, where Stormbringer lay.

'I see your other mistress still shares your bed,' she said. 'And now you need never try to dismiss her again, for that black lord of Nihrain has given you an excuse to forever keep her by your side. Destiny – is that the word? Destiny! Ah, the deeds men have done in destiny's name. And what is destiny, Elric, can you answer?'

He shook his head. 'Since you ask the question in malice, I'll not make the attempt to answer it.'

She cried suddenly: 'Oh, Elric! I have travelled for many days to see you, thinking you would welcome me. And now we speak in anger!'

'*Fear!*' he said urgently. 'It is fear, not anger. I fear for you as I fear for the fate of the world! See me to my ship in the morning and then make speed back to Karlaak, I beg you.'

'If you wish it.'

She walked back into the small chamber which joined the main one.

Chapter Three

'WE TALK ONLY of defeat!' roared Kargan of the Purple Towns, beating upon the table with his fist. His beard seemed to bristle with rage.

Dawn had found all but a few of the captains retiring through weariness. Kargan, Moonglum, Elric's cousin Dyvim Slorm and moon-faced Dralab of Tarkesh, remained in the chamber, pondering tactics.

Elric answered him calmly: 'We talk of defeat, Kargan, because we must be prepared for that eventuality. It seems likely, does it not? We must, if defeat seems imminent, flee our enemies, conserving our force for another attack on Jagreen Lern. We shall not have the forces to fight another major battle, so we must use our better knowledge of currents, winds and terrain to fight him from ambush on sea or land. Thus we can perhaps demoralise his warriors and take considerably more of them than they can of us.'

'Aye – I see the logic,' Kargan rumbled unwillingly, evidently disturbed by this talk for, if the major battle was lost, then lost also would be the Isle of the Purple Towns, bastion against Chaos for the mainland nations of Vilmir and Ilmiora.

Moonglum shifted his position, grunting slightly. 'And if they drive us back, then back we must go, bending rather than breaking, and returning from other directions to attack and confuse them. It's in my mind that we'll have to move more rapidly than we'll be able to, since we'd be tired and with few provisions...' He grinned faintly. 'Ah, forgive me for my pessimism. Ill-placed, I fear.'

'No,' Elric said. 'We must face all this or be caught unawares. You are right. And to allow for ordered retreat, I have already sent detachments to the Sighing Desert and the Weeping Waste to bury large quantities of food and such things as extra arrows, lances and so forth. If we are forced back as far as the barrens, we'll likely fare better than Jagreen Lern, assuming that it takes him time to extend the area of Chaos and that his allies from the Higher Worlds are not overwhelmingly powerful.'

'You spoke of realism...' said Dyvim Slorm, pursing his curving lips and raising a slanting eyebrow.

'Aye – but some things cannot be faced or considered – for if we are totally engulfed by Chaos at the outset, then we'll have no need of plans. So we plan for the other eventuality, you see.'

Kargan let out his breath and rose from the table. 'There's no more to discuss,' he said. 'I'll to bed. We must be ready to sail with the noon tide tomorrow.'

They all gave signs of assent and chairs scraped as they pushed them back and left the chamber.

Bereft of human occupants, the chamber was silent save for the sputtering of the lamps and the rustle of the maps and papers as they were stirred by a warm wind.

It was late in the morning when Elric arose and found Zarozinia already up and dressed in a skirt and bodice of cloth-of-gold with a long, black-trimmed cloak of silver spreading to the floor.

He washed, shaved and ate the dish of herb-flavoured fruit she handed him.

'Why have you arrayed yourself in such finery?' he asked.

'To bid you goodbye from the harbour,' she said.

'If you spoke truth last night, then you'd best be dressed in funeral red,' he smiled and then, relenting, clasped her to him. He gripped her tightly, desperately, before standing back from her and taking her chin in his hand raised her face to stare down into it. 'In these tragic times,' he said, 'there's little room for love-play and kind words. Love must be deep and strong, manifesting itself in our actions. Seek no courtly words from me, Zarozinia, but remember earlier nights when the only turbulence was our pulse-beats blending.'

He was clad, himself, in Melnibonéan war regalia; with a breastplate of shiny black metal, a high-collared jerkin of black velvet, black leather breeks covered to the knee by his boots, also of black leather. Over his back was pushed a cloak of deep red, and on one thin, white finger was the Ring of Kings, the single rare Actorios stone, set in silver. His long white hair hung loose down to his shoulders, held by a bronze circlet. Stormbringer was at his hip and upon the table among the open books was a tapering black helm, engraved with old runes, its crown gradually rising into a spoke standing almost two feet from the base. At this base, dominating the eye slits was a replica of a spread-winged dragon with gaping snout, a reminder that, as emperors of the Bright Empire, his ancestors had been Dragon Masters and that perhaps the dragons of Melniboné still slept in their underground caverns. Now he picked up this helm and fitted it over his head so that it covered the top half of his face, only his red eyes gleaming from its shadows. He refrained from pulling the side wings about his lower face but for the meantime, left them sweeping back from the bottom of the helmet.

Noting her silence, he said, with a heart already heavy, 'Come, my love, let's to the harbour to astound these under-civilised allies of ours with our elegance. Have no fear that I shall not live to survive this day's battle – for Fate has not finished with me yet and protects me as a mother would her son – so that I might witness further misery until such a day when it's over for all time.'

Together, they left the Fortress of Evening, riding on magical Nihrain horses, down to the harbour where the other sea-lords and captains were already assembled beneath the bright sun.

All were dressed in their finest martial glory, though none could match Elric. Old racial memories were awakened in many when they saw him and they were troubled, fearing him without knowing why, for their ancestors had had great cause to fear the Bright Emperors in the days when Melniboné ruled the world and a man accoutred as Elric commanded a million eldritch warriors. Now a bare handful of Imrryrians greeted him as he rode along the quayside, noting the ships riding at anchor with their coloured banners and heraldic devices lifting proudly in the breeze.

Dyvim Slorm was equipped in a close-fitting dragon helm, its protecting pieces fashioned to represent the entire head of a dragon, scaled in red and green and silver. His armour was lacquered yellow, though the rest of his dress was black, like Elric's. At his side was Stormbringer's sister sword Mournblade.

As Elric rode up to the group, Dyvim Slorm turned his heavily armoured head towards the open sea. There was little inkling of encroaching Chaos on the calm water or in the clear sky.

'At least we'll have good weather on our way to meet Jagreen Lern,' Dyvim Slorm said.

'A small mercy,' Elric smiled faintly. 'Is there any more news of their numbers?'

'Before the spy who returned yesterday died he said there were at least four thousand warships, ten thousand transports – and perhaps twenty of the Chaos ships. They'll be the ones to watch since we've no idea what powers they have.'

Elric nodded. Their own fleet comprised some five thousand warships, many equipped with catapults and other heavy war-engines. The transports, though they turned the odds, in numbers, to a far superior figure, would be slow, unwieldy, and of not much use in a pitched sea-battle. Also, if the battle were won, they could be dealt with later, for they would obviously follow in the rear of Jagreen Lern's war-fleet.

So, for all Jagreen Lern's numerical strength, there would be a good chance of winning a sea-fight under ordinary conditions. The disturbing factor was the presence of the supernatural ships. The spy's description had been vague. Elric needed more object-ive information – information he would be unlikely to receive now, until the fleets joined in battle.

In his shirt was tucked the beast-hide manuscript of an extraor-dinarily strong invocation used in summoning Straasha the Sea-King. He had already attempted to use it, without success, but hoped that on open sea his chances would be better, particularly since the sea-king would be angered at the disruption Jagreen Lern and his occult allies were causing in the balance of nature. Once before, long ago, the sea-king had aided him and had, Elric recalled, predicted that Elric would summon him again.

Kargan, in the thick but light sea-armour of his people which gave him the appearance of a hairy-faced armadillo, pointed as several small boats detached themselves from the fleet and sailed towards the quay.

'Here come the boats to take us to our ships, my lords!'

The gathered captains stirred, all of them with serious expressions, seeming, each and every one, to be pondering some personal problem, staring into the depths of their own hearts – perhaps trying to reach the fear which lay there; trying to reach it and tear it out and fling it from them. They all had more than the usual trepidation experienced when facing a fight – for, like Elric, they could not guess what the Chaos ships were capable of.

They were a desperate company, understanding that something less palatable than death might await them beyond the horizon.

Elric squeezed Zarozinia's arm.

'Goodbye.'

'Farewell, Elric – may whatever benevolent gods there are left on the Earth protect you.'

'Save your prayers for my companions,' he said quietly, 'for they will be less able than I to face what lies out there.'

Moonglum called to him and Zarozinia: 'Give her a kiss, Elric, and come to the boat. Tell her we'll be back with victory tidings!'

Elric would never have admitted such familiarity, not even with his kinsman Dyvim Slorm, from anyone but Moonglum. But he took it in good part saying softly to her: 'There, you see, little Moonglum is confident – and he's usually the one with warnings of ominous portent!'

She said nothing, but kissed him lightly on the mouth, grasped his hand for a moment and then watched him as he strode down the quay and clambered into the boat which Moonglum and Kargan were steadying for him.

The oars splashed and bore the captains towards the flagship, *Timber-tearer*, Elric standing in the bow staring ahead, looking back only once when the boat drew alongside the ship and he began to climb the rope ladder up to the deck, his black helm bobbing.

Bracing himself on the deck, Elric watched the backs of the warrior-rowers as they bent to the oars, supplementing the light wind which filled the great purple sail, making it curve out in a graceful billow.

The Isle of the Purple Towns was now out of sight and green, glinting water was all that was visible around the fleet, which stretched behind the flagship, its furthest ships tiny shapes in the distance. Already the fleet was moving into battle order, forming into five squadrons, each under the command of an experienced sea-lord from the Purple Towns, for most of the other captains were landsmen who, though quick to learn, had little experience of sea tactics.

Moonglum came stumbling along the swaying deck to stand beside his friend.

'How did you sleep last night?' he asked Elric.

'Well enough, save for a few nightmares.'

'Ah, then you shared something with us all. Sleep was hard won for everyone, and when it came it was troubled. Visions of pits of monsters and demons, of horrifying shapes, of unearthly powers, they crowded our dreams.'

Elric nodded, paying little attention to Moonglum. The elements of Chaos in their own beings were evidently awakening in response to the approach of the Chaos horde itself. He hoped they would be strong enough to withstand the actuality as they had survived their dreams.

'*Disturbance to forward!*'

It was the lookout's cry, baffled and perturbed. Elric cupped his hands around his mouth and tilted his head back.

'What sort of disturbance?'

'It's like nothing I've ever seen, my lord – I can't describe it.'

Elric turned to Moonglum. 'Relay the order through the fleet – slow the pace to one drumbeat in four, squadron commanders stand by to receive final battle orders.' He strode towards the mast and began to climb up it towards the lookout's post. He climbed until he was high above the deck. The lookout swung out of his cradle, since there was only room for one.

'Is it the enemy, my lord?' he said as Elric clambered into his place. Elric stared hard towards the horizon, making out a kind of dazzling blackness that from time to time sent up sprawling gouts of stuff into the air where it hung for some moments before sinking back into the main mass. Smoky, hard to define, it crept gradually nearer, crawling over the sea towards them.

'It's the enemy,' said Elric quietly.

He remained for some while in the lookout's cradle, studying the Chaos-stuff as it flung itself about in the distance, like some amorphous monster in its death-agonies. But these were not death-agonies. Chaos was far from dead.

From this vantage point, Elric also had a clear view of the fleet as it formed itself into its respective squadrons, making up a black wedge nearly a mile across at its longest point and nearly two miles deep. His own ship was a short distance in front of the rest, well in sight of the squadron commanders. Elric shouted down to Kargan whom he saw passing the mast: 'Stand by to move ahead, Kargan!'

The sea-lord nodded without pausing in his stride. He was fully aware of the battle plan, as they all were for they had discussed it long enough. The leading squadron, under the command of Elric, was comprised of their heaviest warships which would smash into the centre of the enemy fleet and seek to break its order, aiming particularly at whichever ship Jagreen Lern now used. If Jagreen Lern could be slain or captured, their victory would be more likely.

Now the dark stuff was closer and Elric could just make out the sails of the first vessels, spread out one behind the other. Then, as they came even closer, he was aware that to each side of this leading formation were great glinting shapes that dwarfed even the huge battlecraft of Jagreen Lern.

The Chaos Ships.

Elric recognised them, now, from his own knowledge of occult lore. These were the ships said normally to sail the deeps of the oceans, taking on drowned sailors as crews, captained by creatures that had never been human. It was a fleet from the deepest, gloomiest parts of the vast underwater domain which had, since the beginning of time, been disputed territory – disputed between water elementals under their king Straasha, and the Lords of Chaos, who claimed the sea-depths as their main territory on Earth, by right. Legends said that at one time Chaos had ruled the sea and Law the land. This, perhaps, explained the fear of the sea that many human beings had to this day, and the pull the sea had for others.

But the fact was that, although the elementals had succeeded in winning the shallower portions of the sea, the Chaos Lords had retained the deeper parts by means of this, their fleet of the dead. The ships themselves were not of earthly manufacture, neither were their captains originally from Earth, but their crews had once been human, and were now indestructible in any ordinary sense.

As they approached, Elric was soon in no doubt that they were, indeed, those ships. The Sign of Chaos flashed on their sails, eight amber arrows radiating from a central hub – signifying the boast of Chaos, that it contained all possibilities whereas Law was supposed, in time, to destroy possibility and result in eternal stagnation. The Sign of Law was a single arrow pointing upwards, symbolising dynamic growth.

Elric knew that in reality Chaos was the harbinger of stagnation, for though it changed constantly, it never progressed. But, in his heart, he still felt a yearning for this state, for his past loyalties to the Lords of Chaos had suited him better to wild destruction than to stable progress.

But now Chaos must make war on Chaos; Elric must turn against those he had once been loyal to, using weapons formed by chaotic forces to defeat those self-same forces in these ironic times.

He clambered from the cradle and began to shin down the

mast, leaping the last few feet to land on the deck as Dyvim Slorm came up. Quickly he told his cousin what he had seen.

Dyvim Slorm was astounded. 'But the fleet of the dead never comes to the surface – save for...' his eyes widened.

Elric shrugged. 'That's the legend – the fleet of the dead will rise from the depths when the final struggle comes, when Chaos shall be divided against itself, when Law shall be weak and mankind shall choose sides in the battle that will result in a new Earth dominated either by total Chaos or by almost-total Law. When Sepiriz told us this was the case, I felt a response. Since then, in studying my manuscripts, I have been fully reminded.'

'Is this, then, to be the final battle?'

'It might be,' Elric answered. 'It is certain to be one of the last when it will be decided for all time whether Law or Chaos shall rule here.'

'If we're defeated, then Chaos will undoubtedly rule.'

'Perhaps, but remember that the struggle need not be decided by battles alone.'

'So Sepiriz said, but if we're defeated this day, we'll have little chance to discover the truth of that.' Dyvim Slorm gripped Mournblade's hilt. 'Someone must wield these blades – these destiny-swords – when the time comes for the deciding duel. Our allies diminish, Elric.'

'Aye. But I've a hope that we can summon a few others. Straasha, King of the Water Elementals, has ever fought against the death fleet – and he is brother to Graoll and Misha, the Wind Lords. Perhaps through Straasha, I can summon his unearthly kin. In this way we will be better matched, at least.'

'I know only a fragment of the spell for summoning the water-king,' Dyvim Slorm said.

'I know the whole rune. I had best make haste to meditate upon it, for our fleets will clash in two hours or less and then I'll have no time for the summoning of spirits but will have to keep tight hold on my own less some Chaos creature releases it.'

Elric moved towards the prow of the ship, and, leaning over, stared into the ocean depths, turning his mind inward and contemplating the strange and ancient knowledge which lay there. He became almost hypnotised as he lost contact with his own personality and began to identify with the swirling ocean below.

Involuntarily, old words began to form in his throat and his lips began to move in the rune which his ancestors had known when they and all the elementals of the Earth had been allies and sworn to aid one another long ago in the dawn of the Bright Empire, more than ten thousand years before.

> *'Waters of the sea, thou gave us birth*
> *And were our milk and mother both*
> *In days when skies were overcast*
> *You who were first shall be the last.*
>
> *'Sea-rulers, fathers of our blood,*
> *Thine aid is sought, thine aid is sought,*
> *Your salt is blood, our blood your salt,*
> *Your blood the blood of Man.*
>
> *'Straasha, eternal king, eternal sea*
> *Thine aid is sought by me;*
> *For enemies of thine and mine*
> *Seek to defeat our destiny, and drain away our sea.'*

The spoken rune was merely a vocalisation of the actual invocation which was produced mentally and went plunging into the depths, through the dark green corridors of the sea until it finally found Straasha in his domain of curving, coral-coloured, womb-like constructions which were only partially in the natural sea and partially in the plane where the elementals spent a large part of their immortal existence.

Straasha knew of the Ships of Hell rising to the surface and had been pleased that his domain was now cleared of them, but Elric's summons awakened his memory and he remembered the folk of Melniboné upon whom all the elementals had once looked with a sense of comradeship; he remembered the ancient invocation, and felt bound to answer it, though he knew his people were badly weakened by the effect Chaos had had in other parts of the world. Not only humans had suffered; the elemental spirits of nature had been sorely pressed as well.

But he stirred so that water and the stuff of his other plane were both disturbed. He summoned some of his followers and began to glide upwards into the domain of the Air.

Semi-conscious now, Elric knew that his invocation had met with success. Sprawled in the prow, he waited.

At last the waters heaved and broke and revealed a great green figure, with turquoise beard and hair, pale green skin that seemed made of the sea itself, and a voice that was like a rushing tide.

'Once more Straasha answers thy summons, mortal. Our destinies are bound together. How may I aid thee, and, in aiding thee, aid myself?'

In the throat-torturing speech of the elemental, Elric answered, telling the sea-king of the forthcoming battle and what it implied.

'So at long last it has come to pass! I fear I cannot aid you much, for my folk are already suffering terribly from the depredations of our mutual enemy. We shall attempt to aid you if we can. That's all I promise.'

The sea-king sank back into the waters and Elric watched him depart with a feeling of acute disappointment. It was with a brooding mind that he left the prow and went to the main cabin to tell his captains the news.

They received it with mixed feelings, for only Dyvim Slorm was used to dealing with supernaturals. Moonglum had always been dubious of Elric's powers to control his wild, elemental friends, while Kargan growled that Straasha may have been an ally of Elric's folk but had been more of an enemy to his. The four of them, however, could plan with slightly more optimism and face the coming ordeal with better confidence.

Chapter Four

THE FLEET OF Jagreen Lern bore towards them and, in its wake, the boiling stuff of Chaos hovered.

Elric gave the command and the rowers hauled at their oars, sending *Timber-tearer* rushing towards the enemy. So far his elemental allies had not appeared, but he could not afford to wait for them.

As *Timber-tearer* rode the foaming waves, Elric hauled his sword from its scabbard, brought the side wings of his helmet round to cover his face and cried the age-old ululating war-shout of Melniboné, a shout full of joyous evil. Stormbringer's eery voice joined with his, giving vent to a thrumming song, anticipating the blood and the souls it would soon feast upon.

Jagreen Lern's new flagship now lay behind three rows of men-o'-war and behind the flagship were the Chaos ships.

Timber-tearer's iron ram ripped into the first enemy ship and the rowers leaned on their oars, backing away and turning to pierce another ship below the waterline. Showers of arrows sprayed from the holed ship and clattered on deck and armour. Several rowers went down.

Elric and his three companions directed their men from the main deck, standing so that between them they had an overall view of what was going on around them. Elric looked up suddenly, warned by some sixth sense, and saw streaking balls of green fire come curving out of the sky.

'Prepare to quench fires!' Kargan yelled and the group of men already primed for this leapt for the tubs containing a special brew which Elric had told them how to make earlier. This was spread on decks and splashed on canvas and, when the fireballs landed, they were swiftly quenched. 'Don't engage unless forced to,' Elric called to the seamen, 'keep aiming for the flagship. If we take that, our advantage will be good!'

'Where are your allies, Elric?' Kargan asked sardonically, shuddering a little as he saw the Chaos-stuff in the distance suddenly move and erupt tendrils of black matter into the sky.

'They'll come, never fear,' Elric answered, but he was unsure.

Now they were in the thick of the enemy fleet, the ships of their squadron following behind, their great oars slicing through the ocean's foam. The war-engines of their own fleet sent up a constant barrage of fire and heavy stones. Only a few of Elric's craft broke through the enemy's first rank and reached the open sea, sailing towards Jagreen Lern's flagship.

As they were observed, the enemy ships sailed to protect the flagship and the scintillating ships of death, moving with fantastic speed for their size, surrounded the Theocrat's vessel.

Shouting over the waters, Kargan ordered their diminished squadron into a new formation. Moonglum shook his head in astonishment. 'How can things of that size support themselves on the water?' he said to Elric.

'It's unlikely that they actually do.' As their ship manoeuvred into its new position, he stared at the huge craft, twenty of them, dwarfing everything else on the sea. They seemed covered with a kind of shining fluid which flashed all the colours of the spectrum so that their outlines were hard to see and the shadowy figures moving about on their gigantic decks could not easily be observed. Wisps of dark stuff began to drift across the scene, close to the water, and Dyvim Slorm, from the lower deck, pointed and shouted: 'See! Chaos comes! Where is Straasha and his folk?'

Elric shook his head, perturbed. He had expected aid by now.

'We cannot wait. We must attack!' Kargan's voice was pitched higher than usual.

A mood of bitter recklessness came upon Elric, as he gripped the rigging to steady himself on the swaying deck, then he smiled. 'Come then. Let's do so!'

Speedily the squadron coursed towards the disturbing ships of death. Moonglum muttered: 'We are going to our doom, Elric. No man would willingly get close to those ships. Only the dead are drawn to them, and they do not go with joy!'

But Elric ignored his friend.

A strange silence descended over the waters and the rhythmic sound of the splashing oars was sharp. The death fleet waited for them, impassively, as if they did not need to prepare for battle. He tightened his grip on Stormbringer. The blade responded to the pounding of his pulse-beat, moving in his hand with each thud of his heart, as if linked to it by veins and arteries. Now they were so close to the Chaos ships that they could make out better the figures crowding the great decks. Horribly, Elric thought he recognised some of the gaunt faces of the dead and, involuntarily, he called to the sea-folk's king.

'*Straasha!*'

The waters heaved, foamed and seemed to be attempting to rise but then subsided again. Straasha heard – but he was finding it difficult to fight against the forces of Chaos.

'*Straasha!*'

It was no good, the waters hardly moved.

In his wild despair Elric screamed to Kargan: 'We cannot wait for aid. Swing the ship round the Chaos fleet and we'll attempt to reach Jagreen Lern's flagship from the rear!'

Under Kargan's expert direction, the ship swung to avoid the Ships of Hell in a wide semicircle. Spray cascaded against Elric's face, flooding the decks with white foam. He could hardly see through it as they cleared the Chaos ships which had now engaged other craft and were altering the nature of their timbers so that they fell apart and the unfortunate crews were drowned or warped into alien shapes.

To his ears came the miserable cries of the defeated and the triumphantly surging thunder of the Chaos fleet's music as it pushed forward to destroy the Eastern ships. *Timber-tearer* was rocking badly and was hard to control, but at last they were around the hell fleet and bearing down on Jagreen Lern's vessel from behind.

Now they nearly struck the Theocrat's vessel with their ram, but were swept off course and had to manoeuvre again. Arrows rose from the enemy's decks and thudded and rattled on their own. They retaliated as, riding a huge wave, they slid alongside the flagship and flung out grappling irons. A few held, dragging them towards the Theocrat's vessel as the men of Pan Tang strove to cut the grappling ropes. More ropes followed and then a boarding platform fell from its harness and landed squarely on Jagreen Lern's deck. Another followed it. Elric ran for the nearest platform, Kargan behind him, and they led a body of warriors over it, searching for Jagreen Lern. Stormbringer took a dozen lives and a dozen souls before Elric had gained the main deck. There a resplendent commander stood, surrounded by a group of officers. But he was not Jagreen Lern. Elric clambered up the gangway, slicing through a warrior's waist as the man sought to block his path. He yelled at the group: 'Where's your cursed leader? Where's Jagreen Lern!'

The commander's face was pale for he had seen in the past what Elric and his hellblade could do.

'He's not here, Elric, I swear.'

'What? Am I to be thwarted again? I know you are lying!' Elric advanced on the group who backed away, their swords ready.

'Our Theocrat does not need to protect himself by means of lies, doom-fostered one!' sneered a young officer, braver than the rest.

'Perhaps not,' Elric's voice was low and menacing as he rushed towards the youth, swinging Stormbringer in a shrieking arc, 'but at least I'll have your life before I put the truth of your words to the test.'

The man put up his blade to block Stormbringer's swing. The runesword cut through the metal with a triumphant cry, swung back again and plunged itself into the officer's side. He gasped, but remained standing with his hands clenched.

Elric laughed. 'My sword and I need revitalising – and your soul should make an appetiser before I take Jagreen Lern's!'

'No!' the youth groaned. 'Oh, no, not my soul!' His eyes

widened, tears streamed from them and madness came into them for a second before Stormbringer satiated itself and Elric drew it out, replenished. He had no sympathy for the man. 'Your soul would have gone to the depths of hell in any case,' he said lightly. 'But now I've put it to some use, at least.'

Two other officers scrambled over the rail, seeking to escape their comrade's fate.

Elric hacked at the hand of one. He fell, screaming, to the deck, his hand still grasping the rail. The other he skewered in the bowels and, as Stormbringer sucked out his soul, he hung there, pleading incoherently in an effort to avert the inevitable.

So much vitality flowed into Elric that, as he rushed at the remaining group around the commander, he seemed to fly over the deck and rip into them, slicing away limbs as if they were flower-stalks, until he encountered the commander himself. The commander said weakly: 'I surrender. Do not take my soul.'

'Where is Jagreen Lern?'

The commander pointed into the distance, where the Chaos fleet could be seen creating havoc amongst the Eastern ships. 'There! He sails with Pyaray of Chaos whose fleet that is. You cannot reach him there for any man not protected – or not already dead – would turn to flowing flesh once he neared the fleet.'

'That cursed hellspawn still cheats me,' Elric grimaced. 'Here's payment for your information –' Without mercy for one of the men who had wasted and enslaved two continents, Elric stuck his blade through the ornate armour and, delicately, with all the old malevolence of his sorcerer ancestors, tickled the man's heart before finishing him.

He looked around for Kargan, but couldn't see him. Then he noted that the Chaos fleet had turned back. At first he thought it was because Straasha had at last brought aid, but then he saw that the remnants of his fleet were fleeing. Jagreen Lern was victorious. Their plans, their formations, their courage – none of these had been capable of withstanding the horrible warpings of Chaos. And now the dreadful fleet was bearing down on the two flagships, locked together by their grapples. There was no chance of cutting one of them free before the fleet arrived. Elric yelled to Dyvim Slorm and Moonglum whom he saw running towards him from the other side of the deck.

'Over the side! Over, for your lives – and swim as far as you can away from here!'

They looked at him, startled, then realised the truth of his words. Others, from both sides, were already leaping into the bloody water. Elric sheathed his sword and dived. The sea was cold, for all the warm blood in it, and he gasped as he swam in the direction of Moonglum's red head, which he could see ahead and, close to it, Dyvim Slorm's honey-coloured hair. He turned once and saw the very timbers of the two ships begin to melt, to twist and curl in strange patterns as the Ships of Hell arrived. He felt very relieved he had not been aboard. He reached his companions.

'A short-term escape this,' said Moonglum, spitting water from his mouth. 'What now, Elric? Shall we strike for the Purple Towns?' Moonglum's capacity for facetiousness had not, it seemed, been limited by witnessing the defeat of their fleet and the advance of Chaos. The Isle was too far away.

Everywhere, the Chaos ships were disrupting nature. Soon their influence would engulf them, too.

Then, to their left they saw the water froth and form itself into what was to Elric a familiar shape.

'Straasha!'

'*I could not aid thee, I could not aid thee. Though I tried, my ancient enemy was too strong for me. Forgive me. In recompense let me take you and your friends back with me to my own land and save you, at least from Chaos.*'

'But we cannot breathe beneath the sea!'

'*You will not need to.*'

'Very well.'

Trusting to the elemental's words, they allowed themselves to be dragged beneath the waters and down into the cool, green depths of the sea, deeper and deeper until no sunlight filtered there and all was wet darkness and they lived, though at normal times the pressure would have crushed them.

They seemed to travel for miles through the mysterious underwater grottoes until at last they came to a place of coral-coloured rounded constructions that seemed to drift slowly in a sluggish current. Elric knew it. The domain of Straasha the Sea-King.

The elemental bore them to the largest construction and one section of it seemed to fade away to admit them. They moved now through twisting corridors of a delicate pink texture, slightly shadowed, no longer in water. They were now on the plane of the elemental folk. In a huge circular cave, they came to rest.

With a peculiar rushing sound, the sea-king walked to a large throne of milky jade and sat upon it, his green head on his green fist.

'Elric, once again I regret I was unable, after all, to aid you. All I can do now is have some of my folk carry you back to your own land when you have rested here for a while. We are all, it seems, helpless against this new strength which Chaos has of late.'

Elric nodded. 'Nothing can stand against its warping influence – unless it is the Chaos Shield.'

Straasha straightened his back. *'The Chaos Shield. Ah, yes. It belongs to an exiled god, does it not? But his castle is virtually impregnable.'*

'Why is that?'

'It lies upon the topmost crag of a tall and lonely mountain, reached by a hundred and sixty-nine steps. Lining these steps are forty-nine elder trees, and of these you would have to be especially wary. Also Mordaga has a guard of a hundred and forty-four warriors. I'm explicit in giving numbers, for they have a mystic value.'

'Of the warriors I would certainly be wary. But why the elders?'

'Each elder contains the soul of one of Mordaga's followers who was punished thus. They are vengeful trees – ever ready to take the life of anyone that comes into their domain.'

'A hard task, to get that shield for myself,' Elric mused. 'But get it I must, for without it Fate's purpose would be forever thwarted – and with it I might have vengeance on the one who commands the Chaos fleet – and Jagreen Lern who sails with him.'

'Slay Pyaray, Lord of the Fleet of Hell, and, lacking his direction, the fleet itself would perish. His life-force is contained in a blue crystal set in

the top of his head and striking at that with a special weapon is the only means of killing him.'

'Thanks for that information,' Elric said gratefully. 'For when the time comes, I shall need it.'

'What do you plan to do, Elric?' Dyvim Slorm asked.

'Put all else aside for the moment and seek the sad giant's shield. I *must* – for if I do not have it, every battle fought will be a repetition of the one we have just lost.'

'I will come with you, Elric,' Moonglum promised.

'I also,' said Dyvim Slorm.

'We shall require a fourth if we are to carry out the prophecy,' Elric said. 'I wonder what became of Kargan.'

Moonglum looked at the ground. 'Did you not notice?'

'Notice what?'

'On board Jagreen Lern's flagship when you were hewing about you in an effort to reach the main deck. Did you not know, then, what you had done – or rather what your cursed sword did?'

Elric felt suddenly exhausted. 'No. Did I – did it – *kill* him?'

'Aye.'

'Gods!' He wheeled and paced the chamber, slapping his fist in his palm. 'Still this hell-made blade exacts its tribute for the service it gives me. Still it drinks the souls of friends. 'Tis a wonder you two are still with me!'

'I agree it's extraordinary,' Moonglum said feelingly.

'I grieve for Kargan. He was a good friend.'

'Elric,' Moonglum said urgently. 'You know that Kargan's death was not your responsibility. It was fated.'

'Aye, but why must I always be the executioner of fate? I hesitate to list the names of the good friends and useful allies whose souls my sword has stolen. I hate it enough that it must suck souls out to give me my vitality – but that it should be most partial to my friends, that is what I cannot bear. I've half a mind to venture into the heart of Chaos and there sacrifice us both! The guilt is indirectly mine, for if I was not so weak I *must* bear such a blade, many of those who have befriended me might be alive now.'

'Yet the blade's major purpose seems a noble one,' Moonglum

said in a baffled voice. 'Oh, I fail to understand all this – paradox, paradox upon paradox. Are the gods mad or are they so subtle we cannot fathom the workings of their minds?'

'It's hard enough at times like these to remember any greater purpose,' Dyvim Slorm agreed. 'We are pressed so sorely that we haven't a moment for thought, but must fight the next battle and the next, forgetting often why it is we fight.'

'Is the purpose, indeed, greater and not lesser,' Elric smiled bitterly. 'If we are the toys of the gods – are not perhaps the gods themselves mere children?'

'These questions are of no present importance,' said Straasha from his throne.

'And at least,' Moonglum told Elric, 'future generations will thank Stormbringer if she fulfils her destiny.'

'If Sepiriz is right,' Elric said, 'future generations will know nothing of any of us – blades or men!'

'Perhaps not consciously – but in the depths of their souls they will remember us. Our deeds will be spoken of as belonging to heroes with other names, that is all.'

'That the world forgets me is all I ask,' Elric sighed.

As if growing impatient with this fruitless discussion, the sea-king rose from his throne and said: *'Come, I will make certain that you are transported to land, if you have no objection to travelling back in the same manner as you came here?'*

'None,' said Elric.

Chapter Five

THEY STAGGERED WEARILY onto the beach of the Isle of the Purple Towns and Elric turned back to address the sea-king, who remained in the shallows.

'Again I thank you for saving us, Lord of the Sea,' he said respectfully. 'And thanks also for telling me more of the sad giant's shield. By this action you have perhaps given us the opportunity to make certain that Chaos will be swept away from the ocean – and the land, also.'

'*Aahh,*' the sea-king nodded, '*yet even if you are successful and the sea is unspoiled, it will mean the passing of us both, will it not?*'

'True.'

'*Then let it be so, for I at least am weary of my long existence. But come – now I must return to my folk and hope to withstand Chaos for a little longer. Farewell!*'

And the sea-king sank into the waves again and vanished.

When they eventually reached the Fortress of Evening, heralds ran out to assist them.

'How went the battle? Where is the fleet?' one asked Moonglum.

'Have the survivors not yet returned?'

'Survivors? Then...?'

'We were defeated,' Elric said hollowly. 'Is my wife still here?'

'No, she left soon after the fleet sailed, riding for Karlaak.'

'Good. At least we shall have time to erect new defences against Chaos before they reach that far. Now, we must have food and wine. We must devise a fresh plan of battle.'

'Battle, my lord? With what shall we fight?'

'We shall see,' Elric said, 'we shall see.'

Later they watched the battered survivors of the fleet sailing into the harbour. Moonglum counted despairingly. 'Too few,' he said. 'This is a black day.'

From behind them in the courtyard a trumpet sounded.

'An arrival from the mainland,' Dyvim Slorm said.

They strode together down to the courtyard in time to see a scarlet-clad archer dismounting from his horse. His near-fleshless face might have been carved from bone. He stooped with weariness.

Elric was surprised. 'Rackhir! You command the Ilmioran coast. Why are you here?'

'We were driven back. The Theocrat launched not one fleet but two. The other came in from the Pale Sea and took us by surprise. Our defences were crushed, Chaos swept in and we were forced to flee. The enemy has established itself less than a hundred miles from Bakshaan and marches across country – if march is the word, rather it *flows*. Presumably it expects to meet up with the army the Theocrat intends to land here.'

'Aaahh, we are surely defeated...' Moonglum's voice was little more than a sigh.

'We must have that shield, Elric,' Dyvim Slorm said.

Elric frowned, his heart sinking. 'Any further steps we take against Chaos will be doomed unless we have its protection. You, Rackhir, will be the fourth man in the prophecy.'

'What prophecy?'

'I'll explain later. Are you fit enough to ride back with us now?'

'Give me two hours to sleep and then I will be.'

'Good. Two hours. Make your preparations, my friends, for we go to claim the sad giant's shield!'

From two sides now, Chaos enclosed the East and the four men left the Fortress of Evening knowing it was unlikely it would survive. They rode across the waters to the mainland to discover that garrisons were abandoned as men fled away from the dreadful threat of Chaos. It was not until a day later that they came upon the first survivors of the land-fighting, many of them with bodies twisted into terrible shapes by Chaos, struggling along a white road leading towards Jadmar, a city still free. From them they learned that half Ilmiora, parts of Vilmir and the tiny independent kingdom of Org had all fallen. Chaos was closing in, its shadow spreading more and more swiftly as its conquests increased.

It was with relief that Elric and his companions finally reached Karlaak to find it still free from attack. But reports placed the Chaos army less than two hundred miles away and coming nearer.

Zarozinia greeted Elric with troubled joy. 'There were rumours you were dead – killed in the sea-battle.'

'I cannot stay long. I have to go beyond the Sighing Desert.'

'I know.'

'You know? How?'

'Sepiriz was here. He left a gift in our stables for you. Four Nihrain horses.'

'A useful gift. They will carry us far more swiftly than any other beasts. But will that be swift enough? I hesitate to leave you here with Chaos encroaching at such a rate.'

'You must leave me, Elric. If all seems lost here, we shall flee to the Weeping Waste. Even Jagreen Lern can have scant interest in those barrens.'

'Promise me that you will.'

'I promise.'

Feeling a little more relieved, Elric took her by the hand. 'I spent the most restful period of my life in this palace,' he said. 'Let me spend this last night with you and perhaps we shall find a little of the old peace we once had – before I ride on to the sad giant's lair.'

So they made love, but when they slept, their dreams were so full of dark portent that each wakened the other with their groans so that they lay side by side, clinging to one another until the dawn, when Elric rose, kissed her lightly, clasped her hand and then went to the stables where he found his friends waiting – around a fourth figure. It was Sepiriz.

'Sepiriz, thanks for your gift. They will probably make the difference between our being too late or not,' Elric said sincerely. 'But why are you here now?'

'Because I can perform another small service before your main journey begins,' said the black seer. 'All of you save Moonglum have retained weapons endowed with some special power. Elric and Dyvim Slorm have their runeblades, Rackhir, the Arrows of Law, which the sorcerer Lamsar gave him at the time of the Siege of Tanelorn – but Moonglum's weapon has nothing save the skill of its bearer.'

'I think I prefer it thus,' retorted Moonglum. 'I've seen what a charmed blade can take from a man.'

'I can give you nothing so strong – nor so evil – as Stormbringer,' Sepiriz said. 'But I have a charm for your sword, a slight one that my contact with the White Lords has enabled me to use. Give me your sword, Moonglum.'

A trifle unwillingly, Moonglum unsheathed his curved steel blade and handed it to the Nihrain who took a small engraving tool from his robe and, whispering a rune, scratched several symbols on the sword near its hilt. Then he gave it back to the Eastlander.

'There. Now the sword has the blessing of Law and you will find it more able to withstand Law's enemies.'

Elric said impatiently. 'We must ride now, Sepiriz, for time grows desperately short.'

'Ride, then. But be wary for patrolling bands of Jagreen Lern's warriors. I do not think they will be anywhere along your route when you journey there – but watch for them coming back.'

They mounted the magical Nihrain steeds which had helped Elric more than once, and rode away from Karlaak by the Weeping Waste. Rode away perhaps for ever.

In a short while they had entered the Weeping Waste, for this was the quickest route to the Sighing Desert. Rackhir alone knew this country well, and he guided them.

The Nihrain steeds, treading the ground of their own strange plane, seemed literally to fly for it could be observed that their hoofs did not touch the damp grasses of the Weeping Waste. They moved at incredible speed and Rackhir, until he became used to the pace, gripped his reins tightly. In this place of eternal rain, the land was difficult to see far ahead, and the drizzle spread down their faces and into their eyes as they peered through it, trying to make out the high mountain range, which ran along the edge of the Weeping Waste, separating it from the Sighing Desert.

Then at last, after two days, they could observe tall crags and knew they were near the borders of the desert. Soon they were riding through the deep gorges and the rain ceased until, on the third day, the breeze became warm and then harsh and hot as they left the mountains and entered the desert. The sun blazed down and the wind soughed constantly over the barren sand and rocks, its continuous sighing giving the desert its name. They protected their faces, particularly their eyes, with their hoods as best they could, for the stinging sand was ever present.

Resting only for a few hours at a time, Rackhir directing them, they sped further and further into the depths of the vast desert, speaking little, for it was difficult to be heard over the wind.

Elric had long since fallen into what was virtually a mindless trance, letting the horse carry him over the desert. He had fought against his own churning thoughts and emotions, finding it hard, as he often did, to retain any objective impression of his predicament. His past had been too troubled, his background too morbid for him to do much now to see clearly.

He had always been a slave to his melancholic emotions, his physical failings and to the very blood flowing in his veins. He saw life not as a consistent pattern, but as a series of random events. Unlike others, he had fought all his life to assemble his thoughts and, if necessary, accept the chaotic nature of things, learn to live with it, but, except in moments of extreme personal crisis, had rarely managed to think coherently for any length of time. He was, perhaps, because of his outlawed life, his albinism, his very reliance on his runesword for strength, obsessed with the knowledge of his own doom.

What was thought, he asked himself, what was emotion? What was control and was it worth achieving? Better to live by instinct than to theorise and be wrong; better to remain the puppet, letting the gods move him at their pleasure, than to seek control of his own fate, clash with the will of the Higher Worlds and perish for his pains.

So he considered as he rode into the searing lash of the wind, already striving against natural hazard. And what was the difference between an earthly hazard and the hazard of uncontrolled thought and emotion? Both held something of the same qualities.

But his race, though they had ruled the world for ten thousand years, had lived under the dominance of a different star. They had been neither true men nor true members of the ancient races who had come before men. They were an intermediary type and Elric was half-consciously aware of this; aware that he was the last of an inbred line who had, without effort, used Chaos-given sorcery for convenience and for no other purpose. His race had been of Chaos, having no need of self-control or the self-restrictions of the new races who had emerged with the Age of the Young Kingdoms, and even these, according to the seer Sepiriz, were not the true men who would one day walk an Earth where order and progress might become the rule and Chaos rarely exert influence – if Elric triumphed, destroying the world he knew.

This thought added to his gloom, for he had no destiny but death, no purpose save what fate willed. Why fight against it, why bother to sharpen his wits or put his mind in order? He was little more than a sacrifice on the altar of destiny. He breathed deeply of the hot, dry air and expelled it from his stinging lungs, spitting out the clogging sand which had entered his mouth and nostrils.

Dyvim Slorm shared something of Elric's mood, though his feelings were not so strong. He had a more ordered life than had Elric, though they were of the same blood. Whereas Elric had questioned the custom of his folk, even renounced kingship that he might explore the new lands of the Young Kingdoms and compare their way of life with his own, Dyvim Slorm had never indulged in such questioning. He had suffered bitterness when through Elric's renegade activities, the Dreaming City of Imrryr, last stronghold of the old race of Melniboné, had been razed; shock, too, of a kind, when he and what remained of the Imrryrians had been forced out into the world, also, to make their living as mercenaries of those they considered upstart kings of lowly and contemptible peoples. Dyvim Slorm, who had never questioned, did not question now, though he was disturbed.

Moonglum was less self-absorbed. Since the time, many years before, when he and Elric had met and fought against the Dharzi together, he had felt a peculiar sympathy, even empathy, with his friend. When Elric sank into such moods as the one he was in now, Moonglum felt tormented only because he could not help him. Many times he had sought the means of pulling Elric out of his gloomy depression, but these days he had learned that it was impossible. By nature cheerful and optimistic, even he felt dominated by the doom which was on them.

Rackhir, too, who was of a calmer and more philosophical frame of mind than his fellows, did not feel capable of fully grasping the implications of their mission. He had thought to spend the rest of his days in contemplation and meditation in the peaceful city of Tanelorn, which exerted a strange calming influence on all who lived there. But this call to aid in the fight against Chaos had been impossible to ignore and he had unwillingly strapped on his quiver of Arrows of Law and taken up his bow again to ride from Tanelorn with a small party of those who wished to accompany him and offer their services to Elric.

Peering through the sand-filled air, he saw something looming ahead – a single mountain rising from the wastes of the desert as if placed there by unnatural means.

He called, pointing: 'Elric! There! That must be Mordaga's castle!'

Elric roused himself and let his eyes follow Rackhir's pointing hand. 'Aye,' he sighed. 'We are there. Let us rest here before we ride the final distance!'

They reined in their steeds and dismounted, easing their aching limbs and stretching their legs to allow the blood to flow freely again.

They raised their tent against the wind-blown sand and ate their meal in a mood of companionship, created by the knowledge that after they reached the mountain, they might never see one another alive again.

Chapter Six

T HE STEPS WOUND up around the mountain. High above they could see the gleam of masonry and, just where the steps curved and disappeared for the first time, they saw an elder tree. It looked like any ordinary tree but it became a symbol for them – there was their initial antagonist. How would it fight? Elric placed a booted foot on the first step. It was high, built for the feet of a giant. He began to climb, the other three following behind him. Now, as he reached the tenth step, he unsheathed Stormbringer, felt it quiver and send energy into him. The climbing instantly became easier. As he came close to the elder, he heard it rustle, saw that there was an agitation in its branches. Yes, it was certainly sentient. He was only a few steps from the tree when he heard Dyvim Slorm shout: 'Gods! *The leaves* – look at the leaves!'

The green leaves, their veins seeming to throb in the sunlight, were beginning to detach themselves from the branches and drift purposefully towards the group. One settled on Elric's bare hand. He attempted to brush it off, but it clung. Others began to settle on different parts of his body. They were coming in a green wave now and he felt a peculiar stinging sensation in his hand. With a curse he peeled it off and to his horror saw that tiny pinpricks of blood were left where it had been. His body twitched in nausea and he ripped the rest from his face, slashing at others with his runesword. As they were touched by the blade, so they shrivelled, but they were swiftly replaced. He knew instinctively that they were sucking not only blood from his veins, but the soul-force from his being.

With yells of terror, his companions discovered the same thing. These leaves were being directed and he knew where the direction came from – the tree itself. He clambered up the remaining steps, fighting off the leaves which swarmed like locusts around him. With grim intention he began hacking at the trunk which gave out an angry groaning and the branches sought to reach him. He slashed them away and then plunged Stormbringer deep into the tree. Sods of earth spattered upwards as the roots threshed. The tree screamed and began to heel over towards him as if, in death, it sought to kill him also. He wrenched at Stormbringer which sucked greedily at the sentient tree's lifestuff, failed to tug the sword out and leapt aside as the tree crashed down over the steps, barely missing him. One branch slashed his face and drew blood. He gasped and staggered, feeling the life draining from him.

He stumbled to the fallen tree and saw that the wood was suddenly dead and the remaining leaves brown and shrivelled. 'Quickly,' he gasped as the three came up, 'shift this thing. My sword's beneath and without it I'm dead!'

Swiftly they set to work and rolled the tree over so that Elric could weakly grasp the hilt of Stormbringer still imbedded therein. As he did so he almost screamed, experiencing a sensation of ecstatic power as the tree's energy filled him, pulsed through him so that he felt like a god himself. He laughed, as if possessed by a demon, and the others looked at him in astonishment. 'Come, my friends, follow me. I can deal with a million such trees now!'

He leapt up the steps as another shoal of leaves came towards him. Ignoring their bites, he went straight for the second elder and drove his sword at its centre. Again, this tree screamed.

'Dyvim Slorm!' he shouted, drunk on its life-force. 'Do as I do – let your sword drink a few such souls and we're invincible!'

'Such power is scarcely palatable,' Rackhir said, brushing dead leaves from his body as Elric withdrew his sword again and ran towards the next. The elders grew thicker here and they bent their branches to reach him, looming over him, their branches like fingers seeking to pluck him apart.

Dyvim Slorm, a trifle less spontaneously, imitated Elric's method of dispatching the tree-creatures and soon he too became filled with the stolen souls of the demons imprisoned within the elders and his wild laugh joined Elric's as, like fiendish woodsmen, they attacked again and again, each victory lending them more strength so that Moonglum and Rackhir looked at each other in wonder and fear to see such a terrible change come over their friends.

But there was no denying that their methods were effective against the elders. Soon they looked back at a waste of fallen, blackened trees spreading down the mountain side.

All the old, unholy fervour of the dead kings of Melniboné was in the faces of the two kinsmen as they sang old battle-songs, their twin blades joining the harmony to send up a disturbing melody of doom and malevolence. His lips parted to reveal his white teeth, his red eyes blazing with dreadful fire, his milk-white hair streaming in the burning wind, Elric flung up his sword to the sky and turned to confront his companions.

'Now, friends, see how the ancient ones of Melniboné conquered man and demon to rule the world for ten thousand years!'

Moonglum thought that he merited the name of Wolf, gained in the West long since. All the chaos-force that was now within him had gained complete control over every other part of him. He realised that Elric was no longer split in his loyalties, there was no conflict in him now. His ancestors' blood dominated him and he appeared as they must have done ages since when all other races of mankind fled before them, fearing their magnificence, their malice and their evil. Dyvim Slorm seemed equally as possessed. Moonglum sent up a heartfelt prayer to whatever kindly gods remained in the universe that Elric was his ally and not his enemy.

They were close to the top now, Elric and his cousin springing ahead with superhuman bounds. The steps terminated at the mouth of a gloomy tunnel and into the darkness rushed the pair, laughing and calling to one another. Less speedily, Moonglum and Rackhir followed, the Red Archer nocking an arrow to his bow.

Elric peered into the gloom, his head swimming with the power that seemed to burst from every pore of his body. He heard the clatter of armoured feet coming towards him and, as they approached, he realised that these warriors were mere human beings. Though nearly a hundred and fifty, they did not daunt him. As the first group rushed at him, he blocked blows easily and struck them down, each soul taken making only a fraction of difference to the vitality already in him. Shoulder to shoulder stood the kinsmen, butchering the soldiers like so many unarmed children. It was dreadful to the eyes of Moonglum and Rackhir as they came up to witness the flood of blood which soon made the tunnel slippery. The stench of death in the close confines became too much as Elric and Dyvim Slorm moved past the first of the fallen and carried the attack to the rest.

Rackhir groaned: 'Though they be enemies and the servants of those we fight, I cannot bear to witness such slaughter. We are not needed here, friend Moonglum. These are demons waging war, not men!'

'Aye,' agreed Moonglum, disquieted. They broke out into sunlight again and saw the castle ahead, the remaining warriors reassembling as Elric and Dyvim Slorm advanced menacingly with malevolent joy towards them.

The air rang with the sounds of shouting and steel clashing. Rackhir aimed an arrow at one of the warriors and launched it to take the man in the left eye. 'I'll see that a few of them get a cleaner death,' he muttered, nocking another arrow to the string.

As Elric and his cousin disappeared into the enemy ranks, others, sensing perhaps that Rackhir and Moonglum were less of a danger, rushed at the two. Moonglum found himself engaging three warriors and discovered that his sword seemed extraordinarily light and gave off a sweet, clear tone as it met the warriors' weapons, turning them aside readily. The sword supplied him with no energy, but it did not blunt as it might have and the heavier swords could not force it down so easily. Rackhir had expended all his arrows in what had been an act of mercy. He engaged the enemy with his sword and killed two, taking Moonglum's third opponent from behind with an upward thrust into the man's side and through to his heart.

Then they went with little stomach into the main fray and saw that already the turf was littered with a great many corpses. Rackhir cried to Elric: 'Stop! Elric – let *us* finish these. You have no need to take their souls. We can kill them with more natural methods!'

But Elric laughed and carried on his work. As he finished

another warrior and there were no others in the immediate area, Rackhir seized him by the arm. 'Elric –'

Stormbringer turned in Elric's hand, howling its satiated glee and clove down at Rackhir. Seeing his fate, the Red Archer sobbed and sought to avoid the blow. But it landed in his shoulder blade and sheared down to his breastbone. 'Elric!' he cried. 'Not *my* soul, too!'

And so died the hero Rackhir the Red Archer, famous in the Eastlands as the saviour of Tanelorn. Cloven by a treacherous blade. By the friend whose life he had saved, long ago when they had first met near the city of Ameeron.

And Elric laughed until realisation came and he tugged his sword away though it was too late. The stolen energy still pulsed in him, but his great grief no longer gave it the same control over him. Tears streamed down Elric's tortured face and a great, racking groan came from him.

'Ah, Rackhir – will it ever cease?'

On opposite sides of the slain-strewed field, his two remaining companions stood regarding him. Dyvim Slorm had done with killing, but only because there was none left to kill. He gasped, staring around him half in bewilderment. Moonglum glared at Elric with horrified eyes which yet held a gleam of sympathy for his friend, for he knew well Elric's doom and knew that the life of one close to Elric was coveted by Stormbringer.

'There was no gentler hero than Rackhir,' he said, 'no man more desirous of peace and order than him.' Then he shuddered.

Elric raised himself to his feet and turned to look at the huge castle of granite and bluestone which waited in enigmatic silence as if for his next action. On the battlements of the topmost turret he could make out a figure which could only be the giant.

'I swear by your stolen soul, Rackhir, that what you wished to come to pass *shall* come to pass, though I, a thing of Chaos, achieve it. Law will triumph and Chaos will be driven back! Armed with sword and shield of Chaos forging I shall do battle with every fiend of hell if needs be. Chaos was the indirect cause of your death. And Chaos will be punished for it. But first, we must take the shield.'

Dyvim Slorm, not realising quite what had happened, shouted in exultation to his kinsman. 'Elric – let's visit the sad giant now!'

But Moonglum, coming up to gaze down on the ruined body of Rackhir, murmured: 'Aye, Chaos is the cause, Elric. I'll join in your vengeance with a will so long as,' he shuddered, 'I'm spared from the attentions of your hellblade.'

Together, three abreast, they marched through the open portal of Mordaga's castle and were immediately in a rich and barbarically furnished hall.

'Mordaga!' Elric cried. 'We have come to fulfil a prophecy!'

They waited impatiently, until at last a bulky figure came through a great arch at the end of the vast hall. Mordaga was as tall as two men, but his back was bent. He had long, curling black hair and was clad in a deep blue smock belted at the waist. Upon his great feet were simple leather sandals. His black eyes were full of a sorrow such as Moonglum had only seen before in Elric's eyes.

Upon the sad giant's arm was a round shield which bore upon it the eight amber arrows of Chaos. It was of a silvery green colour and very beautiful. He had no other weapons.

'I know the prophecy,' he said in a voice that was like a lonely, roaring wind. 'But still I must seek to avert it. Will you take the shield and leave me in peace, human? I do not want death.'

Elric felt a kind of sympathy for sad Mordaga and he knew something of what the fallen god must feel at this moment. 'The prophecy says death,' he said softly.

'Take the shield,' Mordaga lifted it off his mighty arm and held it towards Elric. 'Take the shield and change fate this once.'

Elric nodded. 'I will.'

With a tremendous sigh, the giant deposited the Chaos Shield upon the floor.

'For thousands of years I have lived in the shadow of that prophecy,' he said, straightening his back. 'Now, though I die in old age, I shall die in peace and, though once I did not think so, I shall welcome such a death after all this time, I think.'

'The whole world seems to sigh for death,' Elric replied, 'but you may not die naturally, for Chaos comes and will engulf you as it will engulf everything unless I can stop it. But at least, it seems, you'll be in a more philosophical frame of mind to meet it.'

'Farewell and I thank you,' said the giant, turning, and he plodded back towards the entrance through which he had come.

As Mordaga disappeared, Moonglum dashed forward on fleet feet and followed him through the entrance before either Elric or Dyvim Slorm could cry out or stop him.

Then they heard a single shriek that seemed to echo away into eternity, a crash which shook the hall and then the footfall returning.

Moonglum reappeared in the entrance, a bloody sword in his hand.

'It was murder,' he said simply. 'I admit it. I took him in the back before he was aware of it. It was a good, quick death and he died whilst happy. Moreover, it was a better death than any his minions tried to mete to us. It was murder, but it was necessary in my eyes.'

'Why?' said Elric, still mystified.

Grimly, Moonglum continued: 'He had to perish as Fate decreed. We are servants of Fate, now, Elric, and to divert it in any small way is to hamper its aims. But more than that, it was the beginning of my own vengeance-taking. If Mordaga had not surrounded himself with such a host, Rackhir would not have died.'

Elric shook his head. 'Blame me for that, Moonglum. The giant should not have perished for my own sword's crime.'

'Someone had to perish,' said Moonglum steadfastly, 'and since the prophecy contained Mordaga's death, he was the one. Who else, here, could I kill, Elric?'

Elric turned away. 'I wish it were I,' he sighed. He looked down at the great, round shield with its shifting amber arrows and its mysterious silver-green colour. He picked it up easily enough and placed it on his arm. It virtually covered his body from chin to ankles.

'Let's make haste and leave this place of death and misery. The lands of Ilmiora and Vilmir await our aid – if they have not already wholly fallen to Chaos!'

Chapter Seven

I T WAS IN the mountains separating the Sighing Desert from the Weeping Waste that they first learned of the fate of the last of the Young Kingdoms. They came upon a party of six tired warriors led by Lord Voashoon, Zarozinia's father.

'What has happened?' Elric asked anxiously. 'Where is Zarozinia?'

'I know not if she's lost, dead or captured, Elric. Our continent has fallen to Chaos.'

'Did you not seek for her?' Elric accused.

The old man shrugged. 'My son, I have looked upon so much horror these past days that I am now bereft of emotion. I care for nothing but a quick release from all this. The day of mankind is over on the Earth. Go no further than here, for even the Weeping Waste is beginning to change before the crawling tide of Chaos. It is hopeless.'

'Hopeless! No! We still live – perhaps Zarozinia still lives. Did you hear nothing of her fate?'

'Only a rumour that Jagreen Lern had taken her aboard the leading Chaos ship.'

'She is on the seas?'

'No – those cursed craft sail land as well as sea, if it can be told apart these days. It was they who attacked Karlaak, with a vast horde of mounted men and infantry following behind. Confusion prevails – you'll find nothing but your death back there, my son.'

'We shall see. I have some protection against Chaos at long last, plus my sword and my Nihrain steed.' He turned in the saddle to address his companions. 'Well, will you stay here with Lord Voashoon or accompany me into the heart of Chaos?'

'We'll come with you,' Moonglum said quietly, speaking for

them both. 'We've followed you until now and our fates are linked with yours in any case. We can do nought else.'

'Good. Farewell, Lord Voashoon. If you would do a service, ride over the Weeping Waste to Eshmir and the Unmapped East where Moonglum's homeland lies. Tell them what to expect, though they're probably beyond rescue now.'

'I will try,' said Voashoon wearily, 'and hope to arrive there before Chaos.'

Then Elric and his companions rode away, towards the massed hordes of Chaos – three men against the unleashed forces of darkness. Three foolhardy men who had pursued their course so faithfully that it was inconceivable for them to flee now. The last acts must be played out whether howling night or calm day followed.

The first signs of Chaos were soon apparent as they saw the place where lush grassland once had been. It was now a yellow morass of molten rock that, though cool, rolled about with a purposeful air. The Nihrain horses, since they did not gallop on the plane of Earth, crossed it with comparative ease and here the Chaos Shield was first shown to work, for, as they passed, the yellow liquid rock changed and became grass again for a short time.

They met once a shambling thing that still had limbs of sorts and a mouth that could speak. From this poor creature they learned that Karlaak was no more, that it had been churned into broiling nothingness and where it had been the forces of Chaos, both human and supernatural, had set up their camp, their work done. The thing also spoke of something that was of particular interest to Elric. Rumour was that the Dragon Isle of Melniboné was the only place where Chaos had been unable to exert its influence.

'If, when our business is done, we can reach Melniboné,' Elric said to his friends as they rode on, 'we might be able to abide until such a time that the White Lords can help us. Also there are dragons slumbering in the caves – and these would be useful against Jagreen Lern if we could waken them.'

'What use is it to fight them now?' Dyvim Slorm said defeatedly. 'Jagreen Lern has won, Elric. We have not fulfilled our destiny. Our rôle is over and Chaos rules.'

'Does it? But we have yet to fight it and test its strength against ours. Let us decide then what the outcome has been.'

Dyvim Slorm looked dubious, but he said nothing.

And then, at last, they came to the Camp of Chaos.

No mortal nightmare could encompass such a terrible vision. The towering Ships of Hell dominated the place as they observed it from a distance, utterly horrified by the sight. Shooting flames of all colours seemed to flicker everywhere over the camp, fiends of all kinds mingled with the men, hell's evilly beautiful nobles conferred with the gaunt-faced kings who had allied themselves to Jagreen Lern and perhaps now regretted it. Every so often the ground heaved and erupted and any human beings unfortunate enough to be in the area were either engulfed and totally transformed, or else had their bodies warped in indescribable ways. The noise was a dreadful blending of human voices and roaring Chaos sounds, devils' wailing laughter and, quite often, the tortured shout of a human soul who had perhaps regretted his choice of loyalty and now suffered madness. The stench was disgusting, of corruption, of blood and of evil. The Ships of Hell moved slowly about through the horde which stretched for miles, dotted with great pavilions of kings, their silk banners fluttering; hollow pride compared to the might of Chaos. Many of the human beings could scarcely be told from the Chaos creatures, their forms were so changed under the influence of Chaos.

Elric muttered to his friends as they sat in their saddles watching. 'It is obvious that the warping influence of Chaos grows even stronger among the human ranks. This will continue until even Jagreen Lern and the traitor kings will lose every semblance of humanity and become just a fraction of the churning stuff of Chaos. This will mean the end of the human race – mankind will pass away for ever, taken into the maw of Chaos.

'You look upon the last of mankind, my friends, save for ourselves. Soon it will be indistinguishable from anything else. All this unstable Earth is beneath the heel of the Lords of Chaos, and they are gradually absorbing it into their realm, into their own plane. They will first remould and then steal the Earth altogether; it will become just another lump of clay for them to mould into whatever grotesque shapes take their fancy.'

'And we seek to stop *that*,' Moonglum said hopelessly. 'We cannot, Elric!'

'We must continue to strive, until we are conquered. I remember that Straasha the Sea-King said if Pyaray, commander of the Chaos fleet, is slain, the ships themselves will no longer be able to exist. I have a mind to put that to the test. Also, I have not forgotten that my wife may be prisoner aboard his ship, or that Jagreen Lern is there. I have three good reasons for venturing there.'

'No, Elric! It would be more than suicide!'

'I do not ask you to accompany me.'

'If you go, we shall come, but I like it not.'

'If one man cannot succeed, neither can three. I shall go alone. Wait for me. If I do not return, then try to get to Melniboné.'

'Elric –!' Moonglum cried and then watched as, his Chaos Shield pulsing, Elric spurred the Nihrain steed towards the camp.

Protected against the influence of Chaos, Elric was sighted by a detachment of warriors as he neared the ship which was his destination. They recognised him and rode towards him, shouting.

He laughed in their faces. 'Just the fodder my blade needs before we banquet on yonder ship!' he cried as he slashed off the first man's head as if it were a buttercup. Secure behind his great round shield, he hewed about him with a will. Since Stormbringer had slain the demons imprisoned in the elder trees, the vitality which the sword passed into him was almost without limit, yet every soul that Elric stole from Jagreen Lern's warriors was another fraction of vengeance reaped. Against men, he was invincible. He split one heavily armoured warrior from head to crutch, sheared through the saddle and smashed the horse's backbone apart.

Then the remaining warriors dropped back suddenly and Elric

felt his body tingle with peculiar sensations, knew he was in the area of influence exerted by the Chaos ship and knew also that he was being protected against them by his shield. He was now partially out of his own earthly plane and existed between his world and the world of Chaos. He dismounted from his Nihrain steed and ordered it to wait for him. There were ropes trailing from the huge sides of the foremost ship and Elric saw with horror that other figures were climbing up them – and he recognised several as men he had known in Karlaak. But before he could reach the ship he was surrounded by all manner of horrifying shapes, things that flew at him cawing, with heads of men and beaks of birds, things that writhed from out of the seething ground and struck at him, things that groped and mewled and screamed, attempting to pull him down to join them. Frantically, he swung Stormbringer this way and that, cutting his way through the Chaos creatures, protected from becoming like them by the pulsing Chaos Shield on his left arm, until at length he joined the ghastly ranks of the dead and swarmed with them up the sides of the great, gleaming ship, grateful at least for the cover they gave him.

He reached the ship's rail and hauled himself over it, spitting bile from his throat as he entered a peculiar region of darkness and came to the first of a series of decks that rose like steps to the topmost one where he could see the occupants – a manlike figure and something like a huge, blood-red octopus. The first was probably Jagreen Lern, the second was obviously Pyaray, for this, Elric knew, was the guise he took when he manifested himself on Earth.

Contrasting with the ships seen from the distance, once aboard Elric became conscious of the dark, shadowy nature of the light, filled with moving threads, a network of dark reds, blues, yellows, greens and purples which, as he moved through it, gave and reformed itself behind him. He was constantly being blundered against by the moving cadavers and he made a point of not looking at their faces too closely, for he had already recognised several of the sea-raiders whom he had abandoned, years before, during the escape from Imrryr.

Slowly he was gaining the top deck, noting that so far both Jagreen Lern and Lord Pyaray seemed unaware of his presence. Presumably they considered themselves entirely free from any kind of attack now they had conquered all the known world. He grinned maliciously to himself as he continued climbing, gripping the shield tightly, knowing that if once he lost hold of it, his body would become transformed either into some shambling alien shape or else flow away altogether to become absorbed into the Chaos-stuff. By now Elric had forgotten everything but his main object, which was to destroy Lord Pyaray's earthly manifestation. He must gain the topmost deck and deal first with the Lord of Chaos. Then he would kill Jagreen Lern and, if she were really there, rescue Zarozinia and bear her to safety.

Up the dark decks, through the nets of strange colours, Elric went, his milk-white hair flowing in contrast to the moody darkness around him. As he came to the last deck but one, he felt a gentle touch on his shoulder and, looking in that direction, saw with heart-lurching horror that one of Pyaray's blood-red tentacles had found him. He stumbled back, putting up his shield.

The tentacle tip touched the shield and rebounded suddenly, the entire tentacle shrivelling. From above, where the Chaos Lord's main bulk was, there came a terrible screaming and roaring.

'What's this? What's this? What's this?'

Elric shouted in impudent triumph at seeing his shield work with such effect: ''Tis Elric of Melniboné, great lord. Come to destroy thee!'

Another tentacle dropped towards him, seeking to curl around the shield and seize him. Then another followed it and another. Elric hacked at one, severed its sensitive tip, saw another touch the shield, recoil and shrivel and then avoided the third in order to run round the deck and ascend, as swiftly as he could, the ladder leading to the deck above. Here he saw Jagreen Lern, his eyes wide. The Theocrat was clad in his familiar scarlet armour. On his arm was his buckler and in the same hand an axe, while his right hand held a broadsword. He glanced down at these weapons, obviously aware of their inadequacy against Elric's.

'You later, Theocrat,' Elric promised.

'You're a fool, Elric! You're doomed now, whatever you do!'

It was probably true, but he did not care. 'Aside, upstart,' he said as, shield up, he moved warily towards the many-tentacled Lord of Chaos.

'You are the killer of many cousins of mine, Elric,' the creature said in a low, whispering voice. 'And you've banished several Dukes of Chaos to their own domain so that they cannot reach Earth again. For that you must pay. I at least do not underestimate you, as, in likelihood, they did.' A tentacle reared above him and tried to come down from over the shield's rim and seize his throat. He took a step backwards and blocked the attempt with the shield.

Then a whole web of tentacles began to come from all sides, each one curling around the shield, knowing its touch to be death. He skipped aside, avoiding them with difficulty, slicing about him with Stormbringer. As he fought, he remembered Straasha's last message: *Strike for the crystal atop his head. There is his life and his soul.* Elric saw the blue, radiating crystal which he had originally taken to be one of Lord Pyaray's several eyes. He moved in towards the roots of the tentacles, leaving his back poorly protected, but there was nothing else for it. As he did so, a huge maw gaped in the thing's head and tentacles began to draw him towards it. He extended his shield towards the maw until it touched the lips. Yellow, jellylike stuff spurted from the mouth as the Lord of Chaos screamed in pain. He got his foot on one tentacle stump and clambered up the slippery hide of the Chaos Lord, shuddering beneath his feet. Every time his shield touched Pyaray, it created some sort of wound so that the Chaos Lord began to thresh about dreadfully. Then he stood unsteadily over the glowing soul-crystal. For an instant he paused, then plunged Stormbringer point first into the crystal!

There came a mighty throbbing from the heart of the entity's body. It gave vent to a monstrous shriek and then Elric yelled as Stormbringer took the soul of a Lord of Hell and channelled this surging vitality through to him. It was too much. He was hurled backwards. He lost his footing on the slippery back, stumbled off the deck itself and fell to another, nearly a hundred feet below. He landed with bone-cracking force, but, thanks to the stolen vitality, was completely unhurt. He got up, ready to clamber again towards Jagreen Lern. The Theocrat's anxious face peered down at him and he yelled: 'You'll find a present for you in yonder cabin, Elric!'

Torn between pursuing the Theocrat and investigating the cabin, Elric turned and opened the door. From inside came a dreadful sobbing.

'Zarozinia!' He ducked into the dark place and there he saw her.

Chaos had warped her. Only her head, the same beautiful head was left.

But her lovely body was dreadfully changed. Now it resembled the body of a huge white worm.

'Did Jagreen Lern do this?'

'He and his ally.'

'How have you retained your sanity?'

'By waiting for you. I have something to do that required me to keep my wits.' The worm-body undulated towards him.

'No – stand back,' he cried, disgusted against his will. He could hardly bear to look at her. But she did not heed him. The worm-body threshed forward and impaled itself on his sword. 'There,' cried her head. 'Take my soul into you, Elric, for I am useless to myself and you now! Carry my soul with yours and we shall be forever together.'

'No! You are wrong!' He tried to withdraw the thirsty rune-blade, but it was impossible. And, unlike any other sensation he had ever received from it, this was almost gentle. Warm and pleasant, bringing with it her youth and innocence, his wife's soul flowed into his and he wept. 'Oh, Zarozinia. Oh, my love!'

So she died, her soul blending with his as, years earlier, the soul of his first love, Cymoril, had been taken. He did not look at the grotesque worm-body, did not glance at her face, but walked slowly from the cabin.

Though he was moved to an aching sadness, his sword seemed to chuckle as he resheathed it.

As he left the cabin, it appeared to him that the deck was disintegrating, flowing apart. Straasha had been right. The destruction of Pyaray also meant the destruction of his ghastly fleet. Jagreen Lern had evidently made good his escape and Elric, in his present mood, did not feel ready to pursue him. He was only regretful that the fleet had achieved its purpose before he had been able to destroy it. Sword and shield both aiding him in their ways, he leapt from the ship to the pulsating ground and ran for the Nihrain steed which was rearing up and flailing with its hoofs to protect itself from a group of gibbering Chaos creatures. He drew his runesword again and drove into them, quickly dispersing them and mounting the Nihrain stallion. Then, the tears still flowing down his white face, he rode wildly from the Camp of Chaos, leaving the Ships of Hell breaking apart behind him. At least these would threaten the world no more and a blow had been struck against Chaos. Now only the horde itself remained to be dealt with – and the dealing would not be so easy.

Fighting off the warped things which clawed at him, he finally rejoined his friends, said nothing to them but wheeled his horse to lead the way over the shaking earth towards Melniboné, where the last stand against Chaos could be prepared, the last battle fought and his destiny completed.

And in his dark, tormented mind he seemed to hear Zarozinia's youthful voice whispering comfort as, still sobbing, he rode away from that Camp of Chaos.

Book Four

Doomed Lord's Passing

For the mind of Man alone is free to explore the lofty vastness of the cosmic infinite, to transcend ordinary consciousness, to roam the secret corridors of the brain where past and future melt into one... And universe and individual are linked, the one mirrored in the other, and each contains the other.

– The Chronicle of the Black Sword

Chapter One

THE DREAMING CITY no longer dreamed in splendour. The tattered towers of Imrryr were blackened husks, tumbled rags of masonry standing sharp and dark against a sullen sky. Once, Elric's vengeance had brought fire to the city, and the fire had brought ruin.

Streaks of cloud, like sooty smoke, whispered across the pulsing sun so that the shouting, red-stained waters beyond Imrryr were soiled by shadow, and they seemed to become quieter as if hushed by the black scars that rode across their ominous turbulence.

Upon a confusion of fallen masonry, a man stood watching the waves. A tall man, broad-shouldered, slender at hip, a man with slanting brows, pointed, lobeless ears, high cheekbones and crimson, moody eyes in a dead white ascetic face. He was dressed in black quilted doublet and heavy cloak, both high-collared, emphasising the pallor of his albino skin. The wind, erratic and warm, played with his cloak, fingered it and passed mindlessly on to howl through the broken towers.

Elric heard the howling and his memory was filled by the sweet, the malicious and melancholy melodies of old Melniboné. He remembered, too, the other music his ancestors had created when they had elegantly tortured their slaves, choosing them for the pitch of their screams and forming them into the instruments of unholy symphonies. Lost in this nostalgia for a while, he found something close to forgetfulness and he wished that he had never doubted the code of Melniboné, wished that he had accepted it without question and thus left his mind unsundered. Bitterly, he smiled.

A figure appeared below him and climbed the tumbled stones to stand by his side. He was a small, red-haired man with a wide mouth and eyes that had once been bright and amused.

'You look to the East, Elric,' Moonglum murmured. 'You look back towards something irremediable.'

Elric put his long-fingered hand on his friend's shoulder. 'Where else is there to look, Moonglum, when the world lies beneath the heel of Chaos? What would you have me do? Look forward to days of hope and laughter, to an old age lived in peace, with children playing around my feet?' He laughed softly. It was not a laugh that Moonglum liked to hear.

'Sepiriz spoke of help from the White Lords. It must come soon. We must wait patiently.' Moonglum turned to squint into the glowering and motionless sun and then, his face set in an introspective look, cast his eyes down to the rubble on which he stood.

Elric was silent for a moment, watching the waves. Then he shrugged. 'Why complain? It does me no good. I cannot act on my own volition. Whatever fate is before me cannot be changed. I pray that the men who follow us will make use of their ability to control their own destinies. I have no such ability.' He touched his jawbone with his fingers and then looked at the hand, noting nails, knuckles, muscles and veins standing out on the pale skin. He ran this hand through the silky strands of his white hair, drew a long breath and let it out in a sigh. 'Logic! The world cries for logic. I have none, yet here I am, formed as a man with mind, heart and vitals, yet formed by a chance coming together of certain elements. The world needs logic. Yet all the logic in the world is worth as much as one lucky guess. Men take pains to weave a web of careful thoughts – yet others thoughtlessly weave a random pattern and achieve the same result. So much for the thoughts of the sage.'

'Ah,' Moonglum winked with attempted levity, 'thus speaks the wild adventurer, the cynic. But we are not all wild and cynical, Elric. Other men tread other paths – and reach other conclusions than yours.'

'I tread one that's preordained. Come, let's to the Dragon Caves and see what Dyvim Slorm has done to rouse our reptilian friends.'

They stumbled together down the ruins and walked the shattered canyons that had once been the lovely streets of Imrryr, out of the city and along a grassy track that wound through the gorse, disturbing a flock of large ravens that fled into the air, cawing, all save one, the king, who balanced himself on a bush, his cloak of ruffled feathers drawn up in dignity, his black eyes regarding them with wary contempt.

Down through sharp rocks to the gaping entrance of the Dragon Caves, down the steep steps into torchlit darkness with its damp warmth and smell of scaly reptilian bodies. Into the first cave where the great recumbent forms of the sleeping dragons lay, their folded leathery wings rising into the shadows, their green and black scales glowing faintly, their clawed feet folded and their slender snouts curled back, even in sleep, to display the long, ivory teeth that seemed like so many white stalactites. Their dilating red nostrils groaned in torpid slumber. The smell of their hides and their breath was unmistakeable, rousing in Moonglum some memory inherited from his ancestors, some shadowy impression of a time when these dragons and their masters swept across a world they ruled, their inflammable venom dripping from their fangs and heedlessly setting fire to the countryside across which they flew. Elric, used to it, hardly noticed the smell, but passed on through the first cave and the second until he found Dyvim Slorm, striding about with a torch in one hand and a scroll in the other, swearing to himself.

He looked up as he heard their booted feet approach. He spread out his arms and shouted, his voice echoing through the caverns, 'Nothing! Not a stir, not an eyelid flickering! There is no way of rousing them. They'll not wake until they have slept their necessary number of years. Oh, that we had not used them on the last two occasions, for we have greater need of them today!'

'Neither you nor I had the knowledge we have now. Regret is useless since it can achieve nothing.' Elric stared around him at the huge, shadowy forms. Here, slightly apart from the rest, lay the leader-dragon, one he recognised and felt affection for: Flamefang, the eldest, who was five thousand years old and still young for a dragon. But Flamefang, like the rest, slept on.

He went up to the beast and stroked its metal-like scales, ran his hand down the ivory smoothness of its great front fangs, felt its warm breath on his body and smiled. Beside him, on his hip, he heard Stormbringer murmur. He patted the blade. 'Here's one soul you cannot have. The dragons are indestructible. They will survive, even though all the world collapses into nothing.'

Dyvim Slorm said from another part of the cavern: 'I can't think of further action to take for the meantime, Elric. Let's go back to the Tower of D'a'rputna and refresh ourselves.'

Elric nodded assent and, together, the three men returned through the caverns and ascended the steps into the sunlight.

'So,' Dyvim Slorm remarked, 'still no nightfall. The sun has remained in that position for thirteen days, ever since we left the Camp of Chaos and made our perilous way to Melniboné. How much power must Chaos wield if it can stop the sun in its course?'

'Chaos might not have done this for all we know,' Moonglum pointed out. 'Though it's likely, of course, that it did. Time has stopped. Time waits. But waits for what? More confusion, further disorder? Or the influence of the Great Balance which will restore order and take vengeance against those forces who have gone against its will? Or does time wait for us – three mortal men adrift, cut off from what is happening to all other men, waiting on time as it waits on us?'

'Perhaps the sun waits on us,' Elric agreed. 'For is it not our destiny to prepare the world for its fresh course? It makes me feel a little more than a mere pawn if that's the case. What if we do nothing? Will the sun remain where it is for ever?'

They paused in their progress for a moment and stood staring up at the pulsating red disc which flooded the streets with scarlet light, at the black clouds which fled across the sky before it. Where were the clouds going? Where did they come from? They seemed instilled with purpose. It was possible that they were not even clouds at all, but spirits of Chaos bent on dark errands.

Elric grunted to himself, aware of the uselessness of such speculation. He led the way back to the Tower of D'a'rputna where years before he had sought his love, his cousin Cymoril, and later lost her to the ravening thirst of the blade by his side.

The tower had survived the flames, though the colours that had once adorned it were blackened by fire. Here he left his friends and went to his own room to fling himself, fully clad, upon the soft Melnibonéan bed and, almost immediately, fall asleep.

Chapter Two

E LRIC SLEPT AND Elric dreamed and, though he was aware of the unreality of his visions, his attempts to rouse himself to wakefulness were entirely futile. Soon he ceased trying and merely let his dream form itself and draw him into its bright landscapes...

He saw Imrryr as it had been many centuries ago. Imrryr, the same city he had known before he led the raid on it and caused its destruction. The same, yet with a different, brighter appearance as if it were newly built. As well, the colours of the surrounding countryside were richer, the sun darker orange, the sky deep blue and sultry. Since then, he realised, the very tints of the world had faded with the planet's ageing...

People and beasts moved in the shining streets; tall, eldritch Melnibonéans, men and women walking with grace, like proud tigers; hard-faced slaves with hopeless, stoic eyes, long-legged horses of a type now extinct, small mastodons drawing gaudy cars. Clearly on the breeze came the mysterious scents of the place, the muted sounds of activity – all hushed, for the Melnibonéans hated noise as much as they loved harmony. Heavy silk banners flapped from the scintillating towers of bluestone, jade, ivory, crystal and polished red granite. And Elric moved in his sleep and ached to be there amongst his own ancestors, the golden folk who had dominated the old world.

Monstrous galleys passed through the water-maze which led to Imrryr's inner harbour, bringing the best of the world's booty, tax gathered from all parts of the Bright Empire. And across the azure sky lazy dragons flapped their way towards the caves where thousands of the beasts were stabled, unlike the present where scarcely a hundred remained. In the tallest tower – the Tower of B'aal'nezbett, the Tower of Kings – his ancestors had studied sorcerous lore, conducted their malicious experiments, indulged their sensuous appetites – not decadently as men of the Young Kingdoms might behave, but according to their native instincts.

Elric knew that he looked upon the ghost of a now-dead city. And he seemed to pass beyond the tower's gleaming walls and see his emperor-ancestors indulging in drug-sharpened conversation, lazily sadistic, sporting with demon-women, torturing, investigating the peculiar metabolism and psychology of the enslaved races, delving into mystic lore, absorbing a knowledge which few men of the later period could experience without falling insane.

But it was clear that this must either be a dream or vision of a netherworld which the dead of all ages inhabited, for here were emperors of many different generations. Elric knew them from their portraits: Black-ringleted Rondar IV, twelfth emperor; sharp-eyed, imperious Elric I, eightieth emperor; horror-burdened Kahan VII, three-hundred-and-twenty-ninth emperor. A dozen or more of the mightiest and wisest of his four-hundred-and-twenty-seven ancestors, including Terhali, the Green Empress, who had ruled the Bright Empire from the year 8406 after its foundation until 9011. Her longevity and green-tinged skin and hair had marked her out. She had been a powerful sorceress, even by Melnibonéan standards. She was also reputed the daughter of a union between Emperor Iuntric X and a demon.

Elric, who saw all these as if from a darkened corner of the great main chamber, observed the shimmering door of black crystal open and a newcomer enter. He started and again attempted to wake himself, without success. The man was his father, Sadric the Eighty-Sixth, a tall man with heavy-lidded eyes and a misery in him. He passed through the throng as if it did not exist. He walked directly towards Elric and stopped two paces from him. He stood looking at him, the eyes peering upwards from beneath the heavy lids and prominent brow. He was a gaunt-faced man who had been disappointed in his albino son. He had a sharp, long nose, sweeping cheekbones and a slight stoop because of his unusual height. He fingered the thin, red velvet of his robe with his delicate, beringed hands. Then he spoke in a clear whisper which, Elric remembered, it had always been his habit to employ.

'My son, are you, too, dead? I thought I'd been here but a fleeting moment and yet I see you changed in years and with a burden on you that time and fate have placed there. How did you die? In reckless combat on some upstart's foreign blade? Or in this very tower in your ivory bed? And what of Imrryr now? Does she fare well or ill, dreaming in her decline of past splendour? The line continues, as it must – I will not ask you if that part of your trust was kept. A son, of course, born of Cymoril whom you loved, for which your cousin Yyrkoon hated you.'

'Father –'

The old man raised a hand that was almost transparent with age. 'There is another question I must ask of you. One that has troubled all who spend their immortality in the Forest of Souls, which surrounds this shade of a city. Some of us have noticed that the city itself fades at times and its colours dim, quivering as if about to vanish. Companions of ours have passed even beyond death and, perhaps, I shudder to contemplate it, into non-existence. Even here, in the timeless region of death, unprecedented changes manifest themselves, and those of us who've dared ask the question and also give its answer fear that some tumultuous event has taken place in the world of the living. Some event, so great is it, that even here we feel our souls' extinction threatened. A legend says that until the Dreaming City dies, we ghosts may inhabit its earlier glory. Is that the news you bear to us? Is this your message? For I note on clearer observation that your body lives still and this is merely your astral body, released for a while to wander the realms of the dead.'

'Father –' but already the vision was fading; already he was withdrawing back down the bellowing corridors of the cosmos, through planes of existence unknown to living men, away, away...

'Father!' he called, and his own voice echoed, but there was none there to make reply. And in some sense at least he was glad, for how could he answer the poor spirit and reveal to him the truth of his guesses, admit the crimes he himself was guilty of against his ancestral city, against the very blood of his forefathers? All was mist and groaning sorrow as his echoes boomed into his ears, seeming to take on their own independence and warp the word into weirder words: 'F-a-a-a-ath-e-er-r-r... A-a-a-a-a-v-a-a-a... A-a-a-a-h-a-a-a-a-a... R-a-a-a... D-a-ra-va-ar-a-a...!'

Still, though he strove with all his being, he could not rouse himself from slumber, but felt his spirit drawn through other regions of smoky indeterminacy, through patterns of colour beyond his earthly spectrum, beyond his mind's conception.

A huge face began to take form in the mist.

'Sepiriz!' Elric recognised the face of his mentor. But the black Nihrainian, disembodied, did not appear to hear him. 'Sepiriz – are *you* dead?'

The face faded, then reappeared almost at once upon the rest of the man's tall frame.

'Elric, I have discovered you at last, robed in your astral body, I see. Thank Fate, for I thought I had failed to summon you. Now we must make haste. A breach has been made in the defences of Chaos and we go to confer with the Lords of Law!'

'Where are we?'

'Nowhere as yet. We travel to the Higher Worlds. Come, hurry, I'll be your guide.'

Down, down, through pits of softest wool that engulfed and comforted, through canyons that were cut between blazing mountains of light which utterly dwarfed them, through caverns of infinite blackness wherein their bodies shone and Elric knew that the dark nothingness went away in all directions for ever.

And then they seemed to stand upon an horizonless plateau, perfectly flat with occasional green and blue geometric constructions rising from it. The iridescent air was alive with shimmering patterns of energy, weaving intricate shapes that seemed very formal. And there, too, were things in human form – things which had assumed such shape for the benefit of the men who now encountered them.

The White Lords of the Higher Worlds, enemies of Chaos, were marvellously beautiful, with bodies of such symmetry that they could not be earthly. Only Law could create such perfection and, Elric thought, such perfection defeated progress. That the twin forces complemented one another was now plainer than ever before, and for either to gain complete ascendancy over the other meant entropy or stagnation for the cosmos. Even though Law might dominate the Earth, Chaos *must* be present, and vice versa.

The Lords of Law were accoutred for war. They had made this apparent in their choice of Earthlike garb. Fine metals and silks – or their like on this plane – gleamed on their perfect bodies. Slender weapons were at their sides and their overpoweringly beautiful faces seemed to glow with purpose. The tallest stepped forward.

'So, Sepiriz, you have brought the one whose destiny it is to aid us. Greetings, Elric of Melniboné. Though spawn of Chaos you be, we have cause to welcome you. Do you recognise me? The one whom your earthly mythology calls Donblas the Justice Maker.'

Immobile, Elric said: 'I remember you, Lord Donblas. You are misnamed, I fear, for justice is nowhere present in the world.'

'You speak of your realm as if it were all realms.' Donblas smiled without rancour, though it appeared that he was unused to such impudence from a mortal. Elric remained insouciant. His ancestors had been opposed to Donblas and all his brethren, and it was still hard to consider the White Lord an ally. 'I see now how you have managed to defy our opponents,' Lord Donblas continued with approval. 'And I grant you that justice cannot be found on Earth at this time. But I am named the Justice *Maker* and have still the will to make it when conditions change on your plane.'

Elric did not look directly at Donblas, for the sight of his beauty was disturbing. 'Then let's to work, my lord, and change the world as soon we may. Let's bring the novelty of justice to our sobbing realm.'

'Haste, mortal, is impossible here!' It was another White Lord speaking, his pale yellow surcoat rippling over the clear steel of breastplate and greaves, the single Arrow of Law emblazoned on it.

'I'd thought the breach to Earth made,' Elric frowned. 'I'd thought this martial sight a sign that you prepared war against Chaos!'

'War *is* prepared – but not possible until the summons comes from your realm.'

'From us! Has not Earth screamed for your aid? Have we not worked sorceries and incantations to bring you to us? What further summons do you need?'

'The ordained one,' said Lord Donblas firmly.

'The ordained one? Gods! (You'll pardon me, my lords.) Is further work required of me, then?'

'One last great task, Elric,' said Sepiriz softly. 'As I have told you, Chaos blocks the attempts of the White Lords to gain access to our world. The Horn of Fate must be blown thrice before this business is fully terminated. The first blast will wake the Dragons of Imrryr, the second will allow the White Lords entrance to the earthly plane, the third –' he paused.

'Yes, the third?' Elric was impatient.

'The third will herald the death of our world!'

'Where lies this mighty horn?'

'In one of several realms,' said Sepiriz. 'A device of this kind cannot be made on our plane, therefore it has had to be constructed on a plane where logic rules over sorcery. You must journey there to locate the Horn of Fate.'

'And how can I accomplish such a journey?'

Once again Lord Donblas spoke levelly. 'We will give you the means. Equip yourself with sword and shield of Chaos, for they will be of some use to you, though not so powerful as in your world. Go you then to the highest point on the ruined Tower of B'aal'nezbett in Imrryr and step off into space. You will not fall – unless what little power we retain on Earth fails us.'

'Comforting words, my Lord Donblas. Very well, I shall do as you decree, to satisfy my own curiosity if naught else.'

Donblas shrugged. 'This is only one of many worlds – almost as much a shadow as your own – but you may not approve of it. You will notice its sharpness, its clearness of outline – that will indicate that time has exerted no real influence upon it, that its structure has not been mellowed by many events. However, let me wish you safe passage, mortal, for I like you – and I have cause to thank you, too. Though you be of Chaos, you have within you several of the qualities we of Law admire. Go now – return to your mortal body and prepare yourself for the venture ahead of you.'

Elric glanced at Sepiriz. The black Nihrainian stepped back three paces and disappeared into the gleaming air. Elric followed him.

Once again their astral bodies ranged the myriad planes of the supernatural universe, experiencing sensations unfamiliar to the physical mind, before, quite without warning, Elric felt suddenly heavy and opened his eyes to discover that he was in his own bed in the Tower of D'a'rputna. Through the faint light filtering between chinks in the heavy curtain thrown over the window slit, he saw the round Chaos Shield, its eight-arrowed symbol pulsing slowly as if in concert with the sun, and beside it his unholy rune-blade, Stormbringer, lying against the wall as if already prepared for their journey into the might-be world of a possible future.

Then Elric slept again, more naturally, and was tormented, also, by more natural nightmares so that at last he screamed in his sleep and woke himself to find Moonglum standing by the bed. There was an expression of sad concern upon his narrow face. 'What is it, Elric? What ails your slumber?'

He shuddered. 'Nothing. Leave me, Moonglum, and I'll join you when I rise.'

'There must be reason for such shouting. Some prophetic dream, perhaps?'

'Aye, prophetic sure enough. I thought I saw a vision of my thin blood spilt by a hand that was my own. What import has this dream, what moment? Answer that, my friend, and, if you can't, then leave me to my morbid bed until these thoughts are gone.'

'Come, rouse yourself, Elric. Find forgetfulness in action. The candle of the fourteenth day burns low and Dyvim Slorm awaits your good advice.'

The albino pulled himself upright and swung his trembling legs over the bed. He felt enfeebled, bereft of energy, Moonglum helped him rise. 'Throw off this troubled mood and help us in our quandary,' he said with a hollow levity that made his fears more plain.

'Aye,' Elric straightened himself. 'Hand me my sword. I need its stolen strength.'

Unwillingly, Moonglum went to the wall where stood the evil weapon, took the runeblade by its scabbard and lifted it with difficulty, for it was an over-heavy sword. He shuddered as it seemed to titter faintly at him, and he presented it hilt first to his friend. Gratefully, Elric seized it, was about to pull it from the sheath when he paused. 'Best leave the room before I free the blade.'

Moonglum understood at once and left, not anxious to trust his life to the whim of the hellsword – or his friend.

When he was gone, Elric unsheathed the great sword and at once felt a faint tingle as its supernatural vitality began to stream into his nerves. Yet it was scarcely adequate and he knew that if the blade did not feed soon upon the lifestuff of another it would seek the souls of his two remaining friends. He replaced it thoughtfully in the scabbard, buckled it around his waist and strode to join Moonglum in the high-ceilinged corridor.

In silence, they proceeded down the twisting marble steps of the tower, until they reached the centre level where the main chamber was. Here, Dyvim Slorm was seated, a bottle of old Melnibonéan wine on the table before him, a large silver bowl in his hands. His sword Mournblade was on the table beside the bottle. They had found the store of wine in the secret cellars of the place, missed by the sea-reavers whom Elric had led upon Imrryr when he and his cousin had fought on opposite sides. The bowl was full of the congealed mixture of herbs, honey and barley which their ancestors had used to sustain themselves in times of need. Dyvim Slorm was brooding over it, but looked up when they came close and sat themselves on chairs opposite him. He smiled hopelessly.

'I fear, Elric, that I have done all I can to rouse our sleeping friends. No more is possible – and they still slumber.'

Elric remembered the details of his vision and, half-afraid that it had been merely a figment of his own imaginings, supplying the fantasy of hope where, in reality, no hope was, said: 'Forget the dragons, for a while at least. Last night I left my body, so I thought, and journeyed to places beyond the Earth, eventually to the White

Lords' plane where they told me how I might rouse the dragons by blowing upon a horn. I intend to follow their directions and seek that horn.'

Dyvim Slorm replaced his bowl upon the table. 'We'll accompany you, of course.'

'No need – and anyway impossible – I'll have to go alone. Wait for me until I return and if I do not – well, you must do what you decide, spending your remaining years imprisoned on this isle, or going to battle with Chaos.'

'I have the idea that time has stopped in truth and if we stay here we shall live on for ever and shall be forced to face the resulting boredom,' Moonglum put in. 'If you don't return, I for one will ride into the conquered realms to take a few of our enemies with me to limbo.'

'As you will,' Elric said. 'But wait for me until all your patience is ended, for I know not how long I'll be.'

He stood up and they seemed a trifle startled, as if they had not until then understood the import of his words.

'Fare you well, then, my friend,' said Moonglum.

'How well I fare depends on what I meet where I go,' Elric smiled. 'But thanks, Moonglum. Fare *you* well, good cousin, do not fret. Perhaps we'll wake the dragons yet!'

'Aye,' Dyvim Slorm said with a sudden resurgence of vitality. 'We shall, we shall! And their fiery venom will spread across the filth that Chaos brings, burning it clean! That day *must* come or I'm no prophet at all!'

Infected by this unexpected enthusiasm, Elric felt an increase of confidence, saluted his friends, smiled, and walked upright from the chamber, ascending the marble stairs to take the Chaos Shield from its place and go down to the gateway of the tower and pass through it, walking the jagged streets towards the magic-sundered ruin that had once been the scene of his dreadful vengeance and unwitting murder – the Tower of B'aal'nezbett.

Chapter Three

Now, as Elric stood before the broken entrance of the tower, his mind was beset with bursting thoughts which fled about his skull, made overtures to his convictions and threatened to send him hopelessly to rejoin his companions. But he fought them, forced them down, forgot them, clung to his remembrance of the White Lord's assurance and passed into the shadowed shell which still had the smell of burned wood and fabric about its blackened interior.

This tower, which had formed a funeral pyre for the murdered corpse of his first love Cymoril and his warped cousin, her brother Yyrkoon, had been gutted of innards. Only the stone stairway remained and that, he noted, peering into the gloom through which rays of sunlight slanted, had collapsed before it reached the roof.

He dare not think, for thought might rob him of action. Instead, he placed a foot upon the first stair and began to climb. As he did so, a faint sound entered his ears, or it may have been that it came from within his mind. However it reached his consciousness, it sounded like a faraway orchestra tuning itself. As he climbed higher, the sound mounted, rhythmic yet discordant until, by the time he reached the final step still left intact, it thundered through his skull, pounded through his body producing a sensation of dull pain.

He paused and stared downward to the tower's floor far below. Fears beset him. He wondered whether Lord Donblas had intended him to climb to the highest point he could easily reach, or the actual point which was still some twenty feet above him. He decided it was best to take the White Lord literally and swinging the great Chaos Shield upon his back, reached above him and got his fingers into a crack in the wall, which now sloped gently inwards. He heaved himself up, his legs dangling and his feet seeking a hold. He had always been troubled by heights and disliked the sensation that came to him as he glanced down to the rubble-laden floor, eighty feet below, but he continued to climb and the climbing was made easier by the fissures in the tower's wall. Though he expected to fall, he did not, and at last reached the unsafe roof, easing himself through a hole and onto the sloping exterior. Bit by bit he climbed until he was on the highest part of the tower. Then, fearing hesitation still, he stepped outwards, over the festering streets of Imrryr far below.

The discordant music stopped. A roaring note replaced it. Swirling waves of red and black rushed towards him and then he had burst through them to find he was standing on firm turf beneath a small, pale sun, the smell of grass in his nostrils. He noted that, whereas the ancient world seen in his dream had seemed more colourful than his own, this world, in turn, contained even less colour, though it seemed to be cleaner in its outlines, in sharper focus. And the breeze that blew against his face was colder. He began to walk over the grass towards a thick forest of low, solid foliage which lay ahead. He reached the perimeter of the forest but did not enter, circumnavigating it until he came to a stream that went off into the distance, away from the forest.

He noticed with curiosity that the bright clear water appeared not to move. It was frozen, though not by any natural process that he recognised. It had all the attributes of a summer stream – yet it did not flow. Feeling that this phenomenon contrasted strangely with the rest of the scenery, he swung the round Chaos Shield onto his arm, drew his throbbing sword and began to follow the stream.

The grass gave way to gorse and rocks with the occasional clump of waving ferns of a variety he didn't recognise. Ahead, he thought he heard the tinkle of water, but here the stream was still frozen. As he passed a rock taller than the rest, he heard a voice above him.

'Elric!'

He looked up.

There, on the rock, stood a young dwarf with a long, brown beard that reached below his waist. He clutched a spear, his only weapon, and he was clad in russet breeks and jerkin with a green cap on his head and no shoes on his broad, naked feet. He had eyes like quartz that were at once hard, harsh and humorous.

'That's my name,' Elric said quizzically. 'Yet how is it you know me?'

'I am not of this world myself – at least, not exactly. I have no existence in time as you know it, but move here and there in the shadow worlds that the gods make. It is my nature to do so. In return for allowing me to exist, the gods sometimes use me as a messenger. My name is Jermays the Crooked, as unfinished as these worlds themselves.' He clambered down the rock and stood looking up at Elric.

'What's your purpose here?' asked the albino.

'Methought you sought the Horn of Fate?'

'True. Know you where it lies?'

'Aye,' smiled the young dwarf sardonically. 'It's buried with the still-living corpse of a hero of this realm – a warrior they call Roland. Possibly yet another incarnation of the Champion Eternal.'

'An outlandish name.'

'No more than yours to other ears. Roland, save that his life was not so doom-beset, is your counterpart in his own realm. He met his death in a valley not far from here, trapped and betrayed by a fellow warrior. The horn was with him then and he blew it once before he died. Some say that the echoes still resound through the valley, and will resound for ever, though Roland perished many years ago. The horn's full purpose is unknown here – and was unknown even to Roland. It is called Olifant and, with his magic sword Durandana, was buried with him in the monstrous grave mound that you see yonder.'

The dwarf pointed into the distance and Elric saw that he indicated something he had earlier taken to be a large hillock.

'And what must I do to gain this horn?' he asked.

The dwarf grinned with a hint of malice in his voice. 'You must match that bodkin there 'gainst Roland's Durandana. His was consecrated by the Forces of Light whereas yours was forged by the Forces of Darkness. It should be an interesting conflict.'

'You say he's dead – then how can he fight me?'

'He wears the horn by a thong about his neck. If you attempt to remove it, he will defend his ownership, waking from the deathless sleep that seems to be the lot of most heroes in this world.'

Elric smiled. 'It seems to me they must be short of heroes if they have to preserve them in that manner.'

'Perhaps,' the dwarf answered carelessly, 'for there are a dozen or more who lie sleeping somewhere in this land alone. They are supposed to awaken only when a desperate need arises, yet I've known unpleasant things to happen and still they have slept. It could be they await the end of their world, which the gods may destroy if it proves unsuitable, in which case they will fight to prevent such a happening. It is merely a poorly conceived theory of my own and of little weight. Perhaps the legends arise from some dim knowledge of the fate of the Champion Eternal.'

The dwarf bobbed a cynical bow and, hefting his spear, saluted Elric. 'Farewell, Elric of Melniboné. When you wish to return I will be here to lead you – and return you must, whether alive or dead, for, as you are probably aware, your very presence, your physical appearance itself, contradicts this environment. Only one thing fits here...'

'What's that?'

'Your sword.'

'My sword! Strange, I should have thought that would be the last thing.' He shook a growing idea out of his mind. He did not have time to speculate. 'I've no liking to be here,' he commented as the dwarf clambered over the rocks. He glanced in the direction of the great burial mound and began to advance towards it. Beside him he saw that the stream was moving naturally and he had the impression that though Law influenced this world, it was to some extent still forced to deal with the disrupting influence of Chaos.

The grave barrow, he could now see, was fenced about with giant slabs of unadorned stone. Beyond the stones were olive trees that had dull jewels hanging from their branches, and beyond them, through the leafy apertures, Elric saw a tall, curved entrance blocked by gates of brass embossed with gold.

'Though strong, Stormbringer,' he said to his sword, 'I wonder if you'll be strong enough to war in this world as well as giving my body vitality. Let's test you.'

He advanced to the gate and drawing back his arm delivered a mighty blow upon it with the runesword. The metal rang and a dent appeared. Again he struck, this time holding the sword with both hands, but then a voice cried from his right.

'What demon would disturb dead Roland's rest?'

'Who speaks the language of Melniboné?' Elric retorted boldly.

'I speak the language of demons, for I perceive that is what you are. I know of no Mulnebooney and am well-versed in the ancient mysteries.'

'A proud boast,' said Elric, who had not yet seen the speaker. She emerged, then, from around the barrow, and stood staring at him from out of her glowing green eyes. She had a long, beautiful face and was almost as pale as himself, though her hair was jet-black. 'What's your name?' he asked. 'And are you a native of this world?'

'I am named Vivian, an enchantress, but earthly enough. Your Master knows the name of Vivian who once loved Roland, though he was too upright to indulge her, for she is immortal and a witch.' She laughed good-humouredly. 'Therefore I am familiar with demons of your like and do not fear you. Aroint thee! Aroint thee – or shall I call Bishop Turpin to exorcise thee?'

'Some of your words,' said Elric courteously, 'are unfamiliar and the speech of my folk much garbled. Are you some guardian of this hero's tomb?'

'Self-made guardian, aye. Now go!' She pointed towards the stone slabs.

'That is not possible. The corpse within has something of value to me. The Horn of Fate we call it, but you know it by another name.'

'Olifant! But that's a blessed instrument. No demon would dare touch it. Even I...'

'I am no demon. I'm sufficiently human, I swear. Now stand aside. This cursed door resists my efforts too well.'

'Aye,' she said thoughtfully. 'You could be a man – though an unlikely one. But the white face and hair, the red eyes, the tongue you speak...'

'Sorcerer I be, but no demon. Please – stand aside.'

She looked carefully into his face and her look disturbed him. He took her by her shoulder. She felt real enough, yet somehow she had little real *presence*. It was as if she were far away rather than close to him. They stared at one another, both curious, both troubled. He whispered: 'What knowledge could you have of my language? Is this world a dream of mine or of the gods? It seems scarcely tangible. Why?'

She heard him. 'Say you so of us? What of your ghostly self? You seem an apparition from the dead past!'

'From the past! Aha – and *you* are of the future, as yet unformed. Perhaps that brings us to a conclusion?'

She did not pursue the topic but said suddenly: 'Stranger, you will never break this door down. If you can touch Olifant, that speaks of you as mortal, despite your appearance. You must need the horn for an important task.'

Elric smiled. 'Aye – for if I do not take it back whence it came, you will never exist!'

She frowned. 'Hints! Hints! I feel close to a discovery yet cannot grasp why, and that's unusual for Vivian. Here –' she took a big key from her gown and offered it to him – 'this is the key to open Roland's tomb. It is the only one. I had to kill to get it, but oftimes I venture into the gloom of his grave to stare down at his face and pine that I might revive him and keep him living for ever on my island home. Take the horn! Rouse him – and when he has slain you, he will come to me and my warmth, my offer of ever-lasting life, rather than lie in that cold place again. Go – be slain by Roland!'

He took the key.

'Thanks, Lady Vivian. If it were possible to convince one who in truth did not yet exist, I would tell you that Roland's slaying of me would be worse for you than if I am successful.'

He put the large key in the lock and it turned easily. The doors swung open and he saw that a long, low-roofed corridor twisted before him. Unhesitatingly, he advanced down it towards a flicker-ing light that he could see through the cold and misty gloom. Yet, as he walked, it was as if he glided in a dream less real than that he had experienced the previous night. Now he entered the funeral chamber, illuminated by tall candles surrounding the bier of a man who lay upon it dressed in armour of a crude and unfamiliar design, a huge broadsword, almost as large as Stormbringer gripped to his chest and, upon the hilt, attached to his neck by a silver chain – the Horn of Fate, Olifant!

The man's face, seen in the candlelight, was strange; old and yet with a youthful appearance, the brow smooth and the features unlined.

Elric took Stormbringer in his left hand and reached out to grasp the horn. He made no attempt at caution, but wrenched it off Roland's neck.

A great roar came from the hero's throat. Immediately he had raised himself to a sitting position, the sword shifting into his two hands, his legs swinging off the bier. His eyes widened as he saw Elric with the horn in his hands, and he jumped at the albino, the sword Durandana whistling downwards towards Elric's head. He raised the shield and blocked the blow, slipped the horn into his jerkin and, backing away, returned Stormbringer to his right hand. Roland was now shouting something in a language com-pletely unfamiliar to Elric. He did not bother trying to understand, since the angry tones were sufficient to tell him the knight was not suggesting a peaceful negotiation. He continued defending himself without once carrying the offensive to Roland, backing inch by inch down the long tunnel towards the barrow's mouth. Every time Durandana struck the Chaos Shield, both sword and shield gave out wild notes of great intensity. Implacably the hero continued to press Elric backwards, his broadsword whirling and striking the shield, sometimes the blade, with fantastic strength. Then they had broken into daylight and Roland seemed moment-arily blinded. Elric glimpsed Vivian watching them eagerly for it appeared Roland was winning.

However, in daylight and with no chance of avoiding the angered knight, Elric retaliated with all the energy he had been saving until this moment. Shield high, sword swinging, he now took the attack, surprising Roland who was evidently unused to this behaviour on the part of an opponent. Stormbringer snarled as it bit into Roland's poorly forged armour of iron, riveted with big unsightly nails, painted on the front with a dull red cross that was a scarcely adequate insignia for so famous a hero. But there was no mistaking Durandana's powers for, though seemingly as crudely forged as the armour, it did not lose its edge and threat-ened to bite through the Chaos Shield with every stroke. Elric's left arm was numb from the blows and his right arm ached. Lord Donblas had not lied to him when he had said that the strength of his weapons would be diminished on this world.

Roland paused, shouting something, but Elric did not heed him, seized his opportunity and rushed in to crush his shield against Roland's body. The knight reeled and staggered, his sword giving off a keening note. Elric struck at a gap between Roland's helmet and gorget. The head sprang off the shoulders and rolled grotesquely away, but no blood pumped from the jugular. The eyes of the head remained open, staring at Elric.

Vivian screamed and shouted something in the same language which Roland had used. Elric stepped back, his face grim.

'Oh, his legend, his legend!' she cried. 'The only hope the

people have is that Roland will some day ride once more to their aid. Now you have slain him! Fiend!'

'Possessed I may be,' he said quietly as she sobbed by the headless corpse, 'but I was ordained by the gods to do this work. I'll take my leave of your drab world, now.'

'Have you no sorrow for the crime you've done?'

'None, madam, for this is only one of many such acts which, I'm told, serve some greater purpose. That I sometimes doubt the truth of this consolation need not concern you. Know you this, though, I have been told that it is the fate of such as your Roland and myself never to die – always to be reborn. Farewell.'

And he walked away from there; passed through the olive grove and the tall stones, the Horn of Fate cold against his heart.

He followed the river towards the high rock where he saw a small figure poised and, when he reached it, looked up at the young dwarf Jermays the Crooked, took the horn from his jerkin and displayed it.

Jermays chuckled. 'So Roland is dead, and you, Elric, have left a fragment of a legend in this world, if it survives. Well, shall I escort you back to your own place?'

'Aye, and hurry.'

Jermays skipped down the rocks and stood beside the tall albino. 'Hmm,' he mused, 'that horn could prove troublesome to us. Best replace it in your jerkin and keep it covered by your shield.'

Elric obeyed the dwarf and followed him down to the banks of the strangely frozen river. It looked as if it should have been moving, but it evidently was not. Jermays leapt into it and, incredibly, began to sink. 'Quickly! Follow!'

Elric stepped in after him and for a moment stood on the frozen water before he, also, began to sink.

Though the stream was shallow, they continued to sink until all similarity to water was gone and they were passing down into rich darkness that became warm and heavy-scented. Jermays pulled at his sleeve. 'This way!' And they shot off at right angles, darting from side to side, up and down, through a maze that apparently only Jermays could see. Against his chest, the horn seemed to heave and he pressed his shield to it. Then he blinked as he found himself in the light again, staring at the great red sun throbbing in the dark blue sky. His feet were on something solid. He looked and saw that it was the Tower of B'aal'nezbett. For a while longer the horn heaved as if alive, like a trapped bird but, after some moments, it became quiescent.

Elric lowered himself to the roof and began to edge down it until he came to the gap through which he had passed earlier.

Then suddenly he looked up as he heard a noise in the sky. There, his feet planted on air, stood grinning Jermays the Crooked. 'I'll be passing on, for I like not this world at all.' He chuckled. 'It has been a pleasure to have had a part in this. Goodbye, Sir Champion. Remember me, the unfinished one, to the Lords of the Higher Worlds – and perhaps you could hint to them that the sooner they improve their memories or else their creative powers, the sooner I shall be happy.'

Elric said: 'Perhaps you'd best be content with your lot, Jermays. There are disadvantages to stability, too.'

Jermays shrugged and vanished.

Slowly, all but spent, Elric descended the fractured wall and, with great relief, reached the first stair to stumble down the rest and run back to the Tower of D'a'rputna with the news of his success.

Chapter Four

THE THREE THOUGHTFUL men left the city and went down to the Dragon Caves. On a new silver chain, the Horn of Fate was slung around Elric's neck. He was dressed in black leather, with his head unprotected save for a golden circlet that kept his hair from his eyes. Stormbringer scabbarded at his side, the Chaos Shield on his back, he led his companions into the grottoes, to come eventually to the slumbering bulk of Flamefang the Dragon Leader. His lungs seemed to have insufficient capacity as he drew air into them and grasped the horn. Then he glanced at his friends, who regarded him expectantly, straddled his legs slightly and blew with all his strength into the horn.

The note sounded, deep and sonorous, and as it reverberated through the caverns, he felt all his vitality draining from him. Weaker and weaker he became until he sank to his knees, the horn still at his lips, the note failing, his vision dimming, his limbs shaking, and then he sprawled face down on the rock, the horn clattering beside him.

Moonglum dashed towards him and gasped as he saw the bulk of the leading dragon stir and one huge, unblinking eye, as cold as the Northern wastes, stare at him.

Dyvim Slorm yelled jubilantly: 'Flamefang! Brother Flamefang, you wake!'

All about him he saw the other dragons stirring also, shaking their wings and straightening their slender necks, ruffling their horny crests. Moonglum felt smaller than usual as the dragons wakened. He began to feel nervous of the huge beasts, wondering how they would respond to the presence of one who was not a Dragon Master. Then he remembered the enervated albino and knelt beside Elric, touching his leathern-covered shoulder.

'Elric! D'you live?'

Elric groaned and tried to turn over onto his back. Moonglum helped him sit upright. 'I'm weak, Moonglum – so weak I can't rise. The horn took all my energy!'

'Draw your sword – it will supply what you need.'

Elric shook his head. 'I'll take your advice, though I doubt whether you're right this time. That hero I slew must have been soulless, or else his soul was well-protected, for I gained nothing from him.'

His hand fumbled towards his hip and grasped Stormbringer's hilt. With a tremendous effort, he drew it from the scabbard and felt a faint flowing leave it and enter him, but not enough to allow him any great exertion. He got up and staggered towards Flamefang. The monster recognised him and rustled its wings by way of welcome, its hard, solemn eyes seeming to warm slightly. As he moved round to pat its neck, he staggered and fell to one knee, rising with effort.

In earlier times there had been slaves to saddle the dragons but now they would have to saddle their beasts themselves. They went to the saddle-store and chose the *skeffla'an* they needed, for each was designed for an individual beast. Elric could scarcely bear the weight of Flamefang's elaborately carved saddle of membraneous wood, steel, jewels and precious metals. He was forced to drag it across the cavern floor. Not wishing to embarrass him with their glances, the other two ignored his impotent struggling and busied themselves with their own *skeffla'an*. The dragons must have understood that Moonglum was a friend, for they did not demur when he cautiously approached to dress his dragon with its high wooden saddle with silver stirrups and sheathed, lancelike goad from which was draped the pennant of a noble family of Melniboné, now all dead.

When they had finished saddling their own beasts, they went to help Elric who was half-falling with weariness, his back leaning

against Flamefang's scaly body. While they tied the girths, Dyvim Slorm said: 'Will you have strength enough to lead us?'

Elric sighed. 'Aye – enough, I think, for that. But I know I'll have none for the ensuing battle. There must be *some* means of gaining vitality.'

'What of the herbs you once used?'

'Those I had have lost their properties, and there are no fresh ones to be found now that Chaos has warped plant, rock and ocean with its dreadful stamp.'

Leaving Moonglum to finish Flamefang's saddling, Dyvim Slorm went away to return with a cup of liquid which he hoped would help revivify Elric. Elric drank it, gave the cup back to Dyvim Slorm and reached up to grasp the saddle-pommel, hauling himself into the saddle. 'Bring straps,' he ordered.

'Straps?' Dyvim Slorm frowned.

'Aye. If I'm not secured in my *skeffla'a*, I'll likely fall to the ground before we've flown a mile.'

So he sat in the tall saddle and gripped the goad which bore his blue, green and silver pennant, gripped it in his gauntleted hand and waited until they came with the straps and bound him firmly into place. He gave a slight smile and shook the dragon's halter. 'Forward, Flamefang, lead the way for your brothers and sisters.'

With folded wings and lowered head, the dragon began to walk its slithering way to the exit. Behind it, on two dragons almost as large, sat Dyvim Slorm and Moonglum, their faces grimly concerned, watchful for Elric's safety. As Flamefang moved with rolling gait through the series of caverns, its fellow beasts fell in behind it until all of them had reached the great mouth of the last cave which overlooked the threshing sea. The sun was still in its position overhead, scarlet and swollen, seeming to swell in rhythm with the movement of the sea. Voicing a shout that was half-hiss, half-yell, Elric slapped at Flamefang's neck with his goad.

'Up, Flamefang! Up for Melniboné and vengeance!'

As if sensing the strangeness of the world, Flamefang paused on the brink of the ledge, shaking his head and snorting to himself. Then, as he launched into the air, his wings began to beat, their fantastic spread flapping with slow grace but bearing the beast along with marvellous speed.

Up, up, beneath the swollen sun, up into the hot, turbulent air, up towards the East where the camps of hell were waiting. And in Flamefang's wake came its two dragon brothers, bearing Moonglum and Dyvim Slorm who had a horn of his own, the one used to direct the dragons. Ninety-five other dragons, males and females, darkened the deep blue sky, all green, red and gold, scales clashing and flashing, wings beating and, in concert, sounding like the throbbing of a million drums as they flew over the unclean waters with gaping jaws and cold, cold eyes.

Though beneath him now Elric saw with blurring eyes many colours of immense richness, they were all dark and changing constantly, shifting from one extreme of a dark spectrum to the other. It was not water down there now – it was a fluid composed of materials both natural and supernatural, real and abstract. Pain, longing, misery and laughter could be seen as tangible fragments of the tossing tide, passions and frustrations lay in it also, as well as stuff made of living flesh that bubbled on occasions to the surface.

In his weakened condition, the sight of the fluid sickened Elric and he turned his red eyes upwards and towards the East as the dragons moved swiftly on their course.

Soon they were flying across what had once been the mainland of the Eastern Continent, the major Vilmirian peninsula. But now it was bereft of its earlier qualities and huge columns of dark mist rose into the air so that they were forced to guide their reptilian steeds among them. Lava streamed, bubbling, on the faraway ground, disgusting shapes flitted over land and air, monstrous beasts and the occasional group of weird riders on skeletal horses who looked up when they heard the beat of the dragon wings and rode in frantic fear towards their camps.

The world seemed a corpse, given life in corruption by virtue of the vermin which fed upon it.

Of mankind nothing was left, save for the three mounted on the dragons.

Elric knew that Jagreen Lern and his human allies had long

since forsaken their humanity and could no longer claim kinship with the species their hordes had swept from the world. The leaders alone might retain their human shape, the Dark Lords don it, but their souls were warped just as the bodies of their followers had become warped into hell-shapes due to the transmuting influence of Chaos. All the dark powers of Chaos lay upon the world, yet deeper and deeper into its heart went the dragon flight, with Elric swaying in his saddle and only stopped from falling by the straps that bound his body. From the lands below there seemed to rise an aching shriek as tortured nature was defied and its components forced into alien forms.

Onward they sped, towards what had once been Karlaak by the Weeping Waste and which was now the Camp of Chaos. Then, from above, they heard a cawing yell and saw black shapes dropping down on them. Elric had not even strength to cry out, but weakly tapped Flamefang's neck and made the beast veer away from the danger. Moonglum and Dyvim Slorm followed his example and Dyvim Slorm sounded his horn, ordering the dragons not to engage the attackers, but some of the dragons in the rear were too late and were forced to turn and battle with the black phantoms.

Elric looked behind him and, for a few seconds, saw them outlined against the sky, rending things with the jaws of whales, locked in combat with the dragons that shot their flaming venom at them and tore at them with teeth and claws, wings flapping as they strove to hold their height, but then another wave of dark green mist spread across his field of vision and he did not see the fate that befell the dozen dragons.

Now Elric signalled Flamefang to fly low over a small army of riders fleeing through the tormented land, the eight-arrowed standard of Chaos flapping from their leader's encrusted lance. Down they went and loosed their venom, having the satisfaction of seeing the beasts and riders scream, burn and perish, their ashes absorbed into the shifting ground.

Here and there, now, they saw a gigantic castle, newly raised by sorcery, perhaps as a reward to some traitor king who had aided Jagreen Lern, perhaps as the keeps of the Captains of Chaos who, now that Chaos ruled, were establishing themselves on Earth. They swept down on them, released their venom and left them burning with unnatural fires, the gouting smoke blending with the shredding mist. And at last Elric saw the Camp of Chaos – a city but recently made in the same manner as the castles, the flaring Sign of Chaos hanging amber in the sky overheard. Yet he felt no elation, only despair that he was so weak he would not have the strength to meet his enemy Jagreen Lern in combat. What could he do? How could strength be found – for, even if he took no part in the fighting, he must have sufficient vitality to blow the horn a second time and summon the White Lords to Earth.

The city seemed peculiarly silent as if it waited or prepared for something. It had an ominous atmosphere and Elric, before Flamefang crossed the perimeter, made his dragon steed turn and circle.

Dyvim Slorm and Moonglum and the rest of the dragon flight followed his example and Dyvim Slorm called across the air to him. 'What now, Elric? I had not expected a *city* to be here so soon!'

'Neither had I. But look –' he pointed with a trembling hand he could hardly lift, 'there's Jagreen Lern's Merman standard. And there –' now he pointed to the left and right, 'the standards of a score of the Dukes of Hell! Yet I see no other human standards.'

Moonglum shouted: 'Those castles we destroyed. I suspect that Jagreen Lern has already divided up these sundered lands and given them to his hirelings. How can we tell how much time has really passed – time in which all this could have been brought about?'

'True,' Elric nodded, looking up at the still sun. He lurched forward in his saddle, half-swooning, pulled himself upright, breathing heavily. The Chaos Shield seemed like a huge weight on his arm, but he held it warily before him.

Then he acted on impulse and goaded Flamefang into speed so that the dragon rushed towards the city, diving down towards the castle of Jagreen Lern.

Nothing sought to stop him and he landed the beast among the turrets of the castle. Silence was dominant. He looked around, puzzled, but could see nothing save the towering buildings of dark stone that seemed to ooze beneath Flamefang's feet.

The straps stopped him from dismounting, but he saw enough to be sure the city was deserted. Where was the horde of hell? Where was Jagreen Lern?

Dyvim Slorm and Moonglum came to join him, while the rest of the dragons circled above. Claws scratched on rock, wings slashed the air and they settled, turning their mighty heads this way and that, ruffling their scales restlessly for, once aroused from their slumber, the dragons preferred the air to the land.

Dyvim Slorm stayed but long enough to mutter: 'I'll scout the city,' and then was flying away again, low amongst the castles until they heard him cry out and saw him swoop out of sight. There came a yell, but they could not see what caused it, a pause, and then Dyvim Slorm's dragon was flapping up again and they saw he had a writhing prisoner slung over the front of his saddle. He landed. The thing he had captured bore resemblance to a human being, but was misshapen and ugly with a jutting underlip, low forehead and no chin; huge, square, uneven teeth bristled in its mouth and its bare arms were covered in waving hairs.

'Where are your masters?' Dyvim Slorm demanded.

The thing seemed to possess no fear, but chuckled: 'They predicted your coming and, since the city limits movement, have assembled their armies on a plateau they have made five miles to the north-east.' It turned its dilated eyes to Elric. 'Jagreen Lern sent greetings and said he anticipated your foolish downfall.'

Elric shrugged.

Dyvim Slorm drew his own runeblade and hacked the creature down. It cackled as it died, for its sanity had fled with its fear. He shivered as the thing's soul-stuff blended with his own and passed extra energy to him. Then he cursed and looked at Elric with pain in his eyes.

'I acted in haste – I should have given him to you.'

Elric said nothing to this but whispered in his failing voice: 'Let's to their battlefield. Hurry!'

Up to join their flight they went again, into the rushing, populated air and towards the north-east.

It was with astonishment that they sighted Jagreen Lern's

horde, for they could not understand how it could have managed to regroup itself so swiftly. Every fiend and warrior on Earth seemed to have come to fight under the Theocrat's standard. It clung like a vile disease to the undulating plain. And around it, clouds grew darker, even though lightning, obviously of supernatural origin, blossomed and shouted, criss-crossing the plain.

Into this noisy agitation swept the dragon flight and they recognised the force commanded by Jagreen Lern himself for his banner flew above it. Other divisions were commanded by Dukes of Hell – Malohin, Zhortra, Xiombarg and others. Also Elric noted the three oldest and wisest Lords of Chaos, dwarfing the rest. Chardros the Reaper with his great head and his curving scythe, Mabelode the Faceless with his face always in shadow no matter which way you looked at it, and Slortar the Old, slim and beautiful, reputed the oldest of the gods. This was a force which a thousand powerful sorcerers would find it hard to defend against, and the thought of attacking them seemed folly.

Elric did not bother to consider this for he had embarked on his plan and was committed to carrying it through even though, in his present condition, he was bound to destroy himself if he continued.

They had the advantage of attacking from the air, but this would only be of value while the dragons' venom lasted. When it gave out, they must go in closer. At that moment Elric would need much energy – and he had none.

Down swept the dragons, shooting their incendiary venom into the ranks of Chaos.

Normally, no army could stand against such an attack but, protected by sorcery, Chaos was able to turn much of the fiery venom aside. The venom seemed to spread against an invisible shield and dissipate. Some of it struck its target, however, and hundreds of warriors were engulfed in flame and died blazing.

Again and again the dragons rose and dived upon their enemies, Elric swaying almost unconscious in his saddle, his awareness of what was going on diminishing with every attack.

His dimming vision was further encumbered by the stinking smoke that had begun to rise off the battlefield. From the horde, huge lances were rising with seeming slowness, lances of Chaos like streaks of amber lightning striking at the dragons so that the beasts hit bellowed and hurtled dead to the ground. Closer and closer Elric's steed bore him until he was flying over the division commanded by Jagreen Lern himself. He caught a misty glimpse of the Theocrat sitting a repulsive, hairless horse and waving his sword, convulsed with mocking mirth. He faintly heard his enemy's voice drift up to him.

'Farewell, Elric – this is our last encounter, for today you go to limbo!'

Elric turned Flamefang about and whispered into his ear: 'That one, brother – that one!'

With a roar, Flamefang loosed his venom at the laughing Theocrat. It seemed to Elric that Jagreen Lern must surely be burned to ashes, but just as the venom seemed to touch him, it was hurled back and only a few drops struck some of the Theocrat's retainers, igniting their flesh and clothing.

Still Jagreen Lern laughed and now he released an amber spear which had appeared in his hand. Straight towards Elric it went and, with difficulty, the albino put up his Chaos Shield to deflect it.

So great was the force of the bolt striking his shield that he was hurled backwards in his saddle and one of the straps securing him snapped so that he fell to the left and was only saved by the other strap that had held. Now he crouched behind the shield's protection as it was battered with supernatural weapons. Flamefang, too, was encompassed by the shield's great power; but how long would even the Chaos Shield resist such an attack?

It seemed that he was forced to use the shield for an infinite time before Flamefang's wings cracked the air like a ship's sail and he was rushing high above the horde.

He was dying.

Minute by minute the vitality was leaving him as if he were an old man ready for death. 'I cannot die,' he muttered, 'I must not die. Is there no escape from this dilemma?'

Flamefang seemed to hear him. The dragon descended towards the ground again and dropped until its scaly belly was scraping the lances of the horde. Then Flamefang had landed on the unstable ground and waited with folded wings as a group of warriors goaded their beasts towards him.

Elric gasped: 'What have you done, Flamefang? Is nothing dependable? You have delivered me into the hands of the enemy!'

With great effort he drew his sword as the first lance struck his shield and the rider passed, grinning, sensing Elric's weakness. Others came on both sides. Weakly, he slashed at one and Stormbringer suddenly took control to make his aim true. The rider's arm was pierced and he was locked to the blade as it fed, greedily, upon his lifestuff. Immediately, Elric felt some slight return of strength and realised that between them dragon and sword were helping him gain the energy he needed. But the blade kept the most part to itself. There was a reason for this, as Elric found out at once, for the sword continued to direct his arm. Several more riders were slain in this manner and Elric grinned as he felt the vitality flowing back into his body. His vision cleared, his reactions became normal, his spirits rose. Now he carried the attack to the rest of the division, Flamefang moving over the ground with a speed belying his bulk. The warriors scattered and fled back to rejoin the main force, but Elric no longer cared, he had the souls of a dozen of them and it was enough. 'Now up, Flamefang! Rise and let us seek out more powerful enemies!'

Obediently Flamefang spread his wings. They began to flap and bear him off the ground until he was gliding low over the horde.

In the midst of Lord Xiombarg's division, Elric landed again, dismounted from Flamefang and, possessed of his supernatural energy, rushed into the ranks of fiendish warriors, hewing about him, invulnerable to all but the strongest attack of Chaos. Vitality mounted and a kind of battle madness with it. Further and further into the ranks he sliced his way, until he saw Lord Xiombarg in his earthly guise of a slender, dark-haired woman. Elric knew that the woman's shape was no indication of Xiombarg's mighty strength but, without fear, he leapt towards the Duke of Hell and stood before him, looking up at where he sat on his lion-headed, bull-bodied mount.

Xiombarg's girl's voice came sweetly to Elric's ears. 'Mortal, you have defied many Dukes of Hell and banished others back to the Higher Worlds. They call you godslayer now, so I've heard. Can you slay me?'

'You know that no mortal can slay one of the Lords of the Higher Worlds whether they be of Law or Chaos, Xiombarg – but he can, if equipped with sufficient power, destroy their earthly semblance and send them back to their own plane, never to return!'

'Can you do this to me?'

'Let us see!' Elric flung himself towards the Dark Lord.

Xiombarg was armed with a long-shafted battle-axe that gave off a night-blue radiance. As his steed reared, he swung the axe down at Elric's unprotected head. The albino flung up his shield and the axe struck it. A kind of metallic shout came from the weapons and huge sparks flew away. Elric moved in close and hacked at one of Xiombarg's feminine legs. A light moved down from his hips and protected the leg so that Stormbringer was brought to a stop, jarring Elric's arm. Again the axe struck the shield with the same effect as before. Again Elric tried to pierce Xiombarg's unholy defence. And all the while he heard the Dark Lord's laughter, sweetly modulated, yet as horrible as a hag's.

'Your mockery of human shape and human beauty begins to fail, my lord!' cried Elric, standing back for a moment to gather his strength.

Already the girl's face was writhing and changing as, disconcerted by Elric's power, the Duke of Hell spurred his beast down on the albino.

Elric dodged aside and struck again. This time Stormbringer throbbed in his hand as it pierced Xiombarg's defence and the Dark Lord moaned, retaliating with another axe-blow which Elric barely succeeded in blocking. He turned his beast, the axe rushing about his head as he whirled it and flung it at Elric with the intention of striking him in the head.

Elric ducked and put up his shield, the axe clipping it and falling to the shifting ground. He ran after Xiombarg who was once again turning his steed. From nowhere he had produced another weapon, a huge double-handed broadsword, the breadth of its blade triple that of even Stormbringer's. It seemed incongruous in the small, delicate hands of the girl-shape. And its size, Elric guessed, told something of its power. He backed away warily, noting absently that one of the Dark Lord's legs was missing and replaced by an insect's claw. If he could only destroy the rest of Xiombarg's disguise, he would have succeeded in banishing him.

Now Xiombarg's laughter was no longer sweet, but had an unhinged note. The lion-head roared in unison with its master's voice as it rushed towards Elric. The monstrous sword went up and crashed upon the Chaos Shield. Elric fell on his back, feeling the ground itch and crawl beneath him, but the shield was still in one piece. He caught sight of the bull-hoofs pounding down on him, drew himself beneath the shield, leaving only his sword-arm free. As the beast thundered above, seeking to crush him with its hoofs, he thrust upwards into its belly. The sword was initially halted and then seemed to pierce through whatever obstructed it and draw out the life-force. The vitality of the unholy beast passed from sword to man and Elric was taken aback by its strange, insensate quality, for the soul-stuff of an animal was different from that of an intelligent protagonist. He rolled from under the beast's bulk and sprang to his feet as the lion-bull collapsed, hurling Xiombarg's still-earthly shape to the ground.

Instantly the Dark Lord was up, standing with a peculiarly unbalanced stance with one leg human and the other alien. It limped swiftly towards Elric, bringing the huge sword round in a sideways movement that would slice Elric in two. But Elric, full of the energy gained from Xiombarg's steed, leapt back from the blow and struck at the sword with Stormbringer. The two blades met, but neither gave. Stormbringer shrieked in anger for it was unused to resistance of this kind. Elric got the rim of his shield under the blade and forced it up. For an instant Xiombarg's guard was open and Elric used that instant with effect, driving Stormbringer into the Dark Lord's breast with all his strength.

Xiombarg whimpered and at once his earthly shape began to dissolve as Elric's sword sucked his energy into itself. Elric knew that this energy was only that fraction constituting Xiombarg's life-force on this plane, that the major part of the Dark Lord's soul was still in the Higher Worlds for not even the most powerful of these godlings could summon the power to transport all of himself to the Earth. If Elric had taken every scrap of Xiombarg's soul, his own body could not have retained it but would have burst. However, so much more powerful than any human soul was the force flowing into him from the wound he had made, that he was once again the vessel for a mighty energy.

Xiombarg changed. He became little more than a flickering coil of coloured light which began to drift away and finally vanish as Xiombarg was swept, raging, back to his own plane.

Elric looked upwards. He was horrified to see that only a few of the dragons survived. One was fluttering down now and it had a rider on its back. From that distance he could not see which of his friends it was.

He began to run towards the place where it fell.

He heard the crash as it came to ground, heard a weird wailing, a bubbling cry and then nothing.

He battled his way through the milling warriors of Chaos and none could withstand him, until he came at last to the fallen dragon. There was a broken body lying on the ground beside it, but of the runeblade there was no sign. It had vanished.

It was the body of Dyvim Slorm, last of his kinsmen.

There was no time for mourning. Elric and Moonglum and the bare score of remaining dragons could not possibly win against Jagreen Lern's strength, which had been hardly touched by the attack. Standing over the body of his cousin, he placed the Horn of Fate to his lips, took a huge breath and blew. The clear, melancholy note of the horn rang out over the battlefield and seemed to carry in all directions, through all the dimensions of the cosmos, through all the myriad planes and existences, through all eternity to the ends of the multiverse and the ends of time itself.

The note took long moments to fade and, when it had at last died away, there was an absolute hush over the world, the milling millions were still, there was an air of expectancy.

And then the White Lords came.

Chapter Five

IT WAS AS if some enormous sun, thousands of times larger than Earth's, had sent a ray of light pulsing through the cosmos, defying the flimsy barriers of time and space, to strike upon that great black battlefield. And along it, appearing on the pathway that the horn's weird power had created for them, strode the majestic Lords of Law, their earthly forms so beautiful that they challenged Elric's sanity, for his mind could scarcely absorb the sight. They disdained to ride, like the Lords of Chaos, on bizarre beasts, but moved without steeds, a magnificent assembly with their mirror-clear armour and rippling surcoats bearing the single Arrow of Law.

Leading them came Donblas the Justice Maker, a smile upon his perfect lips. He carried a slender sword in his right hand, a sword that was straight and sharp and like a beam of light itself.

Elric moved swiftly then, rushed to where Flamefang awaited him and urged the great reptile into the moaning air.

Flamefang moved with less ease than earlier, but Elric did not know whether it was because the beast was tired or whether the influence of Law was weighing on the dragon which was, after all, a creation of Chaos.

But at last he flew beside Moonglum and, looking around, saw that the remaining dragons had turned and were flying back to the West. Only their own steeds remained. Perhaps the last of the dragons had sensed their part played and were returning to the Dragon Caves to sleep again.

Elric and Moonglum exchanged glances but said nothing, for the sight below was too awe-inspiring to speak of.

A light, white and dazzling, spread from the midst of the Lords of Law, the beam upon which they had come faded, and they began to move towards the spot where Chardros the Reaper,

Mabelode the Faceless, and Slortar the Old and the lesser Lords of Chaos had assembled themselves, ready for the great fight.

As the White Lords passed through the other denizens of hell and the polluted men who were their comrades, these creatures backed away screaming, falling where the radiance touched them. The dross was being cleaned away without effort – but the real strength in the shape of the Dukes of Hell and Jagreen Lern was still to be encountered.

Though at this stage the Lords of Law were scarcely taller than the human beings, they seemed to dwarf them and even Elric, high above, felt as if he were a tiny figure, scarcely larger than a fly. It was not their *size* so much as the implication of vastness which they seemed to carry with them.

Flamefang's wings beat wearily as he circled over the scene. All around him the dark colours were now full of clouds of lighter, softer shades.

The Lords of Law reached the spot where their ancient enemies were assembled and Elric heard Lord Donblas's voice carry up to him.

'You of Chaos have defied the edict of the Cosmic Balance and sought complete dominance of this planet. Destiny denies you this – for the Earth's life is over and it must be resurrected in a new form where your influence will be weak.'

A sweet, mocking voice came from the ranks of Chaos. It was the voice of Slortar the Old. 'You presume too much, brother. The fate of the Earth has not yet been finally decided. Our meeting will result in that decision – nothing else. If we win, Chaos shall rule. If you succeed in banishing us, then paltry Law bereft of possibility will gain ascendancy. But we shall win – though Fate herself complains!'

'Then let this thing be settled,' replied Lord Donblas, and Elric saw the shining Lords of Law advance towards their dark opponents.

The very sky shook as they clashed. The air cried out and the Earth appeared to tilt. Those lesser beings left alive scattered away from the conflict and a sound like a million throbbing harp strings, each of a subtly different pitch, began to emanate from the warring gods.

Elric saw Jagreen Lern leave the ranks of the Dukes of Hell and ride in his flaming scarlet armour, away from them. He realised, perhaps, that his impertinence would be swiftly rewarded by death.

Elric sent Flamefang soaring down and he drew Stormbringer, yelling the Theocrat's name and shouting challenges.

Jagreen Lern looked up, but he did not laugh this time. He increased his speed until, as Elric had already noted, he saw towards what he was riding. Ahead, the earth had turned to black and purple gas that danced frenetically as if seeking to free itself from the rest of the atmosphere. Jagreen Lern halted his hairless horse and drew his war-axe from his belt. He raised his flame-red buckler which, like Elric's, was treated against sorcerous weapons.

The dragon hurtled downwards making Elric gasp with the speed of its descent. It flapped to earth a few yards from where Jagreen Lern sat his horrible horse, waiting, philosophically, for Elric to attack. Perhaps he sensed that their fight would mirror the larger fight going on around them, that the outcome of the one would be reflected in the outcome of the other. Whatever it was, he did not indulge in his usual braggadocio, but waited in silence.

Careless whether Jagreen Lern had the advantage or not, Elric dismounted and spoke to Flamefang in a purring murmur.

'Back, Flamefang, now. Back with your brothers. Whatever comes to pass, if I win or lose, your part is over.' As Flamefang stirred and turned his huge head to look into Elric's face, another dragon descended and landed a short distance away. Moonglum, too, dismounted, beginning to advance through the black and purple mist. Elric shouted to him: 'I want no help in this, Moonglum!'

'I'll give you none. But it will be my pleasure to see you take his life and soul!'

Elric looked at Jagreen Lern whose face was still impassive.

Flamefang's wings beat and he swept up into the sky and was soon gone, the other dragon following. He would not return.

Elric stalked towards the Theocrat, his shield high and his

sword ready. Then, with astonishment, he saw Jagreen Lern dismount from his own grotesque mount and slap its hairless rump to send it galloping away. He stood waiting, slightly crouched in a position which emphasised his high-shouldered stance. His long, dark face was taut and his eyes fixed on Elric as the albino came closer. An unstable smile of anticipation quivered on the Theocrat's lips and his eyes flickered.

Elric paused just before he came within sword-reach of his enemy. 'Jagreen Lern, are you ready to pay for the crimes you've committed against me and the world?'

'Pay? Crimes? You surprise me, Elric, for I see you have fully absorbed the carping attitude of your new allies. In my conquests I have found it necessary to eliminate a few of your friends who sought to stop me. But that was to be expected. I did what I had to and what I intended – if I have failed now, I have no regret, for regret is a fool's emotion and useless in any capacity. What happened to your wife was no direct fault of mine. Will you have triumph if you slay me?'

Elric shook his head. 'My perspectives have, indeed, changed, Jagreen Lern. Yet we of Melniboné were ever a vengeful brood – and vengeance is what I claim!'

'Ah, now I understand you.' Jagreen Lern changed his stance and he raised his axe to the defensive position. 'I am ready.'

Elric leapt at him, Stormbringer shrieking through the air to crash against the scarlet buckler and crash again. Three blows he delivered before Jagreen Lern's axe sought to wriggle through his defence and he halted it by a sideways movement of the Chaos Shield. The axe succeeded only in grazing his arm near the shoulder. Elric's shield clanged against Jagreen Lern's and Elric attempted to exert his weight and push the Theocrat backwards, meanwhile stabbing around the rims of the locked shields and trying to penetrate Jagreen Lern's guard.

For some moments they remained in this position while the music of the battle sounded around them and the ground seemed to fall from under them, columns of blossoming colours erupting, like magical plants, on all sides. Then Jagreen Lern jumped back, slashing at Elric. The albino rushed forward, ducked and struck at the Theocrat's leg near the knee – and missed. From above, the axe dashed down and he flung himself to one side to avoid it. Carried off balance by the force of the blow, Jagreen Lern staggered and Elric leapt up and kicked at the small of the Theocrat's back. The man fell sprawling, losing his grip on both axe and shield as he tried to do many things at once and failed to do anything. Elric put his heel on the Theocrat's neck and held him there, Stormbringer hovering greedily over his prone enemy.

Jagreen Lern heaved his body round so that he looked up at Elric. He was suddenly pale and his eyes were fixed on the black hellblade when he spoke hoarsely to Elric. 'Finish me now. There's no place for my soul in all eternity – not any more. I must go to limbo – so finish me!'

Elric was about to allow Stormbringer to plunge itself into the defeated Theocrat when he stayed the weapon, holding it back from its prey with difficulty. The runesword murmured in frustration and tugged in his hand.

'No,' he said slowly, 'I want nothing of yours, Jagreen Lern. I would not pollute my being by feeding off your soul. Moonglum!' His friend ran up. 'Moonglum, hand me your blade.'

Silently, the little Eastlander obeyed. Elric sheathed the resisting Stormbringer, saying to it: 'There – that's the first time I've stopped you from feeding. What will you do now, I wonder?' Then he took Moonglum's blade and slashed it across Jagreen Lern's cheek, opening it up in a long, deep cut which began slowly to fill with blood.

The Theocrat screamed.

'No, Elric – kill me!'

With an absent smile, Elric slashed the other cheek. His bloody face contorted, Jagreen Lern shouted for death, but Elric continued to smile his vague, half-aware smile, and said softly: 'You sought to imitate the emperors of Melniboné, did you not? You mocked Elric of that line, you tortured him and you abducted his wife. You moulded her body into a hell-shape as you moulded the rest of the world. You slew Elric's friends and challenged him in your

227

impertinence. But you are nothing – you are more of a pawn than Elric ever was. Now, little man, know how the folk of Melniboné toyed with such upstarts in the days when they ruled the world!'

Jagreen Lern took an hour to die and only then because Moonglum begged Elric to finish him swiftly.

Elric handed Moonglum's tainted sword back to him after wiping it on a shred of fabric that had been part of the Theocrat's robe. He looked down at the mutilated body and stirred it with his foot, then he looked away to where the Lords of the Higher Worlds were embattled.

He was badly weakened from the fight and also from the energy he had been forced to exert to return the resisting Stormbringer to its sheath, but this was forgotten as he stared in wonder at the gigantic battle.

Both the Lords of Law and those of Chaos had become huge and misty as their earthly mass diminished and they continued to fight in human shape. They were like half-real giants, fighting everywhere now – on the land and above it. Far away on the rim of the horizon, he saw Donblas the Justice Maker engaged with Chardros the Reaper, their outlines flickering and spreading, the slim sword darting and the great scythe sweeping.

Unable to participate, unsure which side was winning, Elric and Moonglum watched as the intensity of the battle increased and, with it, the slow dissolution of the gods' earthly manifestation. The fight was no longer merely on the Earth but seemed to be raging throughout all the planes of the cosmos and, as if in unison with this transformation, the Earth appeared to be losing its form, until Elric and Moonglum drifted in the mingled swirl of air, fire, earth and water.

The Earth dissolved – yet still the Lords of the Higher Worlds battled over it.

The stuff of the Earth alone remained, but unformed. Its components were still in existence, but their new shape was undecided. The fight continued. The victors would have the privilege of re-forming the Earth.

Chapter Six

AT LAST, THOUGH Elric did not know how, the turbulent dark gave way to light, and there came a noise – a cosmic roar of hate and frustration – and he knew that the Lords of Chaos had been defeated and banished. The Lords of Law victorious, Fate's plan had been achieved, though it still required the last note of the horn to bring it to its required conclusion.

And Elric realised he did not have the strength left to blow the horn the third time.

About the two friends, the world was taking on a distinct shape again. They found they were standing on a rocky plain and in the distance were the slender peaks of new-formed mountains, purple against a mellow sky.

Then the Earth began to move. Faster and faster it whirled, day giving way to night with incredible rapidity, and then it began to slow until the sun was again all but motionless in the sky, moving with something like its customary speed.

The change had taken place. Law ruled here now, yet the Lords of Law had departed without thanks.

And though Law ruled, it could not progress until the horn was blown for the last time.

'So it is over,' Moonglum murmured. 'All gone – Elwher, my birthplace, Karlaak by the Weeping Waste, Bakshaan, even the Dreaming City and the Isle of Melniboné. They no longer exist, they cannot be retrieved. And this is the new world formed by Law. It looks much the same as the old.'

Elric, too, was filled with a sense of loss, knowing that all the places that were familiar to him, even the very continents were gone and replaced by different ones. It was like the loss of childhood and perhaps that was what it was – the passing of the Earth's childhood.

He shrugged away the thought and smiled. 'I'm supposed to blow the horn for the final time if the Earth's new life is to begin. Yet I haven't the strength. Perhaps Fate is to be thwarted after all?'

Moonglum looked at him strangely. 'I hope not, friend.'

Elric sighed. 'We are the last two left, Moonglum, you and I. It is fitting that even the mighty events that have taken place have not harmed our friendship, have not separated us. You are the only friend whose company has not worn on me, the only one I have trusted.'

Moonglum grinned a shadow of his old, cocky grin. 'And where we've shared adventures, I've usually profited if you have not. The partnership has been complementary. I shall never know why I chose to share your destiny. Perhaps it was no doing of mine, but Fate's, for there is one final act of friendship I can perform...'

Elric was about to question Moonglum when a quiet voice came from behind him.

'I bear two messages. One of thanks from the Lords of Law – and another from a more powerful entity.'

'Sepiriz!' Elric turned to face his mentor. 'Well, are you satisfied with my work?'

'Aye – greatly.' Sepiriz's face was sad and he stared at Elric with a look of profound sympathy. 'You have succeeded in everything but the last act which is to blow the Horn of Fate for the third time. Because of you the world shall know progression and its new people shall have the opportunity to advance by degrees to a new state of being.'

'But what is the meaning of it all?' Elric said. 'That I have never fully understood.'

'Who can? Who can know why the Cosmic Balance exists, why Fate exists and the Lords of the Higher Worlds? Why there must always be a champion to fight such battles? There seems to be an infinity of space and time and possibilities. There may be an infinite number of beings, one above the other, who see the final purpose, though, in infinity, there can be no final purpose. Perhaps all is cyclic and this same event will occur again and again until the universe is run down and fades away as the world we knew has faded. Meaning, Elric? Do not seek that, for madness lies in such a course.'

'No meaning, no pattern. Then why have I suffered all this?'

'Perhaps even the gods seek meaning and pattern and this is merely one attempt to find it. Look –' he waved his hands to indicate the newly formed Earth. 'All this is fresh and moulded by logic. Perhaps the logic will control the newcomers, perhaps a factor will occur to destroy that logic. The gods experiment, the Cosmic Balance guides the destiny of the Earth, men struggle and credit the gods with knowing why they struggle – but do the gods know?'

'You disturb me further when I had hoped to be comforted,' he sighed. 'I have lost wife and world – and do not know why.'

'I am sorry. I have come to wish you farewell, my friend. Do what you must.'

'Aye. Shall I see you again?'

'No, for we are both truly dead. Our age has gone.'

Sepiriz seemed to twist in the air and disappear.

A cold silence remained.

At length Elric's thoughts were interrupted by Moonglum. 'You must blow the horn, Elric. Whether it means nothing or much – you must blow it and finish this business for ever!'

'How? I have scarcely enough strength to stand on my feet.'

'I have decided what you must do. Slay me with Stormbringer. Take my soul and vitality into yourself – then you will have sufficient power to blow the last blast.'

'Kill you, Moonglum! The only one left – my only true friend? You babble!'

'I mean it. You must, for there is nothing else to do. Further, we have no place here and must die soon at any rate. You told me how Zarozinia gave you her soul – well, take mine, too!'

'I cannot.'

Moonglum paced towards him and reached down to grip Stormbringer's hilt, pulling it halfway from the sheath.

'*No*, Moonglum!'

But now the sword sprang from the sheath on its own volition. Elric struck Moonglum's hand away and gripped the hilt. He could not stop it. The sword rose up, dragging his arm with it, poised to deliver a blow.

Moonglum stood with his arms by his side, his face expressionless, though Elric thought he glimpsed a flicker of fear in the eyes. He struggled to control the blade, but knew it was impossible.

'Let it do its work, Elric.'

The blade plunged forward and pierced Moonglum's heart. His blood sprang out and covered it. His eyes blurred and filled with horror. 'Ah, no – I – had – not – expected *this!*'

Petrified, Elric could not tug the sword from his friend's heart. Moonglum's energy began to flow up its length and course into his body, yet, even when all the little Eastlander's vitality was absorbed, Elric remained staring at the small corpse until the tears flowed from his crimson eyes and a great sob racked him. Then the blade came free.

He flung it away from him and it did not clatter on the rocky ground but landed as a body might land. Then it seemed to move towards him and stop and he had the suspicion that it was watching him.

He took the horn and put it to his lips. He blew the blast to herald in the night of the new Earth. The night that would precede the new dawn. And though the horn's note was triumphant, Elric was not. He stood full of infinite loneliness and infinite sorrow, his head tilted back as the sound rang on. And, when the note faded from triumph to a dying echo that expressed something of Elric's misery, a huge outline began to form in the sky above the Earth, as if summoned by the horn.

It was the outline of a gigantic hand holding a balance and, as he watched, the Balance began to right itself until each side was true.

And somehow this relieved Elric's sorrow as he released his grip on the Horn of Fate.

'There *is* something, at least,' he said, 'and if it's an illusion, then it's a reassuring one.'

He turned his head to one side and saw the blade leave the ground, sweep into the air and then rush down on him.

'Stormbringer!' he cried, and then the hellsword struck his chest, he felt the icy touch of the blade against his heart, reached out his fingers to clutch at it, felt his body constrict, felt it sucking his soul from the very depths of his being, felt his whole personality being drawn into the runesword. He knew, as his life faded to combine with the sword's, that it had always been his destiny to die in this manner. With the blade he had killed friends and lovers, stolen their souls to feed his own waning strength. It was as if the sword had always used him to this end, as if he was merely a manifestation of Stormbringer and was now being taken back into the body of the blade which had never been a true sword. And, as he died, he wept again, for he knew that the fraction of the sword's soul which was his would never know rest but was doomed to immortality, to eternal struggle.

Elric of Melniboné, last of the Bright Emperors, cried out, and then his body collapsed, a sprawled husk beside its comrade, and he lay beneath the mighty balance that still hung in the sky.

Then Stormbringer's shape began to change, writhing and curling above the body of the albino, finally to stand astraddle it.

The entity that was Stormbringer, last manifestation of Chaos which would remain with this new world as it grew, looked down on the corpse of Elric of Melniboné and smiled.

'Farewell, friend. I was a thousand times more evil than thou!'

And then it leapt from the Earth and went spearing upwards, its wild voice laughing mockery at the Cosmic Balance; filling the universe with its unholy joy.

Artwork Portfolio

by James Cawthorn

21 December 1929–2 December, 2008

Rough sketch, 1963, showing Elric and Xiombarg,
previously unpublished.

End-paper sketch, 1989, Elric and Ziombarg again, from a series
commissioned privately to illustrate a copy of the first edition of
Stormbringer (1965), previously unpublished, courtesy Charles Partington.

'Captains of Chaos' sketch, 1963, first published in
Elric: To Rescue Tanelorn, Del Rey, 2008.

A page from an aborted graphic adaptation of *Stormbringer*, 1965,
first published in *Elric: The Sleeping Sorceress*, Del Rey, 2008.

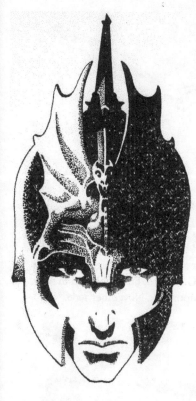

Just published

STORMBRINGER
by Michael Moorcock

J. G. Ballard writes about STORMBRINGER:

"A work of powerful and sustained
imagination which confirms Michael
Moorcock's position as the most
important successor to Mervyn Peake
and Wyndham Lewis. These strange and
tormented landscapes, peopled by
characters of archetypal dimensions,
are the setting for a series of
titanic duels between the forces of
Chaos and Order. Nightmare armies
clash on the shores of spectral seas.
Phantom horsemen ride on skeleton
steeds across a world as fantastic as
those of Bosch and Breughel. Over all
these presides the central figure of
Elric, the haunted warrior-king whose
ambivalent relationship with the magical
sword Stormbringer is the author's most
original creation. The vast, tragic
symbols by which Mr. Moorcock continually
illuminates the metaphysical quest of his
hero are a measure of the author's
remarkable talents."

STORMBRINGER is divided into 3 parts:
The Coming of Chaos, Sad Giant's Shield,
Doomed Lord's Passing.
The jacket is by J. Cawthorn. The price
of the book is only 12s. 6d. (1s. 1d.
postage).

Herbert Jenkins Science Fiction:

THE DEEP REACHES OF SPACE by Bertram A. Chandler 12/6
THE WORLD IN PERIL by Charles Chilton 7/6
THE HAUNTED STARS by Edmond Hamilton (due March 1965) 12/6
MOON BASE by E. C. Tubb 12/6
SPACE BORN by Lan Wright 12/6

HERBERT
JENKINS

SF
&
FANTASY

Publisher's press release for the first edition of *Stormbringer* (1965),
showing with the book's cover artwork, previously unpublished.

Above, below and facing page: Interior artwork (non-Elric), illustrating 'Storm Bird, Storm Dreamer' by J.G. Ballard, first published in NEW WORLDS No. 168, edited by Moorcock, November 1966.

A Scene (Page 81) From 'STORMBRINGER'.

A page from another aborted graphic adaptation of *Stormbringer*,
undated, first published in WEIRD FANTASY No. 2,
edited by David Britton, 1971.

242

Elric illustration left unfinished by Cawthorn, completed by
David Britton, first published in WEIRD FANTASY No. 2.

Title sketch, 1969, from an aborted graphic adaptation of *The Stealer
of Souls*, first published in CRUCIFIED TOAD No. 4, edited by
David Britton, Winter 1974.

Cover artwork for CRUCIFIED TOAD No. 4.

Rough sketch, undated, of Jagreen Lern, first published in *Sieg Heil Iconographers*, by Jon Farmer, Savoy Books, 2006.

Cover artwork for graphic adaptation of *Stormbringer*, Savoy, 1976.

FOR ten thousand years the sorcerer-kings of Melnibone ruled the earth

ten thousand years of a forgotten age, serving the realm of Chaos, while the new creature, man, grew in their shadow. And then Melnibone fell, thrown down amid monstrous wars, shattered by frightful runes. Chaos and Law clashed, striving for mastery of the cosmos, and the earth shook.

It was a time of destiny for men and gods, a time of heroes. Chief among these was Elric, last emperor of Melnibone, lord of dragons. Elric, who had destroyed his homeland in revenge for the death of his sister and lover, Cymoril. Elric, a crimson-eyed albino who drew his strength from a Black Blade which drank the souls of its victims....

STORMBRINGER

Only the island of Melnibone remained untouched by Chaos. Mounted on dragons, Elric, his friend Moonglum of Elwher, and his kinsman Dyvim Slorm, rose from the ruins of Imrryr, the dreaming city, to their final battle with the Chaos hordes. Only Elric could summon the Lords of Law to fight for earth, but his life was slowly ebbing....

Interior artwork for Savoy's graphic adaptation of *Stormbringer*.

WITH DIMMING EYES, ELRIC GAZED UPON THE FULL EARTHLY PANOPLY AND MIGHT OF HIS FOES. THE TENTS OF JAGREEN LERN AND HIS ARMIES CROUCHED BENEATH THE GIANT FORMS OF CHARDROS THE REAPER, MABELODE THE FACELESS, AND SLORTAR THE OLD, MOST POWERFUL LORDS IN THE REALM OF CHAOS.

Interior artwork for Savoy's graphic adaptation of *Stormbringer*.

THE CHAOS SHIPS
FLOATED UPON THE SWIRLING, SEETHING EARTH. AROUND THEM FLUTTERED THE BANNERS OF KINGS AND LORDS WHO HAD SOLD THEMSELVES TO THE DEMONIC CONQUERORS. SOON, ELRIC KNEW, THIS VAST HOST WOULD CEASE TO BE HUMAN, WOULD WARP AND CHANGE...

Above and facing: Interior artwork for Savoy's graphic adaptation of *Stormbringer*.

'Urlik', 1976, a wash drawing to accompany the first-draft screenplay
of an aborted motion picture, *Stormbringer* (based more on the
Eternal Champion series), first published in *Elric: Swords and Roses*,
Del Rey, 2010.

Another *Stormbringer* wash drawing, of an Eldren warrior,
previously unpublished.

James Cawthorn & Michael Moorcock
DREAM OF A DOOMED LORD

As the beast foundered beneath him in blood and screaming metal, Elric of Melnibone hurled himself from the saddle. Iron feet stamped and slid, flailing blades ploughed the earth around him. He rolled and sprang erect, Stormbringer gripped in taut, bone-white hands. A spiked shape lunged, slashing with ragged claws. Storm—bringer smashed into the steel torso, shearing metal, tendons, bones, howling as it fed. Blinding blue sparks leaped crackling along the hellblade, burned in Elric's veins. The plain quivered under his feet, the air sang with power. He began to run, a raging white—masked demon, crimson eyes blazing in the black sockets of his helm. Storm—bringer lashed out, once, twice, and the way ahead was open.

He ran toward the castle.

They had combed the ruins of Melnibone, tower by ragged tower. Dyvim Slorm, inheritor of ten thousand years of brilliant and cruel Melnibonean culture, feared for his cousin's life. Moonglum, being merely human, had greater faith in his friend's ability to survive. When they eventually found him, he was standing at the sea's edge, where blue jade dragons brooded under the cloudwracked sky.

Dyvim Slorm quickened his steps. "Elric! We feared that —" He faltered as he looked into the albino's eyes of sombre crimson. For all his sorcerous learning, he flinched from the import of their fixed, unseeing gaze. He looked away. Moonglum, approaching, called out and pointed to an object in the surf. "What is that?"

Stooping, hands on swordhilts, they saw a sphere of crystal. Trapped in its intricate facets, violet light pulsed and flickered.

Elric ran, eyes slitted against the mounting fury of the violet sun that flared on the horizon. The quartz walls of the castle fed upon the light; shimmering, throwing off spectral rainbows that writhed above the plain. The quartz began to flow, melting and reforming, growing. Battlements soared in grotesque, mountainous conformations. Towers sprouted, bristling with deadly barbs of glass. And suddenly Elric knew, with a certainty which cut through his battle—madness like an icy knife, that there was no enemy in the castle. The castle, itself, was his enemy.

His limbs began to shake. Wrapping both hands about Stormbringer's hilt, he ran on, crimson eyes wide, staring into death.

For a day after Dyvim Slorm shattered the crystal with a single stroke of Mournblade, Elric lay, corpselike, in the Tower of D'a'rputna. To his friends' assertion that it had been a device of Chaos, he later assented, but without conviction. Throughout the little time which remained to him, he was haunted by the thought that, on some unknown field, he was doomed to live and fight again.

'Dream of a Doomed Lord', 1978, first published in SOMETHING ELSE
No. 1, edited by Charles Partington, Spring 1980.

End-paper sketch, 1979, commissioned privately to illustrate a copy of the first edition of *Stormbringer* (1965), first published in *Elric: Swords and Roses*, Del Rey, 2010, courtesy George Locke.

Dear Mike —
An Elric collection, and not a
headband in sight — Jim.

Sketch, first published in *Elric: Swords and Roses*,
from an undated series of six.

Two sketches, previously unpublished, from an undated series of six.

Sketch, previously unpublished, from an undated series of six.

Sketch, first published in *Elric: Swords and Roses*,
from an undated series of six.

End-paper sketch, 1989, from a series commissioned privately to illustrate a
copy of the first edition of *Stormbringer* (1965), previously unpublished,
courtesy Charles Partington.

Rough sketch, 1989, showing Elric and Lord Horror,
first published in *Sieg Heil Iconographers*, Savoy, 2006.

'Elric and Lord Horror', first published in HARD CORE HORROR
No. 2, by David Britton, Savoy, 1990.

'Elric', 1992, first published as cover artwork for THE TIME CENTRE
TIMES Vol. 2 No. 2, edited by D.J. Rowe, Ian Covell, Maureen Cuffe
& John Davey, August 1993.

Self-portrait, 2007, commissioned by Savoy, first published in
Elric: Swords and Roses, Del Rey, 2010.

Elric

(1963)

VERY NICE OF you to devote so much time to Elric – though he doesn't altogether merit it! I'd disagree with the writer when he says, 'I expect the "sword and sorcery" stories are by far the most popular type ... etc.' I think those who like them receive them enthusiastically, but it's a fairly small minority compared with those who like, for instance, 'science fantasy' of *The Dragon Masters* variety and the stuff Kuttner, Brackett and others used to turn out for STARTLING, SUPER SCIENCE, etc. These days people seem to want information of some kind with their escapism – and sword-and-sorcery doesn't strictly supply information of the type required. (The appeal of James Bond appears to be based primarily on the lumps of pseudo-data inserted every so often in the narrative.) The only sword-and-sorcery stuff I personally enjoy reading is Leiber's. Don't go much for Tolkien, Dunsany, Smith, Howard – or Edgar Rice Burroughs in spite of what some critics have said of my books recently.

Though I didn't know SCIENCE FANTASY was due to fold when I wrote it, I wound up the Elric series just in time to catch the last issue quite by coincidence. I had intended to kill off Elric (as is probably plain from the second story in the currently appearing quartet, 'Black Sword's Brothers') and his world, so it is just as well. A story set in a world which so closely borders Elric's that some of the place names are the same will be appearing in FANTASTIC some time this year. This was originally called 'Earl Aubec and the Golem' but the title has been changed to 'Master of Chaos' (the cosmology is identical with the Elric stories' cosmology) and will be, if Cele Goldsmith likes the next one I'm planning, the first of a series showing the development of the Earth from a rather unusual start. It is vaguely possible that Elric will appear in future stories and some of his background not filled in in the concluding stories ('Sad Giant's Shield' in SCIENCE FANTASY No. 63 & 'Doomed Lord's Passing' in SCIENCE FANTASY 64) will be filled in there. But this depends on how the series develops and what Cele Goldsmith thinks of the stories. 'Master of Chaos' is, I think, in many ways my best S&S tale.

It is a great disappointment, however, that SCIENCE FANTASY has folded. Not simply because stories sold to it paid my rent, but because for me and many other writers in this country (particularly, like me, the younger ones) it was an outlet for the kind of story that is very difficult to sell in America – even to Cele Goldsmith who appears to be the most open-minded of the US editors. Particularly this went for the short novel of the 'Earth is But a Star' length and the recent 37,000-word 'Skeleton Crew' by Aldiss. The slow-developing, borderline-mainstream story of the kind Ballard does so well will find more difficulty selling in the States too, though Ballard's 'Question of Re-entry' was of this kind and published in FANTASTIC. It seems a pity that English SF has reached, in people like Ballard and Aldiss, an exceptionally high standard and a strongly English flavour, and now it has no markets here.

The landscapes of my stories are metaphysical, not physical. As a faltering atheist with a deep irradicable religious sense (I was brought up on an offbeat brand of Christian mysticism) I tended, particularly in early stories like 'While the Gods Laugh', to work out my own problems through Elric's adventures. Needless to say, I never reached any conclusions, merely brought these problems closer to the surface. I was writing not particularly well, but from the 'soul'. I wasn't just telling a story, I was telling *my* story. I don't think of myself as a fantasy writer in the strict sense – but the possibilities of fantasy attract me. For some sort of guide to what I see as worth exploiting in the fantasy form, I'd suggest you bear this in mind when you read 'The Deep Fix' which will appear in the last issue of SCIENCE FANTASY along with 'Doomed Lord's Passing', the last Elric story... which might also provide a clue. 'The Deep Fix' will be under a pseudonym [the late James Colvin, ed.].

I am not a logical thinker. I am, if anything, an intuitive thinker. Most facts bore me. Some inspire me. Nuclear physics, for instance, though I know scarcely anything about the field, excites me, particularly when watching a nuclear physicist explaining his theories on TV. My only interest in any field of knowledge is literary. This is probably a narrow interest, but I'm a writer and want to be a good one. I have only written two fantasy stories in my life which were deliberately commercial (sorry, three – one hasn't been published). These were 'Going Home' in SCIENCE FICTION ADVENTURES and 'Kings in Darkness' in SCIENCE FANTASY. The rest, for better or worse, were written from inside. Briefly, physics doesn't interest me – metaphysics does. The only writer of SF I enjoy is J.G. Ballard. The only writer of fantasy currently working in the magazines I like is Leiber. The three works of fantasy I can still re-read and enjoy, apart from those, are Anderson's *The Broken Sword*, Peake's Titus Groan trilogy, and Cabell's *Jurgen*. Anderson has done nothing better than *The Broken Sword*, in my opinion, and I sometimes feel that his talent has since been diverted, even lessened. I feel that writing SF can ruin and bleed dry a writer's talent. The best he can do in this field is improve his technique – at the expense of his art. I think of myself as a bad writer with big ideas, but I'd rather be that than a big writer with bad ideas – or ideas that have gone bad. I tend to think of the SF magazine field as a field in which it is possible to experiment – and sell one's mistakes; but the impulse to sell tends to dominate the impulse to experiment the longer one stays in the field.

And fear of death, incidentally, is probably another source of inspiration in the Elric stories. I don't believe in life after death and I don't want to die. I hope I shan't. Maybe I'll be the exception that proves the rule...

Now for some specific remarks about the Elric material in NIEKAS. Firstly, a few carping points on the spelling. As you'll see from the book *Stealer of Souls*, which I had an opportunity to get at before it was printed, there is an accented é in the spelling of Melniboné. Melnibonay – this accent was, of course, left out of all but the first story. Imrryr is spelled thus. Count Smiorgan Baldhead – not *of* Baldhead (his head was hairless).

A point about the end of 'The Dreaming City': Elric used the wind to save himself, abandoning his comrades to the dragons. This, and Cymoril's death, is on his conscience.

I don't know whether the Imrryrians would have *despised* Elric (second story synopsis, line 1). I think of them as accepting his treachery fairly calmly, and yet bound to do something about it if they caught up with him.

When I wrote this story I was thinking of Stormbringer as a symbol – partly, anyway – of Man's reliance on mental and physical crutches he'd be better off without. It seems a bit pretentious, now. I suppose you could call the Dharzi zombie men, but really I didn't think of them as men at all, in the strict sense. The sea is, of course, an underground sea – and also not 'natural' as Elric discovered. The hill, castle, etc. – all the bits and pieces in this episode – are all underground. There was the intention here to give the whole episode the aspect of taking place within a womb. The Book is a similar symbol to the Sword in this story. Again, in the end of this story, he leaves Shaarilla to her fate – abandoning her. At this period of my writing women either got killed or had some other dirty trick played on them. The only female character who survived was my own La Belle Dame Sans Merci – Yishana. I won't explain that here – too personal...

'The exact nature of the feud is a mystery' ('Theleb K'aarna', line 6): Maybe I wasn't clear enough here – but I have the idea that I explained somewhere how Theleb K'aarna had devised a means of sending Elric on a wild-goose chase by loosing some supernatural force or other against him. This was why Elric wanted blood. That story by the way was the most popular of the first three. I guess a Freudian psychologist would know why...

'Kings in Darkness' I'd rather not deal with, since it was the worst of the series and, as I mentioned, written commercially. Therefore there is little of it which fits in with what I like to think of as the *real* content of the Elric series.

No comments, either, on 'The Flame Bringers' – although I enjoyed writing the Meerclar bit and the last sequence with Elric on the back of the dragon. This, I think, is nothing much more than an adventure story, though it serves to show up Elric's weakness in that the moment things get tough he's seeking his sword again. Also the last bit where the sword returns is a hint of the sword's 'true' nature.

In the book version of the last quartet (of which 'Dead God's Homecoming' is the first part) I've revised the opening a bit. It was – and C.R. Kearns pointed this out and I agreed with him – what you might call a confused start. In the final revision of the short story version I changed it fairly considerably from the original and one or two inconsistencies crept through – I was working hard at the time and was very tired.

I would rather you had left this story out or waited until all four had been published before synopsising it since this is the first part of a novel and many issues are not clarified until the end. I'm not happy with any of the magazine stories as they stand and have made, in places, quite heavy revisions. The last story to be written is, I feel, the best though. A final word – the Lords of Chaos hated Tanelorn not because it was a utopia, but because nearly all those in the city had once owed them, the Lords, allegiance and had forsworn it when they came to Tanelorn (or so the story goes). This is probably the most overtly philosophical or mystical of the Young Kingdom tales, as you say, and took much longer to write than the rest. It could be improved, I feel, by more play on the actual characters involved.

The writer feels that 'Black Sword's Brothers' was the dullest Elric story. It was certainly, as explained above, one of the most patchy from the point of view of construction. It's true, in one sense, that I was losing interest in the Elric series – or rather that I had reached a point before it was written where I had run out of inspiration. But the interest picked up as I began to write and, by the time I'd got into the second part I was enjoying the writing again. I think it's possible to look at the Elric stories as a sort of presentation of the crude materials which I hope to fashion into better stories later. Being non-logical, I have to produce a great deal of stuff in order to find the bits of it I really want. My ideas about Law and Chaos and the rest became clearer as I wrote. Of the four, 'Black Sword's Brothers' and 'Sad Giant's Shield' (the most recently published) are the weakest in my opinion. Both were revised (something I do not usually do with the Elric stories) and both suffered from this revision, I think. My mind was at its clearest (not very clear by normal standards) when I wrote 'Doomed Lord's Passing'. I've found that I can only really learn from my mistakes after they've been published, which is hard on the reader.

Ted Carnell, who handles my other work as well, said that he felt 'Earl Aubec and the Golem' (or 'Master of Chaos') was a sort of crystallisation of everything I'd been working on in the Elric series. Maybe not everything, but I think he's right. 'Earl Aubec' is more a kind of sword-and-philosophy tale than an outright sword-and-sorcery. Elric tales – or the best of them – were conceived similarly.

The writer thinks that John Rackham's fantasies (or properly 'Occult-thrillers') will outlast my stories. I don't think either will last for long, but I might as well admit that I was slightly hurt by this remark, for Rackham's stories that I have read struck me as being rather barren, stereotyped tales with no 'true' sense of the occult at all (whatever a true sense of the occult is). Moreover I know John doesn't believe in his stuff for a second (at least not in any supernatural sense) whereas I believe wholeheartedly in mine, as I've pointed out. It's silly to take up someone's remark like this, especially since it is fair criticism and just a statement of someone's individual taste, but I suppose I'm still young enough to feel defensive about my stories – especially my Elric stories for which I have an odd mixture of love and hate. They are so closely linked to my own obsessions and problems that I find it hard to ignore any criticisms of them and tend momentarily to leap to their defence.

As I said earlier, and Cele Goldsmith said in a supplement to AMRA, sword-and-sorcery seems to appeal to an enthusiastic minority and may receive a large volume of praise from a fairly small section of readers.

When Carnell asked me to think up a sword-and-sorcery series I tried to make it as different as possible from any other I'd read. I'd hesitate to agree that the two best-known magic swords are

Excalibur and Prince Valiant's 'Singing Blade' – Excalibur, certainly, and probably Roland's Durandana. The idea of the magic sword came, of course, from legend, but I willingly admit to Anderson's influence, too. The idea of an albino hero had a more obscure source. As a boy I collected a pre-War magazine called UNION JACK. This was Sexton Blake's Own Paper – Blake was the British version of your Nick Carter, I should imagine, and UNION JACK was the equivalent of your Dime Novels. One of Blake's most memorable opponents was a character named M. Zenith – or Zenith the Albino, a Byronic hero-villain who aroused more sympathy in the reader than did the intrepid detective. Anyway, the Byronic h-v had always appealed; I liked the idea of an albino, which suited my purpose, and so Elric was born – an albino. Influences include various Gothic novels, also. Elric is not a new hero to fantasy – although he's new, I suppose, to S&S.

I cannot altogether agree that Elric remains an essentially simple character. I think of him as complex but inarticulate when he tries to explain his predicament. His taste for revenge seems to be a sort of extension of his search for peace and purpose – he finds, to coin a phrase, forgetfulness in action. Elric's guilt over the slaying of Nikorn was guilt for the *slaying* itself, not because he'd killed a particular man.

I don't know whether I could have left Moonglum out and still kept the stories the same. Moonglum is, apart from everything else, to some extent a close, valued friend of mine who has been a lot of help in various ways over the last few years. If Elric is my fantasy self, then Moonglum is this friend's fantasy self (as I see him at any rate). I am not particularly gloomy by nature. I put Moonglum in to make remarks about Elric when he gets too self-absorbed or too absorbed in self-pity, etc.

A little more of Elric's background and some clue as to why he is what he is will be found in 'Doomed Lord's Passing'. I've been aware of this absence and have tried to rectify it a bit here.

I was pleased that you have used the Grey Mouser as a comparison since, as must now be evident, I'm a great fan of the Mouser's. Perhaps Moonglum also owes a little to the Mouser. As for Elric being an idealist rather than a materialist, this is probably because I'm often told I'm a materialist rather than an idealist. I don't like to be told this, but it could be true.

Elric's disregard for danger is of the nature of panic rather than courage, maybe. The Mouser, on the other hand, seems not to disregard danger – he evaluates it and then acts. Conan – well...

The cosmology of the Elric stories probably owes its original inspiration to two things – Zoroastrianism (which I admire) and Anderson's *Three Hearts and Three Lions*. It was developed from there, of course. This set-up simply is:

COSMIC HAND

"

"

"

"

"

"

Balance

/ \

Law   Chaos

Grey Lords

Elementals

Men

Law Sorcerers   Chaos Sorcerers

Men pledged to Law   Beasts   Men pledged to Chaos

etc.

etc.

I have a more complex chart. The sixth story is the one where the cosmology becomes clearer and the reader should realise the rest as he reads the last stories.

I have probably helped anyone who wants to assess the Elric stories on a slightly different level. Who wants to?

The Secret Life of
Elric of Melniboné

(1964)

Some years ago, when I was about eighteen, I wrote a novel called *The Golden Barge*. This was an allegorical fantasy about a little man, completely without self-knowledge and with little of any other kind, going down a seemingly endless river, following a great Golden Barge which, he felt, if he caught it would contain all truth, all secrets, all the solutions to his problems. On the journey he met various groups of people, had a love affair, and so on. Yet every action he took in order to reach the Golden Barge seemed to keep him farther away from it. The river represented Time, the barge was what mankind is always seeking outside itself, when it can be found inside itself, etc., etc. The novel had a sad ending, as such novels do. Also, as was clear when I'd finished it, my handling of many of the scenes was clumsy and immature. So I scrapped it and decided that in future my allegories would be intrinsic within a conventional narrative – that the best symbols were the symbols found in familiar objects. Like swords for instance.

Up until I was twenty or so, I had a keen interest in fantasy fiction, particularly sword-and-sorcery stories of the kind written by Robert E. Howard, Clark Ashton Smith and the like, but this interest began to wane as I became more interested in less directly sensational forms of literature, just as earlier my interest in Edgar Rice Burroughs's tales had waned. I could still enjoy one or two sword-and-sorcery tales, particularly Poul Anderson's *The Broken Sword* and Fritz Leiber's Grey Mouser stories. A bit before this casting off of old loyalties, I had been in touch with Sprague de Camp and Hans Santesson of FANTASTIC UNIVERSE about doing a new series of Conan tales.

I think it was in the autumn of 1960, when I was working for SEXTON BLAKE LIBRARY and reading SF for SUSPENSE (the short-lived companion to ARGOSY) that I bumped into a colleague at Fleetway Publications, Andy Vincent, who was an old friend of Harry Harrison's (who had also freelanced for Fleetway for some time). Andy told me he was meeting Harry and Ted Carnell in the Fleetway foyer and suggested I went along. As I remember, that was where I first met Harry. Previously, I'd sold a couple of stories to Ted, one in collaboration with Barry Bayley, and had had more bounced than bought. Later on in a pub, Ted and I were talking about Robert E. Howard and Ted said he'd been thinking of running some Conan-type stuff in SCIENCE FANTASY. I told him of the FANTASTIC UNIVERSE idea which had fallen through when FANTASTIC UNIVERSE folded, and said I still had the stuff I'd done and would he like to see it. He said he would. A couple of days later I sent him the first chapter and outline of a Conan story. To tell you the truth, writing in Howard's style had its limitations, as did his hero as far as I was concerned, and I wasn't looking forward to producing another 10,000 words of the story if Ted liked it.

Ted liked it – or at least he liked the writing, but there had been a misunderstanding. He hadn't wanted Conan – he had wanted something on the same lines.

This suited me much better. I decided that I would think up a hero as different as possible from the usual run of S&S heroes, and use the narrative as a vehicle for my own 'serious' ideas. Many of these ideas, I realise now, were somewhat romantic and coloured by a long-drawn-out and, to me at the time, tragic love affair which hadn't quite finished its course and which was confusing and darkening my outlook. I was writing floods of hack work for Fleetway and was getting sometimes £70 or £80 a week which was going on drink, mainly, and, as I remember, involved rather a lot of broken glass of one description or another. I do remember, with great pride, my main achievement of the winter of 1960 or 1961, which was to smash entirely an unbreakable plate-glass door in a well-known restaurant near Piccadilly. And the management apologised...

I mention this, to give a picture of my mood at the time of Elric's creation. If you've read the early Elric stories in particular, you'll see that Elric's outlook was rather similar to mine. My point is that Elric *was* me (the me of 1960/1 anyway) and the mingled qualities of betrayer and betrayed, the bewilderment about life in general, the search for some solution to it all, the expression of this bewilderment in terms of violence, cynicism and the need for revenge, were all characteristic of mine. So when I got the chance to write 'The Dreaming City', I was identifying very closely with my hero-villain. I thought myself something of an outcast (another romantic notion largely unsubstantiated now I look back) and emphasised Elric's physical differences accordingly:

> His bizarre dress was tasteless and gaudy, and did not match his sensitive face and long-fingered, almost delicate hands, yet he flaunted it since it emphasised that he did not belong in any company – that he was an outsider and an outcast. But, in reality, he had little need to wear such outlandish gear – for ... [he] was a pure albino who drew his power from a secret and terrible source.
>
> *The Stealer of Souls*, page 13

The story was packed with personal symbols (as are all the stories bar a couple). The 'secret and terrible source' was the sword Stormbringer, which symbolised my own and others' tendency to rely on mental and physical crutches rather than cure the weakness at source. To go further, Elric, for me, symbolised the ambivalence of mankind in general, with its love-hates, its mean-generosity, its confident-bewilderment act. Elric is a thief who believes *himself* robbed, a lover who hates love. In short, he cannot be sure of the truth of anything, not even of his own emotions or ambitions. This is made much clearer in a story containing even more direct allegory, the second in the series, 'While the Gods Laugh'. Unfortunately, Ted left out the verse from which the title was taken:

I, while the gods laugh, the world's vortex am;
Maelstrom of passions in that hidden sea
Whose waves of all-time lap the coasts of me,
And in small compass the dark waters cram.

– Mervyn Peake,
'Shapes and Sounds'

This, I think, gave more meaning to both title and story which involved a long quest after the Dead Gods' Book – a mythical work alleged to contain all the knowledge of the universe, in which Elric feels he will at last find the true meaning of life. He expresses this need in a somewhat rhetorical way. When the wingless woman Shaarilla asks him why he wants the book he replies [in the magazine version]:

'I desire, if you like, to know one of [misprinted as *or* in magazine version] two things. Does an ultimate God exist – or not? Does Law or Chaos govern our lives? Men need a God, so the philosophers tell us. Have they made one – or did one make them?', etc., etc.

Here, as in other passages, the bewilderment is expressed in metaphysical terms, for at that time, due mainly to my education, I was very involved with mysticism. Also, the metaphysical terms suited the description of a sword-and-sorcery hero and his magical, low-technology world.

It may seem odd that I use such phrases as 'at that time' and so on, as if I'm referring to the remote past, but in many ways, being a trifle more mature, perhaps, happily married with a better sense of direction, etc., all this *does* seem to have taken place in the remote past.

The Dead Gods' Book is eventually located in a vast underground world which I had intended as a womb-symbol, and after a philosophical conversation with the book's Keeper, Elric discovers it. This passage is, to me now, rather overwritten, but, for better or worse:

> It was a huge book – the Dead Gods' Book, its covers encrusted with alien gems from which the light sprang. It gleamed, it *throbbed* with light and brilliant colour.
>
> 'At last,' Elric breathed. 'At last – the Truth!'
>
> He stumbled forward like a man made stupid with drink, his pale hands reaching for the thing he had sought with such savage bitterness. His hands touched the pulsating cover of the Book and, trembling, turned it back ... With a crash, the cover fell to the floor, sending the bright gems skipping and dancing over the paving stones. *Beneath Elric's ... hands lay nothing but a pile of yellowish dust.*

The Dead Gods' Book and the Golden Barge are one and the same. They have no real existence, save in the wishful imagination of mankind. There is, the story says, no Holy Grail which will transform a man overnight from bewildered ignorance to complete knowledge – the answer already is within him, if he cares to train himself to find it. A rather over-emphasised fact, throughout history, but one generally ignored all the same.

'The Stealer of Souls', the third story, continues this theme, but brought in rather different kinds of symbols. Coupled with the Jungian symbols already inherent in any tale using direct mythic material, I used Freudian symbols, too. This was a cynical attempt and a rather vulgar attempt to make the series popular. It appeared to work. 'The Stealer of Souls', whatever else it may be, is one of the most pornographic stories I have ever written. In Freudian terms it is the description of, if you like, a night's love-making.

Which brings me to another point. Although there is comparatively little direct description of sexual encounters in the stories, and what there are are largely romanticised, the whole Elric saga has, in its choice of situations and symbols, very heavy sexual undertones. This is true of most sword-and-sorcery stories, but I have an idea that I may be the first such author to understand his material to this extent, to know what he's using. If I hadn't been a bit fed-up by the big response received by 'The Stealer of Souls' (magazine story, not the book) I could have made even greater use of what I discovered.

Other critics have pointed out the close relationship the horror story (and often the SF story for that matter) has with the pornographic story, so there's no need to go any deeper into it here.

The pornographic content of the Elric saga doesn't interest me much, but I have hinted at the relationship between sex and violence in several stories, and indeed, there are a dozen syndromes to be found in the stories, particularly if you bear in mind my own involvement with sexual love, expression in violence, etc., at the time the stories were first conceived. Even my own interpretation of what I was doing is open to interpretation, in this case!

The allegory goes through all ten stories (including 'To Rescue Tanelorn...' which did not feature Elric) in SCIENCE FANTASY, but it tends to change its emphasis as my own ideas take better shape and my emotions mature. When, in the last Elric story of all, the sword, his crutch, Stormbringer turns and slays Elric it is meant to represent, on one level, how mankind's wish-fantasies can often bring about the destruction of (till now at least) part of mankind. Hitler, for instance, founded his whole so-called 'political' creed on a series of wish-fantasies (this is detailed in that odd book *Dawn of Magic*, recently published here). Again this is an old question, a bit trite from being asked too often, maybe, but how much of what we believe *is* true and how much is what we *wish* were true? Hitler dreamed of his Thousand Year Reich, Chamberlain said There Will Be No War. Both were convinced – both ignored plain fact to a frightening extent, just as many people (not just politicians whose public statements are not always what they really believe) ignore plain facts today. This is no new discovery of mine. It is probably one of the oldest discoveries in the world. But, in part, this is what nearly all my published work points out. Working, as I did once, as editor of a party journal (allegedly an information magazine for party candidates) this conviction was strengthened. The build-up of a fantasy is an odd process and sometimes happens, to digress a bit, like this.

The facts are gathered, related, a picture emerges. The picture, though slightly coloured by the personalities of the fact-relaters, is fairly true. The picture is given to the politician. If the politician is a man of integrity he will not deliberately warp the facts, but he will present them in a simplified version which will be understood by the general public (he thinks). This involves a selection, which can change a picture out of all recognition, though the politician didn't deliberately intend to warp the facts. The other kind of politician almost automatically selects and warps in order to prove a point he, or his party, is trying to make. So the fantasy begins. Soon the real picture is almost irrevocably lost.

Therefore this reliance on pseudo-knowledge, which seems to prove something we wish were true, is a dangerous thing to do.

This is one of the main messages of the Elric series, though there are several others on different levels.

Don't think I'm asking you to go back over the stories looking for these allegories and symbols. The reason I abandoned *The Golden Barge* was because among other things it wasn't entertaining. The Elric stories are meant to entertain as much as anything else, but if anyone cares to look for substance beyond the entertainment level, they might find it.

One of the main reasons, though, for taking this angle when Alan [Dodd] asked me to write a piece on Elric, was because I have been a little disappointed at the first book being dismissed by some professional critics (who evidently didn't bother to read it closely, if at all) as an imitation of Conan. When you put thought and feeling into a story – thought and feeling which is yours – you don't much care for being called an imitator or a plagiarist however good or bad the story. Probably the millionth novel about a young advertising executive in love with a deb and involved with a married woman has just been published, yet the author won't be accused of imitating anyone or plagiarising anyone. It is the use to which one puts one's chosen material, not that material, which matters.

Final Judgement

(1965)

by Alan Forrest

STORMBRINGER IS A magic sword, a great, evil blade with a life of its own. It sucks souls like a vampire sucks his victims' blood. It is the real hero-villain of Michael Moorcock's strange new novel set in a blood-soaked and bewitched world, anti-time and anti-history, in which nightmare armies battle, statues scream and heroines can be turned into big white worms at the drop of a warlock's hat.

Mr Moorcock stirs up this hell-brew with an inventiveness that leaves one gasping. His is the territory that has always been dear to a certain kind of English writer, the genuine exotic, who exists to remind us that we're really a most exotic race.

I'm thinking of people like Mervyn Peake and, in the last few years, Jane Gaskell. *Stormbringer* (Herbert Jenkins, 12/6d.) has, for me, the same kind of offbeat integrity and complete involvement with a dreamworld that impressed me in *The Serpent*, Miss Gaskell's novel about Atlantis.

Mr Moorcock's Bright Empire of Melniboné existed 'ten thousand years before history was recorded – or ten thousand years after history had ceased to be chronicled, reckon it how you will'. It is far from easy to describe, but it is a kind of primitive mythland with touches of Victorian Gothick, Wagnerian darkness and even undertones of the Book of Revelations.

The plot is about the battle between the forces of Law and Chaos for nothing less than the future of the universe. The characters have a kind of human form, but we're told they are less than men, ghostly epic-types who live only to intrigue and slaughter to settle the shape of quality of the world of real men which is to follow them.

So *Stormbringer* is an exciting fantasy about the eternal struggle of Good and Evil. The forces of Order are led by Elric, the last ruler of Melniboné, a red-eyed albino who has little real physical strength, but draws it from the soul-sucking sword. With Stormbringer in his hand, he is ten feet tall and a match for any Theocrat called Jagreen Lern, his warrior-priests and the Lords of Hell. Without the sword, he couldn't take on a reasonably skilled lightweight.

Elric is an excellent character, pretty well-rounded and convincing for a myth-figure. He could have been the familiar strong, but lilywhite hero. Mr Moorcock doesn't make him any such thing.

Elric and Stormbringer – between whom there's a skilfully established love-hate relationship; neither can do without the other – take the field in a world ruled by chance, destiny, sorcery, all the supernatural forces that strangle men's free will. The atmosphere is chilly and oppressive and that's, perhaps, my only quibble at Mr Moorcock's fascinating novel.

I don't ask for sweetness and light from science fiction, fantasy and its associated literatures, but I wish more young writers like Michael Moorcock would show us characters who are real masters of their fate and not just dancing on a cosmic puppet-master's strings.

But I wouldn't have missed *Stormbringer* for anything. The excitement and bloodletting never lets up, from the moment Jagreen Lern kidnaps Elric's wife and Elric and his buddies set hotfoot across the Sighing Desert and the Pale Sea to dish the villains of Pan Tang.

Elric himself is no goodie-goodie, his crimson eyes burning with hate as phantom horsemen bear down on him. 'He was capable of cruelty and malevolent sorcery, had little pity, but could love and hate more violently than ever his ancestors.' He'll lop a man's head off for sheer expediency and ask questions afterwards.

But slowly he emerges as a lone goodish man in a landscape that drips with blood and hate. And Mr Moorcock's landscapes are compelling.

There are dark battlefields where bloody men come screaming out of the night, black-cowled midnight horrors with fixed grins, ghastly wailing winged women running amok with their wings clipped, doom-laden seas where black, rat-infested warships fill the air with fireballs.

Elric fights an army of vampire trees with his vampire sword as they try to tear him apart using branches like superhuman fingers. He takes a journey in time to fight that dead hero of another age, Roland, to get his magic horn.

Is there too much blood? I said the weird inventiveness of it all leaves one gasping. Does it tend to drain one dry? Is there a danger of Mr Moorcock's work becoming a parody of itself as this kind of literature often does? On the strength of this one book, he avoids it by a hair's breadth and I can recommend *Stormbringer*. In a tight corner I would rather have Elric's sword than Arthur's Excalibur for all its malevolent habit of doing what it likes and standing there, alive, sinister and smiling when nearly every other character has had his chips in some way.

Most of all, I feel that Mr Moorcock's battle between good and evil is a sad story. If it did happen in some early world of supernatural twilight, a lot of men died in vain.

Elric fought for a decent world of the future, one that he would never enjoy. What did we get? Buchenwald, the atom bomb and brainwashing. Perhaps Mr Moorcock's world has something? Could the sorcerers have done much worse than that?

The Zenith Letter

(1924)

'Woodlands'
Oakhill Gdns
Woodford Green
Essex

2.7.24

Dear Mr Young,

Many thanks!

The Editor of the Union Jack of course receives letters from readers galore as to his yarns and most of them have something to say about Zenith.

They are not all complimentary, some are very much the reverse; but the Albino is usually liked (or disliked) very much indeed.

That shows, I think, that to them, as to you – and me, Zenith is a living man. It is impossible to feel strongly about a phantasm.

One likes appreciation naturally. Literary art, so far as I understand it, is translation, by means of words, from the mind of the writer to the mind of the reader, of certain interests and emotions. When I read that for you Zenith *lived*, I was delighted to perceive that, so far as you were concerned, I had succeeded.

In 1913, I encountered, in the West End, a true albino, a man of about fifty-five.

He was a slovenly fellow: fingers stained with tobacco, clothes soiled by dropped food. Yet he was dressed expensively, and had about him a look of adequacy.

I should have forgotten him in a day or so; but when, an hour afterwards and five miles away, I sat down to have my lunch, he walked in to the restaurant and sat himself within a few feet of me.

This coincidence made an impression upon my mind, and when I needed a central figure not quite so banal as Blake for the U.J. stories, I re-created this albino fellow "moulded nearer to the heart's desire".

As I expect you will agree, Mr Young, the lordly crook exists in most of us, only he is shackled by conventions and virtues. The Jekyll-and-Hyde trick of setting him free is, of course, a trick of the writer's trade. One cannot, alas, have the excitement of a crook's brief life in actuality; but one can, vicariously, with arm-chair and cigarette, experience not only the actions thereof, but the re-actions also. I am telling you what you have already divined.

Regarding my novels, I regret to inform you that I have written none. The disgusting truth is that novel-writing does not pay. I have planned a novel, and soon I shall write it. I think it will be good, but I do not expect to make more than £50 out of it. That's that. I have to live, Mr Young. Novel-writing is an expensive hobby.

Otherwise, you appear to have read all my long stories. In my opinion (which is probably unreliable on the subject) the best chapters I ever wrote were the first one of two in "The Case of the Crystal Gazer" and the best yarn "The Tenth Case" (published immediately after "A Duel to the Death", in 1918). The Editor liked "The Curse of the Crimson Curtain" (published recently).

In addition to these Union Jack, etc., yarns I have written nothing but newspaper articles, and one or two "shorts" not worth mentioning. I have a single copy of most of my Zenith yarns, but I need these frequently for reference, and further copies are, I fear, largely out of print.

I am now writing an S.B. Library story of which, when it is published, I should like to send you a copy.

That I have awakened so strong an interest in one who is, obviously, intellectually superior to the average reader of the Union Jack, I find both flattering and stimulating.

Sincerely yours,
Anthony Skene

Elric: A New Reader's Guide

by John Davey

E LRIC OF MELNIBONÉ – proud prince of ruins, Kinslayer – call him what you will. He remains, together with maybe Jerry Cornelius, Michael Moorcock's most enduring, if not always most endearing, character.

The first version of this guide to the many and various Elric publications was adapted from *Michael Moorcock: A Reader's Guide* (1991/'92), and attempted to provide a title-by-title breakdown of the books together with the omnibuses in which each appeared. While that is still the case this time, there has been such an explosion in Elric collections over the last twenty years – of which these Gollancz editions are the most recent (and quite possibly the best) – that this version of the guide has had to be rather substantially revamped. It retains its chronological format, but deals with each omnibus as an individual title, rather than including them within the main books' descriptions.

Elric began life in response to a request from John Carnell, editor of SCIENCE FANTASY magazine, for a series akin to Robert E. Howard's Conan the Barbarian stories. What Carnell received, while steeped in sword-and-sorcery images, was something quite different. All in all, nine Elric novellas appeared in SCIENCE FANTASY between June 1961 and April 1964. During that time, the first five were collected as *The Stealer of Souls* (1963). These were later split up and re-collected in, or absorbed into, *The Weird of the White Wolf* and *The Bane of the Black Sword* (both 1977) and were also, as a result of this assimilation, slightly revised. Collectors should note that the true first edition of *The Stealer of Souls* (subtitled by its publishers as '... and Other Stories', against Moorcock's wishes) was bound in orange boards; an otherwise identical but less collectable second printing had green boards.

Stormbringer (1965), conceived as a novel, was first published as such when abridged and revised from the four remaining SCIENCE FANTASY novellas. It was later restored to its original length and further revised, in 1977. The original abridgements basically condensed the first two novellas (plus part of the third) into one section, 'The Coming of Chaos'.

The Singing Citadel (1970) is a collection of four other novellas originally published in various periodicals and anthologies between 1962 and 1967. They were later split up and all but one were re-collected in, or absorbed into, *The Weird of the White Wolf* and *The Bane of the Black Sword* as their events interconnect with those of *The Stealer of Souls*. They were also, as a result of this assimilation, slightly revised. The unused novella, 'The Greater Conqueror' (sometimes erroneously listed as 'The Great Conqueror'), was subsequently collected in *Moorcock's Book of Martyrs* (1976, a.k.a. *Dying for Tomorrow*, 1978), *Earl Aubec and Other Stories* (1993), *Elric: To Rescue Tanelorn* (2008) and *Elric: The Sleeping Sorceress* (2013).

The Sleeping Sorceress (1971) was expanded from a novella of the same name, although it was originally commissioned as a serial for Kenneth Bulmer's magazine, SWORD AND SORCERY, which never appeared. One of its sections retells, from Elric's viewpoint, a part of the Corum novel, *The King of the Swords*. In 1977, *The Sleeping Sorceress* was retitled, with minor textual amendments, as *The Vanishing Tower* (q.v.).

Elric of Melniboné (1972) is a prequel to all other Elric novels. *The Dreaming City* (1972) was a version of *Elric of Melniboné*, published with unauthorised changes. Collectors should note that, in 1977, *Elric of Melniboné* was one of three Elric books published as illustrated editions in slip-cases. This first (in a red case) also had a smaller, limited edition (in a brown case) signed by the author, artist (Robert Gould) and publisher. In 2003, *Elric of Melniboné* was the first novel of Moorcock's to become an unabridged audiobook.

Elric: The Return to Melnibone (sic, 1973) remains, despite its comparative irrelevance to the overall series, one of the scarcest and most sought-after of Elric books. This is the result of its somewhat chequered history, a saga complex enough to rival Elric's own. It is actually little more than a showcase for the exquisite artwork of Philippe Druillet, beginning life in the mid-'60s as double-spread colour illustrations for the first two issues of a French children's magazine called MOI AUSSI, with text by Maxim Jakubowski. In 1969, Druillet illustrated an omnibus called *Elric le Necromancien*, and in 1972 some of this (and new) artwork was put into a twenty-one piece portfolio as *La Saga d'Elric le Necromancien*, this time with text by Michel Demuth. All of this work up until then was unauthorised, but when the portfolio was reprinted and bound (less one piece) in the UK as *Elric: The Return to Melnibone* (text by Moorcock), Druillet threatened to sue! Moorcock was forced to step in on behalf of the British publishers, pointing out that permission had never been granted for Druillet to draw Elric in the first place. In order to avoid messy litigation, it was decided to allow the small print run to expire, never to be reprinted. However, a republication was finally agreed, and the book made available again in 1997 as *Elric: The Return to Melniboné*.

The Jade Man's Eyes (1973) is a separate novella which, in order to bring it in line with the developing series, was revised and absorbed into *The Sailor on the Seas of Fate* as 'Sailing to the Past'.

The Sailor on the Seas of Fate (1976) originally slotted, chronologically, between events in *Elric of Melniboné* and *The Weird of the White Wolf*. One of its sections retells, from Elric's viewpoint, a part of the Hawkmoon/Count Brass novel, *The Quest for Tanelorn*. In 2006, *The Sailor on the Seas of Fate* also became an unabridged audiobook.

The Weird of the White Wolf (1977) is a chronological arrangement of selected contents from *The Stealer of Souls* and *The Singing Citadel*, compiled in order to bring them in line with the developing series. At the time of writing, *The Weird of the White Wolf* is (over-)due to become the third unabridged Elric audiobook.

The Vanishing Tower (1977) is a retitling, with minor textual amendments, of *The Sleeping Sorceress*. Collectors should note that, in 1981, *The Vanishing Tower* was the second of three Elric books published as illustrated editions in slip-cases. This edition (in a pictorial red case) also had a smaller, limited edition (in a brown case) signed by the author, artist (Michael Whelan) and publisher.

The Bane of the Black Sword (1977) is a chronological arrangement of selected contents from *The Stealer of Souls* and *The Singing Citadel*, compiled in order to bring them in line with the developing series.

The somewhat misleadingly titled *Six Science Fiction Classics from the Master of Heroic Fantasy* (1979) is a boxed set of six American paperbacks: *Elric of Melniboné*, *The Sailor on the Seas of Fate*, *The Weird of the White Wolf*, *The Vanishing Tower*, *The Bane of the Black Sword* and *Stormbringer*.

Elric at the End of Time (1984) is a collection of short fiction and non-fiction which actually contains only three Elric-related items among its contents of seven (excluding the introduction). The title story was also published separately in 1987 as a large-format novella (*q.v.*) illustrated by Rodney Matthews.

The Elric Saga Part One (1984) is the first Elric omnibus, and contains *Elric of Melniboné*, *The Sailor on the Seas of Fate* and *The Weird of the White Wolf*. *The Elric Saga Part Two* (1984) is the second omnibus, and contains *The Vanishing Tower*, *The Bane of the Black Sword* and *Stormbringer*.

Elric at the End of Time (1987) is a separate, large-format novella illustrated by Rodney Matthews for whom it was originally written some years earlier. Collectors should note that it was published simultaneously in both hardcover and paperback formats.

The Fortress of the Pearl (1989), the first Elric novel for thirteen years, expanded the saga and slots, chronologically, between events in *Elric of Melniboné* and *The Sailor on the Seas of Fate*.

The Revenge of the Rose (1991) slots between events in *The Sleeping Sorceress* and the stories from *The Bane of the Black Sword*.

In 1992, Moorcock began an ambitious project of re-ordering, revising and republishing much of his back-catalogue in a large set of omnibuses in the UK under the collective title, 'The Tale of the Eternal Champion'. The first of these to feature the albino prince was *Elric of Melniboné* (1993), containing *Elric of Melniboné*, *The Fortress of the Pearl*, *The Sailor on the Seas of Fate* and selected contents from *The Weird of the White Wolf*. The omnibus was retitled in the USA, when the 'Eternal Champion' series began to appear there, as *Elric: Song of the Black Sword* (1995).

The second British omnibus to feature Elric was *Stormbringer* (1993), containing *The Sleeping Sorceress*, *The Revenge of the Rose*, selected contents from *The Bane of the Black Sword*, and *Stormbringer*. This omnibus was retitled in the USA as *Elric: The Stealer of Souls* (1998), not to be confused with a later volume of the same name (*q.v.*).

Collectors should note that, in the UK, 'The Tale of the Eternal Champion' omnibuses were published simultaneously in both hardcover and paperback formats. In the USA, hardcover editions appeared ahead of their paperback versions.

Elric: Tales of the White Wolf (1994) is an original anthology of Elric stories by Moorcock and others, edited by Edward E. Kramer & Richard Gilliam.

Michael Moorcock's Multiverse (1999) is a graphic novel illustrated by Walter Simonson, Mark Reeve & John Ridgway, originally serialised in twelve parts (1997/'98). It contains three interconnecting tales (each illustrated by a different artist), one of which – Ridgway's – is 'Duke Elric'.

The Dreamthief's Daughter (2001) was the first volume of a brand-new Elric trilogy – in fact the only preconceived Elric trilogy – linking the albino with some of the many and various members of the Family von Bek. (When revising his books for the 'Eternal Champion' omnibuses, Moorcock had the opportunity to change several character names in order to bring them in line with the developing 'Von Bek' series, which had begun in 1981 with *The War Hound and the World's Pain* although the name's derivation goes back as far as Katinka van Bak in 1973's *The Champion of Garathorm*.) Collectors should note that, also in 2001 (after the true first edition), *The Dreamthief's Daughter* became the last of three Elric books to date published as illustrated editions in slip-cases. This limited edition, signed by the author and artists (Randy Broecker, Donato Giancola, Gary Gianni, Robert Gould, Michael Kaluta, Todd Lockwood, Don Maitz & Michael Whelan), was followed two years later – still dated '2001' – by a smaller limited edition which was leather-bound and tray-cased. In 2013, *The Dreamthief's Daughter* was retitled and revised as *Daughter of Dreams (q.v.)*.

Elric (2001) is another omnibus, containing *The Stealer of Souls* and *Stormbringer*, as part of Gollancz's 'Fantasy Masterworks' series. In 2008, it was repackaged as part of the same publisher's much smaller 'Ultimate Fantasies' sequence.

The Elric Saga Part Three (2002), another omnibus, contains *The Fortress of the Pearl* and *The Revenge of the Rose*.

The Skrayling Tree: The Albino in America (2003) is the second part of the trilogy beginning with *The Dreamthief's Daughter*. In 2013, *The Skrayling Tree* was retitled as revised as *Destiny's Brother*.

The White Wolf's Son: The Albino Underground (2005) is the third and last part of the trilogy. Although this supposedly – again – final Elric subseries can be read as a standalone adventure (as, indeed, can each volume), brief mention is made of events slotting, chronologically, into those described within *Stormbringer*. In 2013, *The White Wolf's Son* was retitled and revised as *Son of the Wolf*.

The Elric Saga Part IV (2005), another omnibus, contains *The Dreamthief's Daughter*, *The Skrayling Tree* and *The White Wolf's Son*.

Elric: The Making of a Sorcerer (2007) is a graphic novel illustrated by Walter Simonson, originally serialised in four parts (2004-'06), and is a prequel to the novel *Elric of Melniboné*.

Elric: The Stealer of Souls (2008) is the first volume of a series of six Elric omnibuses published (in the order the main novels were written) under the collective title, 'Chronicles of the Last Emperor of Melniboné', each containing fiction and non-fiction. The first volume's fiction includes *The Stealer of Souls* and *Stormbringer*. *Elric: To Rescue Tanelorn* (2008) is the second volume, a collection of Elric (or Elric-related) short fiction. *Elric: The Sleeping Sorceress* (2008) is the third volume, including the novels *The Sleeping Sorceress* and *Elric of Melniboné*. *Duke Elric* (2009) is the fourth volume, including *The Sailor on the Seas of Fate*, the 'Duke Elric' graphic-novel script and a novella, 'The Flaneur des Arcades de l'Opera'. *Elric in the Dream Realms* (2009) is the fifth volume, including *The Fortress of the Pearl*, the *Elric: The Making of a Sorcerer* graphic-novel script and a short story, 'A Portrait in Ivory'. *Elric: Swords and Roses* (2009), the sixth and final volume, includes *The Revenge of the Rose*, a *Stormbringer* (unmade) movie screenplay, and the first of three new novellas, 'Black Petals', from 2008, followed (as yet uncollected) by 'Red Pearls' (2011) and another (forthcoming).

Elric: Les Buveurs d'Âmes (2011) is an original, collaborative novel (in French) by Moorcock and Fabrice Colin, for which there seems no imminent sign of an English-language edition.

Daughter of Dreams (2013) is a revised retitling of *The Dreamthief's Daughter*; *Destiny's Brother* (2013) is a revised retitling of *The Skrayling Tree*; *Son of the Wolf* (2013) is a revised retitling of *The White Wolf's Son*.

Elric of Melniboné and Other Stories (2013) is the first volume of Gollancz's series of seven Elric omnibuses published (in narrative-chronology order) as part of 'The Michael Moorcock Collection', each containing similar long & short fiction and non-fiction to the 'Chronicles of the Last Emperor of Melniboné'. It is followed by *Elric: The Fortress of the Pearl* (2013), *Elric: The Sailor on the Seas of Fate* (2013), *Elric: The Sleeping Sorceress* (2013), *Elric: The Revenge of the Rose* (2014), *Elric: Stormbringer!* (2014) and *Elric: The Moonbeam Roads* (forthcoming, containing *Daughter of Dreams*, *Destiny's Brother* and *Son of the Wolf*).

* * *

First Editions and First Appearances

The Stealer of Souls:

'The Dreaming City', originally in SCIENCE FANTASY
No. 47 (edited by John Carnell), UK, June 1961

'While the Gods Laugh', in SCIENCE FANTASY No. 49,
Oct. 1961

'The Stealer of Souls', in SCIENCE FANTASY No. 51,
Feb. 1962

'Kings in Darkness', in SCIENCE FANTASY No. 54, Aug. 1962

'The Flame Bringers', in SCIENCE FANTASY No. 55,
Oct. 1962

Neville Spearman hardcover, UK, 1963

Lancer paperback, USA, 1967

Stormbringer:

'Dead God's Homecoming', orig. in SCIENCE FANTASY
No. 59, June 1963

'Black Sword's Brothers', in SCIENCE FANTASY No. 61,
Oct. 1963

'Sad Giant's Shield', in SCIENCE FANTASY No. 63, Feb. 1964

'Doomed Lord's Passing', in SCIENCE FANTASY No. 64,
Apr. 1964

Herbert Jenkins h/c (abridged & revised from the
novellas),UK, 1965

Lancer p/b (ditto), USA, 1967

DAW p/b (full length & revised), USA, 1977

Granada p/b (ditto), UK, 1985

The Singing Citadel:

'The Singing Citadel' (novella), orig. in *The Fantastic
Swordsmen* (anthology edited by L. Sprague de Camp),
USA, 1967

'Master of Chaos', in FANTASTIC Vol. 13 No. 5 (ed. Cele
Goldsmith), USA, May 1964

'The Greater Conqueror' (non-Elric), in SCIENCE FANTASY
No. 58, Apr. 1963

'To Rescue Tanelorn...', in SCIENCE FANTASY No. 56,
    Dec. 1962
Mayflower p/b, UK, 1970
Berkley p/b, USA, 1970

The Sleeping Sorceress:
    'The Sleeping Sorceress' (novella), orig. in *Warlocks and
        Warriors* (anthol., ed. Douglas Hill), UK, 1971
    New English Library h/c (expanded from the novella), UK, 1971
    Lancer p/b (ditto), USA, 1972
    DAW p/b (as *The Vanishing Tower*), USA, 1977
    Archival Press h/c (as *The Vanishing Tower*, no dust-wrapper, in
        pictorial red slip-case [also limited in brown slip-case]),
        USA, 1981
    Granada p/b (as *The Vanishing Tower*), UK, 1983

Elric of Melniboné:
    Hutchinson h/c, UK, 1972
    Lancer p/b (unauthorised changes, as *The Dreaming City*),
        USA, 1972
    DAW p/b (unchanged, as *Elric of Melniboné*), USA, 1976
    Blue Star h/c (ditto, no dust-wrapper, in red slip-case [also
        limited in brown slip-case]), USA, 1977

Elric: The Return to Melnibone (illustrated by Philippe Druillet):
    Unicorn outsize p/b, UK, 1973
    Jayde Design outsize p/b (as *Elric: The Return to Melniboné*),
        UK, 1997

The Jade Man's Eyes:
    Unicorn p/b, UK, 1973

The Sailor on the Seas of Fate:
    Quartet h/c, UK, 1976
    DAW p/b, USA, 1976

The Weird of the White Wolf:
    DAW p/b, USA, 1977, comprising:
        'The Dream of Earl Aubec' (a.k.a. 'Master of Chaos')

'The Dreaming City'
'While the Gods Laugh'
'The Singing Citadel'
Granada p/b, UK, 1984

The Bane of the Black Sword:
DAW p/b, USA, 1977, comprising:
'The Stealer of Souls'
'Kings in Darkness'
'The Flamebringers' (a.k.a. 'The Flame Bringers')
'To Rescue Tanelorn...'
Granada p/b, UK, 1984

Six Science Fiction Classics from the Master of Heroic Fantasy:
Six DAW p/bs, boxed, USA, 1979, comprising:
Elric of Melniboné
The Sailor on the Seas of Fate
The Weird of the White Wolf
The Vanishing Tower
The Bane of the Black Sword
Stormbringer

Elric at the End of Time (collection):
NEL h/c, UK, 1984, comprising the following Elric-related items:
'Elric at the End of Time', orig. in *Elsewhere* (anthol., ed. Terri Windling & Mark Alan Arnold), USA, 1981
'The Last Enchantment', in ARIEL No. 3 (ed. Thomas Durwood), USA, Apr. 1978
'The Secret Life of Elric of Melniboné' (non-fiction), in CAMBER No. 14 (fanzine, ed. Alan Dodd), UK, June 1964
DAW p/b, USA, 1985

The Elric Saga Part One:
Doubleday (Science Fiction Book Club) h/c, USA, 1984, comprising:
Elric of Melniboné

The Sailor on the Seas of Fate
The Weird of the White Wolf

The Elric Saga Part Two:
Doubleday (S.F.B.C.) h/c, USA, 1984, comprising:
The Vanishing Tower
The Bane of the Black Sword
Stormbringer

Elric at the End of Time (novella, illustrated by Rodney Matthews):
Paper Tiger large-format h/c & p/b, UK, 1987

The Fortress of the Pearl:
Gollancz h/c, UK, 1989
Ace h/c, USA, 1989

The Revenge of the Rose:
Grafton h/c, UK, 1991
Ace h/c, USA, 1991

Elric of Melniboné (omnibus):
Orion/Millennium h/c & p/b, UK, 1993, comprising:
Elric of Melniboné
The Fortress of the Pearl
The Sailor on the Seas of Fate
'The Dreaming City'
'While the Gods Laugh'
'The Singing Citadel'
White Wolf h/c (as *Elric: Song of the Black Sword*), USA, 1995

Stormbringer (omnibus):
Orion/Millennium h/c & p/b, UK, 1993, comprising:
The Sleeping Sorceress
The Revenge of the Rose
'The Stealer of Souls'
'Kings in Darkness'
'The Caravan of Forgotten Dreams' (a.k.a. 'The Flame
Bringers')

Stormbringer
'Elric: A Reader's Guide' (non-fiction by John Davey)
White Wolf h/c (as *Elric: The Stealer of Souls*), USA, 1998

Elric: Tales of the White Wolf:
White Wolf h/c, USA, 1994, comprising the following
Moorcock items:
'Introduction to *Tales of the White Wolf* (non-fiction)
'The White Wolf's Song'
plus Elric stories by Tad Williams, David M. Honigsberg, Roland
J. Green & Frieda A. Murray, Richard Lee Byers, Brad Strickland,
Brad Linaweaver & William Alan Ritch, Kevin T. Stein, Scott
Ciencin, Gary Gygax, James S. Dorr, Stewart von Allmen, Paul
W. Cashman, Nancy A. Collins, Doug Murray, Karl Edward
Wagner, Thomas E. Fuller, Jody Lynn Nye, Colin Greenland,
Robert Weinberg, Charles Partington, Peter Crowther & James
Lovegrove, Nancy Holder, Neil Gaiman.

Michael Moorcock's Multiverse:
DC Comics large-format p/b, USA, 1999
'Moonbeams and Roses' (non-Elric), illustrated by Walter
Simonson
'The Metatemporal Detective' (non-Elric), illustrated by
Mark Reeve
'Duke Elric', illustrated by John Ridgway

The Dreamthief's Daughter:
Earthlight h/c, UK, 2001
American Fantasy h/c (in slip-case [also limited in tray-case]),
USA, 2001
Gollancz p/b (as *Daughter of Dreams*), UK, 2013

Elric:
Gollancz p/b, UK, 2001, comprising:
The Stealer of Souls
Stormbringer

The Elric Saga Part Three:
S.F.B.C. h/c, USA, 2002, comprising:
   The Fortress of the Pearl
   The Revenge of the Rose

The Skrayling Tree: The Albino in America:
Warner h/c, USA, 2003
Gollancz p/b (as *Destiny's Brother*), UK, 2013

The White Wolf's Son: The Albino Underground:
Warner h/c, USA, 2005
Gollancz p/b (as *Son of the Wolf*), UK, 2013

The Elric Saga Part IV:
S.F.B.C. h/c, USA, 2005, comprising:
   The Dreamthief's Daughter
   The Skrayling Tree
   The White Wolf's Son

Elric: The Making of a Sorcerer (illustrated by Walter Simonson):
DC Comics large-format p/b, USA, 2007

Elric: The Stealer of Souls: Chronicles of the Last Emperor of Melniboné: Volume 1:
Del Rey p/b, USA, 2008, comprising:
   'Putting a Tag on It' (non-fiction), orig. in AMRA Vol. 2 No. 15 (fanzine, ed. George Scithers), USA, May 1961
   The Stealer of Souls
   'Mission to Asno!' (non-Elric), in TARZAN ADVENTURES Vol. 7 No. 25 (ed. Moorcock), UK, Sep. 1957
   Stormbringer
   'Elric' (non-fiction), in NIEKAS No. 8 (fanzine, ed. Ed Meskys), USA, 1964
   'The Secret Life of Elric of Melniboné' (non-fiction)
   'Final Judgement' (non-fiction by Alan Forrest), in NEW WORLDS No. 147 (as 'Did Elric Die in Vain?'), UK, Feb. 1965
   'The Zenith Letter' (non-fiction by Anthony Skene), in *Monsieur Zenith the Albino*, UK, 2001

Elric: *To Rescue Tanelorn*:

Del Rey p/b, USA, 2008, comprising:

'The Eternal Champion', orig. in SCIENCE FANTASY No. 53, June 1962

'To Rescue Tanelorn...'

'The Last Enchantment' (a.k.a. 'Jesting with Chaos')

'The Greater Conqueror'

'Master of Chaos' (a.k.a. 'Earl Aubec')

'Phase 1: A Jerry Cornelius Story', in *The Final Programme*, USA, 1968

'The Singing Citadel'

'The Jade Man's Eyes'

'The Stone Thing', in TRIODE No. 20 (fanzine, ed. Eric Bentcliffe), UK, Oct. 1974

'Elric at the End of Time'

'The Black Blade's Song' (a.k.a. 'The White Wolf's Song')

'Crimson Eyes', in NEW STATESMAN & SOCIETY No. 333, UK, 1994

'Sir Milk-and-Blood', in *Pawn of Chaos: Tales of the Eternal Champion* (anthol., ed. Edward E. Kramer), USA, 1996

'The Roaming Forest', in *Cross Plains Universe: Texans Celebrate Robert E. Howard* (anthol., ed. Scott A. Cupp & Joe R. Lansdale), USA, 2006

Elric: *The Sleeping Sorceress*:

Del Rey p/b, USA, 2008, comprising:

The Sleeping Sorceress

'And So the Great Emperor Received His Education...', orig. spoken-word introduction to *Elric of Melniboné* (audiobook), USA, 2003

Elric of Melniboné

'Aspects of Fantasy (1): Introduction' (non-fiction), orig. in SCIENCE FANTASY No. 61, Oct. 1963

'Introduction to *Elric of Melniboné*, Graphic Adaptation' (non-fiction), in *Elric of Melniboné* (by Roy Thomas, P. Craig Russell & Michael T. Gilbert), USA, 1986

'El Cid and Elric: Under the Influence!' (non-fiction), in
COMIQUEANDO No. 100, Argentina, Aug./Sep. 2007

Duke Elric:

Del Rey p/b, USA, 2009, comprising:

'Introduction to the AudioRealms version of *The Sailor on
the Seas of Fate* (audiobook), USA, 2006

The Sailor on the Seas of Fate

'Duke Elric' (script)

'Aspects of Fantasy (2): The Floodgates of the Unconscious'
(non-fiction), orig. in SCIENCE FANTASY No. 62,
Dec. 1963

'The Flaneur des Arcades de l'Opera', in *The Metatemporal
Detective*, USA, 2008

'Elric: A Personality at War' (non-fiction by Adrian Snook)

Elric in the Dream Realms:

Del Rey p/b, USA, 2009, comprising:

The Fortress of the Pearl

Elric: The Making of a Sorcerer (script)

'A Portrait in Ivory', orig. in *Logorrhea: Good Words Make
Good Stories* (anthol., ed. John Klima), USA, 2007

'Aspects of Fantasy (3): Figures of Faust' (non-fiction), in
SCIENCE FANTASY No. 63, Feb. 1964

'Earl Aubec of Malador: Outline for a Series of Four
Fantasy Novels'

'Introduction to the Taiwanese Edition of Elric', in *Elric of
Melniboné*, Taiwan, 2007

'One Life, Furnished in Early Moorcock' (by Neil Gaiman),
in *Elric: Tales of the White Wolf*, USA, 1994

Elric: Swords and Roses:

Del Rey p/b, USA, 2009, comprising:

The Revenge of the Rose

Stormbringer: First Draft Screenplay

'Black Petals', orig. in WEIRD TALES No. 349 (edited by Stephen
H. Segal & Ann VanderMeer), USA, Mar./Apr. 2008

'Aspects of Fantasy (4): Conclusion' (non-fiction), in
SCIENCE FANTASY No. 64, Apr. 1964

'Introduction to *The Skrayling Tree*', written for Borders,
Inc., 2003

'Introduction to the French Edition of Elric', in *Le Cycle
d'Elric*, France, 2006

'Elric: A New Reader's Guide' (non-fiction by John Davey)

Elric: Les Buveurs d'Âmes (with Fabrice Colin):

Fleuve Noir p/b, France, 2011

Elric of Melniboné and Other Stories:

Gollancz p/b, UK, 2013, comprising:

'Putting a Tag on It' (non-fiction)

'Master of Chaos' (a.k.a. 'Earl Aubec')

Elric: The Making of a Sorcerer (script)

'And So the Great Emperor Received His Education...'
Elric of Melniboné

'Aspects of Fantasy (1): Introduction' (non-fiction)

'Introduction to *Elric of Melniboné*, Graphic Adaptation'
(non-fiction)

'El Cid and Elric: Under the Influence!' (non-fiction)

Elric: The Fortress of the Pearl:

Gollancz p/b, UK, 2013, comprising:

The Fortress of the Pearl

'Aspects of Fantasy (2): The Floodgates of the Unconscious'
(non-fiction)

'Introduction to the Taiwanese Edition of Elric'

'One Life, Furnished in Early Moorcock' (by Neil Gaiman)

Elric: The Sailor on the Seas of Fate:

Gollancz p/b, UK, 2013, comprising:

'Introduction to the AudioRealms version of *The Sailor on
the Seas of Fate* (audiobook)

The Sailor on the Seas of Fate

'The Dreaming City'

'A Portrait In Ivory'

'While the Gods Laugh'
'The Singing Citadel'
'Aspects of Fantasy (3): Figures of Faust' (non-fiction)
'Elric: A Personality at War' (non-fiction by Adrian Snook)

Elric: *The Sleeping Sorceress*:
Gollancz p/b, UK, 2013, comprising:
'The Eternal Champion'
'The Greater Conqueror'
'Earl Aubec of Malador: Outline for a Series of Four
    Fantasy Novels'
The Sleeping Sorceress
'The Stone Thing'
'Sir Milk-and-Blood'
'The Roaming Forest'
'The Flaneur des Arcades de l'Opera'
'Aspects of Fantasy (4): Conclusion' (non-fiction)

Elric: *The Revenge of the Rose*:
Gollancz p/b, UK, 2014, comprising:
The Revenge of the Rose
'The Stealer of Souls'
'Kings in Darkness'
'The Caravan of Forgotten Dreams' (a.k.a. 'The Flame
    Bringers')
'The Last Enchantment' (a.k.a. 'Jesting with Chaos')
'To Rescue Tanelorn...'
'Introduction to the French Edition of Elric'

Elric: *Stormbringer!*:
Gollancz p/b, UK, 2014, comprising:
Stormbringer
'Elric' (non-fiction)
'The Secret Life of Elric of Melniboné' (non-fiction)
'Final Judgement' (non-fiction by Alan Forrest)
'The Zenith Letter' (non-fiction by Anthony Skene)
'Elric: A New Reader's Guide' (non-fiction by John Davey)

Elric: The Moonbeam Roads:

Gollancz p/b, UK, forthcoming, comprising:
Daughter of Dreams
Destiny's Brother
Son of the Wolf.

★   ★   ★

MINUTIAE:

In both of the variant omnibus editions called *Elric: The Stealer of Souls*, the version of *Stormbringer* appears in a definitive, re-revised form, retaining its full, four-novella length but also incorporating some of the pertinent changes from its 1965 abridgement which were lost during its 1977 restoration to full length.

Non-Elric items contained within the *Elric at the End of Time* collection include 'Sojan the Swordsman' (a composite of short tales featuring Moorcock's first ever fantasy hero), 'Jerry Cornelius & Co.' (two essays on that character) and the short story 'The Stone Thing'.

The essay 'The Secret Life of Elric of Melniboné' – between its first fanzine appearance (1964) and its collection in *Elric at the End of Time* – was also in *Sojan* (Savoy Books p/b, UK, 1977). That collection additionally contained another piece of non-fiction, 'Elric', which originally appeared in the fanzines NIEKAS No. 8 (ed. Ed Meskys, 1963, as a letter) and CRUCIFIED TOAD No. 4 (ed. David Britton, 1974).

The French omnibus, *Elric le Necromancien* (Éditions Opta h/c, 1969), collected *The Stealer of Souls* and the full version of *Stormbringer* – plus the novellas 'The Singing Citadel' and 'To Rescue Tanelorn...' – all arranged in correct chronological order some eight years before any English-language equivalents. More recently, in France, the mammoth omnibus, *Le Cycle d'Elric*, collected in a single volume *Elric of Melniboné*, *The Fortress of the Pearl*, *The Sailor on the Seas of Fate*, *The Weird of the White Wolf*, *The Sleeping Sorceress*, *The Revenge of the Rose*, *The Bane of the Black Sword*, 'The Last Enchantment', *Stormbringer* and 'Elric at the End of Time'! There is also a French anthology of Elric stories by hands other than Moorcock's (although he introduces it), *Elric et la Porte des Mondes*, which seems unlikely ever to receive an English-language edition.

Many graphic adaptations of the Elric saga have appeared over the years, mostly starting as comics. Moorcock himself, together with James Cawthorn, plotted a two-part strip in 1972, in which Elric and Conan the Barbarian join forces ('A Sword Called Stormbringer!' & 'The Green Empress of Melniboné' in CONAN THE BARBARIAN Nos. 14 & 15). Cawthorn also produced a one-off graphic adaptation of *Stormbringer* for Savoy Books (1976). Several other Elric one-offs have appeared over the years, drawn by various hands, but the most widely available series for some time were Pacific/First Comics' *Elric of Melniboné* (6 parts), *Elric: Sailor on the Seas of Fate* (7 parts), *Elric: Weird of the White Wolf* (5 parts), *Elric: The Vanishing Tower* (6 parts) and *Elric: The Bane of the Black Sword* (6 parts), all serialised throughout the late-eighties. The first three sets were also compiled as bound graphic novels. The sequence was stopped by Moorcock before *Stormbringer*, due to deterioration in the quality of the artwork, although a new graphic version of the novel, adapted by P. Craig Russell, was finally serialised in the USA for Topps/Dark Horse Comics in 1997 (compiled as a bound graphic novel a year later). Of course, the two most recent Moorcock-scripted tales, 'Duke Elric' and *Elric: The Making of a Sorcerer*, have developed the saga further still, and also recently there has been *Elric: The Balance Lost* (2011/'12), an original 12-part graphic series by Chris Roberson & Francesco Biagini.

Also heavily and ornately illustrated are the various rule books and supplements for Elric-related rôle-playing games from the American companies, Chaosium (whose best-known *Stormbringer* has itself been revised and massively expanded several times) and more recently Mongoose Publishing with their *Elric of Melniboné*.

Elric ephemera has become quite a major industry, and if a long-awaited Elric movie ever comes to fruition, such things can only be expected to blossom. There have already been collectable cards, die-cast miniatures, dolls, jigsaw puzzles, model-kits, posters, T-shirts, 'replica' swords and, of course, records.

Moorcock's musical involvement with several rock bands, including his own, is well known. He wrote an Elric-related song, 'Black Blade', for Blue Öyster Cult, but it is Hawkwind who have used the albino prince to the best effect. In 1985, they released the album, *The Chronicle of the Black Sword*, and went on an accompanying theatrical concert tour – sometimes featuring Moorcock on stage with the band – which also gave rise to a live album, *Live Chronicles*, and video/DVD, some versions of which include Moorcock performances.

Quite what the ever-taciturn Elric would make of all this attention, I am not sure. He has already endured far more than those first nine novellas would have had us believe possible. Have we really now seen the last of him? Only time will tell...

Acknowledgements

The foreword, by Tad Williams, first appeared in *Elric: Swords And Roses*, Del Rey, 2010.

Stormbringer first appeared (serialised) in SCIENCE FANTASY Nos 59, 61, 63 & 64, edited by John Carnell, June & October 1963 and February & April 1964; first published in book form (abridged) by Herbert Jenkins, 1965; published (restored to serial length) by DAW, 1977.

'Elric' first appeared in NIEKAS No. 8, edited by Ed Meskys, 1964.

'The Secret Life of Elric of Melniboné' first appeared in CAMBER No. 14, edited by Alan Dodd, June 1964.

'Final Judgement' (as 'Did Elric Die in Vain?'), by Alan Forrest, first appeared in NEW WORLDS No. 147, edited by Michael Moorcock, February 1965.

'The Zenith Letter', by Anthony Skene, first appeared in *Monsieur Zenith the Albino*, Savoy, 2001.

'Elric: A New Reader's Guide', by John Davey, first appeared in *Elric: Swords And Roses*, 2010, and has been updated for this Gollancz edition.

All artwork by James Cawthorn:

'Elric in the Young Kingdoms' map, 1992 (based on the map by John Collier & Walter Romanski), first published in *Elric of Melniboné*, Millennium Books, 1993.

Stormbringer, title page, first published in *Stormbringer*, Millennium Books, 1993.

Stormbringer, dedication page artwork and thumbnail illustrations, from a series commissioned privately to illustrate a copy of the first edition of *Stormbringer*, all previously unpublished (except Book One, Chapter Five and Book Two, Chapter Four, first published in *Elric: Swords And Roses*, 2010), courtesy Charles Partington.

Stormbringer, interior artwork, from *Sturmbringer*, Heyne, Germany, 1982.

Stormbringer, Book Three title page artwork, from the front cover of SCIENCE FANTASY No. 63, edited by John Carnell, February 1964.

See portfolio for other artwork acknowledgements.

MICHAEL MOORCOCK (1939–) is one of the most important figures in British SF and Fantasy literature. The author of many literary novels and stories in practically every genre, he has won and been shortlisted for numerous awards including the Hugo, Nebula, World Fantasy, Whitbread and Guardian Fiction Prize. He is also a musician who performed in the seventies with his own band, the Deep Fix; and, as a member of the space-rock band, Hawkwind, won a platinum disc. His tenure as editor of NEW WORLDS magazine in the sixties and seventies is seen as the high watermark of SF editorship in the UK, and was crucial in the development of the SF New Wave. Michael Moorcock's literary creations include Hawkmoon, Corum, Von Bek, Jerry Cornelius and, of course, his most famous character, Elric. He has been compared to, among others, Balzac, Dumas, Dickens, James Joyce, Ian Fleming, J.R.R. Tolkien and Robert E. Howard. Although born in London, he now splits his time between homes in Texas and Paris.

For a more detailed biography, please see Michael Moorcock's entry in *The Encyclopedia of Science Fiction* at: http://www.sf-encyclopedia.com/

For further information about Michael Moorcock and his work, please visit www.multiverse.org, or send S.A.E. to The Nomads Of The Time Streams, Mo Dhachaidh, Loch Awe, Dalmally, Argyll, PA33 1AQ, Scotland, or P.O. Box 385716, Waikoloa, HI 96738, USA.